"We're l

Zoey JAN 2009 gaze to her hands as if she couldn't meet his eyes. "Are we? You're not going to give up, then?"

He caught one of her hands and tugged gently until she looked up again. "I'm going to keep looking for Pete until we find her and bring her home."

He watched those blue eyes search his own. Zoey must've found whatever she was looking for in his face. For a moment, she closed her eyes. "Thank you."

He tugged at her hand, gently, so she could pull away if she wanted to. But she didn't. Instead, she opened her eyes and leaned toward him. He watched her blue eyes come closer and then he closed his own eyes.

Kissing Zoey was a revelation. She kissed him open-mouthed, no hesitation, her lips soft and warm . . .

JULIA HARPER IS JUST TOO
HOT TO HANDLE

"A refreshing, funny, tug-your-heartstrings read that deserves a Perfect 10 . . . If you like HOT stories, this is just the book you need."

—RomRevToday.com

"[A] delightful crime caper . . . the story line is fast-paced and jocular . . . Filled with terrific twists, fans will appreciate Julia Harper's HOT thriller."

—*Midwest Book Review*

"A fantastically written story filled with suspense, adventure, and—as the title suggests—steamy scenes. Julia Harper . . . has a flair for creating lovable and interesting characters who are hard to forget."

—Bookloons.com

"One of those books that is so good that it, unfortunately, is over long before the reader wants it to be . . . with unforgettable characters, slick dialogue, and a story that is both romantic and suspenseful. Julia Harper writes hot, sexy characters in fast-moving situations with searing realism."

—RomanceReaderatHeart.com

ALSO BY JULIA HARPER

Hot

for the
love of
pete

julia harper

FOREVER

NEW YORK   BOSTON

Cover design by Melody Cassen

Forever
Hachette Book Group
237 Park Avenue
New York, NY 10017
Visit our Web site at www.HachetteBookGroup.com

Forever is an imprint of Grand Central Publishing. The Forever name and logo is a trademark of Hachette Book Group, Inc.

Printed in the United States of America

First Printing: January 2009

10 9 8 7 6 5 4 3 2 1

*For DOROTHY SINHA, librarian extraordinaire,
talented baker of lamby cakes,
and the very best of friends.*

Acknowledgments

Thank you to Mili Priyanka for her help with Indian culture and cooking—any mistakes are my own—to Susannah Taylor, the most patient of agents, to Melanie Murray and Amy Pierpont, wonderful and wise editors, to Anne Twomey and Claire Brown in the Grand Central Publishing art department for a lovely cover, to Tanisha Christie and Melissa Bullock for their outstanding publicity efforts, and, last but not least, to my copyeditor, Angela Buckley, for making me look good.

Thank you.

for the
love of
pete

Prologue

*H*ad Charlie Hessler known the chain of events his stroke would set off, he would never have run that last lap around the Quantico track. If nothing else, stroking out was counter-productive to what he'd hoped to achieve by hauling his sorry middle-aged ass out every night at seven p.m. But Charlie had no knowledge of future events. As he closed in on the final mile a blood clot hit his brain with catastrophic effect and Charlie collapsed to the grass beside the track.

He wouldn't be found for another fifteen minutes.

Halfway across the country and fourteen hours later, an email was opened on a government computer. The email said that Charlie Hessler was down. The recipient stared for a minute at his lit screen, slowly tapping a finger on his desk. Then a slight smile curved one side of his face and he hit the *delete* button. If Hessler was out of action, then Dante Torelli was without backup and wide open.

Time to take him out.

Chapter One

$\mathcal{T}$hings finally came to a head between Zoey Addler and Lips of Sin the afternoon he tried to steal her parking space.

Okay, *technically,* her upstairs neighbor's name wasn't really Lips of Sin. She knew the guy's occupation but not his name. Since the man was drop-dead gorgeous, Zoey had taken to calling him "Lips of Sin" in her mind. And yes, *technically,* the parking spot in question might not legally have been hers—she hadn't paid for it or anything—but she *had* shoveled it. This was January in Chicago. In Chicago in winter, shoveling out a parking spot made it yours. Everyone knew that.

Everyone but Lips of Sin, that is.

"What the hell are you doing?" Zoey screamed at him.

She body slammed the hood of his black Beemer convertible, which was sitting in her stolen parking spot.

Lips of Sin, behind the wheel of said Beemer, mouthed something she couldn't hear. He rolled down his window. "Are you insane? I could've hit you. Never get in front of a moving vehicle."

Oh, like he had the right to lecture *her*. Zoey straightened, planted both Sorel-booted feet firmly, and crossed her arms. "I shoveled this parking spot. This is *my* parking spot. You can't take it."

Her words emerged in white puffs into the frosty late-afternoon air. They'd already had eight inches of snow the night before, and it looked like it might very well snow again. All the more reason to keep this spot.

The Beemer was at an angle, half in, half out of the parking place, which was almost directly in front of their apartment building. Every other parking space on the block was filled. There was a yellow Humvee, hulking in front of the Beemer, and a red Jeep to the back. Her own little blue Prius was double-parked next to the red Jeep. It was a sweet parking spot. Zoey had gotten up at five freaking a.m. to shovel it before she went to work at the co-op grocery. She'd marked the spot with two lawn chairs and a broken plastic milk crate in time-honored Chicago tradition. Now, returning after a long day of work, it was too much to find Lips in the act of stealing her space.

"Jesus," Lips said. "Look, I'm running a little late here. I promise to shovel you another parking place tonight. Just get out of my way. Please?"

Obviously he wasn't used to begging. Gorgeous guys didn't beg. He had smooth, tea-with-milk brown skin, curly black hair, and bitter-chocolate eyes, framed by lush girly eyelashes. Except the girly eyelashes helped empha-size the hard masculine edges of his face. In fact, the only soft things on his face were the eyelashes and his lips of sin. Deep lines bracketed those lips, framing the cynical corners and the little indent on the bottom lip that made a woman wonder what, exactly, the man could do with that mouth.

Perfect.

He was perfectly perfect in his masculine beauty, and Zoey had hated him on sight. Gorgeous guys were always so damn full of themselves. They strutted around like they were God's gift to women. *Please*. Add to that the fact that the man was always dressed for corporate raiding in suit and tie and black leather trench coat, and he just was not her type.

Lips was getting out of the car now, looking pretty pissed, his black trench coat swirling dramatically around his legs.

Zoey leaned forward, about to give him what-for, when the front doors to their apartment building burst open and a middle-aged guy in a red puffy jacket came running out. He had a baby under his left arm like a football. Zoey froze, her heart paralyzed at the sight. In his right fist was a gun. His bald head swiveled as he caught sight of them, and his gun hand swiveled with it. Zoey's eyes widened, and then a ton of bricks hit her from the side. She went down into the frozen gray slush on the street, and the ton of bricks landed on top of her. An expensive black leather sleeve shielded her face.

BANG!

The shot sounded like it was right in her ear. Zoey contracted her body in animal reaction, trying to make herself smaller beneath the heavy bulk of the man on top of her.

"Get behind the car," Lips breathed in her ear, and she had the incongruous thought that his breath smelled like fresh mint.

Then a flurry of shots rang out, one right after the other, in a wall of sound that scared her witless. The weight lifted from her body, and she felt Lips grab the back of her jacket and haul. She was on hands and knees, but she barely touched the ground before she was behind the Beemer on the driver's side. She looked up and saw Lips crouched over her, a black gun in his hand.

"Don't shoot," she gasped. "He's got the baby!"

"I know." His gaze was fixed over the roof of the car. "Shit."

The word was drowned out by the sound of a revving engine. Zoey looked around in time to see the yellow Hummer accelerate away from the curb, the bald man at the wheel.

"Come on!" She grabbed the door handle of the Beemer and pulled, scrambling ungracefully inside. There was a moment when she thought she might be seriously tangled in the console between the seats, and then she was on the other side, pulling out the passenger-side seat belt. She looked back, and Lips was still standing outside the car, staring at her. "What're you waiting for? We'll lose him."

He narrowed his eyes at her but thankfully didn't argue. Instead he threw back his coat and suit jacket, holstered his gun in a graceful movement Jack Bauer would've envied, and got in the car. He released the emergency brake and shifted into first.

He glanced at her once assessingly and said, "Hold on."

The force of his acceleration slammed her against the Beemer's lush leather seat. Then they were flying, the car eerily quiet as they sped through Evanston.

"Do you think he's a pedophile?" She clutched at the car armrest anxiously.

"No."

The yellow Hummer had turned at the corner onto a medium-sized boulevard lined with small businesses and shops. Zoey was afraid they would've already lost him by now, but two stoplights ahead, the Hummer idled at a red light.

She leaned forward. "There he is. Up ahead at the stoplight."

"I see him." The words were quiet, but they had an edge.

Well, too bad. "Can't you go any faster?"

He sped past a forest green minivan.

"The light changed. He's moving again." Zoey bit her lip, trying to still the panic in her chest. "We can't lose him. We just can't. You need to go faster."

Lips glanced at her. He didn't say anything, but Zoey heard a kind of scraping sound, like he was grinding his teeth. She rolled her eyes. Men had such delicate egos. She hauled her cell out of her jacket pocket and began punching numbers.

"What're you doing?" he asked. The Beemer swerved around a Volkswagen Beetle in the left lane, briefly jumping the concrete divider before thumping down again in front of the Beetle.

Zoey righted herself from where she'd slid against the passenger door. "Calling 911."

He grunted, and she wasn't sure whether that was an approving sound or not. Not that it mattered.

There was a click in her ear and a bored voice said, "911. What is the nature of your emergency?"

The Hummer had turned right at the light onto Dempster. Lips steered the Beemer into the turn going maybe forty mph. The Beemer's tires screeched but didn't skid. Points to BMW engineering.

"A baby's been kidnapped," Zoey said to the 911 operator. "We're chasing the kidnapper."

The operator's voice perked up. "Where are you now?"

"On Dempster, near uh . . ." She craned her neck just as Lips swerved again, nearly sending her nose into the passenger-side window. "Shit."

"I beg your pardon," the operator said, sounding offended.

"Not you. I know we've passed Skokie Boulevard—"

"We're on Dempster and Le Claire," Lips said tightly.

Zoey repeated the information.

"Tell 911 that it's a yellow Hummer," Lips said as he accelerated around a postal truck, imperiling the paint on the Beemer's side. "The license plate's obscured by mud, but there's a dent in the back left panel over the wheel."

The Hummer suddenly swerved into the right lane and took a ramp onto the Edens Expressway.

Zoey gasped in the middle of her recitation. "He's gotten onto the Edens going north."

The Beemer barreled up the ramp and abruptly slowed. In either direction on the freeway, as far as the eye could see, was a four-lane-wide trail of cars.

"Shit," Zoey muttered.

"I beg your pardon," the operator said again. Must get sworn at a lot in her job.

"Not you," Zoey replied and then said to no one in particular, "This is why I never take the Edens after three. They've been doing road construction for, like, ten years here."

"I'll be sure and tell the guy that when we catch up with him," Lips ground out.

If they caught up with him, Zoey thought and bit her bottom lip. The Hummer was already several cars ahead and moving, whereas their part of the traffic jam was stopped dead. There was a good possibility that they'd lose the Hummer in the traffic. She kept her eyes firmly fixed on the massive lump of yellow steel. She wasn't letting it out of her sight. That truck contained a kidnapper with a gun and a very important little piece of humanity. 'Cause the kidnapper hadn't taken just any baby.

He'd taken Pete.

Chapter Two

Thursday, 4:48 p.m.

FBI Special Agent Dante Torelli kept his eyes fixed on the UNSUB in the yellow Hummer, but he was aware all the time of the woman sitting beside him. She strained forward against her seat belt as she talked on her cell, as if she could make the cars ahead move by sheer force of will. And maybe she could. So far she'd appropriated his car, invited herself along on a high-speed chase, and seemed quite comfortable telling him how to do his job.

Dante eased up on the clutch and tapped the accelerator, rolling his nearly new BMW 650i convertible forward a few feet before braking again. He'd been briefed when she moved into the apartment building a couple weeks before, but for the life of him, he couldn't remember her name now. She lived on the second floor, he knew. His place was on the third, next to the couple he was helping guard.

Except it really wasn't his place at all. It was an apartment shared by four FBI agents in twelve-hour shifts of two. He was undercover as a regular city guy, working nine to five during the day and coming home at night to a midpriced apartment. His real job was working the night shift, keeping an eye on a guy named Ricky Spinoza, his girlfriend, Nikki Hernandez, and their toddler daughter. Ricky just happened to be the key witness in a federal trial. Dante and his partner, Jill Petrov, played the part of a boring, happily married yuppie couple. The day shift were a couple of guys young enough to pass as computer geeks working out of their apartment.

Ahead, the Hummer was slowly widening the gap between them. Dante couldn't tell if the driver had noticed yet that he was being tailed. Not that it mattered—neither of them could go any faster in this mess.

His passenger was one of those women who didn't bother with makeup and was in-your-face about not dressing to please a man. Right now she was wearing a navy pea coat, orange mittens, and an orange and purple knitted hat with ear flaps that looked like it was made by colorblind reindeer herders. Red-blond braids snaked out from under the flaps. And she had on a long pink fuzzy scarf that clashed with everything else. Oh, and boots. But not the sexy kind with a heel. Nope. This chick was wearing big ugly boots like something a bear hunter would wear. Except he'd bet his Cartier watch that she'd be more likely to take out the hunter than the bear if she had a gun in her hand.

Dante glanced in the rearview mirror, looking for any way to get around this traffic logjam. The dirty gray Toyota behind him was right on his tail. Even if there was an opening on the side, there was no way he could back up enough to clear the bumper of the SUV in front.

"Shit," he muttered.

The woman shot him a reproving look and went back to talking to 911 on her cell. Like that was going to help. The Chicago PD was notoriously slow to respond. The Hummer would probably be in Wisconsin by the time the local cops showed.

Actually, beneath the god-awful reindeer-herder hat, she had kind of pretty eyes. A clear, sharp blue. Her face was round, not because she was fat, but because that was the way it was shaped, all soft curves. Cheeks pink from the cold, a little nose, and full, sweetheart lips. Her body was probably round, too, somewhere beneath the pink scarf and shapeless coat. When he'd covered her body with his he'd thought he'd smelled something in her hair. Not flowers or perfume. A more familiar scent that he couldn't quite place.

Not, of course, that it mattered what her body looked like or what scent she wore. He was on a job. And with that thought, a realization hit him.

"You were stalling me."

She took the cell away from her ear and looked at him, brows furrowed. "What?"

"That whole parking-place thing. You were stalling me so he could grab the kid."

Her mouth dropped open. "What are you talking—"

He jammed the brake a little too hard, making her jolt in her seat. Then he leaned his arm on the wheel and half turned toward her. "Don't even try an innocent act. We know who you are. We know about your relationship to

Nikki Hernandez. We know you consider yourself that baby's aunt."

Her face had gone blank beneath the multicolored reindeer hat, and for a moment he thought she'd deny it. But then she said, "Pete."

"What?"

"Her name is Pete." She inhaled and laid the open cell in her lap. "And, yeah, I am her aunt—there's no 'consider' about it."

"And did you help this guy"—he jerked his chin in the direction of the Humvee—"kidnap Pete?"

"If you know that I'm Pete's aunt, then you know that I'd never do anything to harm her." She looked at him steadily, her blue eyes clear. "So, no, I didn't help this asshole."

He stared at her a moment longer. She seemed honest, but then there were a lot of sociopaths out there who could lie with a perfectly straight face.

She cleared her throat. "So, you've known all along that my mother fostered Nicki."

He'd turned back to the road, frowning as he watched the traffic creep forward another couple feet. "Yeah. We did a full background on Ricky Spinoza and Nikki Hernandez. And if we hadn't caught you on Hernandez's background, we sure would've when you signed the lease on that second-floor apartment."

"So?"

He clenched his jaw. "So, Spinoza and Hernandez were both clearly instructed to tell no one—*no one*—where we were hiding them."

"Yeah, well, I'm not just anyone," she shot back. "I'm Nikki's sister."

He glared at her a moment. She was a problem that should've been foreseen when they'd done the write-up on Hernandez's file. Foreseen and headed off before she'd gotten the notion to move into the same apartment building where they were holding Ricky and his family in protective custody. If Dante'd been in charge of this operation, he sure would've seen that she was a big fat problem waiting to happen. But Dante had joined the Chicago office only a little over a month ago. He'd not been in on the initial planning of this case.

He grunted and looked away from her. "The brass went back and forth for a whole day on whether or not to let you rent that apartment. In the end they decided it was better to have you where we could keep an eye on you, in case you and Hernandez were cooking something up between you." He looked at her curiously. "That was a gutsy move—taking the place right below where we were holding your sister and her boyfriend in protective custody. Why'd you do it?"

"If you did a background on Nikki, then you know how close I am to her and Pete." Her lush mouth had tightened. "I saw Pete almost every day before they went into hiding. I couldn't stay away from her when Nikki called and said they were coming back to Chicago. I just couldn't."

Dante stared at the traffic ahead as he thought about that. His left calf was beginning to ache from pressing down on the clutch. This was the one problem with driving a stick. It was a bitch in stop-and-go traffic. He eased up on the clutch as they crept forward a couple of feet. The black SUV ahead stopped suddenly and Dante tapped on the brake, the BMW's wheels skidding on packed snow and nearly sliding into the SUV.

Ricky Spinoza was a low-level mob bag man—definitely not the sharpest knife in the kitchen drawer. He'd gotten into debt and decided to fake being robbed of the mob money he'd been carrying—almost a half a million dollars. Unfortunately for Ricky, his acting skills had not been nearly as up to par as he'd thought, and he'd quickly come under suspicion by his mob bosses. He'd been on the verge of being picked up and taken for a final dive off of Navy Pier when Ricky had had the smartest idea of his life: he'd decided to turn state's evidence.

Ricky and his family—his girlfriend, Nikki Hernandez, and their baby, Pete—had been protected by the FBI for a year now, being moved from one place to another. They'd been brought back to Chicago only in the last couple of weeks in preparation for Ricky going on the stand to testify in the biggest mob trial Chicago had seen in decades. The trial to put big Anthony DiRosa—Tony the Rose—away for good. Because, as it turned out, idiot Ricky Spinoza had actually witnessed Tony the Rose popping an underling who had displeased him. The mob boss had a nasty temper, and with Ricky's evidence, it would put him in the federal pen for the rest of his life.

The SUV began to move, and Dante's attention snapped back to the traffic. The cars all rolled forward about twenty feet and then ground to a halt again. They were on an overpass now, the yellow Hummer almost a hundred feet ahead, nearing an exit at a snail's pace.

Dante flexed his hands on the steering wheel. "What's your name?"

"What?" She'd started talking on the phone to the 911 operator again, and now she turned and stared at him as if he'd made a kinky pass.

"Your name. I forgot it from Nikki's file. What is it?"

She scowled. "Zoey."

He glanced at her, brows raised.

She sighed heavily as if the question was a real bother. "Addler. Zoey Addler."

"I'm Special Agent Dante Torelli."

She nodded. "Nikki told me who you guys were, but she didn't have time to give me names."

He cocked an eyebrow in question.

"We met a couple of times to talk," she said. "On the stairwell or in the laundry room. I hadn't seen Pete in all those months you had them in protective custody away from Chicago, and—"

But Dante cut her off with a curse under his breath. The yellow Hummer had reached the off-ramp and was exiting the freeway.

"Dammit!" Dante leaned on his horn. "Tell the 911 operator that he's getting off on Old Orchard."

Zoey relayed the information as Dante rolled down his window and waved at the car ahead. If the SUV moved even an inch, maybe—

But the SUV driver blew his horn back, flipping the bird out the window.

Meanwhile, the Hummer had made Old Orchard.

"Shit." He had literally nowhere to go. The cars were too close together, and even if he could get to the side, there wasn't decent room for a car, because they were on the overpass. "*Shit!*"

"He's pulling into that gas station," Zoey said.

Dante looked, and wonders of wonders, sure enough, the yellow Hummer had pulled into the corner BP not a block from the overpass. The black SUV ahead lurched forward, the traffic awakening sluggishly.

"Blow your horn again." Zoey examined him critically. "Don't you have one of those magnetic police-light thingies to put on the hood of your car?"

He gritted his teeth. "This isn't *Starsky and Hutch*."

"No kidding. Maybe we should get out of the car."

"And do what? Take a flying leap off the overpass?"

"We could run to the ramp—"

He snorted. "And when he takes off we'll be left trying to run down a Humvee on foot."

"Well, we can't just sit here," she said, but he noticed she made no move to leave the car.

His BMW crawled forward another yard, and the UNSUB got out of the parked yellow Hummer.

"Jesus." Dante gripped the wheel. "Where the hell are the cops?"

"Maybe he's just going to leave her there," Zoey said. "Maybe he saw us following him and got scared."

Dante glanced at her in disbelief. *Not likely.* But he didn't want to crush the hope in her voice. The UNSUB pulled open the green and white door to the gas-station convenience store. What was he doing? Taking a leak? He must know he'd been followed.

The SUV ahead stopped suddenly, and Dante again nearly ran into it. He felt his neck muscles contract. The asshole wouldn't stay in the convenience store forever. If he could just get down there. Maybe he should take Zoey's advice and leave her with the car. If he ran down the ramp he could make the gas station in a few minutes.

He unlocked his door.

Zoey leaned forward, staring out her window. "What—?"

He looked over. A little bright green Civic had been parked to the side of the BP station. As he watched, two elderly women hopped out, ran to the Hummer, and got in.

Dante leaped from the BMW and ran down the side of the overpass, his black dress shoes sliding on the ice.

The Hummer pulled out of the BP station and crossed two lanes of traffic, narrowly missing a navy sedan. It bumped over the concrete divider, turned left, and accelerated through the yellow intersection stoplights.

"Fuck!" Dante slammed both fists on the overpass rail, watching helplessly as the Hummer drove by underneath. "Fuck! Fuck! *Fuck!*"

He had no idea who'd taken the kid, he had no idea why he'd let Zoey Addler get in his car, and he had no idea who the second kidnappers were. In fact, the only thing he did know was that under their winter coats, the elderly women had been wearing Indian saris.

Chapter Three

"You are driving too fast, Pratima," Savita Gupta said, clutching both the door and the dashboard of the truck at the same time.

"Pardon me," Pratima Gupta replied tartly to her sister-in-law, "but I was not aware that you knew how to drive, Savita-di."

Pratima steered the very large yellow Humvee truck into a turn, fishtailing just a tiny bit, which was only to be expected. After all, she had never before driven a Humvee truck, a vehicle designed by the US of A army to be used in wars, not on the streets of Chicago. Streets that were even at the best of times slippery with ice. Also, here in the US of A, Pratima must constantly keep in mind that vehicles drove on the *right* side of the street, instead of the more natural left as was done in India.

"Right. Right. Right," Pratima chanted under her breath.

"I may not be able to drive, but only a fool would not understand that you are going too fast," Savita-di said. "And what is that you are saying? I cannot understand you!"

"I am not saying anything, Savita-di," Pratima said cheerfully. "Perhaps you are imagining things."

Savita-di was hunched on the passenger side of the truck, her little round body almost in a ball in the big seat. Her shiny hair was streaked with gray, and she'd had it cut in a bob within a week of their arriving in the USA. Pratima still wore her own long hair pinned up at the back of her head—the same style she had worn since the age of twelve. Savita-di had on a long, puffy, silver down coat, a twin of Pratima's own coat. Although, of course, Pratima's coat was several sizes larger, as she was nearly half a head taller than her sister-in-law. Underneath the coat, Savita-di wore a green and mustard-yellow sari, and on her feet were heavy black boots—Savita-di had a fear of slipping and falling on the icy Chicago sidewalks.

Pratima Gupta and Savita Gupta had known each other for all of their lives. Or at least all of Savita-di's life, for she was the older of the two ladies by one year and nine months. They had grown up in the same middling-sized town in the Marwar region of India, their houses only a stone's throw apart. Naturally they had played together as little children. As young girls they had shared a mutual interest in the English language, which they learned from a battered collection of Victorian romance novels. And eventually, when they had come of age, they had married the brothers Gupta. Savita-di had married the elder, more handsome brother, Pratima the younger but more business-wise brother.

Now, nearly fifty years later, their husbands were dead and their children grown, with families of their own. When Savita-di's youngest daughter, Vinati, had implored her to come to America, naturally Savita-di had asked Pratima to come, as well. They might be only sisters-in-law, but by this time they might as well be sisters in truth.

And if they were sisters in truth, then that would make Savita-di the bossy older sister. "Do you wish us to be arrested by the police?"

Pratima lifted her foot from the gas pedal, because truth be told she did not want to be pulled over by the police. There were two reasons for this. One, that she and Savita-di had just stolen back their precious supply of Grade 1A Very, Very Fine Mongra Kesar. And two, because while Pratima was a very good driver indeed, she did not actually own a driver's license.

"You must look into the box to see if our Grade 1A Very, Very Fine Mongra Kesar is intact," Pratima said in order that her so-bossy sister-in-law would stop complaining about her driving.

They were on Skokie Boulevard now, traveling very fast, but of course *not* speeding. Pratima drove in the direction of their wonderful restaurant. For that was the dream that both women had held in their hearts for many years: a restaurant of their own where they could serve the secret recipes of their youth. Now that dream was so very close to being realized.

"Yes, yes, I am already doing so, Pratima," Savita-di replied rather crossly. She reached to the box sitting on the floor between her feet.

Pratima did not reply, for the other woman's hands were shaking as she pried open the lid of the box. It was a plain wooden box, a little smaller than a shoebox, and not marked at all. One would never know, looking at it, what treasure it hid inside.

"Ahhh," Savita-di breathed as she lifted the lid. "Everything is most wonderful. Our Grade 1A Very, Very Fine Mongra Kesar is intact."

She moved aside the bunched plastic tail of the bag inside the box. Revealed were the dark maroon threads that lay inside the plastic. It was a full kilo of the very finest kesar—*saffron* in English—from Kashmir, India. Mongra kesar was fantastically expensive, legendarily flavorsome, and very, very illegal indeed. It was also the essential ingredient to Mrs. Savita Gupta and Mrs. Pratima Gupta's top-secret Very Special Kesar Kheer recipe. Their kesar kheer was going to be the crowning dish in the wonderful Indian restaurant the sisters-in-law would open in Albany Park. It would make them famous and ensure their restaurant's success, thus making them very, very rich indeed. Pratima had seen grown men weep when the first spoonful of Very Special Kesar Kheer touched their tongues.

Unfortunately, India was quite stingy with its kesar. The Indian government had banned all export of the miniscule annual crop of Mongra kesar for years. This had made it somewhat difficult for Pratima and Savita-di to obtain the kesar, until they had enlisted the daughter of Pratima's aunt's son. This girl most fortuitously worked in the Indian consulate in Chicago and for a small fortune had smuggled the kesar out of India in a diplomatic pouch.

All had been delightful then, the kesar in their possession, the restaurant about to open, everything in readiness.

Until That Terrible Man had walked into the kitchens last week, demanding protection money. Protection money! Here in the US of A? This was the Land of the Free! Most naturally, Pratima and Savita-di had refused That Terrible Man, waving their wooden cooking spoons indignantly. He had left, cursing them in foul language.

And then disaster had struck, for That Terrible Man had returned the next day—this last Tuesday—when Pratima and Savita-di had not been about to protect their invest-ment with their wooden spoons. That Terrible Man had broken several dishes, frightened the elderly man hired to mop the floor, and, most criminal of all, stolen their kesar. He had then held their precious spice as ransom so that they would pay the protection money. What iniquity! Nat-urally they had not the funds to pay the protection money, and naturally they must steal back the kesar to open their restaurant.

"Do you think he will follow us?" Pratima asked now. She looked worriedly into the rearview mirror. She was not intimidated by That Terrible Man, but he was very large and she would not like to meet him whilst driving his stolen yellow Humvee.

"No, I do not," Savita-di stated with certain authority. "How can he? We have taken his Humvee, thus ensuring that he is without a car. I do not believe that anyone will give such an ugly and disagreeable man a lift in their car, no I do not."

"I think you are right, Savita-di."

"Yes, of course I am right," Savita-di said. "Was I not right in saying that That Terrible Man would still have our Grade 1A Very, Very Fine Mongra Kesar in his yellow Humvee truck?"

"Yes, indeed."

"And was I not right in thinking that we would find That Terrible Man by waiting near the BP petrol pump in a stealthy manner because it is where he daily buys an Illinois lottery ticket?"

"This is true," Pratima admitted reluctantly, because Savita-di needed no further encouragement to her already monstrous ego. And besides, it had been Pratima's idea to follow That Terrible Man about all week to find out what places he habituated.

Not that facts ever deterred Savita-di. "And was I not right that That Terrible Man would leave his keys in his vehicle because he is extremely lazy?"

"Ye-es."

"And was I not right—"

At that moment they came to a red stoplight, and Pratima pressed both feet on the brake to stop the enormous yellow Humvee truck. Pratima turned to Savita-di, who looked rather out of sorts as she retrieved her purse, which had been flung against the dashboard by the force of their stop, and opened her mouth.

But the words that Pratima was about to speak were forever erased from her mind, for she heard a small, birdlike sound from the back seat. Pratima's eyes widened as she looked at Savita-di, frozen in place, and then both ladies slowly turned their heads to stare into the back seat.

Where not one, but *two,* babies stared back.

Chapter Four

*W*ho were they? Could you see?" Zoey demanded as Lips threw himself back in the Beemer.

"I don't know," he said tightly, gripping the steering wheel as if he wanted to crush it into powder between his fists.

"But what were they doing?" she nearly wailed. "They looked like little old ladies in saris—"

"They *were* little old ladies in saris."

"So why'd they steal the Humvee? Why'd they take Pete?"

Zoey closed her eyes on the words *take Pete.* Oh, God. Her thirteen-month-old niece was out there somewhere, being driven who knew where by total strangers. She wanted to scream. Pete was like flesh and blood. She'd been there when Pete was born, had helped cut her cord, had held her and watched her tiny, tiny fingers open and close on the first day of her life. She loved the baby almost as much as if she'd given birth to Pete herself.

Zoey bit her lip. "Maybe the sari ladies made a mistake. Maybe they just wanted to try a Hummer out, y'know, drive it around the block. Maybe they'll be back soon."

Lips rolled his eyes at her.

"Okay, that's lame," she conceded. "But they left their little car and . . ." *Oh, shit, her Prius!* Zoey stopped talking, her mouth half open like a freshly pithed frog. "I left my Prius running in front of the apartment!"

He looked at her. "What?"

"My Prius! I saved for three years for that car. It'll be paid off in nine months. I love my Prius!"

"Isn't it a hybrid?" he said slowly and rather pedantically. "I thought hybrids have a radio key. If you took the key with you—"

"I didn't take the key with me!" she yelled at him. She was clearly hysterical now, but dammit, she didn't care anymore. Pete had been stolen by little old ladies in saris, her beautiful car was probably gone, and some human sympathy would be nice right about now.

Not that she was going to get it from the robot sitting next to her. He'd obviously gone into male logic mode. "That was stupid. You should never leave your keys in a parked car. Do you have any idea how many cars are stolen a year because the owner—"

"I know that!"

He looked at her, clearly confused. "Then why leave your keys in the car?"

"Because I was busy keeping you from stealing my parking place!"

The traffic was stopped again, and Baldy the kidnapper still hadn't come out of the gas station. Lips was turned in his seat to face her, so she saw the exact moment when his mouth twitched.

She narrowed her eyes at him. "You think this is funny."

"No, I don't."

"Losing my Prius is *not* funny."

"I didn't say it was."

"But you're laughing at me."

"I'm not—"

"I saw you smile!"

"I don't think you did."

She folded her arms across her chest, perilously close to pouting. "I had to special order the color, too. The light blue is really popular."

"I don't think you have to worry," he murmured softly in a deep voice that no doubt he used in the bedroom to great success. "The police have probably impounded your car by now."

"Shit!"

"Unless it was stolen, of course," he said helpfully. "It takes the Chicago police a while to respond, even to a shooting, and a newer car just sitting there, running in the middle of the street"—he shook his head—"you might as well have written *steal me* on the windshield."

"Oh, gee, thanks. I feel loads better now."

He grinned, flashing movie-star teeth, blindingly white against his swarthy skin, and she had to stop herself from doing a double take. Dear God, the man was gorgeous when he smiled. For some reason she would've never guessed that he had a sense of humor. He seemed so straitlaced, the type of guy who always took himself and everything around him perfectly seriously. It sent her off-balance, realizing that she might be able to connect to him. A sense of humor made him more human, more—

"Damn," he said softly.

She looked up in time to see Baldy come running out of the gas station. The kidnapper stopped suddenly and stared at the place where his Hummer had stood. Then he began miming baffled rage, clutching his head and gesticulating wildly.

"There goes that theory," Lips said.

"What theory?"

He sighed and eyed the traffic in front of them. "The theory that the ladies in saris taking the Hummer was some kind of planned switch-off. It was far-fetched, but a possibility."

Zoey turned to look at Baldy, who was now jumping up and down in the gas-station parking lot. "Yeah, I think that theory might be toast."

Baldy turned and darted around back of the gas station.

"Where's he going?" she muttered.

"Christ, I don't know." Lips sounded fed up and disgusted.

A moment later, a bright red SUV ricocheted back around the gas station, with Baldy at the wheel.

Zoey leaned forward to watch as the truck careened across the lanes of traffic, drove over the concrete street divider, and roared under the overpass. "Did he steal—?"

"Looks like it," Lips growled. "Tell 911."

She'd forgotten the cell phone still open in her lap, but now she picked it up and relayed the kidnapper's new vehicle information to the confused operator. "Did you see the license plates?" she asked Lips.

"Not from this angle."

She grimaced and finally hung up on the operator.

The black SUV ahead of them suddenly surged forward, and Lips cursed under his breath. A couple of minutes later and they were speeding down the off-ramp.

"Are you going to try and follow them?" Zoey asked, though she knew it was probably hopeless.

"No, they're long gone."

"But—"

"Look, there're two cars now, and the cops have to arrive soon. Better we wait so I can brief them and regroup."

He drove the Beemer into the BP gas station and pulled in beside the little frog green Civic the sari ladies had been driving. The car looked like it had been through several Chicago winters, and the rear bumper was hanging at an angle, but there was a brand-new magnetic sign on the driver's-side door that read, THE TAJ MAHAL RESTAURANT, with an address and prominent phone number beneath.

"How are we going to regroup?" Zoey asked.

Lips was already unclipping a little black cell phone from his belt. She caught a glimpse of the gun harness under his left arm.

He frowned at her as he punched in a number and held the cell to his ear. "*I'm* going to regroup by calling in this car's number. *You're* going to go home instead of regrouping. I'll call you a cab and—"

Zoey felt her pulse speed up with alarm. She couldn't let him dump her. He was her only hope of finding Pete. She knew it was irrational, but as long as she was with him she was *doing* something. At home, she'd be merely pacing the floor. Besides, she no longer entirely trusted the FBI to keep Pete safe once they found her again. Right now, she was the only one chasing the kidnapper who was interested purely in Pete's safety and not some stupid mob trial.

She bit her lip and tried to think of a concrete reason for him to let her stay. "Look—"

He held up a hand, cutting her off, and spoke into the cell. "Kev? . . . Yeah, it's—"

He made an impatient face as the person on the other end of the phone apparently started talking fast.

Zoey watched him as his beautiful lips compressed into a frustrated, thin line. "Look, calm down. I've got a lead on the guy who grabbed the kid . . . Yeah . . . That's what I've been trying to tell you. Okay, look, I'm at a BP on Old Orchard Road, just west of 94. Happy?"

Zoey leaned forward urgently, catching his eye.

He held up his hand again, forestalling her. "Okay, I need you to run a license plate, give me the owner, address, everything you got." He rattled off the numbers on the little green Civic. "No, don't hang up." He blew out a frustrated breath. "I need this now, Kev. These women took off in the kidnapper's Hummer. . . . Yeah, you heard me right . . . Look, I need to talk to Headington . . . Yeah . . . Well, then where is he? . . . Okay, I'll wait."

"Who's Kev?" Zoey asked in a stage whisper.

"Tech guy."

"And Headington?"

"My boss, the SAC—Special Agent in Charge." Lips held the phone away from his ear and turned to her. "I'll call you a cab as soon as I get off the phone."

Zoey pasted on a big fake smile. "That's okay; I can hang out with you."

She realized her mistake almost immediately.

His bitter-chocolate eyes narrowed suspiciously at her, and suddenly he looked like an Italian Clint Eastwood. "You can't stick with me. I'm following a kidnapper. This whole thing could get violent."

"Maybe I don't want to just be dumped in this part of town," Zoey shot back. "It'll be dark soon, and—"

"Okay, okay, I'll wait with you for the taxi."

Panic was tightening her chest now. She couldn't let him ditch her. "That's not—"

"Or I'll drive you home myself. Just—" He cut himself off as two Chicago PD cars screeched into the gas station, one on either side of the Beemer.

Zoey blinked. "Wow, that was fast."

She watched as all four front doors on the police cars flew open, the nearest one narrowly missing banging against her door.

"Hey."

But something was wrong. Instead of getting out, the police officers were crouching behind the car doors, and it looked like they had their guns drawn, as if they were really nervous, or as if—

"Out of the car!" one guy boomed.

"Well, shit," Lips said softly. "This day just gets better and better."

He raised his hands.

And the cops opened fire.

"Get down!" Dante pushed her head into her lap and jammed the Beemer into reverse. He backed swiftly out from between the cop cars, the Beemer's engine whining.

He stomped on the brake, whipping the Beemer's front end around, and then accelerated out of the BP gas station.

It took a full second for Zoey to realize that the loud bangs coming from behind them meant that the Chicago PD were still shooting at the car. "Shit! What was that? Why are they shooting at us? I thought you were the good guy!"

Beside her, Dante's hands had tightened into white-knuckled vices around the steering wheel. His face was hard and angry, and she was really, really glad that his expression wasn't aimed at her.

"I *am* the good guy," he said quietly. "And I don't know why they were shouting at us, but you can be damned sure I'm going to find out."

Chapter Five

*W*hy *was* the Chicago PD shooting at him? That was the question that pounded through Dante's mind as he sent the BMW careening through traffic. It sure as hell wasn't standard operating procedure to shoot a man trying to surrender.

Unless, of course, they hadn't wanted him alive.

Sirens were wailing somewhere, but he couldn't see the pursuing cops. Not yet, anyway. Ahead, a cement mixer suddenly loomed, moving so slowly it was nearly at a stand-still. Dante jerked the wheel of the BMW to the right, sliding between the huge truck and a parked blue Mini with barely a hair's breadth to spare on either side. Behind him, tires squealed ominously. He made a left, cruising across two lanes of traffic, and sped down the street. A service alley was on the right, and he stomped the brake, slowing fractionally to make the turn.

The alley had been plowed only half-heartedly. Brown snow was frozen into ruts, the black asphalt beneath broken into chunks. The BMW rattled through the narrow space, barely missing a battered green metal Dumpster. The blackened backs of buildings rose high on either side, blocking the last light of the day.

Out of the corner of his eye, Dante saw Zoey clutch the passenger door. "You all right?"

"Yeah." She glanced at him, the whites of her eyes flashing in the car's dim interior. "Yeah. Was that some kind of mistake? Did they get mixed up about the car the kidnapper was driving, or—?"

"I don't think it was a mistake." Articulating the thought made him swallow with dread.

They were coming up on the end of the alley. It spilled out on another small business street. Dante nosed the BMW forward, looking in both directions before cruising sedately into traffic. There wasn't a cop car in sight.

He fumbled to find the BMW's navigation system button and then turned off the GPS. "Give me my phone."

The open cell was miraculously still in her lap. She handed it over.

"Thanks," he muttered and glanced at the little screen. Kevin had disconnected. "I want you to watch out the back window and tell me the moment you see anyone following us."

"Okay." She twisted in her seat.

Dante punched buttons one-handed as he drove and put the phone to his ear.

Eight rings and then a clatter. "What?" said an adenoidal voice on the other end.

"Kev, what the *hell* is going on?"

"Dante?" Kevin asked as if he had no idea.

Kevin was some sort of certified genius when it came to computers and the Internet, but he was an idiot about people and relationships. He was a young dude, maybe midtwenties, with long reddish hair and a scraggly tuft of fuzz on his chin, which didn't help his appearance. Just the opposite, in fact. Kevin worked in the Chicago FBI office and was one of the few people Dante trusted.

Or at least Dante *had* trusted him until today. "Yeah, it's me. Surprised? I just got shot at by Chicago's finest. You want to tell me why?"

"Hey, man, I don't know. Really, I swear on my mother's grave. I don't know what you're talking—"

Dante pressed the brake to the floor in a controlled movement, bringing the BMW to a halt at a stoplight. Then he said very quietly and very clearly, "Your mother isn't dead, Kev, and I'm sick of you lying to me. Why is the Chicago PD shooting at me?"

"They think you took the baby," Kevin said without hesitation.

Dante blew out a breath. "Why the hell would they think that? I gave you the description of the kidnapper and the vehicle he was driving."

"Yeah, but someone from our office told them you made that up to cover."

"Oh, come on," Dante growled. The light turned and the traffic rolled forward. "All they have to do is ask Jill or Wettstein. They'll tell you that—"

"They can't."

"Bullshit. Look—"

"They're dead."

"What?" he asked, even though he'd heard Kevin's words perfectly well.

"They're all dead."

"Jesus," Dante breathed.

He shot a look at Zoey. She was staring at him, her eyes wide. He'd obviously lost his poker face. But three agents killed? He'd only known Wettstein and his partner to say hello to, and Jill had been his partner for a mere three weeks. He didn't know her well, but he'd seen the photos of her husband and two elementary-school-aged sons. *Jesus.*

What the fuck was going on?

"Why would someone in the office tell the Chicago PD that I'd kidnapped a baby and killed fellow agents? Hell, why would anyone believe that?"

Kevin made a nervous humming sound. "Things are really weird here, man. People aren't talking, and I don't know what's going on exactly."

Dante stopped for a light and sat staring at the glowing red for a moment. Kevin was scared of something—or someone—in the office, that much was obvious. And considering why Dante had really been sent to the Chicago office, maybe Kev wasn't just being paranoid. Because Dante's true mission was to uncover an FBI agent who was in the pocket of the Chicago mob. He'd felt that he was getting close in the last week or so. Maybe someone felt he'd gotten *too* close.

The light changed. Beside him Zoey was very quiet, her eyes worried as she scanned the street behind them.

Dante swallowed and tried to focus. "Is there any word about Spinoza? Did they get him?"

"That I do know. Spinoza and his girlfriend are okay. Apparently they had a fight, Spinoza snuck out of the apartment through the bedroom window, and the girlfriend followed. They weren't even in the apartment when the thing went down; got back and found three dead FBI agents and the baby gone. I heard the mother had to be sedated."

"Okay. Okay." Dante tried to think as he drove the BMW, aware that sweat was beading at the small of his back. This couldn't be happening. How could he have been set up so neatly? How could they—whoever *they* were—have known that he'd be late to work today and unable to help his colleagues? If he'd been on time . . . He swallowed as he made the final connection. They hadn't known he was going to be late. Had he been on time as he usually was, he'd be just as dead as the three other FBI agents. What a lovely thought.

On the other end of the phone Kevin's breathing hitched. "Dante . . ."

"What?"

"There's something else."

"What? Spit it out."

"Charlie Hessler had a stroke last night."

"Fuck," Dante breathed. Charlie Hessler was a friend, a mentor in the FBI, and, at the moment, his link to the outside. "Is he dead?"

"No, he's in the ICU. They don't know yet if he's going to recover. He didn't—"

"Why didn't anyone tell me?" Dante snapped. He braked to a stop at a red light.

On the other end, Kevin breathed nasally, not answering.

Dante blinked hard and thought. Hessler was out, maybe permanently, and it looked like someone was trying to set Dante up to take the fall for three of his colleagues dying. If he didn't figure out what was going on *now* and how to stop it, he was going to end up in jail—or worse, on a metal shelf in the morgue. "Who did you tell where I was, Kevin? I need to know."

"Uh, why?"

"Because the cops arrived only minutes after I told you my location."

"It was these two humorless dudes in suits," Kev whined, "like all the rest of you field ops."

"What were their names?"

"That's what I'm telling you. I don't *know.* I'd never seen them before, and they weren't wearing ID tags."

"Okay." Dante breathed through his nose as he tried to calm his heart rate. "You don't tell them anything else from here on out, you hear me, Kev?"

"I—"

"*Nothing,* got it? Just keep your mouth shut."

"Okay, I got it. I'm not talking. Promise."

Dante felt his jaw tighten. Kevin was going to betray him again; he knew it, and there was nothing he could do about it. The little weasel was his only link to the information department. Best to find out what he needed and hang up fast.

"Is Headington there? I need to speak to him."

"No. I-I don't know where he is right now."

Dante grimaced. He needed to speak with his boss, but he couldn't stay on the phone that long. "Did you get a name for me on that license plate?"

"Yeah, I got it here." There was the clicking of keys in

the background. "It belongs to a woman named Agrawal A-G-R-A-W-A-L, first name Saumya, S-A-U-M-Y-A, lives up in Wheeling." Kevin gave a street number and address.

"Thanks."

"So." Kevin cleared his throat. "So, you going there now?"

"You don't need to know that."

"Okay, okay. I'm just asking."

"Don't ask."

Dante cut the connection, rolled down his window, and threw the cell phone out the window.

Zoey rubbernecked to see where the cell went and then turned to face him. "What's going on?"

"They think I took Pete," he said as he made an abrupt turn onto a busy boulevard.

"You . . ." She stared, open-mouthed. "But that's ridiculous! You were *guarding* her. How could they even think that you'd be in on the kidnapping?"

And this was the weird thing. The Chicago PD was chasing him, his whole career was going down in flames, and he was sitting next to a woman in a goofy reindeer hat. Yet hearing Zoey's absolute faith in him made him feel better.

Not, of course, that he showed it. "The three other agents who were on this assignment with me were shot dead in the apartment, and someone in the local FBI has pointed the Chicago PD in my direction."

Her inhaled breath rasped and she opened her mouth.

He continued before she could voice her fear. "Your sister and Ricky Spinoza are fine. They weren't in the apartment when the agents were killed."

"Nikki wouldn't leave Pete alone."

"Apparently she was arguing with Ricky and followed him out the window in the bedroom." He shrugged. "Probably she figured she'd only be gone a couple of minutes and the FBI agents were in the apartment. In any case, it's a good thing your sister and her boyfriend weren't there."

"Or they'd be dead, you mean," she whispered.

Dante nodded.

"Oh, God, I've got to call Nikki. I've got to see if she's okay."

"She's been sedated," he started, but she was already dialing her cell.

He glanced in the rearview mirror as she held the cell to her ear. As far as he could see they weren't being followed.

Zoey blew out a frustrated breath and snapped her cell shut. "She's not answering."

"Doesn't mean anything," he said soothingly. "My contact says she and Ricky are fine. Try again in a little bit."

"What else did your contact say?"

He shrugged. "He got me the name and address of the owner of that little green car the two old women jumped out of."

"And we're going there?"

He glanced at her and then turned the BMW into a corner gas station, slowing and creeping between cars pumping gas before exiting on the far corner. "See anybody behind us?"

She looked over the headrest. "No."

"Sure?"

He expected a glare but got a steady stare instead. "Yes."

"Good."

They were traveling backstreets now, a residential neighborhood that'd seen better days. The houses here were one-and-a-half story, mostly brick, with aluminum awnings that had probably been installed in the sixties.

"I don't understand how you're going to find Pete," Zoey said beside him. "You haven't forgotten her, right?"

They stopped at a light, and Dante turned his head to eye her. She was chewing on one corner of her lush mouth. "I haven't forgotten Pete."

The light turned and the cars started up again. Dante returned his gaze to the road. He thought about the little girl. He hadn't had much interaction with her—she was mostly in the bedroom with her mother when he'd talked to Ricky—but he remembered huge brown eyes and dark hair curling in wisps about her head. Babies always seemed to have such big heads on such soft, vulnerable necks. Dante tightened his grip on the steering wheel.

"So, how're we going to find her?"

"Trust me." He turned onto a boulevard and headed for the Edens Expressway again. Crosstown traffic was letting up now and they were moving faster, though he still kept his eye on the rearview mirror.

He felt her looking at him. "Trust you? I don't even know you."

His mouth twisted. "Same here."

Her teeth clicked together audibly as she snapped her mouth closed. He would've smiled if the situation weren't so grim. The woman was certainly prickly. They drove in silence for a while. The winter light was fading outside, the dark grays taking over the sky, the city lit by neon and the lights of cars and streetlamps.

He exited the expressway and slowed, looking for the

street. This area was pretty run-down, the old shops along the street mostly boarded up. But there were some signs of a possible revival: a newish drugstore, a big hole where something had been torn down, and evidence that something would be erected in the empty spot.

Dante turned down a cross street, passing an alley, and then turned again. The buildings that backed onto the alley were part of a strip mall. There was a discount dollar store, a liquor store, several windows with newspaper taped over the glass inside, and one shop with a brand-new sign. It read, "THE TAJ MAHAL RESTAURANT."

Zoey straightened in her seat. Dante circled the block and parked on the curb opposite the alley entrance. He craned his neck to peer down the darkening alley. Halfway down, partly obscured by a Dumpster, was an SUV. It was hard to tell in the dusk, but he was pretty sure it was bright red.

Dante smiled in satisfaction. "Bingo."

Chapter Six

The veteran FBI agent watched Kevin Heinz hunch his shoulders and type jerkily at his computer. The FBI agent's office was beside the tech department and if he leaned a little to the side in his desk chair, he had a clear view of Kevin in his little cubical.

Kevin wasn't working out.

The FBI agent closed his eyes and tapped slowly on the arm of his chair. Twenty-five years he'd given the FBI. Twenty-five years of wrestling bureaucracy and watching lesser men advance ahead of him. Hell, he even had a bullet scar on his shoulder and a wall full of commendations. And for what? A measly government pension? No goddamned way.

So he'd gone into business for himself, amassed a nice fortune, and was *this* close to retiring to someplace anonymous when something had put the wind up old Charlie Hessler. Charlie had ordered an internal investigation, sent in Special Agent Dante Torelli undercover, and Torelli had lived up to his reputation as a hotdogger by almost immediately finding a trail—one that led straight to the veteran FBI agent.

A tiny shard of pain pierced his temple. The FBI agent opened his center desk drawer and took out a half-empty bottle of aspirin. He swallowed two, washing them down with cold coffee from the mug on his desk. Torelli should've been killed at the safe house this afternoon. That was the plan: kill the informant and all the FBI agents. Make it look like Torelli had been lured into the mob's pocket and three brave agents had died trying to save Ricky Spinoza's scrawny ass.

Instead what he had was a big old pile of shit: Torelli and Spinoza still alive. Hit men and corrupt Chicago cops to pay off for work they'd screwed up.

The veteran FBI agent tapped his fingers. The key was not to panic. He'd been in the Bureau for twenty-five years. He had balls of steel and was damn smarter than anyone he knew. All he had to do was remain calm and figure another way to off Torelli before he could come in. Before Torelli could destroy him.

The tap of his fingers on the chair arm was the only sound in the room.

Chapter Seven

Thursday, 6:13 p.m.

*T*here's a hole in your roof," Zoey said.

She hadn't noticed the small hole in the Beemer's canopy until they'd been parked for ten minutes. By that time most of the heat in the car had vanished and she'd felt the cold air blowing in the hole.

She stuck a mittened finger in the hole.

"Don't do that," Lips muttered.

She withdrew her finger. "It doesn't help anyway. Just makes my finger cold. Do you have any duct tape?"

"What?" He'd been staring at the back of the Taj Mahal Restaurant this entire time, not talking or anything. He must be a whole lot of fun on a date—*not.* But maybe his dates were happy simply to gaze at his strong, silent profile.

Zoey sighed. "Duct tape. Do you have any duct tape?"

"What for?"

"For the hole in the roof of your car. Duh."

There was a streetlamp halfway up the block. In the reflected light she could see him draw his perfect, straight eyebrows together. "Why would I have duct tape?"

"I dunno. Seems like something a guy would carry around with him in his car."

He turned and looked at her, one eyebrow arched.

"Okay, so you don't have duct tape." Zoey folded her arms. "Sheesh."

He went back to staring at the alley.

Zoey twisted in her seat, drawing one leg up.

"What are you doing?" he asked without turning.

"Trying to get comfortable." She looked at the hole again. It sure was producing a lot of cold air for such a tiny hole. Lips didn't seem like the kind of guy to drive around with a hole in his pretty Beemer . . .

"Hey, that's a bullet hole!" She sat forward to peer at the hole more closely. It was perfectly round. Definitely a bullet hole. "Oh, my God. We could've been shot. Did you know that was a bullet hole?"

She looked at him.

He elevated both eyebrows a fraction of a hair. "Duh."

Okay, maybe she deserved that. Zoey turned around in her seat and peered into the back.

She heard a heavy masculine sigh. "Now what're you doing?"

"Where'd it go? It must've gone out of the car somewhere." She leaned over the seat, squinting at the black back-seat upholstery, nearly diving headfirst into the back floor.

She felt him grab her coat, his grip firm and sure. "Back driver's-side window."

The window had a tiny hole with a spiderweb of cracked glass around it.

"Wow." Zoey faced forward and sat back down. He had his arms crossed now, which was kind of too bad. She wouldn't've minded if he'd kept his hands on her just a little longer. "That's gonna cost to replace."

"My insurance will cover it."

"Your insurance covers gunshot holes?"

He glanced at her. There seemed to be a muscle jerking under his eye.

Zoey held out her palms. "I'm just saying, my insurance probably wouldn't cover it. They'd call it an act of God or something. But, hey, I'm sure you have special top-secret government-agent insurance. Good thing, too, huh?"

He'd turned away, and all she could see was the back of his head and his neatly trimmed dark hair. He had a nice neck. Strong, not too thick, but not weenie-thin. He gave a small sigh.

Zoey clasped her hands in her lap and tried not to think of Pete. Was she crying? Scared out of her wits, riding around with strangers? God, she hoped not.

She sighed softly. "I don't think she's ever been away from either me or Nikki."

She didn't expect Lips to necessarily catch on right away to what she was talking about—her words had been kind of obscure—but he understood. "Pete?"

"Yeah." She shifted in the seat again, the rustle of her coat against the leather loud in the car. "It was mostly me or Nikki with her. Nikki can't afford sitters much."

"Ricky didn't help?"

She shrugged. "There's a reason I call him Ricky-the-jerk."

He nodded.

She laughed, but her breath caught and it came out almost a sob. "Pete didn't remember me, of course, not after six months away. But this last week she was smiling when she saw me. I thought, you know, that we'd eventually catch up."

"You will," he said, and it was the kindest thing anyone had said to her in a long while.

She cleared her throat because it was swelling and she didn't want to start crying in front of him.

"I thought her name was Petronella."

"It is. Petronella Spicy Hernandez. Nikki named her on the spur of the moment. I think she was still under the influence of the painkillers. Anyway, we've been calling her Pete pretty much since she came home from the hospital."

She realized she was jiggling her right knee up and down and stilled it. The car was getting pretty cold, and as it got colder, her bladder seemed to contract. She squirmed around in the leather seat, trying to get comfortable.

She cleared her throat. "Do you know how long we'll be here?"

Lips tore his gaze from the alley to look at her. "As long as it takes."

"But, like, do you think it'll be hours or minutes?"

"Do you have somewhere to go?" He arched his right eyebrow. Was that obnoxious or what? Who went around arching one eyebrow, outside of the movies? She'd bet her last dollar that he practiced in front of his bathroom mirror, probably daily. The sweet guy who'd comforted her about Pete seemed to have evaporated.

He returned his gaze to the red SUV in the alley across

the street. There was a single light, high on a pole in the alley, that had switched on automatically a couple of minutes ago. It was probably meant to deter burglars. At the moment, it was the only thing that made the red SUV visible.

Jerk. Zoey looked at the alley, too. Nothing was moving in the red SUV. Maybe Baldy had gone to sleep in there. Maybe the Indian ladies were off joyriding in Wisconsin with Pete.

"How do we know they're even in the restaurant?" she asked.

"We don't," he murmured. "But the kidnapper is in that SUV, and if he's waiting for the Indian women here, they'll probably show eventually."

"But what if they don't?"

She heard a gritting sound like he was grinding his teeth. "If they don't show, I arrest him and get him to talk."

"Oh." She stretched her legs out carefully. Her bladder felt like a water balloon perched in her pelvis. Any sudden movement and it might burst.

"Can't you hold still?" Lips asked without taking his eyes from the alley.

"I have to pee."

His looked at her and blinked, long girly eyelashes brushing his cheeks. "Oh. Uh . . . the dollar store probably has a restroom. We're behind him and far enough back in the shadows that I doubt he can see you exit the car. Just don't draw attention to yourself."

"I'll try not to jump up and down and wave my arms," she said sweetly. "Be back in a sec."

Zoey grabbed for the handle of the car door. Was it her imagination, or were his cheeks darker? She didn't stay to see. This was already embarrassing enough.

Trudging through the frozen slush in the street and around to the front of the block, she hoped that Baldy wouldn't take off when she was in the store. Just her luck she'd come back and Lips would be gone.

But fifteen minutes later, the Beemer was still sitting at the curb across the street from the entrance to the alley. Zoey opened the passenger-side door and got in, conscious that her nose was running from the cold.

"Hope nobody saw you." Lips had his eyebrows pulled together in stern worry.

Zoey rolled her eyes as she dug a tissue from the pocket of her coat. "Would you rather I peed in your car?"

She dabbed at her nose.

He frowned harder. "I—"

"For God's sake, don't answer that." Zoey opened the paper sack the cashier had given her at the dollar store. "Twizzler?"

He stared at the red licorice candy like it was a turd in her hand. "What?"

"Twizzler." She waved it under his nose. "Do you want a Twizzler?"

"Uh . . ."

She withdrew her hand. "If you don't like cherry licorice, just say so. Jeez."

He seemed mesmerized as she tore open the bag of Twizzlers and took out a piece, biting off the end. She chewed as his gaze fastened on her mouth like he'd never seen someone eat licorice before.

Finally he blinked as if he was coming out of a daze. "Okay."

She stopped chewing. "Okay, what?"

"Okay, I'll try one."

"Oh." She offered the bag again.

He inserted a finger and thumb and drew out one stick of licorice. He bit into it as he returned his gaze to the alley.

"Anybody move while I was gone?" Zoey rummaged in the dollar-store bag and came up with a six-pack of half-pint water bottles—the only kind the store had carried. She peeled one off, gave it to Lips, and took one for herself.

"Thanks." Lips took the bottle absently. "And no, nobody moved."

"How long will we stay here?"

"Until somebody moves or until sunup."

There wasn't much to say to that, so Zoey stayed quiet, slowly chewing her Twizzler. After a minute she rummaged in her bag and got out a roll of silver duct tape. She opened the plastic shrink-wrap around the roll, tore off a palm-sized strip with her teeth, and stuck it on the roof hole.

The tape held for a second and then fell to the floor.

Zoey looked at Lips.

He was watching her with the kind of expression most people reserve for the mentally challenged. "It's too cold."

She scowled. "I know it's cold."

He pointed to the hole. "For the tape to stick."

"Oh."

She put the tape away. There went a dollar down the drain. She took another bite of Twizzler to console herself.

Lips drank some water and recapped his water bottle. "So. What do you do?"

She stopped chewing to squint at him. "What?"

He did the eyebrow thing again. Someone really ought to tell him how irritating that was. "You know, work? What do you do?"

"Oh." She wrinkled her nose and took a slurp of her own mini water bottle. "I'm a poet."

"Yeah?" He stared at her a second, probably trying to figure out if she was kidding or not.

"Yeah." She waited for the sarcastic comment. For some reason most people seemed to think writing poetry was like this really effete endeavor and also incredibly silly at the same time.

"Huh," he said, biting into his Twizzler stick. "I've never met a poet before."

She nodded. That wasn't surprising.

He chewed meditatively for a moment. "What do you do with it?"

"What?"

He waved the Twizzler stick vaguely. "Your poetry. Is it published somewhere? Do they still publish books of poetry?"

"Some. There's small presses, and once and a while a major house comes out with a new compilation. But usually you have to know someone or be dead. Preferably dead." Usually she would be getting defensive at this point—it was amazing how little people knew about poets and poetry—but he really seemed interested in her answer. "Unless you go the vanity press route."

"Vanity press?"

"You know. Little red book with a cardstock cover, staples in the binding, one copy to all your friends and relatives?"

"Oh."

"Yeah. But there are still magazines that take new poems. I've gotten three of my pieces published in the last couple of years."

"Really."

Now he sounded almost impressed, and she could feel her cheeks heating. *Oh, God, don't blush.* It was such a pain having fair skin sometimes. And it was totally involuntary, blushing—it wasn't like it meant anything.

Except now she found herself babbling. "It's not a big deal. They were little magazines; you've probably never heard of them. Actually, the only people who've heard of them are other poets."

"So, I'm only allowed to be amazed if I'm another poet?"

"You're amazed?" Okay, now she was definitely blushing, she couldn't help it. No one, not even her family, had ever said something that nice about her writing.

"Sure. I don't know anyone who has published anything." He looked at her, and his dark brown eyes seemed so sincere.

Good God, the man was dangerous.

"Yeah, well." She cleared her throat. "It's not like the checks they send me will buy more than an order of take-out Chinese."

"So what do you do to pay the bills?"

"I have a day job at a co-op grocery store—The Serene Grape—"

"The Serene Grape?" He looked at her.

"That's what I said."

He stared pointedly at the Twizzler package in her hands. "Isn't that a health-food store?"

"Yeah? So?"

"So, what's with the licorice candy? I thought health-food types don't eat junk food."

She arched her own brow at him—not that he noticed, since he'd gone back to staring at the alley. "Just because I work at a health-food store doesn't make me a food Nazi. Besides, there's nothing wrong with Twizzlers—"

"Red food coloring? Refined sugar? Isn't that bad?"

"I don't eat Twizzlers all the time!" Now she sounded defensive. What was with this guy?

"Don't see how you could. This stuff tastes like cherry-flavored rubber."

"Well, yeah. That's what Twizzlers are." Zoey took another pull on her own stick.

He darted a funny look at her, and for a moment he seemed hypnotized by her mouth.

She stopped chewing. "What?"

He shook his head. "Nothing. I—"

And then everything happened at once. In the alley the back door to the Indian restaurant opened and a scrawny old man emerged. Baldy jumped from the red SUV. Lips cursed, drew his gun, and scrambled from the Beemer just as a lavender minivan rounded the corner. The little old man jumped in the air at the sight of Baldy and ran back into the restaurant, slamming the door behind him. Baldy started shouting and banging on the door, which, being metal, looked pretty solid.

The lavender minivan braked abruptly and then suddenly accelerated past Lips, standing by the side of the Beemer. As it whizzed by, Zoey caught sight of the two Indian women, one waving her arms wildly, the other bent over the wheel of the minivan as if she were on the last lap of the Indy 500. On the side of the lavender minivan someone had painted a lopsided daisy and the words "ARTIE'S FLOWERS."

Lips said a bad word.

Baldy turned at the sound of the revving engine and looked straight at Lips. Even from this far away, Zoey saw his eyes widen. Then he got a gun out and she dove for the floor of the Beemer.

BLAM! BLAM! BLAM!

A squeal of tires.

BLAM! BLAM!

Silence.

Oh, God, had he got Dante? The guy had been a hard-ass, but still, he'd tried her Twizzlers. What if—?

The car rocked as a man got in. Zoey raised her head to peek. Lips was sitting in the driver's seat, staring straight ahead out the windshield. He had a smear of dirt on one perfect cheekbone, and the shoulder of his black leather trench coat was smudged with white salt from the street. He didn't look happy.

Zoey scrambled up from the floor of the car and checked the alley. It was deserted, both minivan and red SUV gone. Even the little old man was still hiding—not that she blamed him, what with the gunfight and all.

The Twizzlers packet had fallen to the floor. She bent, picked it up, and took two out. One she handed to Lips, the other she bit into.

"Man," she said as she swallowed her gummy bite. "Have you got bad karma or what?"

Chapter Eight

Thursday, 7:03 p.m.

*N*eil's nerves had been pretty much shot to hell since the two old ladies had snatched his fucking Hummer, so it wasn't surprising that the sound of his cell going off in his jacket pocket made him jerk the wheel of the red SUV, which nearly sent the big truck into an oncoming bus. Fortunately, he got the SUV back in the right lane in time for the bus to fly by while the driver gave him the bird. At one time in his life, that would've been cause enough for Neil to pull out his Beretta and pop the bus driver.

But he'd turned forty-five just last month, and Neil had found that age was mellowing the fuck out of him. He hadn't killed anyone in nearly six months, and it'd been a good two weeks since he'd broke some little fucker's legs on behalf of Tony the Rose. True, he'd been in a shootout twice today, but that was a pretty small lapse. Ashley had made him do these anger management classes, and while he'd been in AM classes before—court ordered—he'd never paid any attention to them in the past. But when Ash said he needed to take the class and stay awake this time, Neil had figured he'd better do it. Ash was the best thing that'd ever happened to him, and he knew enough not to mess up something that good.

He'd met Ash five years ago now, and she'd knocked him on his ass, metaphorically speaking. Ash was smart and not afraid to show it. She'd stand up to any guy, give as good as she got, and stare them down. It'd taken Neil two years and a pink diamond big as the nail on his pinkie to get Ashley to marry him, and he figured it was about the smartest thing he'd done in his life.

So now, instead of plastering the fucking bus driver's brains against his fucking bus-driver seat, Neil turned off the main street and pulled up beside a brick bungalow. He took a breath, checked the rearview to make sure he'd lost the FBI agent. He hadn't even realized he was being followed until he saw the fucker again at the Indian restaurant. The guy was in plain clothes, but his shiny dress shoes and suit screamed Feeb. Neil snorted and pulled out his still-ringing cell. He checked the screen and nearly had a heart attack on the spot.

Slowly he took two short breaths and one long, like his AM teacher had taught them, and then flipped open the cell. "Yeah?"

There was a pause on the other end and an exhale like someone was blowing smoke, which of course he was, then a high voice that sounded like it was coming from a kid that didn't even have hair on his nuts yet.

'Cept this was no kid. "That you, Neil?"

Deep breath, blow it out slowly. It was supposed to lower his blood pressure, but Neil felt like his heart rate was going through the roof. "Yeah, it's me."

"Go okay?"

Neil shifted a bit in the car seat. Fact was, Tony the Rose wouldn't be calling at all if he didn't already know that the fucking job had gone all to shit in a shit basket. "Not so much."

Another pause while Tony blew more smoke. Way the guy sucked on cigars, he should've had a voice like a steam shovel, instead he was stuck with a little girl's lisp, go figure. "Wanna explain that to me?"

Not so much, but he couldn't tell Tony that. Instead, Neil took another deep breath, hoping he wasn't hyperventilating with all this fucking breathing, and said, "They didn't get the asshole."

"No?"

"No." Neil felt sweat pop out under his armpits, even though the heater on the SUV was only lukewarm. It was never a good thing to be the one to tell Tony bad news. "When I got there, the Feds were shooting at each other and Spinoza was nowhere in sight."

"He wasn't dead on the floor like he shoulda been?"

"No."

"And you didn't shoot him."

"No, I—"

"'Cause you know that's why I sent you over there in the first place, Neil," Tony the Rose said gently in his little-girl voice. "As backup, should that FBI agent screw me over and *not* kill Spinoza like he promised to. Which, as it turns out, he did."

"Ah . . ."

Tony blew smoke into the phone. "So you're sayin' I'm screwed now. Spinoza's still walking around plannin' on testifying against me."

"I guess." Neil swallowed. Turned out the fucking breathing wasn't helping worth a damn. "But I got the kid."

There was a pause from the other end, which Neil couldn't figure was good or bad or just surprised. He'd been a bit surprised himself when he'd had a brainstorm and snatched the kid when Spinoza hadn't been home. This was a clear case of "thinking outside the box," one of the things he'd learned in anger management class. Almost made the $149.99 class fee worth it.

"What am I gonna do with a kid?" Tony asked, and he sounded really interested, like he wanted to hear the answer.

Neil shrugged, even though he was alone in the SUV and there wasn't nobody around to see. "It's the asshole's kid. I thought you could hold it hostage, like."

"That's not a bad idea, Neil," Tony said gently. "If you still had the kid. But you don't, do you?"

Sweat slid down Neil's spine. How did Tony find these things out? It was fucking unnatural. Made working for him a real unsettling job, too. "I don't got the kid, but—"

"Get the kid."

The phone clicked, and then the dial tone buzzed in his ear.

Neil felt like throwing the fucking phone out the window, but the anger management classes called that "counterproductive." Also, he had a call that he still had to make. One that he'd been putting off for the last couple of hours.

Sighing, he punched in the number and waited for Ash to pick up while he tried to think of what to say. 'Cause he was going to have to explain that not only had he lost the asshole's kid and the Hummer, but he'd also lost the other thing in the Hummer.

Which happened to be Neil Junior.

Chapter Nine

Thursday, 7:25 p.m.

It took some doing to get the old guy to open the back-alley door to the Indian restaurant. First, because he must've been scared half to death by all the shooting and yelling, and second, because he didn't seem to speak any English. But despite the language barrier, Dante kept at it, mostly using his kindest tone of voice, with now and then a shouted threat thrown in for variety. In the end, the old man probably let them in more out of exhaustion than fear of the law.

"Thought I'd freeze before he'd open up," Zoey muttered as they tramped in. "How come the cops haven't turned up?"

Dante shrugged, putting away the FBI badge he'd been waving in the old guy's face. "No one called in the shots? Or maybe they're just late."

"Lucky for us. I'm getting tired of getting shot at." Her tone was light, but she wasn't fooling Dante. The woman was scared.

The battered metal door led into a huge kitchen with industrial metal counters and a bank of dented refrigerators and freezers. The old guy was cowering in a corner, holding up a mop, presumably in defense.

Dante sighed and raked a hand through his hair. Way to go. Now he was scaring the shit out of old men. "Uh . . . who owns this restaurant?"

The old man started at the sound of his voice and raised his mop. Not going well. The janitor or whoever he was couldn't've been more than five foot five. He wore a faded blue coverall with a green cardigan over it, and running shoes on his feet. His hair was snow white, and there was white stubble on his jaw. He looked like he might be from the Middle East, but Dante hadn't a clue where exactly.

"The restaurant?" Dante waved his arm but then dropped it when the old man shied. "Owners? Boss?"

Beside him Zoey cleared her throat. He glanced at her in time to see her roll her eyes.

Then she took her package of licorice out of her pocket. "Twizzler?"

Dante stared at her incredulously. Did she really think she could win over this old guy with rubbery red candy? Although, come to think of it, watching her eat Twizzlers had sure impressed him. She had a way of pursing her lips around the red candy stick before she bit into it that had him thinking all sorts of nasty thoughts. Thoughts that made sitting in a car for long periods really uncomfortable.

The old guy reached out a hand that looked more like a

desiccated claw and took a stick of licorice. He opened a maw with a single prominent tooth in the front and maneuvered the Twizzler into the side of his mouth, where presumably he had enough teeth to bite into the stick. Then he chewed happily—and open-mouthed—as he grinned at Zoey, his newest bestest friend.

Thoroughly revolted, Dante looked around the kitchen. The place was obviously not in business—the first clue being that it was now past suppertime and the doors were still locked. But also there were no stacked boxes of supplies, no recipes and orders taped to the walls, no pans waiting to be used. In fact, the kitchen looked pretty pristine. A lone corded phone hung on the wall next to the front counter. Dante went over and picked it up. There was a dial tone but no number anywhere on the phone.

Farther down the painted cinderblock wall there was a single wooden door. Behind him, the old guy was chattering to Zoey in who knew what language. Dante glanced over. Zoey was nodding her head somberly as if she understood every word. Dante caught her eye and tilted his head in the direction of the door. She nodded and edged around a bit, the old guy following her as he chattered, until she'd maneuvered him so that he had his back to Dante.

Dante tried the handle of the wood door. Locked. But it was one of those cheap locks with a push-in button on the inside doorknob. Dante glanced at the old man, still talking away, and took out a ballpoint pen. He pressed the tip into the little hole on the outside doorknob and heard the button pop on the inside.

Opening the door, he ducked in. There was a basic office setup here: a battered wooden desk, a chair, and a gray metal filing cabinet, but no computer. Dante sat in the chair behind the desk and started pulling open drawers. On the third one he hit pay dirt. There was a folder with several bills inside, orders for various supplies for the restaurant. Across one was written the name Savita Gupta, with an address and phone number. Both the address and phone number were different than the ones Kevin had given him from the car license plate.

Dante smiled and reached into his inside suit jacket pocket, taking out the ballpoint pen and a small leather notebook he always carried. He copied the information from the bill before searching the rest of the office. There wasn't much else to find—a few more bills, a newspaper clipping announcing the opening of an Indian market, and a few papers handwritten in a looping language. Dante pocketed these last.

Back in the kitchen, the old guy was still talking up a storm and Zoey's packet of Twizzlers was almost empty, but she had her head cocked toward the man, nodding every once in a while, as if she found every word he said terribly important. Dante paused for a second in the doorway, just watching her. She'd been a pain in the ass earlier, jumping on his car like a lunatic and telling him how to do his job. Yet now she was taking the time to listen to a stranger babble at her in a language she probably didn't even understand. Her head was tilted, a little line between her brows, the multicolored ties from her reindeer hat hanging down on either side of her face. Her full cheeks were flushed from the cold outside, and she looked kinda sexy.

She caught his eye and smiled, her eyes crinkling at the corners, her lush mouth curving, a dimple appearing in one cheek. Dante found himself staring, remembering what that mouth had looked like sucking on candy. This was just bizarre. She was so totally *not* his type. The last few hours had been full of tension and adrenaline. That must be the reason for his fascination. Adrenaline. Everyone knew it was an aphrodisiac.

Dante mentally shook himself and crossed to where she stood with the old man. "Let's go."

She looked dubiously at the old guy, who was still talking. "Shouldn't we offer him a ride home?"

Dante raised his eyebrows. "You're kidding, right?"

She frowned at him. "No. It's dark outside and the neighborhood isn't safe. What if the kidnapper comes back? What if—"

"Okay, okay." Dante held up his hands in surrender. "I'll give him a lift if you can figure out how to tell him that."

She shook her head like he was brain-dead, then turned to the old man. And somehow, without speaking the same language, she conveyed the offer of a lift to the guy. Either that or the man figured they were taking him out to dinner. In any case, he followed them outside the restaurant. He paused to lock the back door, and a few minutes later they were all piling into the BMW.

"Nice," Dante said as he pulled his seat belt out. "That was very nice. But I don't know how he's going to tell us how to—"

From his position smack in the middle of the back seat, the guy pointed, straight-armed, dead ahead.

Dante twitched a smile at the old guy and turned the ignition key. "Right."

"Did you find anything in the office?" Zoey asked.

"Yeah, I—" Flashing blue and red lights suddenly

reflected in his rearview mirror, and Dante felt his pulse kick into heart-attack territory.

"Oh, my God!" Zoey was twisting in her seat to look behind them.

There was nowhere to go, nowhere to turn. The police car was coming up fast on his rear. Dante started to press down the accelerator.

And the flashing cop car sped by them on the left, drove another couple of blocks, and took a right farther down. The cops hadn't been interested in them at all.

"Jesus." He eased off the accelerator, wishing his heart rate could calm down as easily.

"Good thing I used that restroom," Zoey muttered.

Dante shot her a look. Her words were cocky, but her cheeks were pale, and the sight bothered him. She shouldn't be frightened. She was the type of girl who took the world head-on. Much as her sarcasm and orders irritated him, he preferred them to the white face. He needed to get her away from this craziness as soon as possible. Before she was hurt.

A squawk from the back seat interrupted his thoughts, and an arm appeared over Dante's right shoulder, pointing left.

"All right, all right," he muttered as he maneuvered around the truck in front of them. "Just give me a second so I don't rear-end this guy."

A digital song started playing in the car.

"Darn." Zoey fumbled for her phone. Her frown smoothed to an expression of worry when she looked at the caller ID. "It's Nikki."

She flipped open the phone. "Hi, sweetie . . . no, I'm okay . . . yeah, I know."

Dante stopped at a light. "Don't tell her where we are."

She glanced at him. "I'm with a friend. No, it's . . . No, it's okay. No, really . . ." She sighed as Nikki talked for a long bit, then said, "I'll call you later . . . Promise . . . Yes . . . love you, too. Bye."

Zoey shook her head as she hung up. "She's almost insane with worry."

Guilt tightened his chest. "I'm sorry."

"Thank you." Her face was hidden as she put away the cell.

He accelerated as the light changed.

"Shouldn't we switch cars or something?" Zoey asked. "Won't the guys who're chasing you know what car you drive?"

"One thing at a time." He needed to get her to a safe place. The problem was that she was his only witness that he *hadn't* kidnapped a baby and shot three of his colleagues. Sooner or later the fact that she was a witness to the truth was bound to occur to whoever had set him up. The case against him was a whole lot stronger if Zoey were missing. Or dead. Which left a question: Was Zoey safer with him, or by herself?

"Hey, maybe we can break into the city's impounded-cars lot and liberate my Prius," Zoey said.

He widened his eyes in mock admiration. "That *is* a good idea. A Prius is just what I'd like to be driving if we're chased again."

"No need for the macho sarcasm," Zoey huffed. "Besides, who says *you'd* be driving the car?"

Dante didn't bother answering. They were in a neighborhood composed of brownstone duplexes and more modern square apartment buildings. The old guy tapped

Dante on the shoulder, and he took that as a signal to slow down.

"Or I know someone we could ask to borrow her car," Zoey continued. "'Course she drives a Beetle. And it's purple."

The old guy gave a yell from the back, and Dante stomped on the brake in reflex. "Jesus! What?"

He turned to find the old guy scrambling out of the back seat.

"Bye!" Zoey called, and they both watched him skitter across the street and into one of the duplexes. She turned to him with a bright face. "Want to try for the Beetle? Or do you have a better idea?"

Dante put the BMW in gear. "I've got a better idea."

Chapter Ten

Thursday, 8:05 p.m.

"Where are we going?" Zoey asked. It was dark now, the streetlights reflecting off the slush piled against the curbs.

"I need to drop you off," Lips said. The car was shadowed, but she could make out the grim set of his jaw. "Do you have a friend or relative you can stay with?"

"No." Her heart had sped up at his words. The last thing she wanted was to have him dump her somewhere. It was important that she stay with him. Important that she find Pete.

"No one at all? What about the friend who owns the Beetle?"

"She just had a baby. My mother lives in Indiana. I've got one friend who's just left for two weeks in Cancún, and another who lives in a dorm at the University of Chicago."

"A dorm?"

Zoey shrugged, glad that he couldn't see her face. She was skating the truth on all of this, and she wasn't the best liar in the world. "She's getting a law degree."

"You don't have any brothers or sisters?"

"Not besides Nikki." She swallowed. "Well, I've got some foster brothers and sisters from way back, but we're not in touch. I don't even have current phone numbers."

Lips sighed. "Okay. Give me your cell phone."

She dug in her coat pocket and handed it over, mute.

He tapped in a number one-handed and held it to his ear. "Kevin? Yeah, it's me. What's happening?"

He drove silently as Kevin must've said something at length.

"Christ, Kev."

His tone was sharp, and Zoey watched him curiously.

"Look, I need you to trace the money for me. . . . Yeah, I know it won't be easy, but . . . Just do your best . . . Yeah . . . The usual place . . . What about Headington? Christ. . . . Okay."

Lips flipped the phone shut. He had a thoughtful expression on his face.

Zoey couldn't stand the suspense anymore. "What? What'd he say?"

Lips glanced at her as if surprised by her outburst, then looked ahead again. "My boss is unavailable. And, apparently I've got a bank account in the Cayman Islands. Three million dollars was deposited into it an hour ago."

"*What?*"

"Yeah." His voice was awful and low. "Someone has

also made it look like I'm deeply in debt from gambling—as if the mob has a hold on me. Kev's going to try and trace the money trail, but whoever's set me up is pretty good. Kevin's not sure he can do it."

"And if he doesn't?"

"I'll be going to prison." Dante shook his head. "That doesn't matter right now—"

Being set up to go to prison didn't matter? "How can you—"

He rolled down his window.

Zoey's mouth fell open as she realized what he was about to do. "Hey!"

Out the window went her hot pink cell phone.

"Awww!"

"As soon as they figure you're with me, they'll ping it," Lips said ruthlessly.

"I know." She couldn't help her voice sounding resentful. "But it was practically new—"

He raised a hand, cutting her off. "I'll buy you a new one. Now. Where can I take you? What about a different relative? Is your father nearby?"

She shook her head. "He lives in Naperville, but I'm not going to him for help."

"Naperville is only a couple of hours away. Look, you might be in danger. If he's even—"

"I'm not asking my father for help."

Her tone was flat, and she could feel him glancing at her.

She sighed. "He left Mom and me the summer I turned fourteen and didn't keep in touch. I'm not going to him now."

"Fine." He stared out the windshield for a minute. "I'll take you to a motel—"

"I don't have the cash on me."

"I can get you some."

"I'm not taking money from you!"

His jaw clenched. "Look, I'm just offering."

"And if whoever's setting you up finds me at the motel?"

"They aren't going to find you." He glanced into the rearview mirror.

"How do you know?"

He didn't even bother replying.

They drove in silence for a bit, Lips thinking deep, federal thoughts, no doubt, and Zoey readying her argument.

Finally she twisted in her seat to face him. "Look, I know you don't want me here. I know I'm in the way and I'm a pain in the ass, and I admit I'm scared at the thought of being shot at, but I need to do something to help find Pete. I *can't* just sit somewhere and wait while she's out there with strangers."

"I don't—"

"*Please.*"

He was silent a minute, watching the street. Somehow they'd ended up in a nicer area. Zoey didn't recognize the neighborhood in the dark, but it featured shopping centers, restaurants, and all-night groceries.

Finally Lips muttered, "You're not a pain in the ass."

She felt her eyebrows shoot up. She wasn't?

He didn't look at her, keeping his gaze focused on the road instead. The oncoming headlights strobed across his face and made it look like some Greek statue, all hard planes and no color. "And you don't have to be scared. I won't let anyone hurt you."

It was a line straight out of a movie—maybe one

starring Bruce Willis—but Zoey wasn't even tempted to laugh. This guy who didn't even know her cared about her safety. The thought kind of made her shiver. *'Course protecting people is his job,* a practical voice inside her head drawled.

Practical voices could be such downers.

Zoey replied totally without thinking. "Okay."

Okay was a simple everyday word, but it felt like more in this case. Like she'd made a pact with him. He'd keep her safe; she'd trust him to do it. Which was weird, because it wasn't like she did the whole male-protector thing, as a rule. Actually, it was usually the opposite—she hadn't totally trusted a man since Dad had done his walkout when she was a teenager.

"Okay," he replied, and now it was too late. Their pact—if it even was a pact—was sealed.

Dante signaled and turned off the main road, passing little shops lit by strings of white Christmas lights. He drove a couple of blocks and then turned into an upscale mall. Even though it was evening, the lot was crowded; one end of the mall was anchored by a twenty-four-hour health club. Dante slowed the BMW and started cruising up and down the parking lot.

"What are you doing?" Zoey asked. Maybe he felt an overwhelming urge to do bench presses when he was under stress. Except he wasn't parking the car.

"I'm looking."

"For what?"

"Hush," he said absently. "Can't you be quiet for more than two minutes?"

"Hey! I'm a real quiet person. You just don't—"

"Aha!"

"Aha?" Zoey looked at him incredulously. "Who says *Aha?*"

"Bitch, bitch, bitch," he muttered, but he said it lightly, not really paying attention to her because he was parking the car. He set the emergency brake and jumped out without explanation.

"Hey!" Zoey scrambled out of the car, wrapping her arms around herself as the cold winter wind hit her. With the sun down, the temperature had dropped ten degrees or more. Dante was at the rear of the BMW, popping the trunk. She watched as he pulled out a soft-sided toolbox and started rummaging in it. "What—?"

"Really. Try to be quiet now."

Zoey rolled her eyes. He was enjoying being mysterious, she could tell. This silence stuff was just to impress her.

He found a screwdriver and walked to the nearest car. Only now did she notice that it was a black convertible Beemer and . . . She squinted. It looked like the same model as Dante's car.

"Hey."

"Shhh."

He squatted by the back of the car, the skirt of his black trench coat pooling at his feet, and started working on the license plate cover. He had it off in a few seconds and walked over to his Beemer, taking his plates off and switching them with the other black Beemer's. In another few minutes he'd completed the job, stowed away the screwdriver, and slammed the trunk lid shut.

Zoey glanced at Dante as she got back into the car. He had a satisfied expression on his face—not quite a smile, but the kind of look that guys got when they thought they'd been very clever.

"Nice," she said.

He shrugged modestly as he put the car in gear and drove out of the health club parking lot.

"'Course I've seen that in the movies," Zoey continued carelessly.

His too-handsome face fell.

She took pity. "But it was pretty smart anyway."

"Thanks."

She grinned at him.

"I'm hungry." He signaled to get back on the main road. "Let's get something to eat."

"You're taking me out?"

"Yup. To a drive-thru."

"Be still my heart," Zoey muttered.

"Then I'm going to find these old ladies." He looked at her. "And get your niece back."

Chapter Eleven

*T*hat is not the correct way to fasten a diaper such as this one," Savita-di said bossily to Pratima over the wailing of the blond baby she held on her hip.

They were in a tiny basement apartment belonging to Abdul. Abdul was the janitor at their restaurant—a kindly old man who did not seem to have a word of English. He worked extremely slowly, but he was prompt and never missed a day of work. One sometimes had to make compromises, Pratima had found, when one owned a restaurant.

And they must've made a good choice in hiring Abdul, for despite the late hour, he had greeted them with a toothless smile when they'd knocked on his door. At the moment he sat in a rather tattered stuffed green chair watching and nodding as the ladies attempted to diaper the babies.

Fortunately, he'd turned off the blaring TV when they'd entered.

Pratima smiled kindly down at the dark-haired baby girl, who was presently trying her best to crawl away. "If you know so much about diapering babies, Savita-di, perhaps you should diaper the child yourself."

"My hands are full, Pratima, as you can plainly see," Savita-di gasped as the blond baby boy drew breath to blast both ladies again. "This boy is admirably strong."

"But not as pretty as the girl," Pratima retorted. Savita-di had always been partial to boy children, a deplorably old-fashioned prejudice that should have been lost long before the ladies had come to the US of A.

The baby girl suddenly stilled, her eyes caught by the necklace about Pratima's neck. Pratima took advantage of her calm to fasten the sticky tapes of the disposable diaper around the little girl's round tummy. The baby grinned and reached up to tangle her fingers in the delicate gold necklace.

"Ah, ah!" Pratima chided. "Mustn't break auntie's beautiful necklace."

"Hurry, Pratima," Savita-di said breathlessly. "This boy is very strong. And his bottom—pee-yew!"

It was unfortunate that both babies had chosen to dirty their diapers at the same time, but fortunate that they had done so *after* the Gupta ladies had thought to buy a parcel of disposable diapers.

"I am working as fast as I can," Pratima panted as she wrestled a T-shirt onto the wiggling baby. The little girl's clothes needed to be washed after her diaper change, and the T-shirt was the best available clothing for her, though it draped her like a tent.

Abdul said something in his native language.

Savita-di smiled widely at the man. "Yes! Yes!" She leaned to Pratima and whispered out of the corner of her mouth. "What do you think he is saying?"

"How should I know, Savita-di?" Pratima shrugged. "I do not speak Farsi or whatever language he employs. Perhaps he is saying that we have had a nice visit but now it is time for us to leave."

"We cannot leave, as well you know, Pratima. That Terrible Man was at the restaurant. If I had not warned you to drive away in time—"

"Pardon me, Savita-di, but was it not me who had the idea to change the so-large and very visible yellow Humvee for our nephew's purple minivan?"

"Yes—"

"Then I believe I deserve equal share in the praise for eluding That Terrible Man."

"Humph," was all Savita-di said, so Pratima knew that her sister-in-law had taken the point.

Pratima smiled as Savita-di knelt to diaper the boy.

Twenty minutes later, both ladies sat back on Abdul's worn settee and contemplated the babies. The children crawled about the floor like miniature explorers, the boy hauling himself up the leg of the wooden table to stand swaying, the girl gnawing on a metal teaspoon she held in one hand as she crawled.

"What are we to do with them, Savita-di?" Pratima asked wearily.

Babies were very pretty, but such work! One forgot how terribly exhausting one baby was, let alone two. They were a job for younger women. Both sisters-in-law had reached the age when they should only have to play with babies on their knees, then hand them back to their frazzled mothers when the babies became stinky.

"We cannot take them back to That Terrible Man," Savita-di said with certainty.

"No, no," Pratima agreed. "These sweet innocents in the hands of such a man is an awful thought. But perhaps we can take them to a police station?"

"And have the police arrest us at first sight?" Savita-di asked indignantly. "Have you no sense, Pratima?"

"I have sense enough to know we cannot keep these babies."

"If your sense was so wonderful, would we have stolen the yellow Humvee in the first place?"

"Pardon me, Savita-di, but the plan to steal the Humvee was yours, if you will recall."

"Ah!" Savita-di cried as if pinched. "Always you blame me! But what else can I expect from a woman who would flirt with her husband's brother?"

The babies had looked up at the sound of raised voices, and even Abdul stared, puzzled, from his tattered chair. Pratima pursed her lips shut. This was a very old, very painful argument, and one which both Gupta ladies usually avoided at all costs. Savita-di must be frightened indeed to bring it up now.

Pratima inhaled deeply. "What do you suggest we do with these babies, then, Savita-di?"

"I do not know!" Savita-di threw up her arms.

"We cannot leave them with Abdul."

Both ladies watched as the elderly man giggled and poked a bony finger into the baby boy's soft arm.

"Nooo," agreed Savita-di.

"Your daughter Vinati will not be back from her

wonderful vacation in Disney World for another week. And I do not think it wise to consult Saumya about this business, at least not yet. Remember, she was quite rude when we asked for the loan of her extra car."

"Hmm. And we've left the car at that petrol pump," Savita-di mused. "No, no, best not to ask Saumya. Or my nephew Karan, for that matter."

Pratima pursed her lips judiciously. "In fact, I think all the nephews and nieces are far too busy for this matter."

"Very true, very true, Pratima," Savita-di muttered. "Best not to bother the nieces and nephews."

Both ladies stared at the babies for a moment. Pratima felt weary to her bones. It had been a long day, first planning to steal back their kesar, then the actual theft, and then the unpleasant surprise that they'd stolen two babies, as well. She sighed and drew the thin cloth of her sari over her arm. Really, she wasn't as young as she used to be.

Next to her, Savita-di sighed, as well, and spoke. "But maybe there is one nephew whom we might contact."

Chapter Twelve

*F*or a chick who worked in a health-food co-op, Zoey sure liked her junk food.

"Oh, my God! I'd forgotten how good these were!" she mumbled through a mouthful of ButterBurger. "I used to get these when I was a teenager—Culver's was the only burger place I could bike to—and then I found how much fat was in one and quit."

They were eating in the car, which was parked in a dark lot in front of a bakery. There was a neon CLOSED sign over the bakery door, and a glow showed through the plate-glass windows—probably some kind of security light. Actually, it just now occurred to him that it was kind of romantic out here. Dante glanced at Zoey and wondered if the thought had occurred to her, too. Probably not. Most people didn't think running for their lives was all that romantic.

He sighed, took a bite of his Bacon ButterBurger Deluxe with extra cheese, and considered her last statement. "Just how much fat is there in these things?"

Zoey shook her head sagely, her mouth full. She swallowed and took a long draw from her milkshake. "You don't want to know. It's unbelievable, but junk food was such forbidden fruit when I was a teenager."

"Why?"

"Mom was way into whole foods."

He crumpled a napkin. "So where exactly did you grow up?"

"Big farm." She waved a hand as if conjuring the immensity of the space inside the BMW. "Out in the middle of nowhere, Indiana."

"But you had a Culver's within biking distance?"

"Thank God." She swirled a french fry in ketchup and ate it. "My mom was the last of the back-to-earth hippies, only they didn't call themselves hippies by the time she started. Anyway, we raised most of our food ourselves."

"Yeah?" He could totally see her as a girl on some whole-grains-and-turnips commune, running through fields of weeds, bare kid legs flashing, her red-blond hair streaming behind her, shining in the sun. He blinked and took another bite of sloppy burger.

She hadn't seemed to notice his brief reverie. "Yeah. We grew weird heirloom veggies, had apple and pear trees, a couple of beehives, and chickens. Lots of chickens. Oh, and goats."

He glanced at her. She was listing the ingredients to a natural paradise, but her voice was flat. "Sounds perfect."

She pulled a pickle out from her half-eaten burger and nibbled the edge. "You'd think so, wouldn't you."

"Why wasn't it?"

She heaved a small, sad sigh. "Turns out that it takes a lot of work to run a farm, even a half-assed hippie farm. Mom spent all her time milking goats, canning tomatoes, feeding chickens, all that stuff. And she also did weird little crafts, because strangely enough, most shop owners won't take a bushel of apples as payment for a kid's shoes."

"And your father? You said he left when you were fourteen."

"Yeah. He took off with a girlfriend and started a new family. He and Mom really had nothing in common. He was this right-wing, suburban kind of guy, totally the opposite of Mom. It's amazing what hormones will do to the brains of two otherwise perfectly sane humans. I think he was kind of embarrassed by me."

He looked at her.

She shrugged. "Me and Mom didn't really fit into his Middle America idea of happiness, you know? A marriage that didn't work out. A teenaged kid who didn't listen and wasn't as cute as his new babies. I think he sometimes wanted to just forget we even existed. We were a mistake in his otherwise perfect life."

"Huh." He meditated on that as he ate the rest of his burger. "Did he have a job?"

"Uh-huh." She wadded her burger wrapper up into a tiny, tight ball and thrust it into the paper bag the food had come in. "He was a cop."

Dante had been about to turn the car on, and the keys jangled as his hand hit them clumsily. A cop. That might explain her barely concealed hostility at times. Maybe she had a thing about men in law enforcement. Baggage like that could make a relationship die an early death. Huh. Good thing he wasn't interested in a relationship with Zoey.

She was busy wiping her fingers on a napkin and apparently hadn't noticed his distraction. "Mom and Dad met when he arrested her at some sit-in. Either that's romantic or just sad, depending on how you look at it."

"How do you look at it?"

Her fingers stilled. "Sad, I think. They should've never married, should've never had me."

She said it matter-of-factly, but an admission like that couldn't be made unemotionally.

He looked at his hands on the steering wheel, uncertain of what to say. "Well, I'm glad they had you."

He glanced at her as he turned the ignition and caught a fleeting emotion on her face. Uncertainty? Surprise? It might even be gratitude. He wasn't sure, and it was gone as fast as it'd come. Zoey was the kind of girl who would keep a guy constantly on his toes, trying to figure out what she was thinking, watching to see which way her mood would swing. He suddenly wondered if any man had ever penetrated her goofy shell to find the real woman within. What would she do if a guy tried to get that close? Would she even let him?

He put the car in gear, pulled over to a Dumpster, and got out briefly to throw away the trash from their meal.

When he reentered the car she was looking at him. "Are we going to look for Pete now?"

"I need to try my boss again first."

She pointedly fingered the hole in the BMW's canopy.

"Can you trust him? Someone sent the Chicago police on us."

"There's more going on than you understand. Jack Headington is the Chicago SAC—Special Agent in Charge. If someone has set me up in the Chicago FBI office, it isn't him. In fact, he's the one guy I can trust in Chicago."

"Why?"

There was no way he could answer that—without telling her about his undercover operation which he didn't want to do. He ignored her question and pulled out the new cell he'd bought right before the burgers. He'd used most of his cash to get the cell, but it couldn't be helped. He needed a clean phone.

She kind of humphed and folded her arms across her chest.

Dante flipped open the cell and punched in a private number.

Three rings and then it picked up. "Headington."

He exhaled in relief. "It's Torelli, sir."

A gentle sigh on the other end. "Bit of trouble, I hear, Dante."

"Yes, sir."

"Tell me what happened."

The SAC's speaking voice was so quiet that Dante had to strain to hear. Dante had long suspected that the low tone was his boss's way of exerting dominance in a conversation. The person Headington was speaking to had to pay perfect attention to understand what the man was saying. And few were bold enough to ask him to speak up.

"As you know, there was a hit on the safe house," Dante said now.

"The agents assigned to the case are all dead, Dante.

Why aren't you?" The tone was curious rather than condemning.

"I was late for my shift. Sir."

"Late."

Dante winced. "Yes, sir."

"Well, fortunate for you, I suppose. And for the agency. Do you think this mess is related to the problems we've been having in this office?"

"I think it must be, sir."

"Any ideas?"

Dante grimaced, hating to admit it. "Not at the moment, sir."

"Ah." There was a silence from the other end, then, "Did you recover Spinoza's daughter?"

"No, sir."

Where another man would've sworn, Headington was merely silent. Dante glanced in the rearview mirror. He didn't see any cars following them, but he didn't like making this call anyway. Someone on the inside had already betrayed them, and a cell phone call could be traced.

"Then the kidnapper got away." Headington sighed. "I'm told that Spinoza hasn't been contacted yet."

"Do you think the kidnapper will contact Ricky?"

Another sigh. "It's only a matter of time until they do. Are we working under the assumption that the kidnapper was in DiRosa's employ?"

"I think we have to, sir."

"With the child in DiRosa's hands, there's no way that Spinoza will testify on Monday."

"No, sir." Dante pulled the car to a stop at a light and debated for a second. He hated telling him this over a phone, but there was no other way. "I'm not sure DiRosa actually has the baby, sir."

"What?" The word was so low that Dante almost missed it.

"We saw the baby taken from the original kidnapper."

Dante braced himself for a slew of questions about the second kidnappers, but Headington surprised him as always by latching on to a different bit of information.

"We?"

Dante hesitated, eyes narrowed against the glare of oncoming cars. The Chicago office must already know that Zoey was with him. She'd left her car running right in front of the apartment building, and, if nothing else, the Chicago PD had seen her in his car. There was absolutely no reason not to tell Headington, even if they were being listened to.

"Dante?"

He shook his head, trying to clear his brain. "I've got a civilian with me, sir. Nikki Hernandez's sister, Zoey Addler."

"Good God, son, what're you thinking?"

Dante winced. Headington had a point.

"You need to get rid of her, you know that."

"Yes, sir, I do, but I'm worried for her safety."

"Safety? Why wouldn't she . . ." Headington trailed away into a thoughtful silence. "Ah. I see what you mean."

"Yes, sir."

"You both need to come in."

"I—"

"You're a target, Dante," Headington murmured. "Whoever this traitor in our office is, he's powerful, and he's setting you up. Kevin told me that Chicago cops shot at you this afternoon. That takes money and influence."

Dante glanced behind him as he changed lanes. "We already know it's someone high in the office. His use of the Chicago PD is interesting, though. Have you been able to talk to the police? Call them off my tail?"

"I have, but we have no way of knowing how high the corruption goes in the Chicago police department. I can't guarantee that they won't go after you again."

"Damn." Dante grimaced. "We were getting close. Has Kevin gotten into Pearson's financial records?" Pearson was the ASAC in Chicago, a tired, middle-aged man who was only hanging on for his retirement pension.

"Kevin's still going through Fred Pearson's computer." Headington sounded weary. "God, I hope it isn't Fred. I've known him for twenty years."

"Yes, sir." Dante didn't point out that the traitor was bound to be someone Headington knew well.

"In any case, you can't fight this guy on your own." The SAC's voice was commanding again. "Come in. That's an order. We'll put you under guard and you can finish your investigation here."

Dante swallowed. Beside him, Zoey was watching with wide eyes. Dammit, he'd just promised her that they'd go after the kid.

"I'm following a lead on the child, sir," Dante said carefully. "I don't believe anyone else is in a better position to do this right now. Not anyone we can trust. If we can't get that baby back by Monday, then Spinoza won't testify and the judge will probably declare a mistrial."

"You're forgetting that your first priority is the internal investigation," Headington said without inflection. "That's what Charlie Hessler sent you to Chicago to do. That's what's important. I want this rot in my department rooted out and exposed to the light of day. I want it destroyed."

"Yes, sir." He knew the baby wasn't his primary job. But on the other hand . . . "I've got a lead, though. Just twenty-four hours to see if it pans out. That's all I'm asking."

"I don't like this, Dante. We have no way of protecting you out there. We lost three of our finest agents today. What's to stop the traitor from locating you—and killing you and Miss Addler?"

"I know, sir." Dante blew out a breath. "But the longer the baby stays out here, the higher the chance she'll be found by DiRosa's man first. Once that happens you know her life will be in danger."

Silence as Headington made his decision. Whatever he decided, Dante would have to follow his orders. The FBI wasn't an organization that encouraged independent thought.

Finally, the SAC cleared his throat, a sound like dry leaves rustling. "You have until ten hundred tomorrow morning. If you haven't got the child by that time, you're to abort and come in. And bring Ms. Addler with you. She's not safe on the streets by herself. Do you understand, Dante?"

"Yes, sir." It wasn't twenty-four hours, but the SAC giving him until tomorrow morning was better than nothing at all.

"Good."

"Where can we meet?"

"Do you know the Stevenson Expressway overpass just south of Chinatown? Where Canal Street runs under the expressway?"

"I can find it, sir."

"Good. It's out of the way enough not to attract attention, but still an open space. I'll see you there, Dante."

"Yes, sir."

"Be careful, son."

"Yes, sir."

The line clicked as Headington disconnected.

Dante glanced over his shoulder and crossed two lanes to pull into an all-night drugstore parking lot. He palmed the cell and got out of the BMW. Two cars were sitting by the doors to the drugstore. One was a burgundy Buick with a wooden-bead seat cover over the driver's seat. Dante tried the door handle and found it unlocked. He quickly opened the driver's-side door and threw the cheap cell into the back seat.

As he walked back to the BMW, two college-age guys came out of the drugstore, carrying a case of beer. They climbed in the Buick and screeched out of the parking lot.

Dante got back into the BMW and started the car.

"Now are we going after Pete?" Zoey asked.

"Yes. Now we're going after Pete."

Chapter Thirteen

Thursday, 10:08 p.m.

It turned out that Dante's big plan to find Pete involved driving to the residential address he'd gotten from the papers in the restaurant office and staking out the little bungalow there. In the BMW. With the heat turned off.

"Why would someone living in Chicago buy a convertible?" Zoey grumbled. "There's snow on the ground seven months out of the year."

"I wasn't assigned to Chicago when I bought this car," Dante murmured.

She looked at him. The interior of the BMW was dark, but she could make out that he was staring at the fifties cottage across the street. There was a bright streetlamp in front of the house next door that illuminated the cottage pretty well. It was a red brick one-story with green aluminum awnings over the front windows. The house was nearly identical to every other one on the block. Dante didn't seem cold, even though he still wasn't wearing a hat. He appeared perfectly happy to sit all night in a freezing car, in fact.

"Where were you assigned?" she asked. "Before?"

"Milwaukee."

She squinted at him, but as far as she could make out he wasn't smiling. She sighed. "So why aren't we at the address from the car the Indian ladies left at the BP station?"

"Because I got that address from Kevin, which means the rest of the FBI office knows about it, as well. We show up there and I'll get shot at again."

"But what if the Indian ladies went there?"

"Then we're wasting our time sitting here."

She squinted at him again. He didn't look put out by the thought. Maybe he spent a lot of time on useless stakeouts. Maybe he'd entered a Zen stakeout zone.

Well, she hadn't.

"Have you ever thought about bringing along a Game Boy on a stakeout?" She tried to discreetly shift in her seat, because it felt like her ass had gone to sleep. "Or one of those mini TVs that run off the battery of your car. That way you could keep up with *Desperate Housewives*."

"*Battlestar Galactica*."

"Huh?"

"*Desperate Housewives* is a chick show," he said with his gaze still on the little bungalow. "All melodrama and who's banging who."

"Oh, like *Battlestar Galactica* isn't a soap opera."

"At least the writing's good. And the science."

"Science?" She stared. He had to be pulling her leg. "It's science *fiction*. The science is made up."

"That's—"

"And I bet it isn't the science that you watch the show for anyway." She folded her arms across her chest.

He glanced at her, puzzled. "What do you mean?"

"That girl." She nodded, her own eyes on the house now. "The one that wears that red dress. Or nothing. That's why you're watching it."

If the car wasn't so dark she might've sworn that his cheeks got ruddier. "And you're not watching *Housewives* for that guy who does the yards?"

"Nothing wrong with admiring a fine actor." She tried not to laugh. He sounded so disgruntled. Did he really think he was watching *Battlestar* for the science? What a geek! The thought of Dante's suave exterior hiding the heart of a geek hit a tender chord within her. She had a weird urge to lean over and kiss him.

Of course, she didn't. "The point is, you could use a TV or something to keep you awake out here."

"Not having a problem staying awake at the moment." His eyes were back on the little cottage. "Besides, the whole point of being out here is to watch the house."

Zoey shifted again. They'd been sitting here for over an hour with that hole in the ceiling letting in the freezing night air. She glared at it and then turned back to Dante, unable to keep her nagging concerns to herself.

"Shouldn't the old ladies have come home before now if they were going to come home?"

"Not necessarily."

"I mean, what if the address you copied down from that bill at the restaurant belonged to someone else? One of the old ladies' relatives or friends. Heck, we don't even know if the car they were driving originally belonged to them. Maybe they stole it, too, and *that* address isn't theirs, either."

"Doesn't get us anywhere."

"What?"

"Speculating. This is the lead we have. We follow it until it goes somewhere or it peters out. Either way, second-guessing doesn't help."

Zoey bit her lip, staring out of the dark windows into the equally dark neighborhood street. "It's just that I'm wondering where she is."

He frowned. "Who?"

"Pete." She picked at a piece of yarn coming undone from her left mitten, blinking hard to hold back tears. "She must be scared without Nikki—without her mommy. And how do we know that the old ladies are taking care of her? If she's warm and if they fed her? What if—"

His hand covered hers, large and warm. His voice was quiet in the near-dark. "They looked like someone's grandmas. I'm sure they're taking care of the baby. She's safe, she's warm, and she's fed."

He had no way of knowing that. He was just telling her these things to comfort her, they both knew it. But the strange thing was it worked. She did feel a tiny bit better at his words. Or perhaps it was the touch of his hand.

"I hope so," she whispered, "oh, I hope so."

She was on the verge of tears, but she couldn't help it. It had been hours now since the kidnapping. Would she ever see Pete again?

Zoey sucked in a deep breath, trying to keep it quiet. Time to regain some control. Dante had withdrawn his hand, and now hers felt cold again. She rubbed her hands together, hoping the friction would heat them. It didn't work, so she stuck them in her pockets.

"Do you need to call someone?" Dante asked suddenly. His face was still half turned away, watching the house, so she couldn't make out his expression.

"I told you, there isn't anyone I can stay with."

He turned fully to look at her, his face thoughtful. "I remember. But is there someone who might be worried? Besides Nikki, that is. The kidnapping and shooting is probably all over the news by now. Do you have friends who might see it?"

She tucked her chin into the collar of her coat. "People I work with at the co-op. But I'm not that, uh . . ."

"Close to anyone," he said softly.

Well, yeah, but he didn't have to say it out loud. He was looking at her with a sympathetic expression, his mouth softened at the edges as if in pity, and she couldn't take it.

"What about you?" she shot back. "Got anyone to call?"

"I've got family, but they're all on the East Coast."

"Anyone here?"

"No."

She'd scored a point, but the knowledge that he was just as lonely as she didn't make her feel any better.

"You're not married?"

"Nope."

"Girlfriend?"

He smiled. "No. Nosy, aren't you?"

She shrugged, covering a shiver. "Not much else to do in here but talk, is there?"

"Good point." He was back to watching the house.

"Where on the East Coast?"

"My family? New York."

"New York City? Really? I've never met anyone who actually came from New York. Usually it's the other way around."

"Other way around?"

She shrugged even though he couldn't see the movement. "You know, everyone wants to move to New York."

"Huh."

She twisted to a new position. "And you grew up in the city?"

"Sure. Until I went to a boys' boarding school."

"A boarding school?" She'd never met anyone who'd been to a boarding school either. It sounded like something out of Dickens. Totally Victorian. Totally alien. "How old were you when you went?"

"Twelve."

"What was that like?"

He turned his head slightly in the darkened BMW so that he was silhouetted against the window. "It was a boarding school."

She studied his profile. It seemed aloof. Too elegant. Out of her league. But it had once belonged to a little boy. "Boarding schools always sound so impersonal."

He shrugged. "They teach you independence. How to look after yourself, how to be neat. It was a good school. The teachers were first-rate."

"Didn't you miss your family?"

"Everyone misses their family at first."

She was silent, listening to their combined breathing in the dark car.

"Sometimes . . ." He shifted. "Sometimes it was lonely."

His voice was reluctant, as if she'd dragged a shameful admission out of him.

He cleared his throat. "I wasn't real outgoing as a kid."

She imagined him, a beautiful dark boy. A boy she somehow knew would be more sensitive and shy than the other boys. That boy moving to a strange place on his own. A place where he didn't know anyone. That single word—*lonely*—probably didn't begin to describe his experience. Her heart contracted, holding in sympathetic tears for a little boy who no longer existed.

Dante shifted again. Coughed. "So, what about you? Boyfriend?"

She inhaled. He obviously didn't want her sympathy. "Not since Brick the Bastard."

Even with his face half turned away, she could see his eyebrows shoot up. "You dated a guy named Brick?"

She sighed. "I think his mother watched a lot of daytime TV."

"Must've."

She scrunched lower in the seat, trying to conserve what body heat she had left, and yawned. "He was all right except for the fishnet-stocking thing."

He reached to turn the keys in the ignition. "Dare I ask?"

Air blew out of the vents, but it was cool still. "He was a part-time actor—during the day he worked in a boring office. But he was always taking these drag roles that he needed to wear stilettos and fishnet stockings for, and I think he liked it *too* much, if you know what I mean. God, that feels good."

The heat had finally kicked in, and hot air was blowing in her face. Zoey leaned forward, closing her eyes, feeling the warmth wash over her.

Beside her, she heard Dante clear his throat. "So you dumped him?"

"I wouldn't call it dumping," she said lazily, her eyes still closed. "I just didn't catch him when he started sliding away, you know?"

"Yeah, I know."

His tone was a little dark.

She opened her eyes and turned to look at him. What she could see of his mouth was straight and thin. "Suffered some flesh wounds in the dating wars?"

"You could say that."

"Do tell."

He shrugged.

"Oh, come on. We've got all night, we're stuck in this car. You got anything better to do than to spill your guts to me?"

"Put like that, how could I resist?" He turned the car engine off.

"Awww." All the lovely hot air went away.

"We have to conserve the gas. It's got to last us until morning."

"Humph." She huddled into her down jacket, already feeling the heat leaking from her body.

"Here." Dante twisted and leaned over the back seat, coming back up with a tasseled tartan throw. He draped it over her and then began tucking it in all along her body, his hands sure and firm. He pulled the edge of the blanket up around her chin, and she felt his fingers brush tenderly against her skin.

"Better?"

She nodded, mesmerized by his care.

He took his hands away and sat back in his own seat. "Good. Then you're all set to hear the sorry tale of Psychotic Shayna."

"Psychotic Shayna?"

"Fifty-four messages on my answering machine over one weekend."

"Whoa."

"Not only that, but she was convinced I was seeing another woman."

"You weren't?"

"Swear to God." She saw a shadowed movement as he held up his hand. "Besides, we didn't date all that long. The fifty-four messages were only three weeks in."

"Ouch." She winced.

"After that I backed away fast and she latched on to another FBI agent. I heard later that she was kind of a federal agent groupie."

"Huh." She stared into the dark for a moment, thinking. "I bet Psychotic Shayna was a babe."

"Why do you say that?"

"Was the other agent she hooked up with smart?"

"I didn't know him that well, but he never struck me as dumb."

She nodded wisely. "Good-looking, otherwise intelligent FBI agents falling for a crazy woman? You all were blinded by her boobs or butt or both."

"Huh."

"Am I right?"

"I'm gonna take the fifth on that one," he muttered.

"Thought so." Zoey snuggled into her blanket, feeling oddly happy. "Where do you think Baldy the kidnapper is right now?"

Beside her, Dante snorted. "If he's smart he's holed up somewhere warm."

Chapter Fourteen

Thursday, 11:21 p.m.

Neil was halfway to freezing his fucking nuts off.

As it turned out, the red SUV he'd nabbed at the BP station had a defective heater. What kind of a dumb fuck didn't fix his heater in Chicago in winter? This just went to show how little people took care of their stuff anymore. Slobs, all of them.

Neil hunched into himself and slapped his hands against his upper arms. He was parked in an apartment complex on the north side of Chicago. He was sitting here like an idiot because some guy named Sujay Agrawal lived here. Sujay was the nephew or maybe great-nephew of the crazy little old Indian ladies. When he'd tossed the Indian restaurant, Neil had found the guy's name on a piece of paper and pocketed it in case he might need it later, which, as it turned out, he did. Neil intended to brace Sujay, should he ever decide to come home. What the fucker was doing out late on a Thursday night was anybody's guess.

Neil should be home at this very moment, warm under his electric blanket, but truth was, as much as he loved Ash, he wasn't about to face her without Neil Junior. Even spending the night in a fucking freezing SUV with no heat was better than going home and telling Ash he didn't have their baby. He shuddered at just the thought.

Another thing that was bothering Neil: what had those old bats done with his Hummer? He couldn't help but imagine the Hummer on the fucking South Side maybe near Cabrini Green, in which case there wouldn't be anything left of his ride except the grill and maybe not even that. And where the hell had they taken Neil Junior? What were they going to do, sell him to a baby black marketer? He hadn't thought the old ladies were that cold, but then on the other hand, he hadn't thought they'd have the balls to steal his fucking Hummer, either.

And right then Neil made a decision. After he braced the nephew, after he went and found the Indian ladies and got Neil Junior back and got the Spinoza kid back, too, after this whole thing blew over and Ash was talking to him again, after all that, he was finding a new line of work. Maybe see if Tony had a place for him in middle management, something less to do with street work. His anger management teacher droned on about "life reassessment," which, near as Neil could figure, meant thinking about getting either a new wife or a new job or both. Well, he sure as hell wasn't going to ditch Ash, but since he'd just turned forty-five, reassessing his career choice as muscle might not be a fucking bad idea. Too bad his skills mostly ran to breaking legs and intimidating old ladies. Only lately he couldn't even intimidate old ladies.

Neil slumped farther in the seat. Yeah, getting a new job was a priority. But first he had to find Neil Junior and Ricky Spinoza's kid, or the life reassessment wouldn't matter. Because Tony the Rose would kill him.

Chapter Fifteen

Friday, 6:03 a.m.

It was dark when Dante woke. He opened his eyes without moving, assessing his position and his surroundings. It was cold, he was in his own car, and he heard soft breathing coming from the passenger seat beside him. Zoey. He remembered her smooth skin beneath his fingers as he'd tucked her into his blanket. Remembered her husky laughter in the dark as he'd told her stories of his dating mishaps. Remembered the perfume she wore, which he still couldn't place.

He turned his head, wincing as the muscles in his neck protested the awkward angle he'd slept in. Zoey had pulled the blanket up over her nose. Her eyelashes trembled as she slept, the blanket slowly rising and falling with each breath she took. She seemed smaller in sleep, more delicate, more feminine.

Or maybe he was just projecting what he wanted to see. He'd been surprised—pleasantly surprised—by her sense of humor last night. He would've thought the organic, co-op-food type would be humorless in her strict convictions. Except she wasn't strict in her convictions, either, was she? Not if she ate red licorice and craved Culver's ButterBurgers. He shook his head. She was more complicated than he'd first thought.

More familiar.

His eyes narrowed. He was getting too close to her. It was becoming harder to be objective, to see her as a witness to a crime, nothing more. Bottom line, he couldn't afford to trust her, even if a primitive, mindless part of him was telling him just the opposite. Trusting the wrong person at this point could get him killed.

He glanced to the small house across the street. It was silent and dark, the occupants, if there were any, still abed. Dante stretched and yawned. He hadn't meant to fall asleep, but the adrenaline crash must've caught up with him. It didn't matter anyway. He was pretty sure that his unconscious cop brain would've waked him up if anyone had shown last night. No one had.

They were at a dead end.

He could question the occupants of the house, and the neighbors, too, see if they had any information about sari-clad little old lady kidnappers, but essentially his game was done. He had orders to come in this morning. He glanced again at Zoey, sleeping so innocently. She wasn't going to like him leaving the chase.

Dante frowned on that thought and got out of the car, bracing himself against the god-awful cold. Shit, this was not going to be fun. He chose the alley running behind the houses and jogged over to relieve himself.

Five minutes later when he got back in the car, Zoey was just beginning to wake up.

"Oh, my God, it's cold!" she moaned and pulled the blanket all the way over her face.

Dante grinned. "I'm turning on the engine now. We should have heat in another minute."

"I want a hot bath," came her muffled voice from beneath the blanket, "and hot slippers and a hot robe and hot coffee and hot oatmeal."

He raised his eyebrows. "Oatmeal?"

"Oatmeal is very nutritious."

"Not to mention soggy."

"Not with lots of brown sugar and cream—"

"Still sounds soggy."

"And raisins."

"Raisins in oatmeal are disgusting," he informed her kindly.

"Oh, yeah? Well, what do you eat in the morning?"

"Toast, usually."

"Bo-oring," she intoned from under the blanket.

"I wouldn't mind eggs today, though," he mused.

"Bet you like bacon and eggs and hash browns, with the eggs over easy so they're all runny and you can dip the bacon in them."

"Well, yeah."

Her snort puffed up the blanket over her face.

He grinned. "But I usually have just toast and coffee instead. Hard to run off bacon, eggs, and hash browns."

"Oh, my God, you run."

"So?"

"That's what's disgusting. Getting up early and going running, making the rest of us feel guilty."

He peeled back a corner of the blanket to look into clear blue eyes. "I can't see you feeling guilty."

She just blinked sleepy, sexy eyes at him for a minute, and he realized his body was responding.

Then her eyes widened. "I don't suppose there's a potty anywhere nearby?"

He released the blanket edge and sat back. "Nope."

"Damn." She was still a moment. Then, in a burst of speed, she threw off the blanket, grabbed the door handle, scrambled from the car, and disappeared into the same alley he'd used.

Dante took advantage of her absence to run his hands through his hair. He grimaced. God, he probably smelled really rank right about now.

His glum thoughts were interrupted by Zoey opening the passenger-side door and flinging herself back into the car.

"Oh, God, oh, God, oh, God," she chanted as she wrapped the blanket around herself again. "It's *freezing* out there."

"I didn't think it was that bad."

She stared at him incredulously.

"Compared to yesterday. Or the day before."

She scowled. "You didn't have to bare your entire rear end to do what you had to do."

He shrugged.

"It's not fair," she grumbled. "Women are at a stakeout disadvantage. All you guys have to do is unzip and take out your—"

Dante smiled and turned the air up full blast.

Zoey was immediately diverted. "Ohhh, that feels so good."

She leaned into the heater on her side as she had the night before, and Dante again felt a tightening in his gut. Or rather just below his gut. He looked away from the sight of her eyes closed in bliss and tried to control a surge of lust. Maybe it was the husky tone of her voice, or maybe it was the sensual pleasure in the expression on her face. Or, hell, maybe it was just his usual morning woody, pure biological fact, nothing to do with the woman sitting next to him at all. It hardly mattered, in any case. They'd go in today, Headington would debrief him, Zoey would get some protection until this was all over, and odds were that they'd never see each other again.

And that thought shouldn't be such a depressing one.

"I wish I had a brush," Zoey muttered. She took off her hat and unwound her red-blond braids. Her hair was messed up from the hat, but gold threads glinted in the morning sun and he had a sudden urge to touch them.

He looked away. "I wish I had a comb."

"Yeah, you are beginning to look a little scruffy."

He turned the rearview mirror and looked before he realized she was teasing him.

She grinned finger-combing her hair. "You're so vain."

"Am not," he muttered.

"You've got dirt on your forehead."

"Where?" He looked again.

She started laughing.

He knocked the mirror back into place. Being careful of how he looked wasn't vain.

Was it?

"So, what do we do now?" Zoey asked. She was rebraiding her hair now. "Should we try the restaurant again, or—?"

Dante glanced at the dash clock. It was only a little after six. They had a couple of hours until the meet with Headington. Even allowing for morning traffic, that left plenty of time. The least he could do was take her to breakfast before they had to drive to the overpass south of Chinatown. Maybe someplace that had both hot oatmeal and bacon and eggs.

He was opening his mouth to invite her when a light went on in the little house they were supposed to be watching.

Dante straightened. Someone was in there, after all.

Zoey had seen him go on alert. "What?" She glanced at the house and her eyes widened. "Hey . . ."

The front door cracked open and a head peered out. For a moment nothing happened, then a slim figure emerged and scurried down the front steps, stooped, and retrieved the morning newspaper, which had been thoughtfully left on the front walk.

There wasn't much he could do. He was about to hand over the case; it was no longer any of his concern. But even as Dante had the thought, he was putting the BMW into gear and pulling into the empty drive in front of the house.

"That's not one of the women we saw yesterday," Zoey pointed out as they got out of the car. "She's younger."

"I know." Dante strode to the front door and knocked.

Beside him, Zoey had her hands deep in her pockets and was rocking a little from side to side. "It's so darn cold!"

Dante knocked again just as they heard movement from inside.

The door was pulled partially open, a flimsy chain holding it back from opening all the way. A woman peered out, her dark eyes wide. "What is it? Who are you?"

"It's okay," Zoey said before Dante could answer.

"FBI, ma'am." Dante flashed his ID. "I'm Special Agent Dante Torelli. I need to talk to you. May we come in?"

If possible the woman's eyes widened even more. "FBI? What is this about? You must be mistaken. My husband's visa is perfectly in order. It doesn't expire for another eight months. I assure you—"

"Do you know two old ladies who wear saris and drive a little green Civic?" Zoey cut in loudly.

The flow of words abruptly stopped. The woman stared at them a long moment as if stunned, her mouth still half-open. Then she blinked and closed her mouth with a click.

"Oh, God, what have they done now?"

Chapter Sixteen

Friday, 6:34 a.m.

The house was warm, blessedly warm, and while hot, milky tea wasn't the same as hot coffee, it did fine in a pinch. In fact, Zoey thought as she sipped from a delicate china cup, hot tea was just about perfect when your butt was nearly frozen off.

They sat in a small living room done in early Ikea with traces of Indian to give it color. The black sectional sofa had a bright pink embroidered throw over the back, and the lamp on the end table was engraved brass.

Dante set his nearly empty teacup down on a glass coffee table and took out a small cordovan leather notebook from his breast pocket. He flipped to a clean page and looked at the petite Indian woman sitting opposite them. "Can I have your name again?"

"Priyanka Agrawal." She sat at the very edge of her

chair, looking like she might topple forward in her anxiety at any moment.

Dante nodded and wrote her name in his notebook as the woman watched him. He was in some kind of FBI zone, his focus completely on Ms. Agrawal. He sat relaxed but alert, his body leaning slightly toward the young woman, his dark brown eyes narrowed. Zoey felt a small pang of envy. To have all that masculine energy focused on her . . . Hastily she took another sip of tea, because obviously her brain had frozen.

Priyanka Agrawal was in her late twenties, slim and delicate in a way that inevitably made anyone—any *woman*—of European decent feel like a big, hulking troll. She had shoulder-length black hair that swung in a curtain when she moved her head, and even without makeup her face was incredibly lovely. Zoey sighed into her milky tea and wished she could hate the other woman for winning the grand national gene lottery.

"And the names of the two women in saris?" Dante asked.

Ms. Agrawal pursed her lips. "Savita Gupta and Pratima Gupta. What have they done?"

"Kidnapping, vehicular theft."

"Oh, dear God."

"Can you spell their names for me?" Dante murmured, scribbling in his notebook.

She spelled the names, her delicate hands twisting in her lap anxiously.

Dante looked up. "They're sisters?"

"No, oh, no," Ms. Agrawal licked her lips. "The mamis—aunties—aren't related by blood at all. They're sisters-in-law to each other. They married brothers, oh, ages ago, in India."

"They're your aunts?"

"No. My husband's aunties. Well, actually his father's aunties, I suppose. What do you call that in English?"

"Great-aunt?"

"Yes, that's it." She frowned down at her own teacup. "He's going to be so upset when he hears they're in trouble. They drive him mad."

"Where is your husband?"

Ms. Agrawal hunched one shoulder. "In Los Angeles. He's at a conference until Sunday."

"What kind of conference?"

"Computers. He works at the computer lab at Loyola."

Dante nodded. "His name?"

"Karan Agrawal." She spelled it for him, and for a moment the only sound in the room was the scratching of Dante's pen across the page.

He looked up. "Where do your husband's great-aunts live?"

"With us at the moment." Her eyes narrowed. "Although it was really Saumya's turn, the cow. She always manages to get out of family obligations."

"Who is Saumya?"

Ms. Agrawal sighed. "Look, it is an extended family, you understand? Saumya is married to my husband's cousin, Sujay Agrawal. They are all descended from Savita Gupta's elder sister."

"So Saumya is related to the Gupta ladies?"

"No, it is Sujay who is related." Her lovely mouth twisted. "But it is the ladies in the family who must look after the elderly relatives."

"Look after," Dante repeated, frowning. "Are you saying they're senile?"

"No, although they act that way sometimes." Ms. Agrawal rolled her eyes. "They are such pains in the neck. You can't imagine how much trouble they cause. Savita's own daughter, Vinati, won't let her mother live with her. She claims her apartment is too small, but I think she knows her mother would drive her to murder."

"Where does the daughter live?"

"Out in Cicero, but you won't find her there."

"Why not?"

"Vinati has gone to Walt Disney World. In Orlando, Florida," Ms. Agrawal explained, as if Dante might not know where Disney World was. "She left over a week ago and will not be back for another week. It's monstrous! Saumya and I are supposed to take care of the mamis, but of course Saumya has wriggled out. She claims she has pneumonia and thus cannot care for the aunties."

"So, they're staying here with you and your husband?"

"Yes, yes." Ms. Agrawal waved a hand. "They really ought to be in India, cooking and nagging their grandchildren to do better in school. But nooo. They insisted that they must come to America. They said they wanted to see more of the world and that they had lives to lead now that their husbands were dead. Can you imagine? At their ages? Absurd is what it is." She tightened her mouth into a little prune shape.

"I see," Dante said in a noncommittal voice, and Zoey couldn't help but snort. Naturally he'd take the part of the fun-suppressing younger generation.

Dante shot her a repressive look, and Zoey widened her eyes in mock terror.

But Ms. Agrawal wasn't paying attention to their by-play. "They've been living with us for two months, and what a bother they've been! Poor Karan has had a sour stomach the entire time, and if he develops ulcers I will blame them, truly I will."

Dante flipped back a couple of pages in his notebook. "The green Civic they were driving is registered to Saumya Agrawal. That's the same Saumya you've been talking about?"

"Yes. She lent the aunties her old car. It's practically the only thing she has helped with."

"Okay." Dante wrote in the notebook. "But they're driving a lavender Dodge minivan now with the words ARTIE'S FLOWERS on the side. Do you know where they could've got it?"

Ms. Agrawal stared at Dante for a moment. She jumped up and ran to the back of the house. Zoey looked at Dante and then followed her. There was a small kitchen at the back of the house, and Zoey found the other woman standing over her sink, looking out the back window.

"Oh, no," she moaned. "Oh, no! Those wicked aunties have taken Karan's minivan. And look what they have left in its place!"

Zoey followed her pointing finger and looked out the window over the sink. In back of the house there was a rectangular concrete slab, extra parking for vehicles that couldn't fit in the one-car garage. There sat the yellow Humvee, as out of place as a giant cuckoo in a sparrow's nest.

Ms. Agrawal looked like she was in shock, so Zoey took her arm and led her back to her sofa. "It's okay. The police won't blame you for the Humvee. In fact, the owner probably hasn't even reported it stolen."

The other woman didn't seem comforted. "But what about Karan's minivan?"

Dante cleared his throat. "Do you know why your husband's aunts would want to steal the Humvee? And then dump it?"

Ms. Agrawal stared. "Oh, God, who knows? Who knows? My husband will have to bail them out of jail, and there goes our summer vacation to the Wisconsin Dells. He'll—"

"Or kidnap a baby?" Dante cut into the catalog of woes.

"A baby?" Ms. Agrawal's lovely mouth fell open. "They took—"

"Kidnapped," Dante murmured.

"A *baby*?"

He nodded.

"Oh, my God. Oh, my God!" Ms. Agrawal leaped up but then didn't seem to know what to do, so she just stood there. "Karan will lose his work visa. We'll be deported. Oh, my God!"

Dante sat back on the couch, his manner relaxed, but Zoey knew his interest was still totally engaged. "Do you know where they might go?"

Ms. Agrawal's gaze settled on him like a lifeline. "Go?"

Dante shrugged. "They aren't here, are they?"

She gazed around the little room as if one of the sari-clad old ladies might pop up from behind a chair. "No. They didn't come home last night."

Dante's eyebrows shot up. "That didn't worry you?"

"Naturally—"

"Two elderly ladies in a big city like Chicago?"

"I—"

Dante sighed. "Have you reported them missing?"

Ms. Agrawal chewed on the inside of her cheek. "I was going to, but it didn't seem necessary yet. I did call all the family in Chicago. No one had seen them."

Dante simply stared at the woman. The silence grew, and Ms. Agrawal's skin darkened. She couldn't seem to meet his eyes, and even Zoey was feeling guilty.

"Where do you think your husband's great-aunts might be right now, Mrs. Agrawal?"

"I don't know."

Dante sighed and closed his notebook, the movement oddly ominous.

Ms. Agrawal must've thought so, too. She stuttered into speech. "I-I don't know! Really I don't! There's only my husband's brother and sister, and Auntie Savita's daughter, but she's in Disney World in—"

The notebook was flipped open again. "Your husband's siblings' names?"

She sank into the chair, looking dazed, and rattled off a list of names.

"Who else?"

"I don't know!"

"They don't have friends in the city?"

"No."

Dante arched an eyebrow, obviously skeptical. "Not at all?"

Ms. Agrawal shrugged. "They've only been in the US for a couple of months. They spend all of their time on that stupid restaurant they plan to open."

"What about neighbors?"

"No."

"Acquaintances? Clubs or religious groups they might belong to?"

"I told you, they spend all their free time at the restaurant."

"Okay." Dante sighed. "No friends, no acquaintances, no clubs. Only the family you've mentioned: Mrs. Gupta's daughter, your husband, his brothers and their wives, and his cousin. That's it?"

"Well . . ."

Dante looked up. If he'd been a wolf his ears would've pricked forward. "What?"

Ms. Agrawal waved a hand dismissively. "My husband has one more cousin—another of the aunties' nephews—but he doesn't even live in Chicago."

"Where is he?"

"Cairo."

Dante's eyebrows shot up. "In Egypt?"

"No. Cairo in southern Illinois."

Chapter Seventeen

Friday, 7:00 a.m.

$\mathcal{I}$ do not think that the city of Cairo is on this map," Savita-di announced.

Pratima dared not take her eyes from the road, so dangerous was the traffic, but she did consider rolling them. "Cairo must be on the map. Rahul has his wonderful motel there."

Savita-di rustled the enormous map, which she had completely unfolded across the passenger side of the minivan. "I do not see it. I think this map is defective, Pratima."

"The map is not defective, Savita-di," Pratima replied. She inhaled sharply as a massive semi truck attempted to run down the purple minivan. At the last minute the truck swerved away, shaking the minivan in the wind of its passage.

Savita-di was oblivious. "I see a city called Rockford

and one called Davenport, but I do not see a city called Cairo."

Pratima frowned, calling up her hazy knowledge of American geography. "Is the city of Davenport in the state of Illinois?"

"Of course it is, Pratima!" Savita-di rattled her map. "It is on this map, is it not?"

"So you say."

"I say so because it is," Savita-di huffed. "And this map is a map of the state of Illinois. Therefore, Davenport is in Illinois."

"Hmm," Pratima murmured. She was concentrating on passing a tiny striped Mini car and could not help but feel a certain glee when the wheels of the purple minivan splattered brown slush against the little Mini's windshield. In the US of A it was good to drive a big vehicle.

From the back seat of the minivan a small voice sang, "La na la." It was the baby girl, freshly diapered and snuggly belted into a car seat taken from the yellow Humvee. She was munching on a breakfast of cut-up bananas and crackers, bought this morning at the scandalously expensive corner grocery store near Abdul's apartment. Beside the girl sat the boy, belted into the minivan's own car seat. This was a marvelous contraption concealed behind a removable cushion. The Gupta ladies would never have known about the hidden built-in baby car seat if it were not for Abdul, who had shown them. Their janitor might not speak English, but he seemed to have that mysterious knowledge of mechanical things that all gentlemen shared.

"This map is useless," Savita-di exclaimed, throwing

aside the rustling paper. "I shall guide us to this city of Cairo."

Pratima frowned, feeling uneasy. "How can you guide us without the map?"

Savita-di shrugged carelessly. "It is south, yes?"

"Yes."

"Then we simply drive south," Savita-di said. "It will be easy."

Chapter Eighteen

Friday, 7:13 a.m.

Dante held the car door for Zoey as she got in the BMW again. The sun was all the way up now and blindingly bright against the snow cover.

"Where to next?" Zoey asked as she buckled her seat belt. "Are we going to go try the brother and sister? 'Cause if so, I need a coffee. That tea was nice, but I really can't function without coffee in the morning."

"You are so not what I expected from someone who works in a health-food store," Dante muttered.

Dante shut the car door and walked around to his own side. He knew he was putting off telling her. Truth was, he was feeling a little down at the thought of not seeing her again after today. He glanced over his shoulder before pulling the BMW into the street. In the last half hour the neighborhood had waked up. Cars began backing out of driveways, an elderly man stood on his front steps watching a pug make yellow spots in the snow, and clumps of bundled schoolchildren trudged down the sidewalk.

"You're just prejudiced," Zoey said.

He looked at her. "What?"

Her cheeks were pink from walking to the BMW, and for someone who'd spent the night in a car, she looked pretty good. Her eyes were bright from dinging him, her face a little shiny under the ridiculous hat. "Prejudiced. Against people who work in health-food stores."

"Am not."

"Are, too. Why can't I drink coffee if I want to?"

"I thought coffee was bad for you."

"And yet *you* drink it anyway." She nodded wisely, the colorful strings on either side of her face bobbing. "Probably gives you a secret thrill, doesn't it? Drinking something you think is baaad?"

"Hey."

Okay, it was probably morning hormones, but the way she drawled *bad* kind of made him hot. Dante switched lanes, heading toward a main north–south artery. No matter which way he went this time of the day, it was going to take a good two hours to get to Chinatown. Maybe more.

Fortunately, she didn't seem to notice anything as she chattered. "Sorry to burst your little thrill bubble, but coffee's got lots of antioxidants and there're fewer suicides among people who drink coffee."

"You're making that up."

"Am not."

"Huh. Probably they're so high on caffeine they can't think straight to commit suicide."

"Well, yeah." She grinned at him.

He felt his own lips curving back. For such a prickly woman, she sure was sweet in the morning. Which made him feel like a total jerk for what he was about to do to her—dump her. She'd be safe. That was more important than disappointing her. He tried to keep that thought at the forefront of his mind as he pulled into a grocery parking lot. The grocery itself was a specialty store and had only one or two cars in front, but the tiny coffee kiosk in the parking lot was doing a brisk business.

Dante pulled the BMW into line behind a silver Audi and a battered blue Taurus.

He looked at Zoey. She was leaning toward him, studying the hand-lettered sign attached to the side of the kiosk. "What do you want?"

"I'm thinking."

He rolled his eyes and inched the BMW forward as the Audi left.

"You decided where we're going yet?" she asked absently.

The Taurus pulled away and he brought the BMW up to the kiosk.

He rolled down his window.

"Yeah?" The kid inside wore a stained T-shirt under an equally stained apron. He peered out the open half door of the kiosk, apparently oblivious to the cold.

"Large coffee, two creams," Dante said. He glanced at Zoey.

She leaned over nearly into his lap. "Good morning."

The kid focused on her. "Hi."

"Do you make carmellos?"

"Sure."

"Okay, can you make me a double, skim milk with lots of whipped cream?"

"You got it."

"Thank you." She smiled sweetly at the guy and straightened, her silly hat almost brushing Dante's chin. She looked at him. "So where do we go after this?"

He flattened his mouth. "Nowhere. We're going to meet my boss, and he'll take you to somewhere safe until this thing is straightened out."

Her brows knit. "But you said yesterday that someone in the FBI framed you."

He nodded, hating that he had to explain this, wishing that she'd just let him make decisions without arguing. "Someone inside the local FBI is trying to frame me, but Headington, the SAC, is on the case."

"What—?"

"Look, you're not safe with me. I need to make sure you're protected."

"But what about Pete?" Her voice had risen. "You're abandoning her!"

"I'm not abandoning her. My orders are to report in. There are others who can find her."

"The others were the ones that let her get kidnapped in the first place!" She was glaring at him now.

"Hey, you guys want these?"

Dante turned to the coffee kiosk. His face must've been pretty grim, because the barista jerked back, nearly dropping the paper cups he held.

"Yeah." Dante fumbled for his wallet.

"Here," Zoey said curtly. She held out a ten-dollar bill.

"I'll get it." Dante opened his wallet.

"I can pay for my own coffee."

"I said I'll get it." He ignored the ten waving under his nose and gave the barista a twenty.

"Jerk," Zoey muttered.

"You're welcome," he said as he shoved the cup into her hand.

He took a gulp of his coffee, burned his tongue, swore, and pulled out of the parking lot. Beside him, Zoey was silently sipping her own coffee, both hands wrapped around the cup. Which was fine. It didn't matter at all if she wasn't talking to him.

He brought the BMW to a halt at a stoplight, tapping his fingertips on the wheel. "Look. We're going to get your niece back. It's only a matter of time."

She snorted.

He gritted his teeth and accelerated as the light turned. "This thing is dangerous. You know that. I need to get you out of the line of fire."

"Oh, yeah, like you can trust your FBI peeps. Look what happened when you told Kev we were at the BP. The cops showed up minutes later. No way was that a coincidence."

Dante's lips tightened. Actually, Zoey wasn't saying anything he hadn't thought himself. He was pretty certain he could trust Headington, but he didn't know if he could trust anyone else at the office. Which was why he was making sure to arrive at the meeting place early.

Zoey was silent for most of the rest of the drive. When he entered Chinatown on Wentworth, she hadn't spoken to him for forty-five minutes.

Wentworth was the main drag through Chinatown. On either side of the street were stores and restaurants decorated in turn-of-the-last-century Chinese kitsch.

"You're meeting here?" Zoey sounded dubious.

"Close by."

They drove under a red-painted arch decorated with wild-eyed lion dogs. The road twisted to the right as they neared the tangle of Stevenson Expressway and I-94, high overhead. Tall concrete bridges arched into the sky, supported by massive pillars. Dante turned, paralleling the expressway. The sheltered area underneath had been made into a makeshift parking lot. He drove into the lot, crawling between crumbling concrete barriers that separated the road from the parking area. Old snow, ice, and grit crunched under the BMW's tires. Dante turned off the engine, and for a moment they sat in the car, listening to the engine tick as it cooled.

Zoey shivered and wrapped her arms around her waist. "I don't see anyone."

"That's because we're early." Dante unbuckled his seat belt. "Stay here."

He got out of the car, scanning the area. There were a couple of parked cars, old snow drifted over their tops. Long, dirty icicles hung from the edges of the concrete. They trembled as the traffic roared by on the highway overhead. As far as he could see, they were the only people in the parking lot.

The passenger door to the BMW opened, and Dante turned unsurprised to see Zoey get out of the car.

He reached under his overcoat to unholster the Glock. "Stick close to me."

For once she didn't argue. He walked across the garage, checking under and around cars, the progress slow. He could feel Zoey at his back, trailing him and looking under cars when he did. A white van drove under the overpass, slowing on the turn. Dante pulled Zoey into a crouch next to him, partly shielded by a parked car.

The van sped by.

Dante released his breath and stood. He glanced at his wristwatch: 9:39. He had twenty minutes or so until the meet. The cars they'd searched were in a clump in the middle of the parking lot. There were still three or four that he hadn't looked at, parked next to one of the giant concrete pillars. Dante started for them.

"What are we looking for, anyway?" Zoey asked.

"Surprises."

"Great."

He ignored her. The nearest car was an old Cadillac. He bent to peer under it and froze. There wasn't anything under the car, but on the far side, lying on the ground, he could see a tennis shoe and part of a jeans-clad leg. He straightened.

"What are—" Zoey began.

He turned and pressed his fingers to her lips, watching as her eyes widened over his hand. He motioned her behind him and gripped the Glock in both fists. Leading with the gun, Dante whipped around the corner of the Caddy in a crouch.

Oh, shit.

For a timeless moment Dante merely stared. A young man lay on his back on the ground, his face turned slightly to the side, his half-opened eyes dull. A sudden gust of winter wind flattened the thin Dilbert T-shirt against his skinny frame. The Dogbert cartoon in the middle was nearly obscured by the large crusted bloodstain that covered his chest. He would've hated that—Dogbert was Kevin's favorite.

"Oh, my God," Zoey whispered, just as two black SUVs squealed into the parking lot.

Chapter Nineteen

Friday, 9:47 a.m.

Zoey stood frozen as the black SUVs bore down on them from the far side of the parking lot.

"Run to the car!" Dante shoved his keys into Zoey's hands.

Her hands shook and she nearly dropped them. The black SUVs were roaring nearer, and she couldn't just leave Dante here. She couldn't just—

"Go!" he shouted and raised his gun.

Zoey whirled and ran flat out across the parking lot. She was about twenty yards from the car. The ground was uneven, badly plowed, and crusted old snow clumped with chunks of crumbling concrete. Her body jolted with each hard footfall.

BLAM! BLAM! BLAM!

The rapid gunshots echoed off the concrete overhead

like claps of thunder. Zoey chanced a glance over her shoulder and caught an image of Dante that impressed itself on her retinas. Dante stood, legs apart, arms held straight in front of him in a shooter's stance as he returned fire. His long black trench coat hung to his calves, and his face was no longer pretty. It was grim and hard, set in granite. He looked like something out of a western—the lone figure of justice defending an innocent town against evil.

But the two SUVs were almost on him now, and they looked like they were just going to run him down where he stood. A scream ripped from her throat. At the last possible moment, Dante dove behind the Cadillac he'd been standing next to. The lead SUV careened off the old car, smashing it into the Jeep behind it.

Oh, God, Dante must be crushed. Zoey made the last couple of yards to the BMW and scrambled in. She fumbled with the keys, trying to insert them into the ignition, her eyes blurred with tears. Behind her, shots crunched against concrete, a whole series of them, making her ears ring. She got the key in and turned it. The BMW's engine purred to life.

He might already be dead. The treacherous thought popped into her brain. She wasn't an FBI agent. She wasn't trained for anything but ordering oat bran in bulk. He'd told her to run. Shouldn't she do just that? But more shots rang out. They wouldn't still be shooting if he were dead. And the point was moot, because Zoey had already gunned the BMW in the direction of the shooting.

The two SUVs were stopped now, all of the doors flung open. She could see movement behind one of them as a man with a blond crew cut leaned out and fired into the wreckage of the Cadillac and Jeep. The gunshots were immediately returned. Zoey's heart leaped. *Thank God. Thank God Dante isn't dead.*

The Caddy and Jeep were piled together, but the giant concrete pillar behind them had stopped the momentum of the crash. There was a car-wide space between the pillar and the outer wall, and Zoey aimed the BMW at it.

More shots rang out. One of the bad guys turned as the BMW neared, and Zoey actually saw his eyes widen. He brought up his gun, but there was a sudden flurry of shots from behind the Caddy and he went down. Then she was pulling into the space by the pillar. She braked fast and watched as Dante rose up from the wreckage of the cars, firing straight-armed at the SUVs. He dove and rolled over the trunk of the BMW to get to the passenger-side door.

He flung himself into the car. "Go! Go! Go!"

Zoey floored the BMW, fishtailing out from behind the pillar. Something thumped against the rear panel, and then they were out of the parking lot and into the street.

"You okay?" Dante asked. He'd twisted to kneel in his seat and look behind them.

"Yeah, I'm fine." Zoey glanced in the rearview mirror. One black SUV roared on her tail like a demon from hell.

"Shit," Dante muttered.

He ejected the clip from his gun, fumbled under his coat, and came up with another, sliding it into place in one motion. He rolled down the passenger-side window, leaned out, and fired. Zoey braked and jerked the wheel of the car, flying onto an east–west street.

Dante slid on the seat. He grabbed the back of the headrest to steady himself. "Careful."

"Why is there only one?"

"What?" He had his arm out the window again, frigid air blasting in.

Zoey swerved to speed around a panel delivery truck. "The second SUV. Where is it?"

Dante fired his gun, making her flinch and cringe against the steering wheel. Tires screamed behind them, and Zoey heard a smashing roar.

"Serves you right, you son of a bitch." Dante muttered. He grunted and withdrew his arm from the window. "Shot out the first SUV's tires in the parking lot."

She glanced in the rearview mirror. The second SUV was no longer following them. "What do we do now?"

She sped through a light just as it turned red. A car horn blasted behind her.

Dante turned around in the passenger seat. "Slow down, for one."

"Okay." Zoey could feel her face warming. "I'm not used to car chases, you know."

"I know," he said quietly. He'd buckled his seat belt, and now he rested his head against the seat. "You did a good job. A real good job."

"Thanks." She felt shaky, on edge like little prickly needles were riding her bloodstream. "Where should I go?"

Dante blinked. "Turn off here."

Zoey turned the wheel, not quite braking enough. The car slid around the curve, and Dante grunted again.

"Sorry." She grimaced and slowed, glancing at him. "I need to—"

But she didn't finish the sentence, because her thoughts scattered. There was a smear of blood on the console.

"Oh, my God," she whispered. "You've been shot."

Chapter Twenty

$\mathcal{T}$ony the Rose sat at a huge steel and glass desk in his mansion office in one of the most exclusive neighborhoods in Chicago. His office was a dark room because the black vertical blinds were pulled permanently over the windows. Tony didn't like the thought of someone looking in the room from outside. Maybe taking a shot at him from the outside. Better to live in the half light than be highlighted on a stage. Besides, he wasn't too interested in the view: trees with maybe a glimpse now and then of a Rottweiler patrolling the grounds.

On the wall opposite his desk was a fifty-seven-inch flat-screen TV with the sound off. It was tuned to the Weather Channel. A plate of Pepperidge Farm sugar cookies lay on the green ink blotter in front of him. Next to it, a Cuban cigar smoldered in a cut-glass ashtray. Tony sipped espresso from a tiny gold-rimmed glass cup and thought about what a pain in the ass his family was.

"That Fed double-crossed us," Leo, his right-hand man, said. Leo was sitting on the other side of the desk in a red armchair, bony knees poking up. "'Course. Feds always double-cross or fuck things up, you don't mind me saying so."

Tony selected a perfectly round cookie and carefully bit off a quarter, savoring the taste of vanilla. What Leo was really saying was *I told you so,* only he couldn't say that out loud, because Tony would then have to blow his brains out. Which didn't mean that they didn't both know what Leo really meant.

Tony swallowed his bite and said, "Sending Neil was a mistake."

Leo made a big shrug, both hands palms up at shoulder height. "Don't know that it was the Neilster's fault this time, Tony. He said the place was already fucked when he got there. What could he do?"

"Not lose the kid, for one." Tony shoved the rest of the cookie into his mouth and wiped his fingertips on a white paper napkin.

"True."

"Make sure our feeb had Ricky killed, for another. That was the job I sent him to do in the first place. The feeb was supposed to have Ricky killed, Neil was supposed to verify the hit. Simple. Except no one does what they're supposed to do anymore."

"I dunno, Tony. I think the whole thing was a setup."

Tony looked at Leo over the rim of his espresso cup. "Why?"

"The feeb knows we're sending a guy, and when our

guy gets there he finds a whole lot of dead Feds? I think the feeb wanted Neil to go down for his mess. Had nothing to do with popping Ricky."

"So you're saying the feeb never planned to have Ricky killed at all?"

"I think so, Tony. I think so."

"Motherfucker," Tony commented without any real heat. He'd been dealing with Feds for a long time, and like Leo said, they always double-crossed or fucked things up.

"So now we gotta worry about this trial," Leo said, opening an unpleasant topic of conversation.

Tony had been on trial for the last couple of weeks on federal charges. He didn't like to think about the trial too much when he wasn't actually in the courtroom. It gave him heartburn. And he wasn't due back in court until after lunch. He should've had the morning off. But that wasn't going to happen.

Tony grunted and set down his espresso cup. "What about Ricky Spinoza? Can we get to him?"

Leo shook his head slowly, looking like a sad balding basset hound. His face was all vertical lines and drooping jowls, topped by the big dome of his bald head. Two patches of fuzz sat over both ears, making him look vaguely like a morose Bozo the Clown. "They've moved him again. Him and his girlfriend."

"I am not going to be sent down by some two-bit hustler who thinks he can cross me and get away with it."

"No, Tony."

"I'm too old to go to the pen again. I've got gout in my knee."

Leo looked surprised. "Gout? Had an uncle who had the gout. I didn't know people got gout anymore."

"Of course they do," Tony replied. "It's a buildup of uric-acid crystals in the joint. Happens all the time."

"That so? You sure it's your knee?"

"Yeah, it's my knee."

"'Cause my uncle, he had gout in his big toe."

"It's my knee."

"I'm just sayin' I never heard of gout in the knee. Toes, yes, knees, no."

"Leo, would you kindly shut the fuck up about your uncle's gouty toes?"

"Sure, Tony." Leo held his hands wide and shrugged. "I'm sorry to hear you got gout."

Tony nodded. "I want Ricky dead."

"I hear you, but I don't trust that feeb anymore and it'll take too long to find Ricky. He's due to testify in three days."

"We ought to ice the feeb."

"Yeah, Tony, yeah," Leo said in an annoyingly soothing tone. "But maybe later, huh? We gotta keep Ricky from testifying."

Tony drank the last of his espresso and patted his lips with the napkin. Then he sat back in his leather chair, making it squeak a little. "I need that kid. If we have the kid, Ricky doesn't talk."

"Neil said she was gone."

"Neil is a jerkoff who I would never have sent for this job if it weren't for my niece and her mother," Tony growled. "I don't even like Janet."

This was the problem with family. They expected you to hire them just because of blood, never mind if they were screwups. What was worse, they expected you to hire their asshole husbands, too. And in the case of Neil, he had not only his niece, Ashley, hounding him, but her mother, Janet, as well. And though Tony would never say this to anyone, his younger sister kind of gave him the willies. Janet was a coldhearted bitch and a mean one, too.

No one knew how hard it was to be the boss. Tony allowed himself a small moment of self-pity.

Then he looked at Leo. "I'm bringing in Rutgar."

Leo's head jerked back like he'd been popped in the forehead. "Jesus, Tony. Rutgar? He ain't exactly a precision worker."

"He gets the job done. Every time."

"Yeah, but the job's usually a hit, pardon the expression."

"So?"

"So, you want a baby hit?"

Tony shrugged. "I want Rutgar to bring the kid to me."

Leo looked uneasy. "Yeah, but what I'm saying is that Rutgar gets kinda enthusiastic when he's working. People get hurt, and sometimes they ain't the ones supposed to be hurt."

"Doesn't matter. I'm not going to prison again. I need that kid, and I need her fast. If she's a little bruised in the process, well"—Tony picked up a sugar cookie and idly ground it into the plate, watching as it shattered and fell into little pieces—"that's the way the fucking cookie crumbles, isn't it?"

Chapter Twenty-one

Friday, 10:24 a.m.

It's not a gunshot wound," Dante said from the passenger seat.

"How do you know?" Zoey felt tears blur her vision. She blinked them away fiercely. *Not now.* "You're bleeding. You could be in shock and not know that you're hit. We have to get you to a hospital."

But even as she said it, she knew that wasn't possible. They might as well turn themselves in at a police station as go to an emergency room. And after the shootout under the overpass, she very much feared that Dante wouldn't come out of a police station alive.

"The Caddy hit my thigh when the SUVs crashed into it," Dante said beside her. "Must've gotten a cut or something. I'd know if I'd been shot."

She glanced quickly at him. He was yellow under his

naturally swarthy skin. Not a good sign. "How would you know?"

"What?"

"How would you know if you were shot?" They were heading north now, and she'd driven into a commercial area. Zoey searched the stores as she drove by.

"Because I've been shot before."

For a split second she stared at him before she wrenched her gaze back to the road. It'd never occurred to her that he might be hurt in his line of work. Which was silly, of course, considering what they'd both been through since yesterday afternoon, but there it was. It seemed too Hollywood, an FBI agent being shot, too surreal. Not part of her everyday, boring life.

But Dante was sitting next to her, his hair rumpled, his face shiny with sweat, his eyes shut in what must be pain, not looking at all like a *GQ* cover model now. Now he looked like an ordinary man and he was *real*. Suddenly real in a way that he hadn't been before. He was a flesh-and-blood man. One who could feel pain.

One who could be shot and killed.

She drew in a shaky breath. "What—?"

"I'll tell you later," he said quietly, and she felt ashamed. This was a wild adventure for her. She was worried sick about Pete, true, but after this was all over, after they got Pete back, she'd return to her normal, slightly boring life. Whereas for Dante, this *was* his life.

She saw what she was looking for and made an abrupt turn into a corner mall, the kind with an old K-Mart and a row of little discount shops. Dante grunted as he was thrown against the door. She jerked the BMW to a halt in the K-Mart parking lot between a blue sedan and a yellow Jeep.

"I'm sorry," Zoey babbled as she unhooked her seat belt. "Stay here. I'll be right back."

Dante grabbed her arm, his fingers tight even through her puffy coat. "You can't go in there."

"You need bandages," Zoey hissed fiercely.

"How're you going to pay for them?"

"I've got a credit card."

"It'll be traced. I don't want you—"

She turned and placed her hand over the hand that gripped her arm. "Look. They already know we're in Chicago, right? It doesn't matter if they trace my card to a K-Mart."

He stared at her, his bitter-chocolate eyes intent and worried. Then he let go of her arm. "Hurry. I don't want them to find us here."

She nodded and scrambled from the BMW. The wind was cold outside, and she walked swiftly to the automatic sliding doors. Inside, insipid background music played, and once again she felt a sense of disconnect. Zoey grabbed a monster cart and started wheeling it through the aisles. First stop was the pharmacy area. She picked up first-aid supplies, as well as some bottles of painkillers, then looked at the cart and hesitated a moment. She'd only been in the store less than five minutes. It wouldn't take much longer to pick up a few things more.

Twenty minutes later she was through the checkout line and lugging four full plastic bags to the car. She could see Dante frowning as she unlocked the back seat door and threw the bags inside.

"What did you get?" he asked as she buckled her seat belt.

"Supplies." She looked over her shoulder as she backed out of the parking space. When she turned around again, she caught Dante's eye. "What?"

"Looks like you plan on a siege."

She shrugged and put the car in drive. "I like to be prepared."

He didn't say anything for a bit as she drove a couple of miles closer to the Loop. She pulled over into another parking lot and turned off the engine.

"Okay, take off those pants." Zoey leaned over into the back, rummaging in the plastic bags. When she came back up with her first-aid supplies, Dante was looking at her with raised brows.

She rolled her eyes. "Unless you want me to cut them off, Lips."

"Lips?"

She could feel her face go hot. Oh, wonderful. Her mouth had been betrayed by her nervousness.

He reached for his belt buckle. "Did you say *Lips?*"

"No." This was the point when Zoey knew she should politely look away, but she couldn't. She just couldn't. There was something unbelievably erotic about a man undoing his trousers, and her eyes were fixed on his long, dark fingers working at his fly.

"Yes, you did."

"Okay, maybe I did. So what?"

He lifted his hips and slid his trousers down until they bagged around his knees. She noticed sexy gray knit boxers, and then her gaze was caught by the massive bruise on his thigh. It ran from just above the knee to under the edge of his knit shorts and was highlighted by a huge abrasion. Blood must've dried and stuck to the material of his trousers, because fresh blood was welling all along the scrape. The whole thing looked very nasty.

"Shit," Zoey breathed. "You didn't break your leg, did you?"

"No," Dante grunted. "I wouldn't have been able to stand if I had."

"Good point." Zoey unscrewed a bottle of hydrogen peroxide and glanced at him apologetically. "This will probably sting."

He looked resigned. "So what's with *Lips?*"

She began to carefully clean the wound using the hydrogen peroxide and a sterile gauze pad. "Remember when I moved into the apartment building?"

"Yeah, so?"

"So, that first night I went down to use the laundry room and you stole my dryer."

"What?"

"You stole my dryer. You stole my dryer almost every time I used the laundry."

"I did n—"

"You'd go down to the basement, and you'd take all my clothes out of the dryer and steal it. You did. And what was worse, it was always my underwear load. I think you have a panty fetish."

"I do not," he muttered. His sculpted cheekbones were getting ruddy.

"Anyway, I didn't know your name, but I got to calling you Lips of Sin." She had her head down, dabbing at an oozing cut, so she couldn't see his face.

There was a silence in the car, and she began to really

wish that he'd say something. The silence stretched, the only sound in the car their breathing—his deep and even, hers getting just a little ragged.

Finally, she inhaled and said the first thing that came into her mind. "Who was that back there under the overpass?"

She straightened to throw away the soiled gauze she'd been using to clean his scrapes.

He caught her wrist when she swung back. "Zoey."

His hand was hot against the cool skin of her wrist, and his eyes were dark and intense. She stared at him, and for the life of her she didn't know what to say.

He sighed and let go of her wrist. "They were probably professional hit men."

She swallowed, feeling a wave of relief. She got out another square of gauze and tore open the paper wrapper. "No, I mean the dead guy. Did you know him?"

He was silent a moment, and she was conscious of the warmth of his thigh under her fingertips. It was a nicely muscled thigh beneath the bruises and cuts, with a scattering of just enough curly black hair.

"That was Kevin," Dante said at last. "Poor bastard."

She glanced up at him. His lips were set in a grim line.

"Kev, the guy you talked to on the phone?"

"Yeah."

"Wasn't he the guy who gave way where we were?"

He caught her eye. "Yeah, Kev was a weasely guy, but I kind of liked him anyway. It was hard not to."

She stared down at his lap, noticing absently how well the gray cotton fit over his crotch. "Why would they kill Kevin?"

Dante robbed his face looking infinitely weary.

"Because he was one of two people in Chicago who knew that I was working undercover at the Chicago FBI office."

Zoey felt her eyes widen, and her hands stilled over him. "Who was the other?"

"The Chicago office SAC, Jack Headington. The guy we were supposed to meet."

Chapter Twenty-two

*H*er hands were warm and gentle on his bruised skin. For some reason Dante hadn't expected that. Her gentleness was a nice contrast to the stinging pain of the hydrogen peroxide she was using on his scrapes.

"Why were you undercover?" she asked softly.

He blinked and glanced at her. All he could see was the top of her silly multicolored reindeer hat. She was bent over his lap as if doing something entirely different than administering first aid, and he could smell the sweet scent of her hair.

He glanced away, trying to push the inappropriate thought from his brain. "A little over a month ago I was sent in undercover to do an investigation of the Chicago FBI office."

"Like, an internal investigation?" Zoey murmured. He could almost feel the brush of her breath on his leg.

Christ. "Yeah, exactly like an internal investigation. There were suspicions that someone in the Chicago office was crooked."

"Because—?"

"Bad guys being tipped off about raids, evidence disappearing, stuff like that. To top it off, five months ago a mob informant was killed right before a meet with the local cops."

"Couldn't that informant's killing have been job related? It's probably not a very safe profession, tattling on the mob."

Dante smiled grimly. "Yeah, but added all together it set off some alarm bells. The higher-ups decided it was time to send in someone from outside the Chicago office to look into things. Someone who wouldn't be tainted by local loyalties and politics. Someone like me."

"All alone?"

"One guy being transferred in is a lot less suspicious than several."

She sighed and ripped open a new gauze packet. "And the first thing your bosses did was tell this Headington guy? That sounds kind of stupid."

Dante tensed as she poured more hydrogen peroxide in his wounds. The stuff stung like a son of a bitch, and beneath the sting was the pounding ache of his bruised thigh. He wondered idly if he'd be able to walk on the leg tomorrow.

"Jack Headington's the SAC of the Chicago FBI office. He'd have to know why I'd been transferred anyway. Besides, there is no reason to suspect him. He's done decades of exemplary service in the FBI, had several commendations, and never a hint of problems in all that time. In fact, he was the one who initially pushed for an outside investigation."

She snorted. "Probably wanted to be able to keep an eye on what you found."

Dante shook his head. "I don't like that Headington set up the meet but it doesn't necessarily mean that he's the traitor. His phone could've been tapped, he might've told someone in the office he trusted, who knows."

"You have to admit that it doesn't look good."

He shrugged. "*I* don't look good at the moment."

She looked up, her blue eyes disconcertingly close. "Wait. If you were sent in to investigate the Chicago office, why were you guarding Ricky?"

"The corruption within the Chicago office was tied to the mob and Tony the Rose. Guarding Ricky killed two birds with one stone: I needed a cover assignment, and we figured that if I was close to Ricky, I could catch any witness tampering." He hissed as she poured more hydrogen peroxide. "That, at least, turned out to be a good call. Someone certainly tried to 'tamper' with Ricky. Too bad I didn't stop them killing my colleagues and kidnapping Pete."

She shook her down-bent head. "You would've been killed, too. You know that."

He frowned as he watched her clean the wound. He knew it, but it was still hard to accept. Three agents dead . . .

"What about Kevin?" she asked, interrupting his dark thoughts.

He grimaced, remembering again Kev's dull open eyes. "Kevin knew me from a former posting. He was a smart little jerk and figured out what I was doing almost as soon as I walked in the office. But Kevin had a history with the mob. His sister was killed by her mafia boyfriend in New Jersey. He had a deep hatred of the mob so it was pretty unlikely that he was the traitor. Since he was the tech guy, I decided he could help me with my investigation. He was doing computer searches for me."

"Is that why they killed him?"

He sucked in his breath as she poked at a painful cut. "Probably."

"Poor Kevin."

"Yeah, poor Kevin."

"They were going to hang his murder on you, too, weren't they?"

"I don't know."

It had sure looked like a setup. If he hadn't arrived early, the guys in the SUVs would've been there to arrest him for Kevin's murder when he showed up. Or to shoot him as he tried to get away.

"You keep saying *we*," she said. "There must be someone else who knows that you're undercover. Who sent you in?"

"My boss, Charles—Charlie—Hessler."

She looked up excitedly. "So all you have to do is call your boss and tell him . . ." She must've seen the look on his face, because she trailed off. "What?"

"That's one of the things Kev told me yesterday," he said wearily. "Charlie had a massive stroke. He was in the ICU unconscious, last I heard."

"Oh." She looked down.

He watched as she opened a tube of antibiotic ointment and squirted the clear jelly all over his leg. Then she got out a packet of the biggest gauze pads he'd ever seen and laid them in a row on top of the ointment.

She glanced at him. "Can you lift your leg a little?"

"Yeah."

She began to unroll gauze tape around his leg and the bandages.

"So your boss—the only person outside of Chicago who knew about your hush-hush undercover operation—is now out of commission, and your tech support is dead, leaving you only the head of the Chicago FBI—this Headington guy—who may or may not have killed Kevin and sent hitmen to kill us. Have I got that right?"

He looked at her. She seemed pretty calm for someone who'd just described a worst-case scenario. "Yeah, that just about sums it up."

"Sounds like we're screwed." She grinned at him.

That *we* warmed him inside, even though he hated the thought that she was in danger because of him. "It also means that there isn't anyone I trust trying to bring in Pete's kidnapper."

Her hands stilled over his thigh as she seemed to think about that. He wondered if she noticed that one hand was between his legs. Probably not.

He sure did, though.

"They don't want her found," Zoey whispered. "If the Chicago FBI office is crooked—they're not going to want Ricky to testify against Tony the Rose. They don't want Tony convicted." She looked up at him, her eyes wide. "No one's looking for Pete."

Dante didn't point out that no one looking for Pete would be the best thing that could happen. If the traitor in the Chicago FBI sent someone after the child, it wouldn't be to save her.

"We're looking," he said quietly.

She bit her lip and dropped her gaze to her hands as if

she couldn't meet his eyes. "Are we? You're not going to give up, then?"

She was tying the end of the bandage, fumbling as if she were nervous or couldn't see very well. He caught one of her hands and tugged gently until she looked up again. "I'm going to keep looking for Pete until we find her and bring her home."

He watched those blue eyes search his own. Zoey must've found whatever she was looking for in his face. For a moment, she closed her eyes. "Thank you."

He tugged at her hand, gently, so she could pull away if she wanted to. But she didn't. Instead, she opened her eyes and leaned toward him. He watched her blue eyes come closer, and then he closed his own eyes.

Kissing Zoey was a revelation. She kissed him open-mouthed, no hesitation, her lips soft and warm, her tongue wet and erotic. Simply. As if she'd been waiting for this moment from the time she'd flung herself against the hood of his car. She was unsurprised, maybe a little curious, and he wondered if she had any idea how much of a turn-on her forthright sensuality was.

This close, her scent surrounded him. He inhaled and raised his other hand to cradle her head. Her braided hair was springy, tickling his palm. He angled his head and licked into her mouth, discovering sweetness and warmth. He wished he could haul her into his lap, take this embrace to the next level.

She pulled back, breaking the kiss, and looked at him. Her eyes were blue and beautiful and as wise as if she'd lived a hundred years.

And in that moment Dante knew. He'd either made the best decision of his life—or the most stupid.

Chapter Twenty-three

Friday, 11:15 a.m.

He'd overslept.

Neil gripped the wheel of the red SUV and sped through the west side of Chicago, headed for I-57. He should've been out of Chicago hours ago, but the short nap he'd decided to take at five a.m. had turned into an hours-long snoozefest. He could feel a vein throbbing on his temple. His anger management instructor would call the vein an "indicator" and tell him to do some idiot breathing exercises. But then, his instructor had probably never waited up until three freaking a.m. in a freezing truck for an Indian guy and his wife to come home from a party.

It must've been some party, too, 'cause Sujay Agrawal had been leaning on his wife when he'd finally staggered up the steps to his apartment. Neil hadn't had any trouble at all muscling into the Agrawal apartment. Questioning

Sujay had been another ball of wax, though. The guy had hardly been able to string two words together, and his wife had gone into shrill, shrieking hysterics. It'd taken a gag on the wife and a cold shower for Sujay before Neil had found out which way the old Indian ladies might be headed.

Cairo. The fucking armpit of Illinois.

A weird little whistling sound was coming from somewhere, and for a second Neil couldn't place it. And then he realized that the weird little whistling sound was his breath, whistling from between his teeth. He was blowing his fucking top. He stomped on the brake, screeching to a stop at a corner light just as his cell phone rang. Neil froze. He'd already talked to Tony the Rose, but when he'd tried to call Ashley the night before, the answering machine had picked up. And it might make him a dickless wonder, but Neil just hadn't had the guts to try Ashley again today.

He swallowed and picked up his cell, looking at the little itty-bitty window. It flashed Ash's number, like she was screaming at him through the line.

Behind him, someone laid on the horn.

Neil whipped down his window and stuck his Beretta out.

"You want a piece of me?" he screamed, spittle flying through the air. "You want a fucking piece of me?"

The driver's eyes in the pickup behind him went wide, the whites showing all the way around. Then the guy threw his truck into reverse and backed the length of the block, tires squealing, before stopping, switching gears, and speeding away around a corner.

Neil inhaled deeply, withdrew his gun from the window, and tilted his head to the side until his neck cracked. Then he picked up his phone again and answered it.

"Hi, honeybuns."

Chapter Twenty-four

Friday, 11:37 a.m.

Dante tasted like coffee and sex. How the man could walk around in broad daylight without spontaneously combusting was beyond her. Zoey sat back in her own seat and began gathering used gauze pads and wrappers, hoping he wouldn't notice how her hands shook. She looked down, focusing on steadying her hands as she threw trash into one of the plastic grocery bags.

When she looked up, he was gingerly drawing his pants over the bandage she'd made. He winced as the fabric caught on part of the gauze.

Zoey leaned between the seats and dug in one of the remaining plastic bags until she found the bottle of pain-killers. "Here."

He glanced at her and then the bottle, grimacing.

She rolled her eyes and started wrestling open the

packaging. "What? Are you going to be all stoic and deny you're in pain?" The bottle top came off with a pop. She poked a finger through the seal and dug out two red pills. "*Here.*"

One corner of his mouth kicked up as he took the pills from her palm. "Thank you."

His voice was dry, but his dark chocolate eyes were intent on her, and suddenly Zoey didn't know where to look. She busied herself finding a bottle of water.

In the meantime he threw the pills in his mouth and tilted back his head.

She wrinkled her nose as she held out the water bottle. "I don't know how you can do that. I always gag when I try dry swallowing."

He drank from the water bottle, watching her, and then screwed the cap back on the bottle. "They teach us how to dry swallow pills at Quantico."

"Ooo, macho." She buckled her seat belt and started the car. "So, where do we go now?"

"Cairo."

She glanced at him.

He was frowning at her hands on the steering wheel. "Maybe I should drive."

She arched her eyebrows. "With that leg? Not unless you want to cripple yourself."

He opened his mouth.

But she spoke before he could. "I'll drive."

"How much experience do you have driving a stick?"

"Lots. I got us here, didn't I?" She pressed down on the clutch and shifted into first before starting the car. She eased up on the clutch and the car coughed and died.

Dante looked at her. "You're sure."

"That was a fluke. I can drive a stick shift perfectly fine."

"Oh, God," he muttered.

This time she eased up on the clutch very carefully and the Beemer rolled forward.

She shot a triumphant look at him. "So, you think the old ladies are headed for their nephew in Cairo?"

"According to Ms. Agrawal, they're not with any of the family in Chicago." He was still watching her feet.

She eased into traffic. "But Cairo?"

"They're two elderly ladies in a foreign country with not many people they know. So, yeah, I think they've decided to visit their nephew."

"Makes sense, I guess." Zoey chewed on her lip. She'd stopped at a light and was waiting for it to turn. Morning traffic had slowed just a little bit. Even so, the freeway was going to be crowded. "Think I should go south to 55 and take it all the way over to 90/94?"

"Go west until you hit Dan Ryan Expressway," he said absently. He leaned over to check the dash. "We'd better stop for gas soon."

She glanced at the gauge. It showed that she still had an eighth of a tank of gas. "It'll be cheaper if we wait until we're out of the city."

"We have an eighth of a tank."

She looked at him, eyes wide. "Yeah, we have an eighth of a tank."

He exhaled. "You're one of those."

"What *one of those?*"

"One of those women who let the gas tank run down to nothing and then wonder why they run out of gas."

"I am not!" They'd stopped at another light, and she turned to glare at him.

He lifted one eyebrow. How did he *do* that? "Have you ever run out of gas?"

"Well, yeah, but everybody does that."

"I haven't."

"Everybody who's *normal* runs out of gas."

"How many times?"

"How many times, what?" She pressed hard on the accelerator and the BMW jumped forward.

He glanced at her feet worriedly. "How many times have you run out of gas?"

"Not more than three or four or maybe five times—"

"In the last year?" he drawled obnoxiously.

"You realize nobody likes a know-it-all."

But he wasn't paying attention to her words. "Watch for that bus, he's not looking where he's going."

Zoey glanced at Dante thoughtfully. "You weren't worried about my driving before, when I got us out of the parking lot under the Stevenson Expressway."

"I was busy shooting at the guys chasing us."

"So, go find someone to shoot at," Zoey muttered.

He watched her driving for a little bit more and then leaned back against the headrest and closed his eyes. Zoey smirked. Apparently it was easier for him to let her drive his car if he couldn't actually see her doing it.

She passed a school bus and said, "So, have you got family still in New York? Mom or dad?"

"Both parents." He sighed. "And two brothers and three sisters."

"Wow, that's a large—"

"And three brothers-in-law, one sister-in-law, five

nieces, two nephews, four uncles, three aunts, and a dozen or so cousins. *Large* doesn't even begin to cover it."

"That must be really nice."

He grunted.

"Oh, come on! All those kids must be great, especially at Thanksgiving."

"I don't usually go home for Thanksgiving."

"Well, Christmas, then."

"I don't—"

She braked hard at a stoplight. "You don't go home for Christmas? What are you, the Grinch? I bet all those nephews and nieces would love to see you. You're an FBI agent! That's gotta have some cachet with the elementary crowd."

He sighed. "You don't have a large family, do you?"

She thought of the big, mostly empty farm she'd grown up on. "Well, not exactly, but—"

"So you don't know what a pain in the neck they can be. Every time I go home, somebody's not talking to somebody else, my father interrogates me on my job, my mother wonders why I'm not married yet, and inevitably one of the kids is throwing up or coughing."

"Huh."

He opened his eyes and looked at her. "What's that supposed to mean?"

"Nothing." She shrugged. "Huh means huh."

"Oh, please. I have a mother and three sisters, and I know damn well that huh does not mean huh."

"Okay." Zoey gripped the steering wheel tighter, leaning slightly forward. "Okay. I just think you're being a little hard on your fam—"

He snorted.

She raised her voice. "They sound like they love you and are worried about you. It might be irritating at times, but you can't tell me that it's worse than the alternative."

"The alternative being . . . ?"

"Having no family."

She was quiet then, feeling the blush creeping up her face. Dante wasn't talking, either, but she could tell that he was watching her thoughtfully. They passed a Popeyes, and Zoey noticed a gas station up ahead.

"What was your family like, growing up?" Dante asked beside her.

Good God, she hadn't meant to start a conversation like this one. "I already told you, I lived on a hippie farm with my mother. Look, there's a Shell gas station. Should I stop for gas there?"

He watched her a moment more—a disconcertingly perceptive gaze—and then he glanced ahead. "Sure."

She felt like closing her eyes in relief. Dante was too aware. She wasn't sure she was ready for his intense intelligence to be turned on her. Yet at the same time she knew she was drawn to that part of him. Was provoking that part of him. And what was worse, she couldn't seem to help herself.

Chapter Twenty-five

Friday, noon

The veteran FBI agent watched from his office as news of Kevin Heinz's death spread through the tech department. There were whispered conversations, a few angry exclamations, and even some sobs. But overall the result was oddly homogenous: a kind of frightened pall loomed over the tech department. He snorted. They were techies; they weren't used to being the ones targeted in the line of work. Even Kevin, who'd grown increasingly paranoid in the last twenty-four hours, had been laughably easy to take down.

Unlike Torelli.

He sighed and swiveled his chair to stare out his office window. Killing Torelli was his prime concern now. After this morning he very much doubted Torelli would come in from the field—the young agent wasn't stupid.

Torelli was probably heading for a bolt hole at this very minute, assuming he wasn't still chasing after Spinoza's child. Of course it didn't really matter where Torelli was heading because the veteran FBI agent had long ago to make preparations for any eventuality. He opened a drawer in his desk and took out a palm-sized electronic devise. Once switched on, the screen showed a satellite map. In the middle, a small red dot blinked.

It was moving south.

Chapter Twenty-six

Friday, 1:26 p.m.

Zoey wasn't a bad driver, Dante had to admit. She was light on the brake and she didn't accelerate too fast. 'Course that didn't mean he liked her driving his car. But since he didn't have a whole lot of choice in the matter, it was just as well that she was a good driver. Especially as it had begun to snow in the last half hour.

If only her taste in music were as good as her driving.

"What is this stuff?" He frowned at the car radio, which was blasting something with a lot of twang.

"Where have you been living? Under a rock?" Zoey shouted over the moaning vocals. "This is the Dixie Chicks."

"Great," Dante muttered under his breath. Figured she would like country, possibly the sappiest music ever invented by mankind. Was there anyone who took banjos seriously?

Apparently there was. Zoey glared at him, somehow having heard him over the wailing. "That just shows how narrow-minded you are."

Dante straightened. "I am not narrow-minded."

"I bet you've never listened to country, have you?"

"Not if I can help it."

"You just don't like it because you don't think it's cool."

"That and the banjos." Dante glared out the window. They had taken the Dan Ryan south to I-57 and were now nearly to the outskirts of the southern suburbs. "We ought to stop to find something to eat before we get too far out."

"Okay. Where are the wipers?"

He pointed.

She switched them on. "Where do you want to eat?"

"Pick a place."

Twenty minutes later they were pulling out of another Culver's.

"Isn't it amazing how many of these things there are?" Zoey asked as she took the ButterBurger he handed her. She was eating as she drove, but she seemed to be handling the wheel okay.

Dante frowned down at his Mushroom & Swiss Burger. He wasn't sure he'd be able to eat it without slopping it all over himself. "What? Fast-food places?"

"No, silly. Culver's. I never noticed them before."

He watched her take a big bite of ButterBurger and couldn't help smiling. She was enjoying the burger so much. "Well, you've noticed them now."

They ate in silence for a bit before Zoey wadded up her

ButterBurger wrapper and threw it in the paper bag. "So, if you don't like country, what kind of music do you like to listen to?"

He opened his mouth to reply, but she answered her own question. "Alternative rock, right? I bet you listen to the bands that were playing when you were a teenager. Boooring."

He felt his mouth twitch. "Now who's being narrow-minded?"

She glanced at him, blue eyes sparkling under the reindeer hat. God, the woman loved to argue.

"I'm wrong?" she asked. "Oh, come on, don't tell me you like white-boy rap?"

He shook his head and gingerly bent forward to pull out a flat CD folder from under the passenger seat. He unzipped it and flipped through the clear plastic sleeves until he found what he wanted.

"Listen."

He popped the CD in the car player. A rich baritone rolled out from the speakers, singing about Mack the Knife.

Zoey burst into laughter.

Dante frowned at her. "What?"

She gasped through her giggles. "Frank Sinatra?"

"It's Harry Connick Jr."

"Whatever. You have the musical taste of an eighty-year-old. Figures."

"What's that supposed to mean?"

"Just what I said. You've got senile taste in music."

"You're saying I'm an old man?"

"Yeah." She gave him a cheeky grin. "Yeah, I am."

Great. Just what a guy liked to hear: that the woman he

wanted a relationship with thought he was a decrepit old man. It was enough to—

Dante blinked and backed up mentally. *Wanted a relationship with?* Where the hell had that come from? He'd known Zoey less than twenty-four hours. They had nothing in common, not even musical tastes. Sure, he was attracted to her—what guy wouldn't be attracted to her softness, the goofy things she said, and her unabashed sexuality? But a relationship was a whole different thing.

Maybe he just wanted to get her into bed and his mind was trying to justify the urge by making it into a relationship thing. Didn't most guys start wondering what it would be like to sleep with a woman when they'd been around them long enough? Like, ten minutes. And he'd been around Zoey for a whole lot longer than ten minutes. So, it was only natural to wonder if she'd be as enthusiastic in bed as she was about everything else. Or as verbal. 'Cause the thought of her chattering as he entered her soft, warm, slippery female flesh was oddly erotic to him and—

Christ!

Dante inhaled softly and glanced at Zoey. She was still babbling about Frank Sinatra and the Rat Pack and seemed totally oblivious to his thoughts. Just as well. He flipped to another section of the CD holder and took out a different CD. He switched it with the one in the player.

Zoey watched him.

Another male voice, this one raspy and higher. She looked at him curiously.

"Sammy Davis Jr.," he said.

She started laughing again. "Oh, God, he's even worse! You're stuck in the sixties. No, the fifties! All you need is a woman in pearls and a bouffant to serve you meat loaf when you walk in the door and yell, 'Honey, I'm home!' "

"I don't even like meat loaf," he protested.

For a moment Dante saw Zoey in pearls and a funny reddish-blond bouffant—and nothing else. The weird part was that she looked really, really good that way. Maybe he *did* have a fixation on the fifties.

Hastily he flipped to the very back of the folder and took out the last CD. He inserted it in the player.

A sultry, clear soprano sang in lilting Spanish.

Zoey frowned, opened her mouth, paused, and slowly closed it again.

Dante smiled, leaning his head back and losing himself in the melody. The smooth feminine voice slid over him. The only sound in the car was her voice, the hum of the engine, and the soft shush of the windshield wipers.

The singer's voice died away on a liquid whisper. Dante opened his eyes, pushed the stop button, and looked at Zoey.

She had her brows knit. "Who was that?"

"Doris Day."

"No!"

He nodded, pleased at her incredulity. "Yup."

"The one who did those dumb movies with Rock Hudson?"

He winced. "She recorded that before she was in the movies."

"Huh." She stared thoughtfully at him a moment.

"Want to hear more?"

"Sure."

He pressed play and sat back, closing his eyes. He felt absurdly happy that she liked his Doris Day CD.

"How long do you think it'll take to get to Cairo?" Zoey asked after a while.

He didn't bother opening his eyes. "Five hours."

"Have you ever driven to Cairo?"

"No."

"Then how do you know it'll take five hours to get there?"

He sighed. "Do you argue about everything with other people, or just with me?"

"I—"

"Or"—he opened his eyes and frowned—"do you just argue with men?"

"Hey!"

He glanced at her, eyebrows raised.

She glared back. "What's that supposed to mean? I like men just fine."

"I didn't say you didn't *like* men. I said that you argue all the time with—"

She grabbed the rearview mirror and twisted it out of shape, then leaned over to peer in it.

"Watch the road." He reached over and caught the wheel to keep the car straight.

Zoey was still peering at herself, oblivious. "Do I look like a woman who doesn't like men?"

"Would you keep your eyes on the road?"

She glared at him and returned her gaze to the road. "Well, do I?"

He shrugged, letting go of the wheel. "You are wearing a reindeer hat—"

"A what?"

"Watch the road!"

"I am watching the road!" she bellowed back at him. "And I'm not wearing a reindeer hat!"

"Whatever it is, it's not particularly attractive." Actually, as he said the words he realized that while he'd thought her hat ugly at first, now he kind of found it cute. *Not* that he had any intention of telling her that.

"It's warm," Zoey said.

"I'm sure it is."

She glared at him.

"What?" he asked.

"Have you been to Cairo?"

They'd managed to get to the outskirts of Chicago. Suddenly, flat white fields appeared out of nowhere, as if to remind him that they were in the Midwest. Dante shivered. God, he hated the country. No cover, totally exposed if someone decided to start shooting at you. And now the snowflakes had turned into big wet monsters, splatting against the windshield.

He gritted his teeth, trying to keep his voice even. "No, I've never been to Cairo."

"So you know how long it'll take to get there, how?"

"Because it's about four hours to St. Louis. Cairo's farther south. Add another hour and you've got five hours."

"Counting potty breaks?"

He looked at her.

She widened her eyes. "What?"

Dante closed his eyes and counted to ten. "You can't go five hours without a pit stop?"

"Well"—she knit her brow as if calculating—"no."

"You can't hold it in for five hours," he repeated neutrally. She must be making it up just to bother him.

"I said, *no*. Is that something they taught at Quantico, too? How to hold your pee?"

Or maybe not.

He sighed. "Fine, we can stop. But if you buy anything, we need to use cash from now on. That gas station we stopped at has to be the last place we use a credit card."

"I got some cash when I used my credit card."

"That was good thinking."

She rolled her eyes. "Gee, thanks."

He felt his jaw tighten. How she could take an ordinary compliment and turn it into an insult he didn't understand.

She cleared her throat. "I'm sorry."

He glanced at her in surprise.

Pink was staining her cheeks, and it made her look adorable. "I can be kind of bitchy sometimes."

He felt a smile curve his lips. "No problem. I kind of like bitchy women."

And his smile widened as he watched her blush deepen.

Chapter Twenty-seven

Friday, 5:04 p.m.

"You must drive slower, Pratima," Savita-di chided. "The snow is coming down more swiftly, and I do not think you are very experienced at driving in snow."

Pratima was driving the purple minivan through the countryside, which, unfortunately, was enveloped by a snowstorm. She held the steering wheel very tightly because, though she was loath to admit it to Savita-di, she was in fact quite frightened. They were on interstate highway 57. At least Pratima hoped they were on highway 57, for Savita-di's ability to read maps was quite poor indeed, and they had spent most of the day somewhat lost. Pratima privately thought that they might've even ventured into the state of Indiana at one point earlier this afternoon.

Now, however, they were in Illinois, and the land was becoming bumpy as they drove south. Snow blew across the highway in an irritating manner. Only a very good driver, in her opinion, would be able to negotiate these very dangerous conditions.

Which made Savita-di's snide remarks all the more irksome.

Pratima pursed her lips. "You are wrong, Savita-di. I am perfectly experienced at driving in—"

Savita-di made a rude sound with her lips. "Yes, and I suppose you were very experienced when you slid into that light pole in the JCPenney parking lot, denting the fender on our nephew's car?"

"That," said Pratima, enunciating very clearly, "was two months ago, and it is really too bad of you to bring it up now. I think you are jealous because *you* have never learned to drive."

"Jealous? Jealous of you? I think you are the jealous one, Pratima. Was not my husband the elder of the two brothers we married? And was he not the handsomer, as well? I think you know this very well or you would not have tried to flirt with him so long ago."

Pratima frowned. Truly it was most irritating to be castigated so often for something that happened almost forty years ago and which was not as Savita-di portrayed it, to boot. She opened her mouth with the thought that she might point this out, but Savita-di still held the conversational floor.

"I could learn to drive if I wished to," she sniffed.

This was so patently a lie that Pratima did not even bother to reply.

From the back seat, a small voice piped up. "Nah ah nah."

Savita-di immediately twisted in her seat to look in back. "Is that my handsome boy? Is he so smart? So brave?"

Pratima rolled her eyes. The baby was only making baby sounds. How such nonsense syllables could be construed as intelligence she did not understand.

"Would my fine boy like some Goldfish crackers?" Savita-di crooned.

Another baby voice spoke up from the back, this one loud and imperative. "*Gah!*"

Pratima smiled. The baby girl was so sweet, so pretty, so demanding of what she wanted. Girls were not supposed to demand what they wanted when Pratima had been young. Instead, they were supposed to be docile and obedient and were to always worry for the welfare of others. But she thought it was not such a bad thing for a modern girl in the US of A to demand what she wanted.

"Ah! This one eats like a little pig," Savita-di exclaimed. "She will grow fat."

"Not as fat as that boy," Pratima shot back.

"Humph."

There was a silence broken only by the crunch of crackers in childish mouths and the demand for more. Then inevitably a long, drawn-out wail came from the rear.

Pratima flinched in reaction. "Ow, ow, ow. So loud are these babies!"

"Perhaps we should pull over," Savita-di shouted over the now double sirens.

"Yes, yes, Savita-di, I will exit the highway as soon as I am able."

Fortunately, there was a bright green sign informing them that the exit to the next town was just four miles ahead. A further sign—this one blue—offered two gas stations, a variety of cheap fast-food restaurants, and a motel.

Pratima switched on her turn signal, driving up the off-ramp to the accompaniment of twin wails. She drove into the first petrol station and switched off the minivan.

The crying in the back seat rose to a crescendo.

"I will take the boy in to be changed," Savita-di shouted over the bellowing.

"Yes, yes, please," Pratima screamed back.

Savita-di got out of the minivan, ran around the side, and opened the door. The minute the boy was lifted from his car seat, his cries died. He nuzzled a tear-stained face into her soft neck.

"There, there, my fine prince. Auntie Savita will make everything better."

She closed the minivan's side door and hurried with the baby to the door of the convenience store.

Pratima twisted in her seat to look at the girl baby. The child stared back, her tiny bottom lip trembling.

"Oh, so sad," Pratima crooned. "Is there nothing to console you?"

The baby whimpered, thrusting a finger inside her mouth, and gnawing. Quite obviously she was teething. Even as she gummed her finger she sobbed again.

Pratima knit her brow. The baby needed something cold to soothe her inflamed gums. It hurt simply to watch such a little one in pain. She glanced at the convenience store. Savita-di had still not emerged and probably would not for some time. She always took too long in restrooms, and that was without the added chore of the baby boy.

Pratima unbuckled her seat belt. "Stay here, little one,

and do not move. I will return shortly with an ice for your sore gums."

She hurried from the minivan, walking as quickly as was possible in the slippery snow. Inside the convenience store, she found a freezer and chose a rather battered box of orange-flavored ices. Pratima emerged from the convenience store clutching the precious box of ices to her chest. But when she looked at the purple minivan, she screamed and dropped the box into the dirty snow.

For That Terrible Man was jumping into the minivan. He started the van and drove off with the Grade 1A Very, Very Fine 1 Mongra Kesar and, much more importantly, the baby girl inside.

Chapter Twenty-eight

Friday, 5:20 p.m.

Zoey chewed her lip as she peered out the windshield. They were in southern Illinois now, and the weather was getting worse. Dante had insisted on driving for a couple of hours between Kankakee and Champaign, but his jaw had been tight as he drove, and she could tell that his leg was bothering him. When they'd stopped at a rest stop just past Champaign, Zoey had told him that she'd drive and he hadn't even argued. She glanced at him out of the corner of her eye. He'd taken another painkiller, but he still sat stiffly, like he was in pain. She wished that they'd been able to take him to an emergency room. What if something was worse with the leg than bruises?

She tapped her brake as they passed a semi pulled off the road. The snow wasn't wet anymore—the temperature had dropped, and hard, dry snow had begun to drift across the road. Zoey had slowed to fifty-five mph, but if the snow kept piling up or the roads got slick . . .

Beside her, Dante shifted in his seat. "We may have to pull over if this weather keeps up."

She shrugged. "It's okay for now."

He shifted again and grunted.

She looked at him. His face was pale. "Does your leg still hurt? Maybe you should take another pill."

"I'm fine."

She studied him a moment, then turned back to the road. He obviously wasn't fine, but he was in some kind of male stoic zone. "Okay."

He tapped his fingers on his good knee. "So, you been in Chicago long?"

"Four years. I moved there right out of college."

"You're twenty-six?"

"Twenty-seven. I was working, so it took me five years to graduate."

He nodded. "Where'd you go?"

"Indiana University in Bloomington. You?"

"NYU, then Quantico."

"And you majored in, what? Law enforcement or something?" She signaled to pass a dump truck.

He cleared his throat. "Ah, actually art history."

She glanced at him quickly. "You're kidding."

His mouth was in a flat line. "No. What did you major in?"

He looked kind of embarrassed, which only intrigued her. "English lit, but we're talking about you. How'd you get from art history to the FBI?"

He sighed. "I always wanted to go into law enforcement, but the family business is in art and antiques."

"Your parents have an antiques shop?"

"Ah, it's a little more than that."

"A little more." She looked down at her hands, gripping the wheel of a car that probably cost more than twice her yearly wages. "How much more?"

"Don't do that," he said quietly.

"Do what?"

He shook his head, glancing out the window a moment. "My family has an international art auction house. It was founded by my grandfather over fifty years ago. We have branches in Hong Kong, Milan, London, and New York."

"We?"

He shrugged. "I inherited stock from my grandfather, so yeah, *we*. Everyone else in my family works at the business in different capacities."

"Everyone but you," she said softly. He must've had nearly overwhelming pressure to join the family business. The fact that he'd opted for the FBI instead proved a strong and stubborn will.

"Yeah, everyone but me," he answered. "Now, those were some awkward Thanksgivings and Christmases—the first couple of years after I'd made my decision."

"But they did accept your career in the end, right?"

He shrugged one shoulder. "Sure."

She glanced at him. He was staring straight ahead out the windshield, his mouth firmed into a grim line. "You don't sound convinced."

He sighed, and his hand dropped to his leg, brushing the fabric stretched taut over the bandage underneath. "I grew up in a family devoted to the arts and business. My siblings and I all went to private boarding schools, we spent summers in Europe . . ." He trailed off, shaking his head. "To them I'm basically a cop. It's not just that they don't get why I'm an FBI agent, it's more than that. Like I announced one day that I was going to become a wombat. Totally alien."

Zoey cleared her throat, realizing for the first time that Dante wasn't only from a different world, he was from a different class. Mom had been pleased when Zoey had gotten into Indiana U, but it wouldn't have been such a big deal if she hadn't. If anything, Zoey was more educated than the rest of her family, whereas Dante's family thought he'd stepped down in choosing the FBI. Wow.

Just . . . wow.

She glanced at him again, remembering something he'd said when they'd begun this discussion. "You never answered me. What didn't you want me to do?"

He grimaced. "Girls—women—get weird when they find out I've got money."

"Weird how?" But she thought she knew. She'd started stiffening up the moment she'd figured it out.

"They either see me as a meal ticket or they get defensive, like I'm judging them on their manners or something—and finding them lacking. Either way, it tends to spoil a relationship."

"Huh. Bet it does." Zoey kept her eyes on the road and wondered if he knew he'd used the word *relationship* in connection with her. Well, kind of in connection. Close, anyway. She shook the thought out of her mind. "You don't have to worry with me, though."

"Yeah?"

"Yeah. First of all, I've got more cash than you at the moment. And secondly, if you don't like my manners, you can go blow."

His head reared back. "You're telling me to go blow?"

She pursed her lips. "Only if you find my manners offensive."

"Huh. That's pretty tough talk for a poet."

"Watch it. Poets are notoriously sensitive. You don't want to piss me off."

He snorted. "I'll try to keep that in mind."

"You do that." She felt herself smiling now for no particular reason.

They were silent for a bit until they passed an Illinois DOT sign indicating that there was a gas station at the next exit. Zoey flipped on her turn signal. "I want to stop up here."

Dante looked out the window at the rolling, white, frozen fields. "Here?"

"Yeah. I need a restroom."

"Already? This is the second stop since lunch."

"I bet you're really fun on dates," Zoey muttered.

He arched his brows, looking patrician and insulted at the same time. "What's that supposed to mean?"

"Are your dates allowed to use the restroom? Or do they have to hold it in through dinner?"

"Most people can make it all the way through a meal without getting up."

"You are dating females, right?" she asked sweetly.

She waited for his comeback, enjoying the whole snarky exchange, but he didn't say anything.

She glanced at him as she turned into the gas station. "Dante?"

"Look," he said. He tilted his chin at the front of the convenience store. Two older ladies were swaying there, and beneath their long down jackets they had on saris.

"Oh, my God!" Zoey's heart sped up and she involuntarily jerked the wheel, making the car swerve.

"Watch it." Dante's words were sharp, but his voice was even. "Pull in beside the store, over there."

Zoey followed his directions, stopping the car smoothly. She put the car in park and looked at him.

"Wait here," he said.

He'd already drawn his gun. He got out of the car, holding the gun down by his leg where it was partially hidden in the folds of his long leather trench coat. Zoey watched him stroll toward the women. He must be working hard to appear casual, because his limp was slight. He seemed in no particular hurry, but her pulse was pounding. She could see now that one of the women held a child in her arms, a blue jacket hood pulled up over the little head.

Dante stopped a few feet away and reached under his coat. When his hand came back out, it was empty. He'd put away his gun. He approached the ladies and said something to them. Even from inside the car, Zoey could hear both women shriek.

She couldn't stand this anymore. Zoey scrambled from the driver's side of the car, the snowflakes stinging her face as she ran to the door of the convenience store. Both women were wailing, crying as if their favorite dog had died, and the baby was screaming, too, its little face pressed to the shoulder of the woman carrying it.

Dante turned as Zoey approached. He frowned. "I thought I told you to stay in the car."

"I couldn't," she panted. She reached for the baby. "I—"

But the baby's head had turned at the sound of her voice. Zoey stared into big, watery blue eyes and a square little

face topped with blond curls beneath the blue hood. The
baby blinked and buried his face back into the woman's
neck, bawling.

"Zoey?" Dante's voice was urgent. "Zoey?"

She looked at him blankly. "That's not Pete."

Chapter Twenty-nine

Friday, 5:43 p.m.

𝒩ot Pete?" Dante looked from Zoey to the two elderly Indian ladies. Had he accosted the wrong women? Except they'd reacted to the name Gupta, and there couldn't be another pair of Indian ladies in saris running around southern Illinois.

"That's not Pete," Zoey repeated. Her face was white, her big blue eyes stark.

"You're sure?" he asked idiotically. Out of the corner of his eye he saw the Indian ladies exchange a glance. He shifted slightly, blocking access to the parking lot. "Zoey?"

She shook her head. "I-I don't know who this baby is."

He might've done the totally unprofessional then and pulled her into his arms to comfort her, but the taller of the two Indian ladies tapped him on the sleeve. "Are you a policeman?"

"I'm FBI, ma'am. Why—"

But the short lady rounded on him. "That Terrible Man stole the baby! You must go after him at once."

"What man, ma'am?"

"The Terrible one!" the taller lady said, apparently under the impression he hadn't heard the first time.

Dante sighed and rubbed the spot between his eyes where a headache was brewing. "It's cold out here. Let's go inside where the baby can be warm." He stopped in sudden realization. "Whose baby is this? It doesn't belong to you, does it?"

The ladies exchanged another look.

The taller lady began, "He—"

But the shorter lady stepped on her foot, making her cut off her words with a squeak.

"He is our baby," the little round woman said.

Dante looked between the blond, light-skinned child to the Indian woman. "I see."

"Savita-di, you are only making matters worse," the taller woman scolded. She turned to Dante. "The child was in That Terrible Man's car, along with the baby he stole."

"Wait. You mean—"

But Zoey interrupted him. "He stole—kidnapped—*two* babies?"

The taller lady nodded vigorously. "Yes! Yes, he is a most vile man."

"But where is the other—?" Zoey started.

"This is what we are trying to tell you!" Savita Gupta said. "He took our minivan with the child inside!"

"Oh, my God!" Zoey said.

"Can we go in the building?" Dante asked.

No one listened to him.

"He is iniquitous!" the tall lady was sputtering. "A terrible, terrible man, and I do not know what he will do with that sweet, innocent baby, no, I do—"

"Look," Dante said loudly. "Let's go inside before the remaining baby freezes, shall we?"

"You don't have to yell," Zoey muttered.

He rolled his eyes but refrained from snapping back, since she was obviously under strain. He herded the women inside the little convenience store. There was a fast-food sub shop to one side of the store, and Dante found them all a table. The baby by this time had stopped whining and appeared to have fallen into an exhausted sleep. He was a chunky little kid and looked too heavy for the woman holding him.

Dante sighed. This was the problem growing up with an old-fashioned mother. He spoke to the shorter Indian lady. "He looks heavy. Why don't I give you a break?"

He could feel Zoey's startled glance, but he kept his own gaze on the Indian woman. She narrowed her eyes at him, but her arms must've been aching. She nodded reluctantly.

He took the warm little body—amazing how solid babies were—and settled the sleeping child against his shoulder. "Now. What are your names?"

The ladies exchanged looks again. This time it was the smaller lady who spoke. "I am Mrs. Savita Gupta, and this is my sister-in-law, Mrs. Pratima Gupta. We are respectable ladies, and—"

"What were you doing stealing a Humvee, then?"

Mrs. Savita Gupta's eyes widened, as if surprised at his

sharp tone. What was with all the women around him not taking him seriously?

"Well?"

"He stole our kesar," Mrs. Pratima Gupta blurted.

Dante blinked. "Your—"

"Our Grade 1A Very, Very Fine Mongra Kesar. *Saffron*," the short one exclaimed.

Dante looked from one woman to the other and shook his head. "Why in the world would he steal your saffron?"

"Because it's expensive. It's a spice," Zoey said. She frowned. "Or maybe an herb. Anyway, we sell it in bulk at the health-food store I work at. Saffron comes from the stigmas of crocus flowers. There are only two or three stigmas per flower, and they're really small. You have to pick a lot of flowers to get a little saffron, so it's pretty expensive."

"Oka-ay."

The taller lady—Mrs. Pratima Gupta—leaned forward. "We used a very large portion of our savings to buy our Grade 1A Very, Very Fine Mongra Kesar. This is the very best kind of saffron in the world and most important for the dishes at our new restaurant. So when That Terrible Man took it, we knew we had to steal it back. He kept it in his very big truck, and we bided our time, and when he wasn't looking, we took the truck!"

"So he would not be able to follow us," the shorter lady said.

Now his head really did hurt. "And you didn't go to the police because . . . ?"

Both ladies looked slightly chagrined.

Savita Gupta cleared her throat. "We did not purchase the saffron, hmm, exactly *legally.*"

Dante's eyebrows shot up. "You have contraband saffron?"

Both ladies drew back as if he'd blurted out a foul word. Pratima Gupta shook her head. "Not—"

"But what about Pete?" Zoey cut in. "I don't understand. Was she in the Humvee when you stole it? Did you have her until recently? How was she? What happened?"

Mrs. Pratima Gupta immediately turned solicitous. "What a pretty baby. So sweet and adorable! When we, er, *took* the Humvee from That Terrible Man, we found the babies in the back. Such a surprise, you cannot imagine. I thought poor Savita-di might have failure of the heart. And what could we do?" She shrugged elaborately, appealing to Dante and Zoey as if their actions were perfectly practical. "We could not go to the police because of the saffron, and the babies could not be returned to such a Terrible Man, so naturally we took them with us."

Amazingly, Zoey was nodding along with this nonsense, as if she agreed completely.

"And you drove some three hundred miles with two kidnapped children, why?" Dante drawled.

The ladies flinched again and glanced at each other. The little one licked her lips nervously. "We did not think our nephews or nieces in Chicago would, hmm, *understand* precisely our reasons for keeping the babies safe—"

"Kidnapping," Dante muttered.

"Uh, yes." She turned to Zoey, perhaps realizing Zoey was the more sympathetic party. "We decided it might be wise to leave Chicago just for a bit, until That Terrible Man gave up looking for us—"

"So we came to visit our nephew, Rahul, who owns a very nice motel in Cairo," Pratima Gupta finished triumphantly.

Both ladies looked at him as if that wacky explanation made any sense at all. Even Zoey was looking at him expectantly. The baby in his arms chose that moment to stir. He opened wide blue eyes and stared up into Dante's face. He must not've liked what he saw, because his little mouth opened wide, like a baby bird wanting a worm, except instead of a cheep what came out of his mouth was a loud, drawn-out scream.

Dante winced, his headache now full-blown. He looked over the head of the screaming child and asked the final, unanswered question:

"So who the hell does this kid belong to?"

Chapter Thirty

Friday, 6:25 p.m.

*A*shley was going to fucking kill him.

It was Neil's only thought as he stared, stunned, down at the strange little girl. Ashley would fucking *massacre* him. He'd stolen back the wrong kid.

It'd been pure luck that he'd seen the purple minivan with the big daisy on its side from the highway. The van'd been stopped at a gas station, and he'd had to find a place to turn around, praying the whole time that it was the right fucking minivan and that it'd still fucking be there when he fucking got back. It'd seemed like his luck had finally taken a turn for the good when he'd snatched the van out from under the old biddys' eyes.

Only to turn around three exits later and find that Neil Junior wasn't in the van. Now he was stuck with a naked girl baby with a shitty diaper.

Somebody fucking hated him.

The baby girl smiled up at him and kicked her legs, nearly sending her full, smelly diaper into his stomach. She seemed to enjoy having a bare ass. Kinda like Neil Junior. Ashley used to say how Little Neil liked to wait until she took his diaper off and then take a wizz into the air. Neil had thought it pretty funny at the time. Of course that was before he had to change a diaper full of shit himself.

He glanced around the rest-stop men's room, scowling. Had he known that the girl was a girl, he wouldn't've brought her in here. It wasn't right, a little girl lying not five feet from a urinal. Fucking disgusting was what it was.

A guy with long stringy hair in a ponytail strolled in and glanced at the naked baby. Neil bared his teeth at him and Ponytail did an about-face, rethinking his need to take a piss. Fucking pervert. Served him right. This was why these plastic changing gizmos in the men's can were an oddity of nature. Guys were not supposed to have to deal with baby crap. That there was clearly a woman's job, and guys who went around changing babies in the men's can were clearly pussies.

Except there wasn't a woman around to change this baby, and the kid smelled like a sewer. Neil sighed and grimly started mopping shit.

Ten minutes later, he held a dripping baby girl over the sink. He'd finally decided to hose the kid down, which should've been simple but had somehow turned into a water park. He stared glumly at the baby. She grinned back, her pudgy legs bicycling in the air. Her dimpled pink butt was now clean and smelling of the cheap sink soap, but it was still totally bare. He didn't have a diaper.

Behind him, a guy in designer sunglasses and a tur-
quoise ski jacket entered the restroom. He was holding a
kid on one hip and a blue and white striped diaper bag over
the other shoulder.

He looked at the plastic changing gizmo—littered with
the baby girl's clothes—and then over at Neil. "Uh, you
gonna be done soon?"

"Yeah," Neil grunted, still holding a wriggling, wet
baby girl. "You have a spare diaper on you?"

"Uh . . ." The guy looked at him, obviously not wanting to give up a *baby diaper,* for chrissake. Fucking prick.
See? This was the kind of guy who changed his kid in the
men's can: a fucking pansy.

The baby girl chose that moment to pee, a tiny yellow
trickle running down her leg and into the sink.

Pansy Boy cleared his throat. "I've got an extra diaper,
but they're for boys."

Neil curled his lip. "So? What'll that do? Give her a
package?"

"Uh, no." Pansy Boy knit his eyebrows. "Well, they all
have packages, babies I mean. When they're wearing these
disposable diapers. Even the thinnest leave kind of a bulge,
ah, in the crotch area. And when they pee . . ."

Neil growled and grabbed a bunch of paper towels to
dry off the baby's butt. "Give it."

"Ah, okay," Pansy Boy stuttered. He rummaged in his
blue-striped diaper bag and came up with a blue plastic
diaper. Natch.

He held it out.

Neil snatched it out of Pansy Boy's hand and laid the
baby down on the plastic changing table. She immediately
tried to roll off.

"Fuck!" Neil dropped the diaper and grabbed her. But the kid didn't like being restrained. She let out a bellow and began screaming like something out of a horror movie.

"Gotta watch that," Pansy Boy yelled over the noise. "Have to keep one hand on the kid at all times, otherwise they try to jump."

Neil glared. "Thanks."

"No problem." The guy bent, picked up the diaper, and gave it back.

Neil could feel Pansy Boy breathing down his neck as he tried to open the diaper one-handed.

"Other way around," Pansy Boy yelled.

Neil looked at him.

"The diaper." Pansy Boy gestured. "The Velcro strips need to be on the bottom."

Neil closed his eyes and briefly considered popping the guy right there in the men's can. But then he might never get the diaper on the kid. His anger management instructor called this "envisioning consequences." So Neil envisioned himself running from the men's restroom with a peeing, naked-assed kid under his arm. Not a good scenario.

He took a deep breath. "Show me."

Fifteen minutes later, Neil had sweat dripping off his nose and Pansy Boy's hair was standing on end, but the baby girl was dressed. She'd stopped screaming at the top of her lungs midway through, but the kid Pansy Boy held had taken up the slack in the meantime.

"Jeez," Pansy Boy said now. "Babies can be quite a handful, can't they?"

That remark was so fucking dumb-assed that Neil didn't even bother answering. He felt like he'd gone five rounds with a grizzly bear on steroids. Instead he picked up the baby girl and slung her under his arm. She began chewing on his right thumb.

"I gotta say I admire you," Pansy Boy said as Neil neared the door.

Neil half turned. "Yeah?"

Pansy Boy smiled. "Yeah. I used to think guys who changed baby girls in the men's room were, y'know, wusses."

Chapter Thirty-one

Friday, 6:42 p.m.

"You can't arrest them—they're little old ladies," Zoey hissed as she bent over the Beemer's steering wheel.

"Who brought illegal saffron into the country," Dante murmured back. He held a road map up under the ceiling light. "Have you any idea how many laws they probably broke?"

"It's saffron, not opium!"

"Is everything all right?" the taller Gupta lady called from the back seat. She and her sister sat on either side of the little blond boy.

"Fine! Just fine," Zoey sang back. Under her breath she muttered, "Gestapo."

"I didn't say I was going to arrest them," Dante muttered.

"Humph."

Dante cleared his throat and shook out the map. He'd decided without consulting anyone else that they would all go to the motel the Gupta ladies had been heading to in the first place. He hadn't offered an explanation, but Zoey assumed that he didn't want to drive back to Chicago on the roads tonight. Either that, or maybe he thought Pete was still in southern Illinois. Hard to figure out someone else's train of thought when they weren't talking to you.

The two Mrs. Guptas said they had no idea who the little boy between them was. Maybe Tony the Rose's henchman was a specialist in kidnapping babies and always traveled with a few in his Humvee. Zoey wrinkled her nose at her own rather dark humor. What they did know—maybe the only thing they knew for sure right now—was that Tony the Rose's employee had kidnapped Pete. *Again.* Which brought her back to the one guy she could blame all of this on, Ricky Spinoza. Pete was the only good thing that'd come out of stupid Ricky-the-jerk's life, and she was worth ten of him. *Oh, please let Pete be safe.*

Zoey tightened her lips as she looked for the exit. *I will not cry. I will not cry.* The snow was falling thick and fast now, sticking to the faces of road signs and obscuring the letters.

"I think it is here," one of the Mrs. Guptas said from the back seat.

"No, no, Savita-di," the other Mrs. Gupta said. "Do you not remember that we passed a Kentucky Fried Chicken sign before the proper exit?"

"And what if the Kentucky Fried Chicken sign is no longer there?" the first lady shot back. "What then, Pratima Gupta?"

What then, indeed? Zoey thought.

Beside her, Dante cleared his throat. "I think the exit we're looking for is the one after this, actually. There's a sign for the motel right there." He nodded with his chin to a dim billboard by the side of the road. The Beemer's headlights briefly lit a familiar chain logo, and then they were past.

"See? What did I tell you, Pratima?"

Zoey rolled her eyes. These ladies had obviously known each other waaay too long. She squinted, looking for the exit.

"Here," Dante said.

She'd almost driven past the exit. Hastily she clicked on her turn signal and steered the Beemer to the off-ramp. The motel sign was lighted and clearly visible from the top of the ramp. Zoey pulled into the nearly full parking lot and under the concrete awning next to the front doors. The tiny lobby was lit, but no one was in sight inside. A neon NO VACANCY sign flickered above the door.

"Are you sure your nephew will have room for us?" Dante asked, echoing her own thoughts.

"Naturally," the shorter Mrs. Gupta said airily. "We are his aunts, after all."

Dante glanced wryly at Zoey, and for a moment she felt a familiar connection with him. Funny how close you could become to a person in so little time. He hastily looked away again.

Zoey sighed and opened her car door.

Inside, the motel lobby was so warm that the windows had steamed up in places. No one was behind the counter, but TV gunfire and spaceship noises were coming from the back room. Zoey inhaled. Spicy cooking smells also came from the back room.

The shorter Mrs. Gupta marched to the counter and tapped the bell imperiously.

Nothing happened.

She frowned and banged on the little bell, making it clatter obnoxiously.

"There is no room!" a male voice shouted from the back. A short, dark man in a burgundy velour bathrobe stomped out of the back room. "I tell you there is no bloody room! Shoo, now, and stop ringing my—" His words ended in a kind of gurgling squeak as he caught sight of the Mrs. Guptas.

"Rahul Agrawal," Savita Gupta said. "Is this any way to speak to your dear aunties?"

"No, Mamiji, oh, no," Mr. Agrawal stuttered. He leaned to the side to peer behind her as if expecting more elderly relatives to pop out. "I was just surprised by the, uh, *delight* of your unexpected arrival."

"Humph," Pratima Gupta snorted. "We need a room, several rooms, actually, for ourselves and our friends."

"But Mamiji," the poor man protested. "There are no empty rooms in my motel. The snowstorm has made many travelers stop tonight. We are full."

"Maybe we should check a different motel," Zoey began but then jumped when Savita Gupta let out a loud wail.

"Do you hear this, Pratima? Do you hear this? Our nephew will throw his elderly aunts into the cold and dark, with a snowstorm raging outside."

"Oh, if only his mother were still alive," Pratima Gupta replied. "What a sweet, hospitable woman she was. She would cry with shame were she to hear how her only son will throw—"

"All right, all right!" Mr. Agrawal held out both hands in surrender. "Perhaps I can find an empty room."

"And for our friends?" Pratima Gupta demanded.

"I don't know if—"

"His poor mother!" Savita Gupta cried.

"Yes!" Mr. Agrawal shouted. "Yes, a room for your friends!"

"How kind." Pratima Gupta smiled benevolently at him. "And how is your lovely wife? Is that her cooking I smell?"

Dante cleared his throat. "I'm sure we can get a pizza or—"

"Oh, no!" Savita Gupta looked scandalized. "My niece will be most happy to serve us dinner."

Mr. Agrawal didn't seem nearly as certain as his aunt, but he led them all behind the counter and into the back rooms. This was obviously where his family lived. There was a large main room, serving as both living room and dining room. A kitchen was at one side, the TV perched on a counter dividing the two rooms. Two open doors led off the main room into bedrooms. There were three small children sitting on the floor in front of the TV, apparently enthralled by what looked like a very violent science-fiction show. A slender woman in a bright blue sari stood in the kitchen, and she turned as Mr. Agrawal led them in.

"My aunties have come to visit," Mr. Agrawal said rather helplessly. He looked at the shorter Mrs. Gupta. "Mamiji, you remember my wife, yes? And this is . . ." He gestured to Dante and trailed off uncertainly.

"Dante Torelli, ma'am. How do you do?" Dante said. "And Zoey."

Zoey couldn't help but notice that he gave her no description, not even "my friend, Zoey."

"Hello." Mrs. Agrawal nodded and smiled.

"My wife speaks only a little English, but she understands it very well," Mr. Agrawal said. He stared at the baby in his aunt's arms as if noticing him for the first time. "What—?"

Mrs. Savita Gupta ignored her nephew and moved past him to sit at a wood dining room table.

Mr. Agrawal blinked, clearly confused. He shrugged and seemed to give up the idea of introductions altogether.

"Please sit, Mamiji." He pulled out one of the wood dining table chairs for Pratima Gupta. "I'm sure there is something about that my wife can serve you."

But that lady was already moving swiftly, apparently unfazed by the sudden appearance of four extra guests for dinner. She called to the eldest child, and the girl rose obediently to run into the kitchen. Her mother gave her a stack of plates, and the little girl solemnly took them to the table. Zoey smiled and helped her to set the plates around the table as Mrs. Agrawal brought several steaming platters into the dining room.

"Please, eat." Mr. Agrawal gestured and smiled at her, and Zoey couldn't help but think how nice the poor man was even if she'd appeared out of nowhere to eat his food.

Her nose caught the appetizing scents rising from the platters and her stomach took over. After a day and a night and another day of eating nothing but junk food, this was nirvana. One platter held a kind of savory lentil stew, another was filled with hot chickpea dumplings, and a third held steaming flatbread. Zoey took some of each, careful not to overfill her plate so that there would be enough to go around. One of the Agrawal children kneeled in the chair next to her and grinned when she helped him choose a piece of bread.

The meal was nice. It was more than nice, it was a welcome break from constant fear and confusion. If only Pete were here, it would be perfect.

And on that thought, the wonderful bread in Zoey's mouth turned to ashes. Where was Pete now? Halfway back to Chicago? She closed her eyes and remembered long-lashed brown eyes and the rings of baby fat around Pete's little wrists. So small, so fragile. Zoey would never forgive herself if something happened to the baby.

On her other side Dante leaned toward her, placing his hand over hers on the table. His bitter-chocolate eyes were intense and solemn. "We're going to find her, I promise."

Chapter Thirty-two

Friday, 8:35 p.m.

Naturally the motel room had only one bed.

Dante shouldered open the door and walked inside. Zoey followed behind him, holding a pile of towels, mini soap, and shampoo. Mr. Agrawal had told them this room was closed for repairs—something about the ceiling. Sure enough, a two-foot hole in a corner of the ceiling exposed dangling wires. At this point, as long as it had heat and a shower, Dante could care less. Although two beds would've been nice.

He sighed and plopped the plastic grocery bags from the car on the fake wood bureau. All motel rooms had the same long, low bureau, usually with a TV perched on one end, and no one ever used the drawers. Why a bureau? Why not a table?

Dante shook his head, knowing he was delaying the

inevitable argument. He locked the outer door and shot a glance at Zoey. She looked really tired. Beat, as if she'd lost all of her usual forthright energy. All of her optimism. And she had, hadn't she? They didn't have the baby; he hadn't found her niece for her. He'd failed her.

Dante watched as she dragged off her goofy hat and threw it on the one armchair by the bed. Underneath, her red-blond hair was in the messy braids she'd made this morning in the car. Long strands of hair had come undone from the braids and hung to her shoulders.

He sighed and took off his suit jacket. "I'll take the chair."

She looked up. "What?"

"The chair." He gestured with one hand as he loosened his tie with the other. "I can sleep there."

He'd thought she'd be grateful, or at the very least understanding.

She snorted.

He frowned. "What?"

"It's a king-sized bed. I think I can get through one night without leaping to the other side and attacking you."

He felt himself flush. "That's not—"

But she waved a dismissive hand at him. "I call dibs on the shower."

And she disappeared into the bathroom.

Dante stared at the closed bathroom door. Huh. Damned if he'd ever understand women, especially *this* woman. He didn't know whether to be grateful that he wasn't going to have to spend another night upright, or insulted that she apparently had no qualms about sharing a bed with him.

He pulled off his tie, folded it neatly, and laid it on one end of the dresser. Then he hung her idiot reindeer hat on the back of the chair and sat to unlace his shoes. God, he'd give half his pension to have a clean set of clothes right now. He was in the act of shrugging out of his holster when he heard the shower go on in the bathroom.

He paused and listened. The water made that muted roaring sound motel showers did, a product of too-thin walls and cheap showerheads. He almost thought he heard her voice. He held his breath, looking toward the bathroom, straining to hear with every pore in his body. Was she singing? Her voice came again, and he felt his mouth curve into a grin, his face almost aching with the unaccustomed use of muscles. It'd been a while since he smiled so widely. But her voice . . . he couldn't help himself. He could barely pick up the sound, but her voice was low and scratchy and not a little off-key. He let his hands fall to the chair's arms, laid his head against the tall back, and closed his eyes, just listening to Zoey sing in the shower.

She sang in short bursts, interrupted by mutters, pauses, and gasps, and he felt his smile drain away as he imagined what those gasps meant. Her face under the shower spray, the spray making her gasp, the water trickling down past her arched neck, down over her strong shoulders, to run in little streams over her breasts. White, full breasts that would feel heavy in his hands. *Oh, shit.* Having imagined that far, it was impossible not to see the rest. Zoey standing naked under the shower, slowly rubbing soap over belly and thighs and rounded hips. Her fingers stroking lower, tangling in red-gold curls, disappearing into . . .

The shower stopped and Dante's eyes popped open. He could hear her draw back the shower curtain and then a sigh. God, he had to get off this. But his mind's eye helplessly filled in details. Zoey taking one of those awful thin motel towels off the rack, rubbing it over her arms and legs and belly, stepping from the tub, her bare toes curling into the wisp-thin bath mat. There was something wrong with that. Did other guys fantasize about a woman's bare feet? Unless they had some kind of foot fetish?

Dante shook his head. He was tired. Bone-tired, and it was affecting his thoughts. And the kiss they'd shared only this morning had been truly spectacular.

The bathroom door opened. Zoey walked out wearing dark pink sweatpants and an orange sweatshirt with a cartoon little girl on it. She had a towel wrapped around her head and a bundle of clothes in her arms.

"All yours."

"Uh, right." He grabbed his suit coat and folded it over his arm as he stood, because otherwise the bulge in his trousers was going to make her think he was a pervert.

"When I shopped, I got you a change of clothes," she said cheerfully.

"Really?" He grinned. "Thanks."

She set her bundle of clothes on the bureau and rummaged around in one of the plastic bags. "Here they are."

She tossed a pair of gray sweatpants at him and then a navy sweatshirt. Dante caught both and held up the sweatshirt. It had I LOVE NY emblazoned across the front with a heart for the love.

"Funny," he muttered.

"Think so?" Zoey took out a plastic-wrapped package. "And I got you these, too."

She tossed the package at him.

He still had his hands full of the sweatshirt. The plastic package bounced off his chest and fell at his feet. It was a packet of men's white briefs. High-waisted. With a red and blue striped waistband. Like Fruit of the Loom, only knockoffs. He hadn't worn briefs like these since he was fourteen. Maybe thirteen. He looked at her.

She widened her eyes. "What?"

"Tighty-whities?"

"They were cheap."

"Huh." He bent and picked up the package, straightening in time to catch a smirk on her face. "You got these on purpose."

She hastily smoothed out her expression. "I don't know what you're talking about."

"Yeah, right." He stalked to the bathroom and shut the door.

The counter was tiny, and he had to pile the clean clothes on the toilet tank. Then he turned on the shower and stripped. He unwound the bandage from his leg and looked at the bruise underneath. The abrasions were beginning to scab over, and for a moment he considered taping a plastic bag over the wounds. But it seemed like too much trouble, and he was tired. He stepped into the tub.

The shower head was one of those cheap little gizmos that produced either a trickle or a stinging spray. This one was of the stinging spray variety, but Dante didn't care. The water was hot, thank you, God, and he just stood under it for a moment and let it beat against the back of his head. The background ache in the bruised leg receded a little as the hot water ran over his thigh and loosened the muscle. He sighed in relief. Then he reached for the tiny bottle of motel shampoo. There was less than a quarter of the bottle left, but it was enough. He scrubbed his scalp and then washed his face, the stubble of his beard scraping his palms. He'd have to ask Mr. Agrawal if he had any disposable razors behind the desk.

Another five minutes and he stepped out of the shower, feeling the pull on his injured leg. With the water turned off he could hear the TV from the outer room. He dried off with the too-small remaining towel and rubbed a clear patch in the fog on the mirror. He looked like shit, but shit that felt a whole lot better. There were bags under his eyes, and his hair stood in spiky tufts. He ran his hands through his hair to comb it and glanced at the counter. Zoey had left a tube of toothpaste with a wet toothbrush poking out of one of the plastic motel cups. A brand-new wrapped toothbrush was sitting next to the toothpaste, and Dante felt a wash of gratitude. She might've bought him idiot shorts, but she'd thought about toothbrushes.

Dante brushed his teeth, pulled on the sweatpants and sweatshirt, and took a breath before snapping off the light and leaving the bathroom. He double-checked that the outer door was locked as he passed it. Then he looked in the main room.

The bedspread was piled in a messy lump beside the chair. She was sitting up on one side of the bed with the covers over her knees, the TV clicker in one hand. Her long wet hair trailed onto her sweatshirt, partially obscuring the cartoon on the front. She was staring at the TV, her brows slightly pulled together.

She didn't look up as he entered. "Did you know that male penguins have to stand with an egg on their feet for a month in the dark?"

He looked at the TV. A bunch of stoic guy penguins were standing around in near-darkness, huddled against the Antarctic wind, speckled eggs perched on their feet. "Sucks to be a male penguin."

"Hmm." She clicked the TV off. "Is this okay?"

He shook out his trousers and held them upside down to find the leg creases. "What?"

"This side of the bed." She frowned at him. "What are you doing?"

"Folding my pants."

She watched as he folded the trousers along the crease and laid them on top of his tie on the bureau.

"Oh, my God."

"What?" He picked up his jacket and frowned at a tear in the lining. Dammit, the entire suit was probably a loss.

"You're one of those guys," Zoey said.

He dropped the jacket on top of the pants and glanced at her. "What're you talking about?"

She stared back, her expression as horrified as if he'd strangled a kitten in front of her. "You're *neat*."

"And you're not," he said mildly.

He put away the rest of his clothes and turned off the light over the bureau before walking over to pick up the bedspread.

That was apparently too much for Zoey. "Oh, my God," she muttered again and slumped on the bed, pulling the covers over her head.

Dante felt his mouth quirk. He finished folding the bedspread and laid it on the chair by the side of the bed—his side, since Zoey was taking up the other. The bed sank as he got in, and he winced. The springs were probably broken. He looked at Zoey. All he could see was the top of her head, damp springy curls against the white pillowcase.

He reached over and pulled down the edge of the sheet,

revealing her lovely scowling face. He smiled at her. "This side is fine. Thanks for asking. 'Night."

He turned and reached to the wall light on his side of the bed, flicking it off and making the room black.

Dante settled back against his hard, thin pillow.

In the warm darkness, he heard a feminine sigh and felt the bed vibrate as she turned over.

"Good night."

Chapter Thirty-three

Friday, midnight

Rutgar pressed the END button on his cell phone and smiled a small smile. A new job. This was good. He placed the cell phone in the pocket of his leather coat and slid from the barstool. The bartender glanced at him sideways, then ducked his head and pretended to wipe a glass when Rutgar caught his eye.

A man became lazy without work. It was good, then, to have work. Rutgar walked down the shadowy bar, watching as both men and girls turned their heads so they would not meet his gaze. This fear of him both amused him and made him satisfied. Those that turned away were smart. It was true: Rutgar was a dangerous man.

He walked out into the cold street. The wintry night wind blew snow against his face and numbed his lips. It reminded him of Poland. Fucking Poland. Cold and stupid and backward. There was nothing in Poland but thin, diseased whores and bad food. Rutgar had left Poland as soon as he was able. He had come here, to Chicago, land of small cell phones and big guns. It was good here in Chicago. The work was good. The money was very good. But Rutgar still hated the cold.

Tony the Rose had said that this new job was about old women. And a baby. A girl baby. It was perhaps a boring job. Two old women and a baby would not be a challenge. They would whimper in fear of Rutgar. And Tony the Rose had said that Rutgar should be careful. If Rutgar followed Tony the Rose's instructions, the job would be very boring. One should always find what interest one could in a job. Perhaps he would not follow the instructions exactly.

Rutgar smiled a small smile as he walked the dark Chicago street.

Chapter Thirty-four

Saturday, 6:15 a.m.

The room was black when Dante woke, and the darkness disoriented him for a moment. He lay still, letting his mind flip through possibilities until he lit on the right one and remembered where he was. Then he inhaled. The motel room smelled faintly of disinfectant, some kind of laundry detergent, and her. He could smell Zoey. He lay with his eyes closed and breathed her scent, and it finally came to him, there in the twilight, when his mind was at its most vulnerable, lost between waking and sleeping. Vanilla. The scent she wore was vanilla. Or maybe it was her own scent, the scent of her body, of *her.* That made sense. Zoey was home and hearth at her most basic level. Vanilla suited her.

He opened his eyes again and could see now, faint shapes in the dark motel room, the silhouette of the chair beside the bed, the outline of the TV, and a thin crack of light at the curtained window. There must be a light in the parking lot.

He turned his head and saw her shadowed form. She was facing him on her side, her body rising and falling gently with her sleeping breaths. He could hear the sigh of each breath as she exhaled, could almost feel the brush of air from her body. He inhaled her scent again, and his body pulsed with arousal. He wanted to touch her, feel if her skin was as soft as he imagined, brush the covers down and lie over her. Part her legs and enter her warmth.

Someone knocked on the door. Dante turned his head to look. Zoey's breath hitched, and she murmured in her sleep.

The knock came again, a frantic pattering of blows on the wood.

He got up and grabbed his gun from the holster, then walked to the door with the gun held down by his side.

The knocking started again, this time continuing, along with an elderly feminine voice. "Mr. Torelli! Miss Zoey!"

Dante cracked the door.

Both Mrs. Guptas were standing in the hallway. They wore matching terry-cloth robes, one in green, and the other in blue. The shorter lady had a sleeping baby on one shoulder and a cell phone in the other hand.

She held out the cell when she saw him. "That Terrible Man has called me from my sister's telephone. She left it in the purple minivan, and now he has it. He says he works for Mr. DiRosa and that he wants the baby boy."

Dante took the phone with his left hand and spoke into it. "Yeah?"

"You got my kid," a gravelly voice said on the other end.

"Dante?" Zoey called sleepily from the bed.

"*Your* kid?" Dante motioned the ladies into the room and shut the door, locking it behind them. He placed his Glock back on top of the bureau. "What do you mean, your kid?"

"I mean you've got Neil Junior. My son."

Dante glanced at the sleeping baby. His curly blond head was resting on Mrs. Gupta's shoulder. He looked angelic. Hard to believe this was the son of a man who worked for Tony the Rose.

"The baby is your son?"

"What are you, deaf?" the voice growled. "Yeah, that's my kid, and I want him back."

Dante's jaw tightened. "Do you have Ricky Spinoza's daughter?"

Zoey sat up in the bed and clicked on the bedside light. She looked at him with worried blue eyes. Dante noticed with one part of his brain that her hair fell in long corkscrew curls like she was some kind of Pre-Raphaelite maiden. Gorgeous.

"Yeah, I got Spinoza's girl." On the other end of the phone a long baby wail went up, and Dante winced. The gravelly voice yelled over the wail, "I wanna make a trade."

Dante sat on the end of the bed. This had to be some kind of a trick. Tony's henchman wouldn't give up the Spinoza child this easily. But he played along. "Okay. How do you figure?"

"We meet and exchange kids. Simple."

Simple if it wasn't a trap. Dante narrowed his eyes, trying to think out angles. "Where do you want to meet?"

"You know the rest stop on I-57, south of Marion?"

They'd passed it last night. "Yes."

"Okay. I wanna meet there. No one else, just you and me. You come alone. No cops, you capisce?"

Dante rolled his eyes. This guy got his dialogue straight out of a TV mob show. "Yeah, sure. What time?"

The wail crested on the other end, stopped as the baby probably took a breath, and started again even louder. "Make it seven-thirty. I can't wait to get rid of this kid."

Dante met Zoey's wide blue eyes. "Seven-thirty it is."

The other end disconnected, cutting off the baby in midcry.

Dante pressed the END button and looked at Mrs. Pratima Gupta. "We're going to trade the babies. Can I borrow your phone in case he calls back?"

But before the woman could speak, her sister let out a scream. "You will give this innocent child to That Terrible Man? Why?"

Dante winced at her cry. It was awfully early in the morning for all this noise. "He says that's his son. That would explain why he had the kid in his truck with him."

"His . . ." Mrs. Savita Gupta stared at the child as if he'd turned into a purple squid. The little boy yawned, opened his eyes, and smiled at her. "How is this possible?"

"The wonder of genetics, I guess."

Zoey had gotten out of the bed by now, and she stood staring at him. "Are you really going to get her back, Dante?"

He looked her square on, putting every ounce of sincerity he had in him into the one word. "Yes."

She closed her eyes for a second. When she opened them again her mouth was trembling. She nodded at him and went into the bathroom.

Dante followed her with his eyes until his gaze met that of Mrs. Pratima Gupta. That lady looked pointedly from him to the bed—which had obviously been slept in by two people—and raised her eyebrows. Dante felt the same way he had when his Nona had caught him snitching freshly baked cookies meant for a family dinner. The difference being, of course, that he'd only been seven then.

"This is awful," Mrs. Savita Gupta wailed, breaking his silent stare-off with her sister-in-law. "I cannot give this precious baby up to That Terrible Man, no matter what."

"And what will you do, Savita-di," the taller woman said. "Adopt this boy child? At your age?"

Oh, low blow.

Mrs. Savita Gupta turned dark red and inhaled.

"It's his son, ma'am," Dante said soothingly before she could speak. "The baby girl *isn't* his child, and it's very important we get her back."

Mrs. Savita Gupta's lips collapsed into a trembling frown. "But—"

"Savita-di," Mrs. Pratima Gupta said. "We cannot keep this little boy. He will miss his family. His father and his mother. Let Agent Torelli return him to where he belongs."

The shorter woman blinked as if keeping tears at bay, but she nodded.

Dante blew out a relieved breath. "Good. Give us a moment to get ready, and we'll meet you in the motel lobby."

Mrs. Pratima Gupta nodded, her mouth firm. "We will be there, Mr. Torelli."

He ushered them to the door and almost had it closed when Mrs. Savita Gupta suddenly whirled back around, hand held out to stay him.

"The kesar!"

"What?"

But Mrs. Savita Gupta's face had turned stricken. "Our Grade 1A Very, Very Fine Mongra Kesar that we told you about! That Terrible man still has it. It was in the purple minivan when he stole it."

"You'll get our saffron back for us?" Mrs. Pratima Gupta asked. "Please?"

"Yeah, I'll try. Promise." Dante watched smiles light up the elderly ladies' faces.

"Oh, thank you! Thank you!" Savita Gupta exclaimed. "It is so important to us. This saffron is very, very special."

"I understand, but don't thank me until you have the saffron in your hands. Speaking of which"—Dante glanced behind him into the motel room—"I'd better get dressed."

"We will meet you in the lobby," Mrs. Pratima Gupta said. "Hurry."

She took her sister-in-law's arm and hustled her down the hallway.

Right. Dante closed the door. Time to get ready for a hostage exchange.

Chapter Thirty-five

Saturday, 7:01 a.m.

Zoey found herself clutching the armrest on the passenger side of the Beemer as Dante drove. She closed her eyes and tried to relax her stiff fingers. God. She was so close. If nothing went wrong she'd hold Pete's solid little body in her arms in half an hour. The anticipation after the past two days of anxiety was almost too much. She just wanted to feel Pete's warm weight, see her wide brown eyes, and know that nothing bad would happen to her. Half an hour.

If nothing went wrong.

Zoey glanced at the back seat. Neil Junior sat in a car seat borrowed from the Agrawals and was happily gnawing on cold flatbread left over from last night's supper. The roads were pretty clear this morning, considering the snowstorm the night before, but the sky was dark and grim and the sun seemed to be giving up the fight to rise.

"I'm going to need you to stay in the car," Dante said. His eyes were focused on the highway, narrowed and intent and very, very serious. He had said hardly anything at all to her since receiving the call this morning.

"Okay," Zoey said. "As long as you bring back Pete."

He glanced at her, and something softened in his face before he turned his gaze back to the road. "We're going to have to drive straight to Chicago after we get her. God only knows where they've stashed Spinoza, but he needs to know that we've got his daughter back so he'll testify."

Zoey opened her mouth and then closed it again. It hadn't even occurred to her to think about what they would do once Pete was safe again. But now that she considered the matter, she felt uneasy. Her first, instinctive reaction was to spirit Pete far, far away from Chicago. That wouldn't work, though, would it? Ricky-the-jerk needed to testify in the mob trial that'd been going on for the last couple of weeks. She knew Tony the Rose was on trial for various terrible mob activities, including murder. Everyone in Chicago knew what the crimes were—they'd been detailed in the *Chicago Tribune* for months now. Tony the Rose should be sent to prison. She knew that.

She knew that, but she didn't want Pete back in danger.

"There's the rest stop," Dante muttered as he flipped on his turn signal.

Zoey clenched the armrest again, leaning forward in anticipation.

Dante took the exit, breaking as they neared the rest stop. The access road forked before the building, one sign directing campers and trucks to the right, the other instructing cars to park to the left. The rest stop center was the usual dark brown building, long and low, crouched in the center of converging walkways. To the right was a small wood playground, black plastic swings frozen to the snowdrift underneath. To the left of the building was a vending machine shelter and beyond that a small stand of trees, bare and forlorn in winter.

"He should be driving that purple minivan with the big daisy the Guptas had on Tuesday. That's the car he stole from them yesterday," Dante said. "Unless he's switched vehicles."

This early in the morning there were only a few cars pulled up outside the rest stop. For a moment, Zoey's heart stopped. She didn't see a purple minivan. Then an SUV backed away from a parking space and revealed the minivan.

"There it is," she whispered.

"I see it," Dante muttered. He pulled into a parking spot and turned off the Beemer's engine. He glanced at the minivan, then at her. "Stay put. Got it?"

Zoey nodded, biting her lip nervously. His gaze dropped to her mouth and then back up to meet her eyes. She stared back, watching as his bitter-chocolate eyes narrowed, focusing solely on her. He leaned forward and time seemed to still, everything going silent except for the thumping of her heart.

Then he blinked and straightened. "Okay."

He opened the car door and climbed out.

Zoey watched Dante unbutton his trench coat and reach inside, probably checking his gun. Then he strode toward the purple minivan, the black leather whipping around his ankles in the wind. The look was only a little spoiled by the gray sweatpants and dress shoes he wore underneath.

She exhaled slowly. What had just happened? Had she imagined that he'd almost kissed her? Or had proximity to a drop-dead-gorgeous guy blown all her intuitive fuses, making her think there was something going on when nothing existed at all? Okay, no. A girl knew what a girl knew. Dante had come very close to kissing her. And she'd analyze that fact in great detail later.

Right now she had to focus on her niece.

Dante was still twenty or so feet from the purple minivan when the driver's door opened. Dante stopped and reached under his long trench coat. The bald guy that they'd seen on Tuesday emerged from the van. He was walking slowly and holding his hands in front of him. Zoey saw his mouth move, but from this distance and inside the Beemer, she couldn't understand what he said.

A squeak came from the back seat and Zoey twisted to look. Neil Junior was awake. He caught sight of her and his mouth turned down. Tears shone in his eyes.

Zoey glanced at the men. Neil Senior was approaching Dante slowly.

The baby sobbed.

"Okay, okay," Zoey whispered as she unbuckled her seat belt. Why she was whispering when the men outside couldn't possibly hear her, she didn't know.

Zoey got out of the car on the side away from the men and opened the back door. Neil Junior kicked impatiently in his car seat as she wrestled with the buckles. She picked him up and held him against her hip. Neil Junior thumped his big baby head against her shoulder, apparently happy now that he was being held. She absently pulled his jacket hood over his head as she watched the men. They'd stopped again, and she could hear Dante's voice, but not what he was saying.

A man with two little boys came out of the rest stop. One of the boys pulled at his father's jacket, halting him. The child gestured at the vending machine area, his mimed plea quite obvious.

Zoey shifted Neil Junior's weight, hitching him higher on her hip. She absently patted his rump.

Neil Senior's head snapped up as he looked in their direction, and for a horrible timeless moment, Zoey thought she'd somehow blown the trade-off.

Then Dante turned, too, and she heard a car behind her. She looked. A highway patrol car cruised into the rest-stop parking lot.

Things happened fast after that. Neil Senior drew a gun and fired at the cop car, blasting a hole high on the windshield.

"Get down! Get down!" Dante yelled, running for the vending-machine shelter.

The man with the kids stared, startled, for a moment before comprehension must've kicked in. He fell flat to the ground, covering his sons.

The highway patrol car screeched to a halt, the driver's door flying open as the officer inside took cover behind the open door and the car.

Neil Junior had jerked in Zoey's arms at the sound of the shots, and now he opened his mouth wide, crying in fear.

"Throw down your weapon!" the patrolman bellowed. "Ma'am, get back in your car!"

Zoey realized that he was talking to her. She ducked, instinctively holding her hand over Neil Junior's head.

Neil Senior crouched behind a row of metal trash cans, his cover barely adequate. He answered the officer's demand with a flurry of shots. *CRACK! CRACK! CRACK!* echoed off the rest-stop building. Dante was flat on his belly by the vending-machine shelter.

Zoey flinched against the side of the car with each shot. Neil Junior was shaking in her arms, and Zoey suddenly realized that Pete was still in the purple minivan. All alone. Probably terrified. The patrolman had his weapon pointing in Neil Senior's direction, but with so many people in the area, he must be afraid to shoot. He was stymied. As soon as Neil Senior had a chance, he'd run back to the minivan and get away.

And take Pete with him.

Zoey swallowed. She and Neil Junior were shielded from where Neil Senior hid. There were a few cars parked between them and the purple minivan, but there were more spaces than cars. Spaces that left no cover. Neil Senior wouldn't fire at a woman carrying his own child, would he? That is, if he knew it was his child.

Zoey ran behind three cars, sliding to a stop next to the rear end of a blue Ram pickup. She peered around the back bumper, holding Neil Junior's face against her shoulder. There was a fifteen-foot gap between her and the next car, and she wasn't sure how to bridge it.

More shots. She glanced at the rest-stop center. Dante was leaning around the corner of the vending-machine shelter, his gun held in straight arms, shooting toward the row of garbage cans where Neil Senior hid. A bullet hit a can with a *BANG!* and knocked it over.

Zoey couldn't wait any longer. She might not have a better chance. She ran to the next set of cars and kept running behind them. She paused at the last car to glance at the rest stop. Dante had stopped firing, but he and Neil Senior were yelling at each other. She couldn't make out exactly what they were saying, and it didn't really matter. She took a deep breath and ran to the purple minivan. The sliding side door was unlocked, and she hauled it open, conscious all the time of just how big a target her back made.

Pete was in a child car seat, screaming at the top of her lungs. The wail became a duet as Zoey shoved Neil Junior into the empty car seat next to her and strapped him in. She climbed through the seats to the front. Only then did it occur to her that she just might've made a very big mistake. She hit the auto locks before checking the ignition. Thank God. The keys were dangling from the ignition. Zoey turned on the engine with shaking hands, reversed out of the parking place, and sped away from the rest stop.

Leaving Dante behind.

Chapter Thirty-six

Saturday, 7:37 a.m.

Dante watched helplessly as the purple minivan with the big white daisy accelerated out of the rest stop with Zoey at the wheel.

"Hey!" Neil Senior yelled from behind a trash can. "Hey! What the fuck're you doin'?"

And for once Dante sympathized with the man. What the fuck was Zoey doing? Maybe she was just getting the babies out of the line of fire. Maybe she would turn around at the next exit and come back when things were safe.

Maybe, but Dante wasn't betting the house on it.

Pure, pissed anger shot through him. She'd played him for a fool. He needed to finish this so he could go after Zoey and tell her just exactly what he thought of double-crossing, baby-stealing little jerks.

"Throw down your weapon!" he bellowed at Neil Senior.

"Fuck you!" Neil Senior replied. "You set me up, asshole."

And he let loose a volley of shots in Dante's direction to hammer home the point.

Shit. Dante flattened himself on the freezing concrete floor of the vending-machine shelter. The sad thing was, Neil Senior kind of had a point. It had looked like a setup when the highway patrol had wandered in. Not that that was sufficient reason to start shooting in an area with kids present. Behind him, he heard one of the boys whimper. The kids and their father were out in the open, on the side-walk leading to the main building. The potential for trag-edy was pretty high here.

Dante peeked around the side of the shelter. The cop was still behind his car door—and probably would stay there if he was smart. Neil Senior had three orange garbage cans to hide behind, even with one having been knocked on its side.

Dante inhaled deeply to calm his voice. "Look, Neil, I'm freezing my ass off here. Can we go inside where it's warm, maybe talk this out?"

Neil snorted explosively behind the trash cans. "Yeah, you wanna try talking calmly with my wife, she finds out her kid is gone? Again?"

Dante's eyebrows shot up. "Huh. Didn't know you were married."

"What, you think Neil Junior appeared outta nowhere?"

"Good point."   •

There was a pause. A radio squawk came from the highway patrol car.

"That your partner, took off with Neil Junior and the little girl baby?" Neil asked.

"No."

"Girlfriend?"

"Not exactly."

"Then what is she?" Neil asked as if he really wanted to know.

"A pain in the ass," Dante said before he could think.

Neil chuckled. "Yeah. Them's the best kind. Take my advice, you find a woman who makes you want to spit nails and at the same time turns your balls blue, that's the one you want to marry."

Oh, for God's sake. Advice on his love life from a criminal kidnapper of babies just seemed like too much on top of everything else.

Dante bit back a sarcastic reply and went for something a little more neutral. "Huh."

Okay, so sue him. It was hard to think of the right thing to say under the circumstances.

But Neil seemed perfectly happy with monosyllables. "Yeah, once I met my Ash, it turned my whole fucking world around. She's got me eating a high-fiber diet and exercising, you know? And now I've started these anger management classes, which are fucking stupid, but Ash thinks they've helped me."

Lying on cold concrete, with the feeling beginning to go in his fingers, Dante couldn't help but wonder what Neil had been like before the anger management classes.

"Uh, y'know, good for you and all that," the father said from the rest-stop walkway, "but do you mind if I get my kids inside?"

"Hey, don't you—" Neil began in an un-anger-management shout, but he was interrupted.

A powder pink Caddy drove into the rest stop. The cop got on his mike and boomed, *"Pink Cadillac, stop. Stop your car immediately. Do not come any closer. This is a dangerous situation—"*

He was continuing to boom orders because the pink Caddy was meandering through the parking lot, apparently oblivious that it was entering a shootout. A gray puff of hair was just visible over the driver's side dash, a tweed hat on the passenger side.

"Ma'am! Please stop your car RIGHT NOW!"

The car did stop. It pulled sedately into the handicapped parking spot, right smack in front of the rest-stop walkway.

"Do not get out of the car!" The patrolman boomed hopelessly.

Dante shook his head. You had to feel for the guy.

Both car doors creaked open and there was a pause.

The patrolman tried one more time. *"Pink Cadillac! Do not exit your car. Do not—"*

To no avail. A tiny elderly woman in a purple wool coat hopped down from the driver's side. Opposite her, a man in a tweed hat and overcoat climbed out. The man braced his hand against the car hood for a moment and then started inching toward the rest stop.

"Every blamed rest stop," the old man panted. "We're losing time here, Bernice. We'll never make Memphis by noon."

"I wonder if they have the vending machines with flavored coffee here," the elderly woman said. "Wouldn't that be nice? A hot coffee?"

"Coffee!" The old guy snorted. "Last thing you need is coffee."

"*Get back in the car!*" the patrolman boomed optimistically.

"And maybe a bun, if they have them," the old lady was saying as they neared the garbage cans.

Dante watched with the fatalistic feeling one had when the blond teenager went to investigate the noise in the basement in a horror movie. Neil Senior jumped up, bumped the old lady, grabbing her keys out of her hand, and ran to the Caddy.

"Hey!" the old guy sputtered.

Neil got in the Caddy and reversed out of the handicapped parking spot just as a phalanx of highway patrol cars roared into the rest stop, sirens wailing, lights flashing. Backup had finally arrived for the lone patrolman. The Caddy sped away. The patrol cars slowed, then sped up again, chasing Neil.

Dante stood and brushed off his knees.

"Thief!" roared the old guy.

"Careful of your blood pressure, Joe," the old lady admonished.

The father helped his two crying kids up. The younger one looked from the parking lot where Neil had fled to the vending-machine shelter. His tears abruptly stopped, and he gazed up at his father.

"Can I have a candy bar?"

Chapter Thirty-seven

Saturday, 8:26 a.m.

Neil pressed the accelerator to the floor, but the pink Caddy wouldn't go any faster than eighty. It was a pure fucking miracle that he'd lost the four highway patrol cars, all things considered. The world was full of black SUVs, yellow Jeeps, and red Porsches, but did he get to steal one? Noooo. The old geezers had to be driving a fucking Caddy, and a *pink* fucking Caddy at that. He looked like a Mary Kay lady. The only thing worse would be driving around in a neon orange hot-dog truck with a big sign that read, ESCAPING CRIMINAL RIGHT HERE. Jesus Christ!

The cell phone in his pocket went off, nearly giving him his fifth heart attack of the morning. He fumbled for the crappy little piece of plastic while trying to keep his eyes on the road. A battered pickup chose that moment to pass him on the right, would you believe it, and Neil rolled down the window to give the guy the finger good and proper. Then he looked at his phone, hoping to hell and back that it wasn't Tony the Rose on the other end. He hadn't spoken to Tony since yesterday afternoon, before he'd caught up with the Indian ladies. Tony thought he was still headed for Cairo. He hadn't told Tony that he'd had the Spinoza baby and now had lost her again. He really wasn't looking forward to having to tell Tony that. But as it turned out, it wasn't Tony on the other end of the phone. It was worse.

Neil swallowed hard. He'd've ignored the now-shrill ringing of his phone, but he'd already ignored calls from Ashley twice today. She'd notify the cops if he didn't answer this time. The woman was a pistol.

Neil thumbed the Answer button. "Hi, honeybuns."

"Where are you, Neil Maurice Janiowski?" his wife demanded.

"Uh, I'm heading down a county highway in southern Illinois."

"Toward home, I hope."

Neil winced. In fact, he was heading sort of north and west. He'd just decided that probably it'd be better not to tell Ash that fact when the cell crackled in his ear.

"You're not heading home, are you, Neil?"

"See, honeybuns, I had some trouble—"

"I don't want to hear about your trouble," Neil's bride blasted in his ear. "You want to see trouble, you keep my baby from me one more night, you hear me, Neil?"

"I—"

"What were you doing taking Neil Junior on a hit in the first place?"

Ash had asked the same thing the last time she'd called.

It seemed to be a sore point with her. "I had to pick him up from day care, Ash. You know that."

"And you didn't have the time to bring the baby home to his mama before going to shoot it out with the FBI?"

"No. See, I—"

"I can't believe my own husband took my own baby on a hit," Ash muttered.

"Well—"

"And what kind of hit gets this messed up, I ask you?"

"Uh . . ."

"You think Uncle Tony was setting you up, Neil? Do you think?"

Neil blinked. It hadn't occurred to him that Tony might want him dead. The thought made his mouth all dry, which was pretty fucking uncomfortable.

But Ash hadn't waited for his answer. "Uncle Tony sets you up, I'm telling Mama about it. This's no way to treat family."

"Now, don't get too excited, honeybuns. You know the doctor said—"

"I want my baby back, Neil!"

"Just as soon—"

"I want him back like *yesterday!*"

"It's just that—"

"I miss him so much, and I want to hold him and know he's safe. Neil?"

Neil breathed through his mouth, because he thought he'd heard something over the crappy fucking cell line. "Honeybuns?"

"I want my baby." Ash's words ended on a little squeak.

Neil felt his face go hard. She was crying. His Ash was crying. He hated when Ashley cried.

"Look, I'm going to bring the baby back. You know I fucking will. Just as soon as I—"

"Neil, you do have the baby, don't you?" Ash's voice was cold. Cold like winter in fucking Siberia.

One thing Neil had learned in his marriage to this woman: don't come between Ash and her baby.

"I'm going to get him just as soon as I can, honey."

There was a silence, broken only by Ash's harsh breathing. Neil felt his blood run cold. Really. Like he had fucking cubes of ice clunking along in his veins and crashing into his heart. Ash's hormones were kind of berserk at the moment. Neil could've gone his whole life without the knowledge of what berserk hormones could do to an otherwise sweet-as-sugar woman.

Finally, Ash spoke. "You better do that, Mr. Boo. I'm giving you until tonight, and then I'm coming after my baby and I'm coming after you."

She hung up.

And even the knowledge that she'd used her pet name for him couldn't keep Neil from shivering. He needed to find Neil Junior. He needed to find the Spinoza kid again. And he needed to bring them back to Chicago in the next twelve hours. Or one very angry, very hormonal woman was going to do it for him.

Neil turned the big pink Caddy onto the next road. He was headed south now, toward I-57. Towards Cairo.

Chapter Thirty-eight

Saturday, 8:31 a.m.

Zoey pulled off the county road and killed the purple minivan's engine. Then she just sat, staring at her hands on the steering wheel. They were shaking. She would put it down to over half an hour of stereo baby screaming from the back seat, but she knew it was more than that.

She'd betrayed Dante.

It was a stupid thought. She'd known the man for only two days. He was an FBI agent doing a job. This was work for him. He didn't care about Pete the way she did. To him, her niece was a missing piece he needed in order to bring a mobster to trial. He might care for the baby's safety, but he didn't care for Pete herself.

Zoey did. Her first loyalty was to Pete and her sister, Nikki, plain and simple.

And yet she still felt guilty. Dante had trusted her. He'd

told her to stay in the car while he went out to face gunfire. She'd lied to him, betrayed his trust, and stolen Pete. By now he might very well be in the back of a patrol car under arrest. She blew out a breath and closed her eyes. Well, it was over and done now. There was no going back—Dante would never trust her again after this.

She straightened and twisted to look into the back seat. The babies were both slumped in their car seats, having cried themselves to sleep. Pete's head was tilted to the side, one finger caught in her mouth. Small pink lips pursed around the digit. Neil Junior's chin was on his chest, both pudgy baby hands stretched on either side of his car seat, limp. Zoey found herself almost smiling. He looked like a passed-out drunk. What was she going to do with him? He wasn't hers to take care of. He had parents—presumably. Or at least a homicidal father who wanted him back. The last thing she needed was to give Neil Senior another reason to follow her. If only there was someone to care for the baby, just for a little while. Someone who would look after—

A cell rang in the car, a tinkling melody. Zoey looked wildly around before realizing that there was a cell in the console. She picked it up and looked at the screen. It read SAVITA, except Mrs. Savita Gupta didn't have her cell phone at the moment.

Zoey answered. "Hello?"

"Where are you, Zoey?" Dante's voice was quiet, which only made her nervous.

She closed her eyes, relief washing over her. "Dante. You're okay."

"Yeah, I'm fine. Now tell me where you are."

"I can't. I'm sorry, but I can't let you take her back."

"Jesus, Zoey. You knew I needed to bring Pete back to Chicago so Ricky can testify. I'll be taking her to Nikki Hernandez, as well. Don't you want Pete to be with her mother?"

"I want Pete alive, and I know Nikki wants that, too."

"I'll keep her safe, Zoey."

"You didn't before."

There was silence from the other end. Zoey closed her eyes. God, she hadn't wanted to say that, but it was true. The FBI had failed Pete, failed *her*. That was how Pete had ended up with a gunman in the first place.

"I'm sorry," she whispered.

"Zoey," he said low, "don't do this."

She inhaled. "What happened after I left?"

"Neil carjacked a pink Cadillac, and what looked like most of the Illinois highway patrol took off after him."

"Was anyone hurt?"

"Just my feelings."

She winced. "How did you get out of there?"

"There was enough confusion that I slipped away and drove off when the highway patrol went to question the guy with the two boys. I didn't think it was a good idea to stay and get picked up by local law enforcement. My BMW has a bullet hole in the passenger-side door now, by the way."

"That was there from yesterday."

"Really? You didn't tell me."

"I forgot."

There was a brief silence on the line, and the wind whistled past the doors of the purple minivan.

"Zoey, bring her back," Dante said.

"I need to keep her safe. Chicago isn't safe for Pete."

"I'll make sure she's safe."

"You can't."

"You mean you don't believe I can."

She was silent, because there really wasn't anything to say to that, was there?

She heard him sigh. "Please, Zoey."

She inhaled to steady her voice. "I'm sorry."

And she hung up.

She stared at the cell phone in her hand for a moment. Then she inhaled and punched in a number.

The other end rang five times before Nikki answered. "Hello?"

"Nikki, I've got Pete."

"Zoey?" Nikki's voice sounded dazed. Then she seemed to understand. "You have Pete? Oh, God. Oh, God." She started crying.

Zoey blinked hard, staring out the window of the van. "Are you okay?"

"Okay?" Nikki choked. "Yeah, we're okay. How's my baby? Is Pete okay?"

"Yeah, she's fine."

"God. I've got to tell Ricky. Wait until he hears—"

"Nikki, you can't tell Ricky."

"What? Why not? You should see Ricky, he's been so sad without the baby."

Zoey rolled her eyes at that. Ricky-the-jerk had never been particularly loving with Pete before. "You can't tell Ricky because I'm not bringing Pete back to Chicago."

"What do you mean—"

"Shhh. Listen. The FBI's crooked in Chicago. We can't trust them to keep Pete safe."

"But Zoey," Nikki said quietly, "Ricky's told me he

won't testify unless he can see Pete with his own eyes. You keep her away and he's not going on the stand."

Zoey swallowed. "I know the trial is important. I know Tony the Rose is an evil man. But Pete's safety has to come first."

"And how're we going to keep her safe by ourselves?"

That had been something she was worried about, too, but Zoey kept her tone brisk. "I'll hide Pete. It'll be okay."

"But—"

"You can't tell Ricky, though. If anyone finds out where I am—where Pete is—she's in danger again."

There was silence on the other end.

"Nikki?"

"I just want to see Pete."

"I know, honey, I know. But she's safer this way. If I bring her back to Chicago, we can't protect her."

"You sure?"

"Yes. But you can't tell Ricky."

A long sigh.

"Nikki?"

"Okay. Okay. I won't tell Ricky. But Zoey, you've got to promise to keep her safe."

"I will."

"Kiss her for me," Nikki whispered. "Tell her I love her."

Zoey closed her eyes. "I will."

"Bye." There was a click as Nikki hung up.

God, what had she done? Zoey leaned her head against the seat back and watched the snow blow across a field. The wind knocked against the purple minivan, rattling it. It looked like another snowstorm was brewing. Was this the right choice? Dante was strong and determined, and she knew that if it was in his power he would keep Pete safe. But it hadn't been in his power before, and if he took Pete back to Chicago, at some point it wouldn't be in his power again. Her real problem was that she didn't trust his instincts, didn't trust his decision to take Pete back to Chicago. Maybe she couldn't let herself trust him.

Or anyone but herself.

What a thought. But this wasn't the time to sit debating whatever emotional baggage lay inside her. She had two babies in the back seat, bad guys and one really good guy after her, and no plan.

Okay. The first thing to do was to find a safe place for Neil Junior. Someone who would take care of him temporarily until Dante or social services could take the child. And now that she thought of it, she already knew the right person. The Gupta ladies were still at their nephew's motel, and Mrs. Savita Gupta had obviously been sad to see Neil Junior go. Zoey could drop Neil Junior there and then call Dante and let him know where the baby was when she was far enough away.

Zoey looked around. She was in a little wooded area off some kind of farm field. She'd left the highway as soon as she could after escaping with the babies. If she headed to the motel again, it would be best to do so without getting back on the highway. The motel was west of where the van sat, but these back roads twisted, not always going straight west or north.

Zoey reached over and popped the glove compartment. An avalanche of papers fell out onto the floor of the van. She whispered a curse and started sorting through them. Car maintenance bills, insurance forms, and the manual to the minivan. No maps.

She got out and went to look in the back of the van. The snow was about a foot deep, compacted by the wind and crusted. Her boots crunched through the top crust unevenly, and she held on to the van's sides to keep her balance as she made her way to the hatch. Inside the back were a big bag of disposable diapers—hallelujah!—a small cardboard box with Indian writing on the back, an old blanket, and a giant bag of kitty litter. Crumpled under the diapers was an Illinois state highway map. Ha! She grabbed the map, shut the hatch, and waded back to the driver's-side door. When she looked in the back, Pete had turned her head to the other side, but both babies were still asleep.

Zoey fastened her seat belt and started the engine.

Chapter Thirty-nine

Saturday, 8:45 a.m.

Rutgar drove down the flat highway toward Cairo and thought about his favorite subject.

Guns.

In Poland, where he had grown up in a colorless rat-infested tenement, one was not allowed to own guns. The communist government forbade it. This was not to say that there were not men who possessed guns, for there were. Hard men, men who ruled the tenements like barbarian kings. But even these men had access only to old guns. Guns that had been made in the old Soviet Union. Their guns were not like the guns one could own in America.

In America one could be a connoisseur of guns.

The first time that Rutgar had attended an American gun show, his heart had stood still in his body. There were many guns there. Thousands of guns. Perhaps millions of guns. Guns manufactured to shoot wild elephants. Guns so small one could fit them entirely in one's mouth like a hard candy. Guns with scopes and tripods and silencers. Guns made by armies, and guns made to defeat armies.

America was rich with guns, Rutgar thought. He smiled a small smile.

He drove south toward the state of Missouri, although that was not his destination. The car he drove was a black Mercedes-Benz G500 SUV. It was a big car. It was an expensive car. If Rutgar could take this car across the ocean to Poland, to that dirty tenement he had grown up in, those barbarian kings would bow down to him. He would be the king of all the barbarian kings.

But there was nothing in Poland, so he did not do this.

He had a job to do. Tony the Rose had told him that Neil Janiowski had followed the two Indian women to southern Illinois. Everything else Rutgar had needed to know he'd found very quickly. The trail that Neil had left behind him had been easy to trace; the people he'd asked about the women were easily convinced to talk when a knife was pressed to their throat. Perhaps Neil was too stupid to know to cover his tracks. It did not matter. Rutgar knew the cars the two old women might be driving, the people they knew and would feel safe with, the places they might run to hide.

Not that hiding from him would do them any good. He had guns. They did not. His guns were: a semiautomatic Glock, a sawed-off shotgun fitted with a pistol grip, a military-grade sniper's rifle with night scope and laser sight, and a subcompact Beretta. He wore the Beretta in a leather holster on his right hip. Like Han Solo, perhaps.

He looked in the side mirror before passing a semi. The semi was going maybe fifty-five mph. Thus Rutgar could easily pass the truck without going over the speed limit. It was important not to arouse suspicion.

Rutgar smiled a small smile as he drove.

Chapter Forty

Thank God for gas stations that took credit cards at the pump. Zoey winced, watching the numbers flicker rapidly by as she pumped. Looked like minivans took considerably more gas than Priuses. She was aware that using the credit card might alert somebody to her location, but she wasn't about to leave the babies in the car by themselves to go into the station to pay. Using a credit card was a risk she'd just have to take.

They were somewhere south of Carbondale, closer to the interstate than she wanted to be, since that was where the gas stations were to be found. Zoey wasn't exactly sure of their location because as it turned out, her directional skills even with a map were kind of sketchy. She should've found Mr. Agrawal's motel already. Instead, she'd gone in circles—or maybe squares—on back roads so small they didn't even have names. Hence the need to stop for gas.

The gas nozzle started gurgling, signaling that the tank was nearly full. Zoey stepped back, wary of being splashed, and waited for the last gurgle before taking the nozzle out of the gas tank and returning it to the pump. She grimaced when she saw the total. Sheesh. At this rate she was going to max out her credit card. And considering that she seemed on indefinite hiatus from her job at the whole-foods store, that was a serious worry.

Zoey considered her job—and whether she still had one—as she walked to the windshield squeegee thingy. They were at a little gas station—only four pumps—and the wind was whipping across the frosty asphalt. The convenience store next to the gas station looked like the kind that would have ancient peanuts and candy bars and a ladies' room that would make you want to put paper on the toilet. Just as well she hadn't used it.

A huge, square black SUV pulled up to the pump across from the purple minivan. Zoey poked at the dark blue water in the little squeegee box—it looked viscous. The windshield wipers on the purple minivan were worn and worked only intermittently. The windshield had a gray film from salt, dirt, and snow spray, and it was getting close to opaque. Zoey walked back to the van with the squeegee as a young guy got out of the black SUV. He had ash blond hair and was wearing a brown leather jacket. Wow. The jacket probably cost a couple thousand dollars. Maybe he was the local drug pusher. Zoey watched him stroll into the dinky convenience store as she gingerly washed the windshield. These communal washer thingies always gave her the heebie-jeebies. Who knew how many mashed-up bug guts were in the dark blue soup?

Zoey finished washing the windshield and the back window before the guy came out again. She threw the squeegee back in the icky water as he started pumping gas. He'd never looked in her direction, but something about the guy made her nervous. Zoey trotted back to the mini-van and got in. The babies were still asleep in back, but she knew from experience that wouldn't last long. She needed to get Neil Junior to the aunties so both babies could have something to eat and a chance to move around.

On that thought, she started the van and pulled away from the pump.

The blond guy looked up. She shuddered, looking away quickly, but not before she'd seen his eyes.

They were pale gray.

Chapter Forty-one

Saturday, 11:16 a.m.

Dante stared at the two elderly ladies and felt his blood pressure shoot through the roof. "She was here?"

Mrs. Savita Gupta exchanged a look with Mrs. Pratima Gupta. The look clearly said, *This man has lost his marbles.* Possibly this was because he'd already asked the question three times since he'd arrived at their nephew's motel.

"Ye-es. Zoey left not half an hour ago. We fed the babies and cleaned them, and then she said she had to leave." Mrs. Savita Gupta smiled. "It was very kind of her to bring back the boy baby."

Dante pressed two fingers to his pounding temple. *Kind.* Yeah, that would be the first word he would use to describe Zoey. Right before *double-crossing, sexy,* and *a pain in the goddamn ass.* How the hell had he not passed her on the highway?

Some of his thoughts must've shown in his face. Mrs. Pratima Gupta leaned forward anxiously. "Would you like some tea?"

Tea was the very last thing he needed, but it wasn't the Gupta ladies' fault he'd been a half step behind Zoey all morning. He'd been almost at the Cairo exit when he realized that there were highway patrol cars stopped ahead of him on the shoulder. That had necessitated a hasty exit to nowheresville and a stroll about the countryside before he could find another entrance to 57. By the time he'd gotten to the motel, he'd lost over forty-five minutes. Still, he'd held out hope that he'd find Zoey here. Now he wasn't even sure where to look next.

Dante found himself sitting on the saggy couch in Mr. Agrawal's back rooms with a mug of hot tea pressed into his hands. Mrs. Agrawal was in the kitchen doing something, and she flashed a shy smile at him. She probably thought he spent all of his time chasing crazy women with babies. The kids were in their usual spot, grouped in a tight knot in front of the TV with Neil Junior in the place of honor in front. For a moment, Dante was mesmerized by the flashing colors and boinking sounds. Neil Junior would probably fit right in here. He'd grow up watching cartoons and eating curried lentils and flatbreads, a blond cuckoo in another bird's nest.

Then Dante mentally shook himself.

He looked up at the Gupta ladies, hovering solicitously. "Did she give you any idea which way she might be heading?"

The ladies exchanged another look, then Mrs. Pratima Gupta said, "She did not say."

"But she still has your purple van?"

"Our nephew's purple van," Mrs. Pratima Gupta corrected. "She said she'd bring it back to Chicago for us. We've decided to stay and visit with Rahul and his wife for a bit."

"We will bring back Neil Junior to Chicago when we return," Mrs. Savita Gupta said. "Perhaps we can bring him to his mother. I do not like the father. Shooting at you! How awful!"

"Yes, terrible," Pratima Gupta said. "Until we return to Chicago, Neil Junior may visit with us. I believe he likes it here with our nephew's children."

"Great." Dante took a sip of hot tea. Wasn't like he had anything else to do.

Both ladies looked sad that they couldn't help him, and Dante felt guilty for a moment.

Mrs. Pratima Gupta perked up. "She brought us back our Grade 1A Very, Very Fine Mongra Kesar."

"Yeah? Hey, that's good." Zoey was dealing in illicit spices. Whoopee.

Mrs. Savita Gupta cleared her throat. "I wondered . . . if you no longer need my cell phone, perhaps you could give it back?"

"Oh!" Mrs. Pratima Gupta exclaimed. "I forgot to ask for my cell phone from the girl."

Dante looked up. Zoey still had Mrs. Pratima Gupta's cell phone?

"You never use it anyway," Mrs. Savita Gupta said. "I do not think you know how to use it properly, Pratima."

"I do, too," the other lady shot back indignantly.

"You insisted that the phone be able to take photos," Mrs. Savita Gupta tutted. "And do you ever take any photos with your fancy cell phone, Pratima? No, you do not. I do not believe you know how to take photos with a cell phone. I think—"

"I need to borrow your phone for just a little while longer." Dante drained the last of the tea—he was beginning to actually like the stuff—and stood.

"Please. Use it as long as you need it," Mrs. Savita Gupta said.

"Great. Thanks."

Mrs. Pratima Gupta looked uncertain—she was probably wondering if she'd ever get her own cell back at this point—but Dante didn't have time to explain. He thanked both ladies, waved to Mrs. Agrawal, and dashed out of the motel.

The cell phone was in the BMW, stuck in the console where he'd left it. Dante checked the battery—nearly full—then scrolled down the list of phone numbers until he came to Pratima Gupta and pressed the Call button. The other end started ringing.

He watched out the window as he listened. It'd begun to snow again—great puffballs that would pile up rapidly. Maybe she'd ditched the phone. Or she simply wouldn't answer again. Or she couldn't answer. The possibilities were making his muscles tense with anxiety. He rubbed his sore leg and—

"Hello?" Her voice was breathless.

For a moment all he could do was close his eyes in relief.

"Hello?" She sounded sharp.

Well, he wasn't in a good mood, either. "Zoey, where the hell are you?"

"Dante?"

"Yeah."

"Someone's following me."

He straightened, his mind suddenly narrowed to a sharp, pinpoint focus on her. "Where are you? Are you on a major road?"

"I'm on I-24, headed south. I passed Vienna a while back, but I-I don't know what exit I'm near."

He fumbled with the glove compartment one-handed and took out a highway map, searching for I-24. "What does the car following you look like?"

"It's a big black Mercedes-Benz SUV. Dante, it was at a gas station with me earlier."

"Okay." Dante started the BMW and headed for the highway, one hand holding the cell to his ear. "Don't stop, don't get off the highway. Just maintain your speed."

"Dante . . ." He could hear fear in her voice, and it twisted his gut.

"What is it?"

"Something's wrong with the van," she said, her voice thin. "It's pulling hard to the right. I think I'm going to have to stop."

Dante felt panic threaten to close his throat. He swung the BMW onto I-57, headed north. On the map, 57 and 24 met farther north, but there wasn't a direct route to her from here. "Are you near an exit? Maybe a town with a gas station?"

"No."

"Or a fast-food place?" He floored the accelerator, the

needle on the speedometer climbing past ninety mph. "Somewhere with people?"

"I just passed a rest-stop sign. It's in twenty miles."

"Okay, I want you to get off at the rest stop. Park as close to the front of the building as possible, but don't get out of the car. Do you understand?"

There was silence from the other end of the phone.

"Zoey?"

More silence.

"Zoey!"

The line was dead. Dante pressed End, then immediately redialed the number. Two clicks and then a recorded message with a mechanical voice informing him the number was not available at this time.

"Shit! Fuck! Son of a bitch!" Dante threw the phone on the passenger-side seat.

He didn't know if her cell had died, if she'd hung up on him, or she was just out of range. To compound that worry, he was at least thirty minutes away from Zoey's rest stop.

And he had no idea if she'd heard his last instructions.

Chapter Forty-two

Saturday, 11:23 a.m.

Zoey glanced in her rearview mirror. The black clouds overhead made the winter light dim, the color bleeding from the landscape, leaving everything a dreary gray. Shapes became hard to see in the half light. Most cars had their headlights on now. But the black Mercedes-Benz SUV following her hadn't turned his on. The big truck blended into the coming shadows, moving like a silent, ominous wraith behind her.

Zoey swallowed and concentrated on driving. The steering wheel was shuddering hard beneath her hands, numbing her fingers. She didn't know exactly what was wrong with the tire, but the shudder was increasing and the minivan was pulling hard to the right. If she'd been in a safe area, a suburban neighborhood or a lighted, busy mall, she'd have stopped the van long before this.

If the tire had a leak or a weak point, it could blow at any minute, and she wasn't sure she'd have the strength to control the van. And if the minivan broke down here on the highway . . .

She peered in the rearview mirror again. The boxy black SUV still followed, dark and shadowy behind her. It never allowed the space between the cars to increase or decrease. She'd tried speeding up, and he had sped up, too. When she tapped her brake, he slowed, as well. He kept a constant two car-lengths behind. A moderate distance, a polite distance, precisely what a high school driving instructor would approve of.

Zoey stifled a hysterical giggle.

She was in the middle of nowhere. On either side of the road, gray-white fields rolled away to the horizon, dotted here and there by farmhouses in the distance. The traffic was sparse. Zoey looked at her odometer. She had about five miles to go before she hit the rest stop. Okay, so all she had to do was keep calm, drive to the rest stop. And what then? Dante hadn't said he was nearby. Maybe he was calling the highway patrol for her. Maybe—

The black SUV sped up, coming up close on her left. Zoey pressed the accelerator down, but the wheel was shaking so badly now that she was having trouble keeping control of the van. She glanced wildly to her left. The SUV's windows were black, either from the dim light or because they were tinted. Either way, it gave the truck an eerily humanless appearance, as if the vehicle was driving itself.

As she watched, it swerved at her. The SUV hit her minivan with a *thud* and a long screech as the vehicles scraped against each other. Zoey felt her gut dive. The wheel spun in her hands, twisting violently beyond her control as the van went into the gravel on the side of the road. The van tipped horribly and she was sure—absolutely sure—that they were going to roll.

She wrenched at the wheel, pulling with all her strength, and the van crashed back onto the highway, speeding for the ditch that divided the lanes. Zoey twisted the wheel, gradually, oh so gradually, correcting the course of the van, until it straightened. Then they were speeding down the highway in the left lane. The blue rest-stop sign shot by on the right, flashing in her headlights.

She craned her neck, searching behind her. The SUV was in the right lane, almost kissing her right bumper. It was only a matter of time before he tried running her off the road again. As she watched, he veered toward her.

Zoey stomped on the brakes. The purple minivan swerved wildly, and for a heart-attack-inducing moment she thought she'd blown the tire. Then the van steadied. The black SUV was ahead of her now, slowing, as well.

Zoey accelerated fast, driving onto the shoulder and passing him. She hit the rest-stop off-ramp, still on the shoulder.

BANG! The tire blew and the van skewed across the road. Zoey wrestled the wheel, praying and cursing at the same time. From the back seat, Pete let out a scream. Somehow she'd slept through the wild ride, but the tire exploding had woken her up. The van was still going, humping up and down as they rolled on the rim of the torn tire.

Zoey's face was wet, from tears or sweat she couldn't tell. Maybe it was a combination of both. They were almost there, almost at the rest-stop building, and she didn't know what to do. Dante had told her to stay there, had told her to wait, but she couldn't see anyone else. The Mercedes-Benz SUV was on her tail again, following patiently like a wolf trailing a wounded deer. When she stopped, all he had to do was shoot out the window, kill her, and take Pete. She'd failed.

She'd failed . . .

Chapter Forty-three

Saturday, 11:51 a.m.

By the time Dante slammed onto the rest stop exit ramp his shirt was sticking to his back with sweat. He'd not heard from Zoey in almost half an hour. He wasn't even sure she'd be here, but he had nowhere else to look. The purple minivan hadn't been on the highway.

The rest stop looked deserted. A white sedan and a green pickup were pulled up to the walkway in front of the building. No other cars were in sight. Dante slowed, peering at the building. It was well lit, but no one moved inside. If she hadn't made the rest stop, maybe she'd been forced off the road. He hadn't seen a car in the ditch along the highway, but he'd been speeding. Dante pushed down on the accelerator, driving for the rest-stop exit.

BLAM!

His first thought was that he was being shot at. But

then more gunfire blasted the air and he realized the sound came from the other side of the rest stop. Where the trucks parked.

Dante spun the steering wheel hard, the BMW's tires squealing as he wrenched the car back into the truck exit. He stomped on the accelerator and sped up the exit, going the wrong way. Not that it mattered—no trucks were on the exit road. He could see a couple of semis parked ahead, motors running. The drivers had probably stopped in the early hours of the morning and were settled in their warm cabs, still snoozing. Beside the semis, there were only two other vehicles in the parking lot: a black SUV lurking in the scanty cover of leafless trees, and the purple minivan with the big lopsided daisy.

Relief swept his chest. At least he'd found her.

The purple minivan was parked right in front of the building, under one of the large streetlights. The day was so dark that the streetlight had halfheartedly lit, glowing pale orange. The van's headlights were off, and it was canted at an odd angle. Dante didn't have time to try and figure out what was wrong with the minivan, though, because a shot ricocheted off the front right panel of his BMW. Sparks flew into the swirling snow.

"Fuck!" Dante skewed the BMW in close to the purple minivan, between it and the big SUV. The BMW jolted as it hit the curb. Dante climbed over the console and out the passenger-side door. Behind him, the driver's-side window shattered, chunks of glass hitting him in the back.

Dante crouched behind the car and drew his Glock. He straight-armed over the trunk and fired three shots in rapid succession.

CRACK! CRACK! CRACK!

Behind him, the driver's-side door of the van opened. The sound of a hysterically crying baby flooded the cold air.

"Stay inside!" Dante bellowed. "Get down!"

The van door slammed shut just as the shooter opened fire again. A shot pinged off the BMW trunk. Dante flattened himself to the freezing asphalt. *BANG! BANG! BANGBANGBANG!* He lost count of the shots fired. They were high-powered and deafeningly loud, and Dante felt like his ass was sticking in the air, bare and exposed. The BMW shook. He glanced at the minivan behind him and his blood ran cold. The side panel was riddled with holes. Jesus. If Zoey and the baby weren't hit, it'd be a miracle.

That thought lit a fire in his blood. He belly-crawled to the front of the BMW, the shots still pinging against his car and the asphalt, then raised his fist over the hood. He couldn't aim without looking, and he wasn't about to raise his head and have it blown off, but he could give the guy a taste of his own medicine. He squeezed off five shots, his hand jerking up with each round, his wrist aching.

His ears were ringing from the gunshots, both his and the other guy's, so it took a moment for him to hear the siren. It was growing louder, obviously nearing their spot. The shooter stopped, and a second later the black SUV fired up. It roared past the van and BMW. Dante scrambled around the car to get cover as it left.

The black SUV disappeared down the exit ramp.

Dante stood and wrenched at the purple minivan door. The front seat was empty. His heart sank right into his gut. He hauled open the side door and met Zoey's blue eyes. She was crouched on the floor, holding the screaming baby.

"Are you all right?" he yelled at her.

Adrenaline was pounding in his arteries, and he wasn't sure he could keep his voice down even if he wanted to.

Zoey started to nod. He grabbed her and pulled her from the van, scaring the baby into renewed wails of terror.

"You're sure? You're sure you're all right?"

He didn't give her time to answer. He knocked the stupid reindeer hat from her head, thrust his fingers into her hair, feeling for blood, feeling for her life.

"Dante, I'm okay," she said, her voice small. "Pete's okay."

He moved his hands to her neck, running his fingers around under her hair. "Don't ever do that again."

"I—"

"Shut up. Let me see. I have to make sure."

He pulled her jacket open and thrust up her shirt, glaring at the bare, unbroken skin on her belly, then whirled her around, patting for blood or other injuries. Finally he knelt and ran his hands down over hips and thighs, calves, and ankles. She stood still, clutching the baby. He pulled his hands away and looked at them. They were shaking like an old man's.

Damn her. Damn her to hell.

He stood and seized her shoulders, pulling her into a kiss that smashed her lips against her teeth and put the baby's wails right in his ear. He didn't care. It was as much punishment as relief, and he didn't have the time for finesse or gentleness. He tasted sweetness, tasted *her,* and then heard the sirens coming fast.

Fuck. He looked up as flashing lights swung in from the opposite side of the rest-stop building. The cruiser had driven into the car side of the rest stop. It was only a matter of minutes before they realized where the shots had come from and drove to this side.

He looked at the baby, red-faced and with snot running over her wide-open lips. "You checked her?"

"Yeah, I—"

"Get in my car."

"But the baby seat—"

"I've got it." He didn't wait for her to move but reached past her into the van. He found the buckle that held the seat in place, popped it open, and wrenched the awkward contraption out. He turned to find that Zoey had already got in the BMW with the baby. Smart girl.

"Hey!" One of the truckers had ventured from his cab. The man was walking across the parking lot toward them. "Hey, you all okay?"

Dante didn't bother answering. He flung the baby seat into the back of the BMW, then grabbed a big bag of diapers from the van and Zoey's purse. He threw them both in the BMW, slammed the door shut, ran around to the driver's side, and slid in.

"What are—?" Zoey started.

"Just shut up," he growled.

He reversed the BMW, then sped down the exit. The first cruiser was still in the car side of the rest stop, but a second one entered the truck side. Dante watched in the rearview mirror as the cruiser skidded to a stop, the trucker spotlighted in the headlights.

Then they were on the highway, and he pressed the accelerator down. He had Zoey and he had the baby, and they were both safe.

That was more than enough for now.

Chapter Forty-four

Saturday, 12:45 p.m.

*I*s not this child a wonder?" Savita-di gushed as she watched the boy baby bang a wooden spoon against a cooking pot. "Already he has a musical talent!"

Pratima winced as the boy struck the pot particularly hard. "He is a wonder indeed, Savita-di."

"Perhaps we should tune the television to an educational program," Savita-di said. "I am not sure this program is appropriate for a small, impressionable child."

She frowned at the television in the motel room their nephew had given them. The room was rather small, and several of the walls came together at odd angles, making the room seem even more cramped. There were two beds, but one was right against the wall, and the quilts on top of the beds did not match. Pratima had begun to suspect that their room was usually used as a storage space, and up until a few minutes ago Savita-di had been bewailing the cheapness of nephews who stuffed their aunts into closets.

A squawk came from the television. On the screen, a pretty blond girl was earnestly singing into a microphone. Or at least she thought she was singing.

Pratima frowned at her sister-in-law. "*American Idol* is most educational, Savita-di."

"It is a rerun."

"Yes, but is it not very helpful for the boy's musical talent?" Pratima inquired. Really, that girl's hair could not be naturally blond—she had a dark stripe down the middle of her head like a skunk in reverse. Also, her singing was simply atrocious.

Savita-di closed her mouth.

Pratima smiled and looked back at the TV. Mr. Simon Cowell would have something sharp to say to the skunk girl.

"That man reminds me of my late husband somehow, Pratima," Savita-di muttered.

Pratima shot her sister-in-law a sharp glance. Actually, now that she thought about it, Mr. Cowell was a bit like her deceased brother-in-law. Sharp. Sarcastic. Impatient with the weaknesses of others. And, of course, quite, quite handsome. Pratima hesitated. Perhaps this would be the moment to discuss that long-ago time when they were young. She had thought the years would heal whatever wounds had been incurred, but instead, though the hurts were scarred over, they seemed to be festering beneath the surface. In such a case, she knew, often the only choice was to lance the infection. Unfortunately, lancing was very painful and might only make things worse.

Beside her, Savita-di sighed. "I do not know how we will return to Chicago."

"Does it matter?" Pratima asked soothingly. "The snow is falling very rapidly outside and it is very cold. Here in this room we are warm and cozy."

"But what of our restaurant?" Savita-di said. "We were due to open it next week, and hardly anything is prepared. Do not think that Abdul will work when we are not there to oversee him."

Pratima watched closely as the skunk girl finished her song on a screech and Mr. Cowell narrowed his eyes in preparation. Could not Savita-di learn to be quiet and enjoy quality television?

"Rahul says the roads may be impassible tomorrow," Pratima told her sister-in-law. "And in any case, I think it would be most imprudent to try and drive in these conditions."

Savita-di frowned. Such a contrary thing! She would now take the opposing opinion, Pratima was sure, and advocate driving to Chicago this very night. How she, Pratima, had been able to withstand this stubborn need to always be in control on the part of her sister-in-law for so many weary years—

The flimsy door to the room suddenly flew open and crashed against the wall. Savita-di gave a startled cry— really it was more of a squeak—and Pratima merely stared.

That Terrible Man stood in the doorway.

"No! No! No!" Savita-di screamed—she was rarely caught off guard for long. "You must go! Do not disturb us, you Terrible Man! Do not think to—"

But in the midst if this diatribe, just when Savita-di had

really built up a head of steam, a small sound was heard. All in the room paused and turned to the source of this tiny sound—the baby boy.

He smiled and repeated it. "Da!"

He held out small, chubby arms toward That Terrible Man, and really it was remarkably similar to one of those television shows one saw on the Lifetime network. Perhaps one involving angels. For a transformation overcame That Terrible Man's face. He did not exactly become softer—hard to look softer with eyebrows as thick and black as That Terrible Man had—but his face no longer looked quite as menacing as it had before. Perhaps there was even a twinkle in his bloodshot black eyes, although that may have been the cheap lightbulbs her nephew used in his motel rooms.

The gun in That Terrible Man's hand shook, and he spoke one word. "Son."

Pratima sighed, leaned forward to pick up the television remote control, and clicked the TV off, just when Paula was talking earnestly and looked like she might burst into tears. A pity, really.

She turned to Savita-di. "Well, this is a fine mess."

Chapter Forty-five

Saturday, 12:48 p.m.

Dante's face looked like it was carved from stone.

Zoey swallowed and nuzzled her nose into Pete's baby curls, wondering what that kiss had meant. There had been anger in it—she'd have to be dead not to notice that emotion—but beneath had been something else. She wished she could rewind to those seconds when his mouth had pressed so savagely against hers. Maybe she could take notes this time, figure out exactly what he meant. And this time she would try to make his mouth soften. But his kiss had been so fast, so violent, she knew that there hadn't been time for her to respond, to make him soften.

She sighed. She was probably overthinking the whole thing.

Pete had fallen asleep almost as soon as the car had started. Poor baby, she must be exhausted from crying.

She smelled like baby shampoo and baby sweat, and Zoey inhaled gratefully. It was so wonderful to be able to hold Pete, to feel the baby's weight in her arms, to know she was safe, at least for now.

That thought made her glance at Dante. "I'm sorry. I couldn't trust the FBI again, not with Pete's life. I—"

"You couldn't trust me," he clipped out.

Zoey inhaled. "It wasn't you, Dante. It was the FBI. They—"

His mouth turned down into a thin, hard, nasty line. "It was me. Don't try to pretend otherwise. I had the baby. You didn't trust me to take her back to Chicago. You didn't trust me to keep her safe."

He was so angry. She could feel his anger coming in waves off of him; it was almost like a physical barrier between them. She didn't want this awful distance between them. It felt so wrong.

Zoey tried again. "Dante, I—"

"I don't want to talk about it."

She closed her eyes and sighed. She was so tired. It was as if all her vitality had been drained from her body. She just felt gray and wrung out. Pete smacked her lips, still asleep, and clutched a tiny fist into Zoey's hair. Zoey'd forgotten to pick her knitted hat back up when Dante had flung it aside. Her head was bare, her hair tangled and coming down from the braids she'd fixed it in this morning. She probably looked like a mess.

She glanced at Dante's iron profile and sighed silently. Not that it mattered. He hadn't looked at her with much interest before now, and he sure wasn't going to start at this point. The thought shouldn't have depressed her further, but it did.

Dante had turned off I-24 a while back. They'd been driving on a county road, but now he signaled and turned off that, as well. The BMW fishtailed a little on the turn, and Dante tapped the brake. The snow was coming down in big fluff balls that stuck to the windshield and then were swept away by the wipers.

She shuddered. With the driver's-side window broken, the car was freezing. Sitting right next to it, Dante must be even colder than she was, but he didn't show it. He'd duct-taped one of the plastic bags over the window, but there was still an arctic draft. And the bag looked like it might come down at any moment.

"Where are we?" Zoey asked. The road was drifted with snow, and Dante had slowed the BMW down to under forty mph.

He glanced at her for the first time since they'd entered the car. "I'm heading east. To the Shawnee National Forest. I have a friend who has a summer cabin on the Ohio River. It's an hour or so away. Maybe more."

"That's where we're going? To your friend's cabin?"

"Yeah."

She watched the snow swirling over the hood for a moment, feeling the exhaustion drag at her limbs. "Nikki came to our house the summer Dad left."

She felt more than saw him still. He didn't look toward her, but she knew he was listening.

Zoey brushed a damp curl on Pete's forehead. "I was fourteen and Nikki was only eight. We were fostering other kids that summer, a boy and two other girls, but they were reassigned soon after Dad skipped. Mom wouldn't let social services take Nikki, though. She said Nikki had already been through enough upheaval, that it wouldn't be fair to her to move Nikki again."

She chuckled, a sound that emerged dry and sad. "Except I don't know if we were all that good a place for Nikki to be. Mom was in denial and angry because Dad had left us, and I was just angry. Angry all the time."

He cleared his throat. "It must've been a hard time for all three of you."

"Yeah." She watched Pete's soft little eyelashes flutter. "But you know, Nikki used to climb in bed with me at night sometimes. I don't know if she'd had a bad dream or she was just lonely, but I'd wake up all sweaty and there's be a skinny little hand clutching at my arm. She never let go even when she was asleep. She was a sweet kid, you know. I think she'd figured that she had to be appealing to survive the foster-care program."

Dante glanced at her. "Did she stay at your place the entire time she was growing up?"

"Mostly. There were stretches when she'd be placed with an aunt or grandmother, but her family was pretty messed up and her mother was in and out of prison. She spent most of her time with us."

He nodded.

Zoey wet her lips. "Nikki is my sister. I've spent over a decade looking after her. So when she called and said Ricky had done something really dumb and they were going into hiding"—she shrugged—"we kept in touch. I know Nikki wasn't supposed to tell anyone where they were, but I'd helped raise Pete. Nikki depends on me."

"So you dropped your own life and came running when they came back to Chicago?"

"No." She frowned. That sounded so pathetic. "But I

wanted to be near Pete and Nikki. I wanted to know they were safe." She took a deep breath, because he wasn't going to like what she said next. "You should know that Ricky's told Nikki that he won't testify unless he can see Pete with his own eyes. You're going to have to get her back before he's due on the stand if the trial's to continue."

His lips tightened and he frowned, but then he glanced at Pete in her arms. "Is she really okay?"

Zoey smoothed a hand over the curls stuck to Pete's sweaty forehead. "Yes. She's just tired."

"Good." He turned back to the road. His lips compressed. "I . . . was worried."

She looked at him. His face was unreadable, his expression still grim, but he'd asked. He'd admitted it.

She inhaled and stared down at Pete's curls. "I was so scared, Dante. The minivan's tire blew or something, and I could hardly keep it on the road, and that black Mercedes-Benz SUV was following me the entire way. He was right behind me. Even before the tire blew he'd tried to force us off the road. I didn't know if we'd make the rest stop, and even if we made the rest stop, what I would do then, and the entire time Pete was screaming from the back seat."

She stopped because she was trembling and babbling at this point. He must think her an idiot. She'd been the one to run away from him with Pete. He probably thought it served her right for some psycho hit man to come after her.

He was silent a minute. Outside, the blizzard had grown worse, the snow driving hard against the windshield. The wipers struggled to keep up, and the plastic bag on his window snapped in the wind.

"I didn't think I'd get there in time," Dante said so low

she almost didn't make out the words. "I thought I'd get there and find . . ."

He didn't finish the words.

She looked at him. He was still grim, still unreadable, but she knew now that his granite mask hid fear.

Fear for her.

"When I saw your BMW come into the rest-stop parking lot, I knew . . ." Zoey swallowed and continued, her voice raspy. "I knew we were all right. I knew you'd save us."

It was a small change, and maybe no one else in the world would've noticed it, but Zoey saw. Dante's face relaxed. His shoulders lost their tense hunch, his fingers flexed on the wheel, and he almost—almost—smiled.

Zoey felt her own lips curve as she buried her nose in Pete's baby neck.

Chapter Forty-six

Saturday, 2:03 p.m.

The snow was getting worse.

Zoey chewed on her lip, staring out the windshield. The sun was totally obscured behind the storm clouds. Dante had slowed the car again, so that they seemed to crawl through a wall of white fluff that came out of the cold gray and swirled away again as they passed. On either side of the road the Shawnee National Forest rose up, silent and dense. Even at the slower speed, Dante was still having trouble. Every now and again, the car would slide with a stomach-dropping lurch and he would silently and grimly wrestle it back into the middle of the road.

They hadn't spoken in forty-five minutes. Zoey didn't want to break his concentration, didn't want to voice any doubt in his ability to get them all to safety. But if the car got stuck and he couldn't get it going again . . . If he couldn't find the house he said his friend had . . . She swallowed. It was so cold out.

They hadn't passed another car in the last two hours. They'd stopped briefly by the side of the road an hour back so that she could hook up the car seat and strap in Pete. Even then, as she'd struggled for ten minutes, no one had come by.

They were in the middle of nowhere.

The back end of the car spun, fishtailing across the road. Zoey grabbed for her armrest as they swerved. Dante's lips were peeled back in a grimace as he fought the car. There was a thud as Zoey's side of the car hit a snowbank.

Everything was still again. White flakes silently fell outside. Dante drew a breath and peeled his hands off the wheel to set the brake. "Are you okay?"

Zoey stared back at him. His cheeks and chin were dark from stubble and he had bags under his eyes, but he looked more attractive to her than he had two days ago. Which didn't make any sense.

"Zoey, are you okay?"

"Yes. Yes, I'm fine."

Pete let out a sob from the back seat.

"Shoot, I hoped she'd stay asleep," Zoey muttered. She reached back to pat the baby. "It's okay, sweetie. It's okay."

Pete's lower lip puckered and trembled, and she had two big, fat tears in her eyes. She sobbed, her little hands reaching for Zoey.

"Dammit," Dante muttered.

At first Zoey thought he was mad because the baby had woken up. But he got out of the car, opened the back-seat door, and released the baby. Pete sobbed harder. Zoey waited for Dante to lose his temper—not many men could handle a crying baby.

"Yeah, I know. I'm not the one you want," he said wryly over the baby's wails. He picked Pete up and pulled her pink hoodie over her head before getting back in the front seat with her. "Here."

Pete grinned, showing a row of tiny teeth, and bounced in Dante's hands.

Zoey took the baby, holding her close. "Thank you."

Pete bounced on her lap for maybe two seconds and then made a determined lunge for the dash.

"Whoa, sweetie!" Zoey caught her before she could fall on the floor of the car headfirst.

Pete didn't take kindly to being saved. She let out an angry scream.

Zoey looked at Dante apologetically. "She's tired of being in the car."

"Yeah, I know," he muttered. "So am I." He reached over and popped the glove compartment, rummaging for a moment. Pete followed his hand with her eyes, even though her mouth was still wide open on a cry. He grunted and came back up with a small, colorful plastic packet. "Here."

Zoey took the packet. Inside the clear plastic, jewel-colored candies were stuck together in a clump. "Gummi Bears?"

He shrugged. "Last time I was home I got corralled into taking my sister and nephew to a park."

Zoey's eyes widened. "You let your sister put her child in *this* car?"

"Hey." He looked defensive. "I'm not that bad."

"Yes," Zoey muttered under her breath. "You are."

But she was only hassling him. The truth was, she was pretty impressed with how well he was taking a screaming baby. Ricky had a tendency to run from the room when his daughter started crying. Not that Ricky was on anyone's top-ten-fathers-of-the-year list, but still.

She was impressed.

Zoey tore open the little packet and pried an orange Gummi Bear from its fellows. Normally she'd cringe at the thought of feeding pure sugar to a baby, but in an emergency . . .

Zoey would've taken an oath that Pete had never seen a Gummi Bear before in her short little life, but the baby sure knew what to do with the candy. She grabbed the treat and stuck both fist and sweet into her mouth.

"I think she likes that," Dante said.

"Colored sugar? Ya think?" But Zoey smiled at him and kissed Pete's sticky cheek.

Dante quirked an eyebrow at her before shoving down the hand brake. He put the BMW into reverse and looked over his shoulder as he backed out of the snowbank.

Except that instead of backing, the car lurched and then whined as the wheels spun on snow.

Dante muttered something and put the car into second gear. He eased down on the accelerator, but the car didn't move at all this time.

He closed his eyes. "Wonderful."

"We're stuck?" Zoey asked, a really stupid question under the circumstances.

Dante must've thought so, too. He grunted and opened the car door, letting in a whirl of snow. "Stay here."

Then he shut the door behind him.

"He'll get us out," Zoey whispered into Pete's hair.

She gently patted the baby's padded bottom until Pete wriggled again. The only place the baby could sit was on Dante's seat, so Zoey placed her there. The car rocked as Dante slammed the car trunk. Pete leaned forward determinedly until she could place her palms flat on the seat. She grinned at Zoey in triumph, the dissolving Gummi Bear sticking out of a corner of her mouth like a stogie.

"Aren't you brilliant?" Zoey said.

Pete chortled and walked her baby hands forward until she could grasp the bottom of the steering wheel. Zoey winced. Dante's seat and wheel were going to be covered in sticky baby fingerprints when he came back. On the other hand, Pete wasn't crying anymore. The baby levered herself up on the steering wheel until she could stand.

"Ya!" she cried. "Yayayaya!" Each *ya* was accompanied by a bounce, her bottom sticking out on the bend.

Dante opened the door. Pete turned in his direction, and for a moment man and baby contemplated each other.

"I believe that's my seat," Dante said.

"Come here, Pete." Zoey picked her up, and when the baby got that uncertain look that meant she was thinking about crying, she gave her a red Gummi Bear. Nikki would have a cow if she found out about this.

Dante by this time was behind the wheel. He put the car into reverse and eased down on the accelerator. The wheels spun.

"Dammit." He sighed and looked at her. "You're going to have to take the wheel while I push."

"Okay."

Zoey watched him get out of the car. She leaned over the back seat and strapped Pete into the car seat with her red Gummi Bear. Then she crawled over the console, swearing under her breath when she hit her thigh against the shift. Dante's side of the car was even colder than hers. The plastic bag over the window didn't seem like any barrier at all against the blizzard outside.

She settled behind the wheel and watched Dante plow through the snowdrift to the hood. He was spotlighted in the headlights, his head bare, his hair flattened by the wind. He braced his hands on the hood and nodded at her. Zoey shifted into reverse and pressed down on the accelerator. Dante leaned into the hood, his eyes narrowed against the driving snow. The car rocked. Zoey pressed just a little harder. The engine whined; the tires spun against snow. Dante hunched his shoulders, bent over the hood. Almost . . .

The car suddenly broke free of the snowbank, zooming backward. Zoey hurriedly tapped the brake. Dante ran to where the car sat. She set the brake and got out of the car.

"We did it!" she screamed into the blizzard.

Dante grinned and grabbed her shoulders. He kissed her, quick and hard, his lips cold. She gasped, her mouth opening beneath his, and for a moment she breathed him in, his strength, his masculinity.

Then he pulled his head back. "Get in the car."

Zoey nodded and ran around the front of the car. Her brain seemed to have frozen along with her bare fingers. From the back, Pete was making grumpy sounds. "Just a sec so I can settle her."

He nodded, not even looking at her. He was frowning at something on the dash.

Zoey leaned over the back seat to take a look at Pete. Okay, maybe he was one of those people who kissed casually. You know, like, hello (kiss), good-bye (kiss), it's

Wednesday (kiss.) Of course most people she knew who were casual serial kissers were women. Or gay. Dante wasn't gay.

Pete let out a howl of pure frustrated toddler fury. Zoey felt in her pocket and came up with the squished bag of Gummi Bears. She gave the entire thing to Pete, who crowed. She was going to Bad Aunt Hell. She showed Pete how to take out two Gummi Bears from her bag of candy, one for each hand. Pete let the bag drop, and Zoey pocketed it surreptitiously before she turned back around and put on her own seat belt.

Maybe Dante didn't mean anything by the kiss or, worse—she glanced at the front where he was peering under the steering wheel—maybe he regretted kissing her already. Oh, ouch.

"Okay, we're ready," she said to Dante. He didn't really regret kissing her, did he?

But he simply nodded and drove, leaving Zoey to stew in her own doubts.

Chapter Forty-seven

Saturday, 3:02 p.m.

$\mathcal{T}$he veteran FBI agent picked up his buzzing cell phone. The screen showed only a number—not a name—but he knew who the call was from.

He answered the phone with a demand. "What have you got?"

On the other end there was a burst of static and then clearly a man's voice saying, "—driving difficult. We're still picking up the signal, though."

"Don't stop, then," the FBI agent snarled. "I need him out of the picture."

"Yes, sir. Road conditions—" Static cut in and the line was lost.

Dammit. He tried redialing the number and got only an out of service message. He'd sent his best men down there.

They should've found Torelli by now and taken both him and the woman out. Why would—

The phone rang again.

He grabbed for it, pressing the answer button on the second buzz. "Yes?"

"He's headed into the Shawnee National Forest, sir."

The FBI agent frowned. "Why would he go there?"

"It doesn't matter," the voice replied. "The roads are tough and there's only a few ways out. We'll have him soon."

"Good." He felt tension ease in his shoulders. When this was done he was going to schedule a sauna and a massage at his health club. Stress could kill a man—just look at Charlie Hessler, lying in the ICU. "Make sure you do."

Chapter Forty-eight

Saturday, 3:13 p.m.

$\mathcal{K}$issing Zoey—*again*—had been a really stupid thing to do. Dante peered through the windshield at the nearly obscured road and was careful not to look in Zoey's direction. The snowstorm had come back with a vengeance, and he had to keep the windshield wipers on, the defrost blasting at full force to clear the windows. Outside it was pure white. He could see only twenty feet or so in front of the car, and not even that at times.

God only knew what Zoey was thinking right now. She could be contemplating marriage or she might think he wanted to jump her. Which, yeah, okay, he *did* want to jump her, but not in a pressuring way and certainly not at the moment. Too much was going on, and only a horny bastard would be thinking of sex right now and wondering if she'd go for it if he did make a move.

But he wasn't thinking of sex. Right.

Dante blew out a breath. Maybe when this was all over, when they'd gotten Pete back and Tony the Rose was convicted and Dante somehow cleared his name of corruption and murder charges, maybe then he could ask Zoey out on a date. He could take her to a nice restaurant, Italian or French—

Vinyl screeched in his head. He couldn't picture Zoey enjoying a French restaurant. Actually what he pictured was Zoey making fun of the waiter with a fake French accent. He winced. Oookay, well, then, they could maybe take in a play or . . . good God, he had no idea where he'd take Zoey on a date. Christ, he was a loser.

"Where would you go on a first date?" he asked, confirming the loser label.

"The Field Museum," Zoey said without missing a beat.

"Yeah?"

She nodded decisively. "Definitely. You can talk about the exhibits, and if things get awkward and you realize that there's nothing to talk about because he's a nonverbal Neanderthal, you can still look at the stuff. Also, you can figure out lots about a guy by what he goes to see."

Dante felt his eyebrows draw together. "Like what?"

Zoey twisted in her seat so that she was facing him, one knee drawn up. "Okay, what's the first thing you see when you walk into the Field Museum?"

"Uh . . . actually, I've never been to the Field Museum." Or any other museum in Chicago, for that matter, although he didn't say that. Truth was, he'd been working like a dog for the last couple of months.

Zoey stared. "You haven't?"

Definite loser territory. "No."

She sighed heavily as if in sympathy for his total loser-ness. "Okay, you know what the Field Museum is, don't you?"

He started to nod, but she wasn't taking any chances this time.

"Like, this really cool natural history museum in a classical building with dryads or whatever all over the front. There are natural history exhibits, and a bug collection, and an Egyptian exhibit, and a life-size wigwam. Anyway, the first thing you see when you walk in is Sue the Tyrannosaurus rex, and this is a test."

"How?"

"Do you go look at Sue or not?" She paused, waiting for his answer.

Dante shrugged. "Sure. Why not?"

"Oh, you'd be surprised how many people book on past a Tyrannosaurus rex, standing right there, with its tiny little forelegs raised and its giant teeth snarling."

From the back, Pete said, "Gah!" as if in agreement.

Dante blinked. "Okay, then what?"

"So then you watch how the guy looks at the T. rex," Zoey said. "Does he walk around it? Does he read the explanation sign? Does he stand and stare?"

"Which is best?"

"Stand and stare. This shows that he's man enough to admit he's a little in awe of a creature that could've swallowed him whole a bamillion-zillion years ago."

"Huh." Dante squinted, trying to think if he'd've passed this test if he'd unknowingly been given it. Almost certainly no. "And then?"

"Then you have to decide where to go first."

He glanced at her, brows raised. She looked totally serious. Just how many guys had she given this test to, anyway?

"Like, do you go to see the Egyptian tomb or the gems and rocks or the American Indian displays or the scary stuffed animals—"

Scary stuffed animals?

"—or do you go deep into left field and try out the children's exhibits first?"

"What's in the children's exhibits?" he asked without thinking.

"Giant disgusting bugs," Zoey said promptly.

"Huh." Actually the giant disgusting bugs sounded kind of tempting.

"But there's also the exhibit on digging up fossils and one on how chocolate is made."

Dante nodded sagely, as if he were deeply contemplating the history of chocolate versus an Egyptian tomb.

Zoey gave a kind of wiggle in her seat. "So?"

"Bugs."

"Really?" Her eyes had gotten wide, like he'd done something wonderful. "I've never gone to the museum with anyone who picked the bugs first."

He glanced at her nervously. "Is that good or bad?"

"I don't know," she said thoughtfully. "It's hard to say. Either you've got hidden depths of childishness or you're just trying to impress me with your quirkiness."

He shot a look at her.

"Okay, so maybe you're not trying to impress me." She frowned for a second and then perked up. "Did you know they have an entire bug digestive tract you can walk into? It's totally gross."

"Sounds like a date," Dante said and then could've kicked himself.

But Zoey didn't seem fazed. "We should pack a lunch, though."

"We should?"

"Unless you like overpriced salads or overpriced McDonald's."

"Uh, no."

"I can bring a lunch."

"What would you bring?"

"Tofu sticks and soy milk," she said promptly. "Come on! What did you think? I can pack a perfectly nice lunch."

He felt his lips curving. "Yeah? Like what?"

"Oh, I don't know . . ." She stared out the dark windshield for a moment, thinking. "Do you like curried chicken salad?"

"Sure."

"I make it with golden raisins and celery. And pickles. I always think pickles make a picnic lunch." She narrowed her eyes at him. "Which do you like? Sweet or sour?"

"Both."

God, he was enjoying this. He should be worried about his life, his career that was spiraling down the toilet, and the fact that they were driving through a snowstorm with no shelter in sight. But for this moment in time he was content to listen to Zoey plan a hypothetical picnic lunch at the Field Museum.

"Okay, so both sweet and sour pickles." Zoey ticked her menu off on her fingers. "Curried chicken salad sandwiches, maybe some black olives, sweet red pepper and celery sticks—"

"More celery?"

"It's important to have vegetables," she said sternly. "And strawberries and chocolate for dessert."

"No cookies?"

She looked at him. "You're one of those."

"One of what?"

"Guys who like cookies."

He frowned. "Isn't that all guys?"

"No. On the other side of the spectrum is the Cheez Doodle guy."

"Ah. Then I'm definitely in the cookie camp."

"Okay, so I pack some cookies, as well." She looked at him. "Chocolate chip, I presume."

"Is there any other?"

"Evidently not." She heaved an exaggerated sigh. "Okay, so I'll make chocolate chip cookies the night before. How does that sound?"

"Perfect."

And it did. The idea of spending the day wandering the Field Museum with Zoey sounded really good. She'd make bizarre comments about the stuffed animals, drag him through all the children's exhibits, and tease him into buying her a souvenir from the gift shop. He'd follow her lovely swaying ass all day like some enchanted rube until she'd walked herself into near exhaustion. And full of chocolate chip cookies and pickles, she'd become unwary and maybe she'd invite him into her messy apartment—it was bound to be messy—and he'd move in on her, filling his hands with soft, plump woman curves, and the smell of vanilla, feeling a little guilty and a whole lot aroused. Then he'd ease her down on her couch or bed, it really didn't matter, and cover her softness, and open her sweet mouth beneath his, and then—

Shit!

Dante straightened, darting a guilty look at Zoey. God, it must be the lack of sleep. He didn't usually go off into erotic daydreams . . . well, no more than the average guy. And who got turned on by the Field Museum? It must be the proximity to her, the constant sound of her voice, and the scent of vanilla in her hair. Sometimes he found himself leaning closer, trying to make out if he really could smell vanilla or if it was just stuck in his brain.

"Oh, my God," Zoey murmured beside him, and he was so lost in his own obsessive thoughts that he nearly didn't hear her.

"What?"

Dante looked up and saw it, too. Thank God.

They'd found the cabin.

Chapter Forty-nine

Saturday, 4:16 p.m.

Neil stared at the blue bowl in front of him. The bowl contained what looked like soupy rice pudding, only it was a kind of light greenish-yellow color. The color reminded him of the yellow used on emergency vehicles. Neil tried to remember the last time he'd eaten rice pudding. It was probably sometime when he was a kid. He fucking hated rice pudding.

Neil looked up at the two old Indian ladies. They were all in the apartment at the back of the motel. It belonged to their nephew, a squirrelly guy who was out tending the motel counter. His wife was in the kitchen doing something with the stove, and his kids were all in front of the TV, watching cartoons.

Neil cleared his throat. "So, what d'you call this sh—uh, stuff again?"

The taller Indian lady beamed. "It is our Top Secret Very Special Kesar Kheer. Try it. You will like it."

The shorter Indian lady snorted. She sat across the table from Neil with Neil Junior in her lap. She was spooning the milky soup into his son's mouth, and Neil Junior was leaning forward to demand more. The baby obviously liked it, but then again, Neil had seen his son eat a worm once and like that, too.

"Yeah, well, I ought to get on the road soon," Neil said, but not very convincingly, since there was a blizzard raging outside at the moment.

The smaller Indian lady must've thought so, too. She scowled at him. "You cannot take this child into a snowstorm. Even a criminal such as yourself must see this is so."

"Listen, you—" Neil started, and the kids and the woman in the kitchen all looked around. Even Neil Junior frowned at him, a smudge of milk on his cheek. Neil felt his face go hot.

The taller lady started talking fast. "This is our very best dish, our top-secret Very Special Kesar Kheer. It will be the centerpiece of our restaurant. It will bring people from all over Chicago to come and eat at our restaurant."

"The restaurant you vandalized," the shorter lady snarled.

The taller lady shot the shorter one a look and she shut her mouth abruptly.

"Try it," said the taller lady.

And figuring that he couldn't stall anymore and since there really was a fucking snowstorm howling outside, Neil sighed and spooned up greeny-yellow rice pudding.

It entered his mouth and he froze. He tasted something wonderful. Something high and sweet that made him think of hot, sunny summer days as a boy and the first time he'd hit Billy Johnson and broken his nose.

Neil opened his mouth in wonder. "This is good!"

Chapter Fifty

*I*n the end, Dante had to break a window to get into the cabin.

Zoey sat, trying to control her shivers, and watched as he built a fire in the huge fieldstone fireplace. His friend's cabin was lovely. She'd been expecting a little shack on a lake, the kind with an ancient screened-in porch and maybe a ceiling fan to combat the heat in summer. Instead, the "cabin" was worthy of a home in the Alps. The walls were some kind of hardwood, polished to a high shine. They were in a huge great room that took up most of the first floor. The central ceiling was vaulted, with an overhanging upper master bedroom. Lush multicolored rugs decorated the weathered tile floor, and the brown and red sofas where she sat in front of the fireplace were huge and comfy. Apparently they were close to the Ohio

River, too, although she hadn't been able to see it with the snowstorm.

It was a perfect place for a relaxing vacation if only there was a speck of heat. Because right now the inside was only a little warmer than the blizzard raging outside the building. Zoey shuddered and cuddled a sleeping Pete closer.

Dante must've seen her shiver, even though she'd tried to hide it.

He looked up, frowning. "I've got the furnace going, but it may be a couple of hours before it's able to heat up this space."

He glanced at the cavernous ceiling overhead.

Zoey nodded, clenching her teeth to keep them from chattering. "What about the water heater?"

"It's lit, but again, it'll take a couple of hours for the tank to get hot." He bent over the wood piled in the fireplace, carefully stacking pinecones against the bigger pieces.

"At least we have a furnace and a water heater," Zoey said as she watched him. "I'm so glad you found this place."

She didn't want to sound ungrateful. Shelter of any kind was far superior to having to spend a night in the car. She shuddered. Every now and again, there'd be an article in the newspaper about some poor soul dying because their car had gotten stuck in a blizzard. It seemed to happen less often with the advent of cell phones, but even when the highway patrol knew about someone stuck on the road, they still had to get to them. Zoey glanced at the dark picture window, half covered with snow, frozen on the glass. The roads were pretty much impassable at the

moment. It occurred to her that even though she'd been
unable to put her trust in Dante, he'd come through for her
anyway. He'd found shelter and warmth for her and Pete
when they needed it most.

"There we go," Dante muttered.

Zoey looked over. There was a tiny flame flickering
against the bigger logs. As she watched, the pile of pinecones caught and the fire leapt up. Dante crouched on
his heels in front of the fireplace, watching the fire, his
black leather trench coat pooled around his feet. One arm
leaned against a knee. His hair was a little matted and his
shoulders slumped with fatigue, but the firelight glowing
on his face cast his eyes into shadows, brought the planes
of his face into elegant relief. Zoey looked away, aware
that her breath had caught from the sheer impact of his
masculinity. Dear God, he was sexy.

"I think that'll do," he said now. He rose and replaced
a box of matches on the long fieldstone fireplace mantel.
Then he stretched, completely oblivious to her arousal.

Or maybe not. His eyes caught hers and he stilled for
a moment, his arms raised behind his head. Something
seemed to flare in their bitter-chocolate depths. But perhaps it was the reflection of the flames.

He cleared his throat and looked away. "I'm going to
have a look at the stores. Tom might've left some canned
food."

He turned on his heel and walked into the kitchen
area—open like the rest of the house. There was a big
stainless-steel refrigerator, the door propped open to keep
it fresh while not in use. Beside it, the huge stove was
also stainless steel—and a little intimidating, to tell the
truth. A long black granite countertop divided the kitchen

area from the great room. Several stools stood under the counter, so that it could double as a breakfast bar. To one side of the kitchen was a door with what must be a walk-in pantry. Dante disappeared inside.

Zoey sighed and rested her cheek on Pete's soft curls. She'd just about kill for a bath right now. She'd taken a shower last night, but that had been two gunfights and a chase before. She eyed the fire. Maybe if they set a kettle on top of the coals . . .

Dante reappeared with a can in each hand. "We've got a choice. Chicken noodle soup or baked beans."

"Oh, soup, definitely." If he could be cool about all the sexual tension flying through the air, so could she.

Of course, that was assuming he even felt any sexual tension. Wouldn't that just be a bummer? If all the heat was on her side? He'd think she was some kind of desperate single chick if he knew. Just the impression she wanted to make.

Some of her thoughts must've shown on her face.

His head reared back. "You sure?"

"Yep," she chirped like a lunatic chipmunk.

"Uh, okay." He started to say something else, but Pete twitched and woke up at that moment.

Zoey glanced down at the grimacing baby. "I really ought to change her. And she needs a bath. Can we heat a little water, do you think? Can you find a kettle or pot to put on the fire?"

"Sure. I'll get it." He began rummaging in the kitchen.

Pete let out a squawk.

"Come on, stinky." Zoey knelt on the rug in front of the fire and began unwrapping Pete. Even through the layers of clothes she could tell this was going to be a major diaper change.

Ten minutes later, Pete was naked and trying to get away.

"It's cold in the rest of the cabin, can't you tell that?" Zoey muttered as she grasped a leg.

"Gah!" Pete shouted.

"Here." A hand appeared over her shoulder with a big metal spoon. Pete immediately grabbed for it. "I've got some water heated on the fire."

"Thanks," Zoey panted.

She snatched up Pete, spoon and all, and plopped her in a huge soup pot placed on the floor beside the fire. Dante poured a little warm water into the pot. Pete immediately hit the water with her spoon, splashing it all over the place.

"Hey," Zoey muttered and wiped water out of her eye.

Pete giggled.

"Can you hand me the dish soap?" she asked Dante.

He gave her the blue bottle. "Aren't you supposed to use baby soap on babies?"

"Yeah," Zoey grunted, soaping a wiggling arm. "But I think in this case, filth wins out over delicate skin."

"But what if it gets in her eyes?" Dante persisted. Who knew a man could be so concerned over a baby's bath?

"I won't let it get in her eyes."

An epic struggle later, and Pete was cruising a brown and red sofa, one hand holding on for balance, one hand still clutching her spoon. She wore a diaper and a white adult T-shirt Dante had found. The T-shirt was down to her toes and she looked like a little angel in a robe.

"She looks adorable," Dante said. He sounded perplexed.

"Yeah, adorable." Zoey pulled her soaked sweatshirt away from her chest. "It's either perfectly adorable or child of Satan. There's no in between."

She shivered. Pete seemed to be oblivious to the chill that hung in the rest of the room, starting only feet from the fire, but Zoey wasn't. Especially with her sweatshirt now sopping wet.

"God, I wish I could take a bath, too," she muttered.

"Why don't you?" Dante asked. "Pete and me can try out the chicken noodle soup. The fire should've warmed it by now." He gestured to the small pot sitting on the edge of the coals.

She glanced at him. "I think I might freeze."

"Ah." He looked at the fireplace and then Pete. "Well, ah, we—I—can turn my back. You can stay in front of the fire. Really, it's okay. The baby will keep me occupied."

"Well . . ."

"I think I saw some clothes in the upstairs bedroom. Let me get you something." And he dashed up the stairs before she could say anything.

Zoey looked at Pete.

Pete grinned and blew a spit bubble.

If only the rest of the house was as warm as it was by the fire. But the heat had hardly made a dent in the bone-deep chill of the room, and the only hot water was what they heated over the fire. She'd have to take a sponge bath with the kettle of water if she wanted to get clean.

Dante came back down the stairs with a bundle of clothes in his arms. "See if any of this will fit."

Zoey picked out a red cotton T-shirt, a Nordic cardigan, and a pair of silk long john bottoms. "If you're sure."

"Sure I'm sure," Dante said. He was watching Pete and didn't seem to be worried about Zoey at all.

"Okay." Zoey turned to the fireplace and pulled her damp sweatshirt over her head.

Chapter Fifty-one

So, apparently he was trying to nominate himself for the Martyr of the Year award.

Dante sat on the floor facing the couch. He watched Pete sidestep down the couch. He watched the baby, but his entire attention—his entire focus—was on the small, quiet sounds going on behind him. The rustle of cloth against skin. The sigh as she drew something over her head. The sounds of Zoey undressing.

The baby sidestepped over to him, grinning, and he held out a spoonful of noodles. "Want some soup, kid?"

She gurgled and snatched a chubby fistful of noodles, which she then smashed into her mouth. The baby moved away from him along the couch, chanting, "Mm. Mm. Mm." as she went.

"Guess she likes soup," Zoey said from behind him.

"Sure looks like it." Could he be any more lame? "There's some more in the pantry. I'll heat up another can when you're done."

"Thanks. Hot soup would be wonderful."

"Too bad we can't make grilled cheese sandwiches, too."

"Ooo! With tomatoes? That would make it perfect."

She gasped a little and he heard a splash. Was she washing her face? Smoothing the cloth over her shoulders? Soaping her bare breasts? And could he just keep his mind from conjuring up the images?

He cleared his throat. "Is the water warm enough?"

"Yep." A sigh. "It's warm, but not hot, if you know what I mean."

"Oh, God, I wish," Dante said.

"What?"

"Nothing." He scooped up some broth and a piece of chicken for Pete, who had cruised near again. The baby opened her mouth wide like a baby bird and then chomped down on the spoon. She grinned up at him, a dribble of soup at the corner of her mouth. He dabbed at it with the spoon.

"You're good with her," Zoey said.

"Thanks."

"I thought you said you didn't spend much time with your nephews and nieces."

"I don't." He stared down into the cooling pot of chicken noodle soup.

"Then you must be a natural with kids."

"I guess."

"I don't think Ricky knows what to do with her. He gets impatient that she doesn't have a real long attention span at the moment. He'll try to tickle her right before bedtime and get her all worked up. It's like he doesn't know how to play with her."

"There are a lot of guys who aren't too sure what to do with a kid." Jesus, he wasn't defending Ricky Spinoza, was he?

"Actually most of the time he just ignores her."

He frowned. What kind of an asshole ignored his own kid? He wasn't too sure what to do with a kid himself, but if he fathered a child, he damn well would learn. "What does your sister see in him, anyway?"

She sighed. "I don't know. Nikki has always been a magnet for guys who aren't good for her."

"Yeah?"

"She used to run around with the biggest losers when Mom was taking care of her."

"What about you? Were you wild as a teenager?"

Behind him he could hear the sound of trickling water as she squeezed the washcloth over the kettle. He stared up at the ceiling. There was a stain around the fan, indicating water damage. Probably a leak from the roof. He'd only been in the cabin once before—a guys' boating weekend two years before. He hadn't noticed the water damage at that time, but then again, he hadn't spent a whole lot of time gazing at the ceiling, trying not to hear the sounds of a beautiful naked woman taking a sponge bath right behind him.

Not that trying not to hear was working out all that well.

"Not really. I guess I kind of felt that Nikki had the wild-child act covered for both of us. Mostly I went out with artsy guys or the computer geeks at school."

"So you had to be the good girl."

"I wouldn't say that." Clothes rustled behind him.

"Really? You sure spend a lot of time taking care of your sister now."

"But—"

"And what about your mom after she divorced? You said you were angry, but it sounds like you didn't act out. What did you do, repress all your anger?"

"Now, wait—"

"Or did Nikki end up being the surrogate for the anger you felt?"

"What are you, a shrink?" The words sounded like a joke, but her voice was stiff.

Way to turn off the lady, Torelli.

Pete sat suddenly, her diapered bottom thumping against the floor. She abandoned her spoon and scurried on all fours toward Zoey.

"Hey." Dante instinctively followed her with his eyes, only remembering just in time not to look behind him.

"What're you doing, you little imp?" he heard Zoey ask. He could almost make out her shape on the edge of his vision. He swallowed.

"No, that's my water." A splash. "Can you hold her?"

"Uh . . ."

"It's okay, you can look."

He looked.

Actually it was both okay and not okay. On her lower half, Zoey wore panties. On her upper half she wore the wiggling baby. Between her and the baby was a T-shirt, but as far as Dante could tell, Zoey wasn't wearing it. The thin cloth was held in place by Pete's little body. With every squirm, the baby threatened to dislodge the T-shirt.

Squirm, baby, squirm! Oh, he was going to hell for his thoughts.

"Uh, let me take her." Dante reached for Pete, but she evidently didn't want to move. She started kicking, nearly propelled herself from Zoey's arms. When Dante did get a grip on her, the back of his fingers were pressed against soft feminine flesh.

"Thanks."

Zoey wasn't looking at him. She had the T-shirt pressed against her chest like one of the more modest goddesses in a Renaissance painting. He could see the side of her breast, the part that curved just under her arm, and the sight made him aware that he was fully—painfully—hard.

Dante blew out a breath. "No problem."

He took the child and stood. When Pete started to whine he swung her in a wide circle that took them both across the room. The baby squealed with joy. Dante felt the pull of his injured leg, but he ignored it.

"Like that, do you?" he muttered to the little girl. He swung her up again. Anything to get his mind off the half-naked woman across the room.

"Don't let her get cold," Zoey warned.

"I won't." Dante still wore his black leather trench coat. He tucked the baby into it now and tied the front so that her head stuck out the top like a little papoose. He walked to the window with her.

It was dark outside already.

"Too bad we can't see the stars," he whispered to the small face.

The wind moaned outside as it battered snow against the window. A crust was frozen to the glass in an arc at the bottom. Trees seemed to be blowing across the field that surrounded the house, but it was hard to tell in the blackness.

"It's cold and stormy outside, but we're safe and warm in here," he murmured to Pete.

The baby sighed and laid her head against his chest. Dante paced slowly in front of the windows, careful to always keep his back to the fireplace and Zoey. He should've been bone tired, but every cell of his body was on the alert, attuned to the woman across the room.

"How is she?" Zoey asked quietly.

He turned.

She half lounged on one hip in front of the fireplace in an unconsciously classical pose, holding out long strands of hair to the warmth of the fire. Her hair was drying in red-blond corkscrew curls. Titian. That was what the color of her hair was called. After the Renaissance painter.

It was an old-fashioned color, not much favored by twenty-first-century style. When women deliberately chose a color for their hair nowadays, they went for white blond or deep red or stark black. Not soft, glowing orange, a color that picked up the firelight and seemed to throw it back. And of course her skin was that translucent white that only seemed to exist in paintings anymore. She wasn't even wearing the sweatshirt he'd found for her; instead she had a towel wrapped around her upper half, her white shoulders gleaming in the firelight. She was a siren sent from some distant past to tempt a mostly modern man. If she—

"Dante?"

He tore his gaze from her and glanced down at the baby. She was drooling on his shirt. "She's asleep."

"Oh, I'm—"

"It's too cold in the rest of the house still." He strode to the fireplace and gently laid Pete on the couch. He took off his trench coat and dropped it on the couch beside the baby to keep her from rolling off. "I'm going to get some pillows and blankets and bring them down here."

"Well, that's—"

He turned his back and fled into the cold upper story of the house. But even as he did so, he knew.

He was going to have to return and face Zoey.

Chapter Fifty-two

Saturday, 6:54 p.m.

Zoey sighed and turned to the fireplace. Dante had seemed okay earlier in the evening, but now he was being curt with her. Maybe it was just fatigue. Maybe she was just imagining the whole thing, but she didn't think so.

Pete made a sound and turned on the couch cushions, and Zoey leaned over to check on her. She didn't want the baby to roll off the couch. When Dante returned, maybe they could make a bed for Pete on the floor and—

"Why haven't you put on that sweatshirt?" Dante's harsh tones made her start.

Zoey looked up. He was standing over her like a censoring father, his arms full of bedding.

The image had all sorts of bad connotations for her, but she cleared her throat before she spoke to keep her voice calm. "I didn't want to get the shirt wet while my hair dried."

He tossed the bedding on the floor, nearly hitting her feet. "It's dry enough now, isn't it?"

"Almost, it should—"

"Then put on a shirt, for chrissake." He stalked off without waiting for an answer.

Zoey jumped to her feet and viciously jerked some pillows and a blanket into a little bed for Pete on the floor.

When Dante stomped back into the room, she was pulling blankets into a bed for herself on the floor several feet from Pete. Except Dante didn't really stomp—he made no noise when he walked—but the emotion behind his walk sure was a stomp.

"What are you doing?" he demanded.

He dumped his new load of bedding right on top of the pallet she'd been making.

Zoey straightened slowly. "I was making a bed for myself."

"We're sleeping together," he said flatly.

"What?"

"You heard me." He thrust aside the pile of bedding, including her little pallet and unzipped a sleeping bag. "I'm not letting you out of my sight again. You took off last time I did that. We're sleeping together."

"First of all, I am not sleeping with you—"

"You never struck me as a prude," he shot back.

He shrugged out of his gun holster and placed it on the fireplace mantel. Then he squatted to spread the open sleeping bag on the big rug in front of the fire.

"And secondly, you don't have the right to talk to me like that!"

It was his turn to straighten slowly, and when Zoey saw his face she almost took a step back.

"I don't have the *right?*" he asked softly.

"No." She stood her ground, feeling her own anger begin to crest her levee. "I'm not some stupid piece of ass you've picked up for the night. I'm—"

"You're the woman who's been using me for the last three days."

"I didn't use—"

He stepped into her personal space, so close his chest nearly brushed the towel covering her breasts. "You lied to me. Abandoned me in that rest stop—"

"I was trying to protect my niece!"

"And took off without a backward glance," he ground out.

In any other circumstances, his nearness to her would mean that he was going to kiss her, but Zoey wasn't about to mistake the anger in his face for lust. She felt a twinge of guilt. She had lied to him. She had used him. But there had been extenuating circumstances.

"Listen," she tried in a lower tone. "I'm sorry I hurt your feelings, but my loyalty to my sister, to Pete, superseded anything I owed to a guy I hardly knew."

"Hardly knew?" His head reared back.

Zoey winced. Poor choice of words. "I thought we were over all this. You seemed to understand my reasons just this afternoon."

"Yeah, but then apparently I'm nearly a stranger to you."

Zoey inhaled slowly. Someone had to keep their temper in this discussion. "I didn't know you when I got into your car. That's what I meant. Now—"

"Now you think you know me?"

"I-I don't . . ." She took a breath. "Yes. Yes, I know you."

He actually laughed, and it sure wasn't a sweet little chuckle. This was more in the line of an evil cackle. "You don't know me at all."

"I—"

He ripped his sweatshirt off over his head.

For a moment Zoey was stunned by his bare chest. He was muscled, his skin smooth and dark, with only a thin patch of black, curling hair between his pectorals. She was nearly overcome by an urge to lean forward and lick a dark, tight nipple. Her eyes snapped up, shocked.

Just in time to see him shove his face into hers. "You lie to me, you don't trust me, and now you're parading around in a towel like I'm some sort of neutered—"

"I told you, I didn't want to get my shirt wet. And it's not as if I'm acting like a slut—"

"No, you're acting like a woman who wants to be fucked."

"Oh!" She narrowed her eyes to slits. "That is so typical of a guy—"

He snorted.

"Like I'd be coming on to you in the middle of a god-damned blizzard!"

"If you're not coming on to me in a goddamned bliz-zard, then why're you prancing around half-naked?"

"I'm not prancing around," she ground out, "and I'm not half-naked, and for future reference, if I were going to come on to you, I'd be a whole lot more obvious."

"Oh, yeah?"

"Yeah!"

"And what's more obvious than this?" He hooked his finger in the top of her towel and flicked it contemptuously.

"This!" And she flung the towel to the floor.

His eyes dropped to her naked breasts.

Her nipples tightened in the cold air. *Wait.* Okay, maybe her last action was just a little hasty. Zoey started to raise her arms to cover herself, but he caught her wrists.

"Don't."

Suddenly the cabin was very, very quiet. She could hear the fire snap, she could hear the wind blowing outside, she could hear Pete's gentle breathing.

And none of it mattered.

At the moment the only thing that mattered in the entire world was Dante's dark eyes, drinking in the sight of her naked breasts.

"Dante," she whispered.

He didn't look up. "You have the most beautiful skin I've ever seen. It's almost incandescent."

"I don't—"

His eyes flicked to hers, and she saw that his expression hadn't softened. If anything it had become harder, more intent. He looked like a predator sighting prey.

"Hush," he said low. "You set the rules, you made the move. You can't back away now."

She hadn't known she was making rules, at least not consciously. How had she gotten here? She wasn't sure she was ready for this. If they could just slow down . . .

She opened her mouth to say just that, but he murmured, "Hush," again.

And then he lowered his head to her breast.

She gasped. He tongued her nipple before he sucked it

into his mouth, shockingly hot after the chill of the cabin air. Oh, God. Maybe she should just stop thinking altogether. He sucked strongly on her nipple, and if he hadn't been holding her by her wrists still, she might've staggered. The shock streaked right down her belly, almost painful in its intensity, to land at her most vulnerable point. She contracted internally, nearly groaning.

And then he licked across her chest to her other breast and she did groan aloud. His tongue was so hot, his fingers so hard. He took that nipple into his mouth and sucked again, and she felt herself melt at her center.

He pulled away to stare at her and she looked down. Her nipples stood out, red and shining with his saliva, and the sight was incredibly sexy.

Incredibly erotic.

Dante obviously thought so, too. "You're beautiful," he said, and his voice was a deep growl, so removed from his usually cultured tones that it was shocking. "Lie down on the sleeping bag."

She blinked and sat, feeling dazed. This was surreal—it couldn't be happening.

He stood over her and toed off his shoes, stripped off his socks, and hooked his thumbs into the sweatpants he wore to skim them down over his hips. He straightened and looked at her. He hadn't worn the tighty-whities she'd gotten him at the Kmart so long ago, it seemed. He was naked under the sweatpants, and his cock was red and erect and obviously meant for her. She stared, taking in the elegant, narrow line of hair that arrowed down from his navel, his black, curling pubic hair, and his penis, long and hard, glistening just a bit at the blunt head. She swallowed and didn't know if she was breathing anymore.

"Take off the long johns."

He waited, poised, until she obeyed, then he bent and reached for the pocket of his trench coat.

Zoey watched, terribly conscious that she lay before him naked. Her skin felt oversensitive, like she was new-born, without defenses or shell. He ripped open the condom packet he'd taken from his pocket and unrolled it over his penis. She felt her eyelids drift lower as she watched him handle himself, felt the moisture between her legs. She shifted, deliberately opening her thighs, posing for him.

He looked up and said almost casually, "I may not be able to last long the first time. But I'll make sure you come."

She swallowed. She'd never heard a man so self-assured, so certain that he could give her an orgasm. In any other circumstances she might laugh at his arrogance, but right now . . . Right now she believed him.

He knelt between her legs and looked at her without touching. His gaze moved from her knees, up over thighs, to her center. She knew she was wet with moisture for him. His gaze lingered there and his nostrils flared before he continued up over her belly to her breasts and then her face.

"Open your legs more."

She swallowed. Without clothes, he could've been from a different time, a different place. His face was dark, his cheeks flushed high up under his eyes. His arms had beautiful biceps, his shoulders broad and delineated with lean muscle. His thighs were covered in curling black hair, and where they touched her thighs, the contrast in their skin tones was stark.

She looked at his face again and his eyes held hers, demanding, almost desperate. It was this last that made her spread her legs apart further, until the tendons in her thighs ached. He might be the conqueror, the one issuing orders, but her very submission compelled him. She was just as much in control as he.

He leaned forward, bracing one hand on the sleeping bag near her shoulder. With the other he held his cock, and she felt it nudge against her slippery folds. His eyes looked into hers, and he thrust. Deeply. Strongly. Completely into her. His pubic bone settled against hers and he filled her to the brim.

She gasped. It was so intimate, so real, and so sudden. He hadn't wasted time on preliminaries, and she wasn't sure she was prepared. At least mentally. Physically she was more than ready.

He watched her face as he shifted, settling his hips more fully on hers. Both of his forearms were braced on either side of her now, his upper body held barely off of hers.

He raised his eyebrows, his face entirely serious, maybe a little cruel, and he unconsciously repeated her thoughts. "Ready?"

She gulped and ran her fingertips along his ribs, wrapped her legs around his hips. "Yes."

He nodded, his teeth gritted, no longer capable of speech, it seemed.

And then he hammered into her. His body moved fast, his cock sliding in and out in a desperate pace, and she gasped. Holding on, trying to keep up, unable to control the sensations washing over her body. His hips thrust against hers, hitting her hard, giving her no time to assimilate the feeling.

"Dante," she gasped.

He hung over her like a dark god, his eyes intense, his mouth grim. A bead of sweat ran down his temple, and he grunted on each thrust, his breath fast and hard as he labored.

"Dante." She couldn't stop it, couldn't restrain herself. It was too late. Everything was out of control.

So she set herself free. She hitched one leg up over his hip, almost to the small of his back, and made herself completely open to him.

Completely vulnerable.

His pubis rubbed roughly against her clitoris with each thrust, his penis invading and withdrawing again and again, until she no longer thought, no longer felt, she only flew. Higher, higher, until warmth spread from within her, growing in a cumulus cloud of pleasure, widening, overcoming, consuming everything in its path.

"Dante!" she cried, and somewhere close she heard his breathing catch.

She opened her eyes and watched as he shook, his head flinging back, his eyes blind.

And he came within her.

Chapter Fifty-three

Saturday, 7:37 p.m.

No one ever thought about the weather.

Rutgar grunted as the Mercedes-Benz SUV tried to spin off the road. The road was very difficult now. The plows still plowed, but the snow blew over the road within minutes of being cleared. And the plows could dump a mountain of salt and sand and it would not make a difference. Some things man couldn't control, and very bad weather was one of them.

So he was pleased to see the exit sign. Even with four-wheel drive, he did not want to stay on the road any longer tonight. It was good to reach his destination.

He had been lucky this morning. He had recognized the purple minivan with the big painted daisy. Neil had given the van's description to Tony the Rose. Tony the Rose had given the information to Rutgar. So when he saw the van, he'd known that it was connected to the Indian woman. How, he wasn't sure. He'd followed the purple minivan before confronting the driver. And this strategy had proven to be prudent. He'd seen the red-haired woman bring two babies into the motel. Later he'd watched as she came back to the purple minivan with only one baby. The dark-haired child, the Spinoza offspring.

Having to give up his prey at the rest stop had been frustrating. Very frustrating. For some time afterward, Rutgar had been gripped with a terrible rage that made it impossible to think. But when his anger had cleared, he'd seen that he already had a ready-made plan. He would go to the motel. The motel where the other baby had been left.

He didn't know who stayed at the motel, but he could guess. And even if he were wrong, it would make very little difference. The inhabitants would be made to tell him where the redheaded woman had gone.

Rutgar pulled off the road and killed the engine. He had planned for possible bad weather. In the back of the black SUV there was freeze-dried food, water, a kerosene stove, a winter camping tent, and the warmest down sleeping bag available. The catalog he'd bought it from said that the sleeping bag was the same one mountain climbers took up Mount Everest.

Not that he'd need it tonight.

Rutgar pulled on down mittens over his fingerless gloves, drew his hood tight, and climbed from the SUV. He waded through the drifting snow to the back of the truck and opened the tailgate. Inside was his gun box. He flipped it open and looked for a moment at his guns. They gleamed in the truck's overhead light.

Then he selected the Glock from the gray foam padding. He put one clip in his pocket and loaded the other in the gun. He put the silencer attachment in his pocket, as well. It was not good for aim, but if he was close, perhaps it made things easier. He put a double-edged army knife in his left pocket and slung the sniper's rifle over his shoulder. Then he closed the tailgate and looked at the building across the road. Only one room was lit. The natural place to start.

Rutgar smiled a small smile and loped across the road.

Chapter Fifty-four

Saturday, 7:42 p.m.

He slumped over her, his cock still buried deep inside her, and let her warmth seep into his bones. Maybe into his soul. The fire was hot on his left side, in contrast to the rest of his bare back, which was chill from the cabin air. He didn't care. Her breasts were soft, her hips were soft, her belly was soft. He could stay here forever.

"Is the baby still asleep?" she murmured.

She sounded sleepy. Satiated. He felt a grin stretch his lips. He'd done that to her, reduced her to mumbled syllables. She'd nearly screamed his name at her peak, and it was a sound he wasn't ever going to forget, no matter how long he lived.

"She's asleep," he whispered into the hair at her temple. It was slightly damp—with sweat, he was pretty sure, not her bath.

"That's good."

It must've been lemon-scented dish soap, because her hair seemed to smell of it. He nudged aside the tickly curls, burrowing his nose into her neck. She smelled of lemon and vanilla, and him. That brought another smile to his lips. He hoped she smelled of him all over.

"I came," she said now.

He raised his head high enough so that he could look into her bright blue eyes.

She was flushed, whether because of what she'd just said or because of their exertion before, he wasn't sure.

She cleared her throat. "You said you would make sure I came. I just wanted you to know that I did."

"I know."

"Oh."

She looked embarrassed, so he kissed her, and then realized that he hadn't even kissed her during their lovemaking. Well, he'd make up for it now.

Her mouth was warm and soft, and it opened easily beneath his. He took the invitation and ran with it, thrusting his tongue into her warmth, wanting to explore all of her. To inhale all of her. She moaned a little beneath his mouth, and he felt his cock twitch with renewed life. That reminded him of the condom. He licked around her lips one last time, then gingerly rolled off her.

"Cold," she whimpered and drew a blanket over herself.

"I know. I'll be right back."

The tiled floor was icy on the soles of his feet. He hurried across it, conscious that he wasn't at his sexiest, buck naked and shivering.

When he returned from the bathroom, Zoey was curled

on her side under a pile of blankets. He checked Pete—still
asleep in her little cocoon. She'd flung a pudgy arm over
her head, and he carefully tucked it beneath the blankets
again. Then he grabbed a couple more condoms out of his
overcoat pocket and dived beneath the covers with Zoey.

She squealed.

"Shhh." He glanced at Pete, who was fortunately still
asleep.

"You're cold," Zoey grumbled.

"And you're warm. Deliciously warm."

He pulled her soft heat into himself and curled his longer body around hers. She fit perfectly—round hips against
his groin, the soles of her feet pressed to his calves, and
her head just under his chin. He looped his arm over her
shoulder and palmed a warm breast. Perfect. How could
this woman, who seemed so totally different from everything he'd thought he'd wanted, be so perfect?

"So, have you been carrying condoms around in your
coat pocket all this time?" Zoey asked slowly.

He raised his head to peer at her. Her eyes were shut,
and her expression didn't look particularly concerned.

He let his head flop back. "No."

"Then . . . ?"

"Got them from Tom's bathroom cabinet earlier."

She snorted. "Good thing they were there."

He circled her nipple with his middle finger, feeling the
texture. "Oh, I think I could've figured something out if
we didn't have them."

"Humph." Her voice was muffled because she'd drawn
the covers up over her chin. "You sound pretty certain of
yourself."

He pinched her nipple between finger and thumb, and

her words ended on a gasp. His eyes closed. Desire crackled through his system, sudden like summer lightning. He
wished he could make a clever comeback right now. He
wished he was the kind of guy who could talk in bed,
say sexy things. But he wasn't. What he felt—especially
what he felt with Zoey—was too strong, too intense, too
intimate.

He pushed aside her hair and kissed the nape of her
neck, open mouthed. At the same time he trailed his hand
down her belly to press her back against his erection. She
probably wanted nothing more than to sleep right now, but
he couldn't help it. The urge was on him, strong and hard,
and he couldn't speak.

She twisted suddenly in his arms and pressed her wet
mouth to his. He was grateful, so grateful, that she was
responsive. He kissed her with urgent desperation, as if
he hadn't just come in her minutes before, and for a moment his own intensity startled him. Then she was pressing
her tongue into his mouth, and the thought was caught in
the whirlpool of his emotions and swept away. She bit his
lower lip. He couldn't think, couldn't speak, all he could
do was try to control the raging lust that shook his body.
Try not to frighten her with his own animal nature.

"Shhh," she murmured.

He felt her push him back, lay him flat, his bare arms
outstretched and helpless outside the covers.

"Shhh." She climbed on top of him, pressing her palms
into his chest. Her mouth was hot on his face, his throat.

"Shhh."

She'd found one of the condoms, and he watched as she
sheathed him, her beautiful breasts swaying as she leaned
over his groin, the touch of her fingers almost too much

to bear. She straightened and looked at him, her sky blue eyes fathomless and mysterious. Did she know? Did she know he was completely in her power? Helpless to deny her anything at this moment?

She must've sensed a little of that, for she smiled slowly, her mouth curving at one corner. Then she grasped his hard cock and placed it at her warm, sweet entrance. She pressed down.

He closed his eyes. He wanted to thank her, to tell her how grateful he was that she was allowing him in, letting him make love to her, but then she seated herself fully and the wonder of her tight softness enveloping his cock blasted all intelligent thought from his mind.

She leaned down, his own personal sex goddess, and licked his nipple.

He groaned.

She kissed his chest, tonguing her way to his throat, and every small movement was reflected in the hot, tight muscles that held him.

"Do you like that?" she whispered, and if he could talk he would've shouted *yes!* and then cursed her for a sadist. But since he couldn't speak, he merely groaned again.

"I think you do," she murmured into his ear.

She rocked gently against him, her breasts brushing his chest.

"It's all right," she said. "I'll take care of you."

He swallowed and thrust up at her. She gasped, and that made him almost smile. She wasn't as serene as she played.

She covered his mouth with her own, and he arched his head up to seize her lips. He thrust deeply inside of her as she ground her hips down on him. Her face was slanted, her mouth open, and he could hear her panting breath, feel the urgent movement of her body, sense the pounding of her heart. She took his face between her palms, holding him as she kissed him.

And he broke. He was going to come, was going to leave her behind, and he didn't want to. He ran his palms down her back until he reached her hips. One hand wrapped around her buttock, his fingers lodged firmly in her crease; the other hand he pressed into her pubic hair. He'd lost whatever skill he'd ever had, but he searched delicately, and he knew he'd found the right spot when she stilled and her kiss became distracted.

He held her then and fucked her hard. His tongue thrust into her mouth, his cock thrust into her pussy. Heaven played behind his closed eyes. And all the while he fingered her clit, never stopping, never letting up until she tore her mouth from his and moaned, low and shaking. He thrust one last time, twisting up, feeling her shudder above him, and then he was lost himself.

Lost as he poured his whole heart into Zoey.

Chapter Fifty-five

Zoey rested her head against Dante's chest, listening to the slow thump of his heart. The fire had died down a bit, but the room had warmed up in the last couple of hours. The heat must've finally kicked in. Beside them, Pete still slept on her little pallet. She didn't usually sleep all the way through the night, so Zoey figured it was only a matter of time before they had company. But right now, they were for all intents and purposes alone.

Alone together.

She watched as one of Dante's chest hairs wrapped itself around her index finger. "Did you dream last night?"

"No."

"Do you usually dream?"

"Sometimes."

"Do you remember your dreams?"

He exhaled. "What?"

His voice sounded sleepy. Exhausted.

The corner of her mouth curved up. She ought to let him rest. He had, after all, put in a full day.

But she didn't. "At night when you dream, do you remember?"

She felt him shift as he canted his head to look down at her. "Only the awful ones."

She tilted her own face to look up at him. "Awful ones? Like nightmares?"

He laid his head back down with a thump. "No, mostly bad memories. Ones that replay themselves in my mind over and over."

She tapped her finger against his chest. "Sounds like nightmares to me."

"Well, they don't involve purple monsters."

She watched her fingers trace his right nipple. "Do you dream about being shot?"

He stilled.

She didn't look up at him. "That's the scar from where you were shot, isn't it? The round one on your back."

He sighed. "Yeah, it is. But I don't usually dream about that."

"You don't?"

"It wasn't such a big deal."

Zoey thought about that for a moment. Getting shot sure sounded like a big deal to her. She didn't like to think about him hurt. Bleeding and wounded. In the hospital. Who had come to visit him during that time? Who had cared for him?

She pushed the thought aside and asked, "How long ago did it happen?"

"Six months."

She drew in her breath and raised herself onto an elbow. "You were shot only six months ago?"

He raised an eyebrow. "Yeah?"

"You could've died!"

"It wasn't—"

"If you had died six months ago I would've never have known you, Dante. We would never have met."

He stared at her, a little puzzled.

"Don't you get it? We would never have met!" And she punched him lightly on the shoulder.

"Ow." He pulled her down to his shoulder again. "But I didn't die, and we did meet. There's nothing to get upset about."

This was such a guy statement that Zoey had no words for a moment. "It would've been terrible if we'd never met."

He kissed her, slowly and thoroughly. "But we did."

She sighed. It had been a nice kiss. "What bad memories?"

"Huh?"

"You said you dreamed about bad memories sometimes."

"Oh. Cases that didn't go well. Bad guys that got away."

"Really? I wouldn't have thought any bad guy could get away from you."

He snorted. "You'd be surprised. Sometimes we know who did the crime but we have no evidence. Or sometimes we think we have a case locked up and the witness refuses to testify."

She let that comment lie. "I dream of flying."

She felt him look at her. "Like Superman? Or do you have wings?"

"No wings, but I'm not Superman." She thought a moment. "I just think really hard about flying, and then I do."

"Huh." He was silent a moment. "I always figured it would be harder than that."

"Really?" She twisted to look up at him. He was frowning like flying in your dreams was a deep problem. "How would you fly?"

He shrugged. "I don't know. But I think it would involve a lot of work and probably wings. Even Superman has a cape."

"Superman doesn't need his cape to fly."

"Yes, he does."

"No! Duh! His cape doesn't give him magical powers."

"Then why does he wear it?"

"Because it looks cool."

"Huh. So, you're saying that blue tights, a red Speedo, and a red cape are cool."

Zoey squinted. "I didn't say that—"

"You said the cape was cool."

"Ye-es, but I didn't mention the rest."

They were silent a moment, maybe contemplating red Speedos. Pete grunted and rolled over.

Dante cleared his throat. "So, you're saying if I wore a red cape and nothing else—?"

"Oh, yeah." No question there. Zoey closed her eyes, happily drawing the picture in her mind. In her picture, he was wearing the red boots, too, but she wasn't going to tell him that.

"Good to know," he murmured and yawned.

She yawned, too, in reaction. "And in my dreams, when I'm flying without a cape or wings?"

"Yeah?"

"I think I may be invisible, too."

His lips brushed her forehead. "Go to sleep."

Chapter Fifty-six

Sunday, 6:54 a.m.

The smell of vanilla-scented warmth was the first thing Dante was aware of when he came slowly awake the next morning. The fire had died to glowing embers and the room was mostly dark, the winter sun not yet up. He buried his nose into the delicate curve where Zoey's shoulder flowed into her neck, content just to lie still. Sometime during the night, Pete had woken and Zoey had taken the baby into their pallet. Now she lay with her arm curled around the baby, both breathing in soft unison. Dante watched them. His chest tightened almost painfully as he looked at Zoey's strawberries and cream skin. Pete's dark curls, lying against her arm, were in stark contrast. He realized all at once that if they had a child together she might have the same coloring as Pete. His dark skin and hair against—

Thud. Somewhere at the back of the house something

fell. Dante raised his head. It might be snow falling from the roof, or it might be—

A muffled crunch.

He rolled naked from the sleeping bag in one swift, adrenaline-induced surge. His holstered gun was on the mantelpiece, and he strode over to get it.

"Dante?" Zoey blinked sleepily from the pallet.

He drew the gun from the holster, its weight bringing a fierce calm. He looked at Zoey. "Take the baby upstairs and find a place to barricade yourself in. Don't come out until I tell you to."

She didn't argue, didn't say a word, merely scooped up Pete and ran to the stairs.

Zoey was three-fourths of the way up the stairs when the gunman rounded the corner from the pantry. The bastard was all in black, wearing night-vision goggles and carrying a fucking automatic. Dante squeezed off two rounds in the guy's direction before diving behind the sofa. The automatic weapon chattered to life, spraying the back of the couch. Dante cowered, flinching involuntarily from the stuttering shots, feeling a sting at his side.

If he stayed here it was only a matter of time before the shooter got lucky or his backup arrived or both. Dante didn't have much choice. He belly-crawled swiftly to the end of the sofa and made himself roll into the open. He'd gambled, but it paid off. The gunman was still focused on the other end of the couch, and in the split second it took him to adjust his sight, Dante popped him twice in the head. The gunman fell backward, his weapon inscribing an arc of bullet holes into the ceiling. Then it fell silent.

Dante lay still a second, waiting to see if another gunman would reveal himself. His breath was harsh in his ears, and his side burned.

No one appeared.

He levered himself from the floor and ran to the guy he'd hit. The gunman had been a blond man, his hair shaved militarily short. There was a bullet hole below one eye and a chunk of forehead missing. Definitely down. The dead man had an earpiece in one ear with an attached receiver. Dante knelt and took it out, holding it to his own ear. He heard the hiss of dead air, but nothing else. He tapped the receiver. Immediately, a single tap came back, confirming that there was at least one other attacker out there.

Dante glided to the window over the kitchen sink, the Glock held in both fists pointed at the floor. It was still dark, but the window was big and looked out over a field in back of the cabin. He waited, breathing in and out softly, straining to hear anything.

Nothing moved.

After a few minutes, he checked in the pantry and saw the broken pane in the single window, high on the wall. He shut the door to the pantry and shoved a chair beneath the doorknob. It wouldn't stop an intruder, but the sound of the chair falling would alert him if anyone else came in that way.

Next he went to the windows in the breakfast nook and paused, checking there. It wasn't until he went to the windows by the front door that he hit pay dirt. He could just make out a SUV parked near the road. The truck was big, but it didn't have the sharp corners of the Mercedes-Benz from yesterday.

They hadn't been able to get in the drive because of the snow. The drive was maybe fifty feet long, with a handful of tall evergreens lining one side, their branches and shadows merging into one black mass in the still-dark morning. The SUV was almost completely concealed beneath the branches of an evergreen near the end of the drive. Dante stared, his eyes straining to pierce the dark. A single shadow was moving toward the house rapidly, ducking from tree to tree. Dante inhaled and flattened himself to the side of the window, watching. To his right was the window, to his left the front door.

The second gunman made the front of the house and kept coming straight for the door. Dante dropped his gaze to the locked doorknob. It was a pretty brass thing but hardly effective. He watched, fascinated as the doorknob jiggled and something snapped. The door opened. The second gunman stepped inside. He wore camouflage and a bulletproof combat vest.

Dante laid his Glock against the side of the man's head. "Don't move."

The man whirled. Dante fired, but the guy didn't drop. *Shit.* Dante grabbed the barrel of the automatic the guy held and shoved it to the side, just as the intruder started squeezing off rounds. Gunshots blasted across the room.

Something shattered.

Then Dante yanked hard and pulled the automatic from the other man's grasp, throwing it across the room. The intruder spun, kicking him in his injured thigh. Shards of pain spun against Dante's vision. He fired the Glock again, but the shot went wide. The intruder slammed a fist against Dante's wrist and he dropped the gun. Then the other guy was on him, pummeling with gloved hands. Dante fell back, spinning against the wall near the door. If he went down, if the other guy won, there would be nothing between the assassin and Zoey. Zoey would be killed.

He couldn't lose.

He caught a swinging arm and drew the other guy toward him. Then they were both tumbling out the door and into the frosty early morning air. Dante hit the ground, his shoulders instantly numbed by the snow, and rolled. A fist slammed into the snow where he'd lain. Dante drew back his own fist and hit the guy hard in the neck. He was at an extreme disadvantage here, naked and weaponless against an armored assailant. Dante bunched his fist and hit again, but his blow glanced off the other man's shoulder as the gunman rolled.

The attacker elbowed him in the belly, and the air whooshed from Dante's lungs. All at once the attacker was on him, an arm under Dante's chin, pressing his whole weight down on Dante's windpipe. Dante gasped, grappling for the guy's face, his eyes, his nostrils, anything. But the man arched his head away and Dante's fingers slipped off. His back was ice-cold, burning from the snow. His ass was numb. He saw stars that weren't there.

He could not lose.

Dante reached for the guy's face with his left hand, at the same time punching him under the arm. The attacker grunted, but his hold didn't loosen. Dante's lungs were aching, dry and icy cold. His vision was going black around the edges. Dante slid his right hand along the other man's side, feeling, searching. He could hear himself making odd grunting noises. If it wasn't there, if he couldn't find it, he was screwed.

Zoey was screwed.

Then his fingers felt what he needed. Dante wrapped

his hand around the other man's knife and withdrew it from the vest's sheath. He brought it down hard into that vulnerable area just above the vest, put the strength of his arm into the blow, and drove the hunting knife into the other man's neck.

The attacker slumped against Dante, his body heavy and lifeless. Hot blood splattered against Dante's chest. He gasped, his throat aching as he inhaled. Then he pushed the other man off him and staggered upright.

Dante looked down. The snow was trampled where they'd fought, and droplets of scarlet blood, crystallized against the white, stood out clearly. His opponent was still, his eyes wide open and staring into nothing. Dante swallowed. The other man's eyes had been blue and he looked young. Maybe he had been young, but not anymore. Now he wasn't anything but dead.

Dante was suddenly conscious that his bare feet were burning. He limped to the house, his arm held against his aching side.

To the east, dawn was just beginning to light the sky.

Chapter Fifty-seven

Sunday, 7:40 a.m.

There hadn't been any gunshots for about fifteen minutes. At least she thought it was about fifteen minutes. Zoey glanced around the posh bathroom. No clocks.

She and Pete sat in an enormous Jacuzzi bathtub in the corner of the bathroom, the highest point of the cabin, as far as she could make out. The bathroom walls were redwood, the sink, toilet, and floor tiles a mottled stone color that probably cost a fortune. Behind her and Pete, the windows over the Jacuzzi soared into a vaulted ceiling. The windows faced east and were just brightening with day. It was probably the fanciest bathroom she'd ever been in, and she didn't want to die here.

Pete squirmed in her arms. The baby had waked with the first gunshot and had whimpered for a bit before quieting. Thank God. Zoey strained to listen in the silence.

She hoped, she really hoped, that the gunmen didn't get past Dante. Because if they did, all she had for defense was a toilet plunger. Probably the red rubber wouldn't stop bullets.

Pete scrunched up her face and whimpered.

"Shhh, sweetie," Zoey whispered. "Let's stay still. Maybe we can take a nap here together."

But Pete wasn't going for that silly idea. She arched her back and cried.

"Shhh! Shhh!" Zoey hissed desperately.

The baby squirmed, pushing her hands against Zoey's chest, hitting her painfully in the breast.

"Petey—"

Pete let out a long, drawn-out scream of frustration.

"Okay!" Zoey opened her arms, but that wasn't what the baby wanted, either. Pete fell dramatically to the floor of the tub and lay there, screaming beside the toilet plunger.

"Hush. Oh, baby, please hush."

There was no way they hadn't been heard. The gunmen would find them, if they'd gotten through Dante. And where was Dante? He was one man—one *naked* man—fighting who knew how many other men. What if he was already dead? What if the gunmen were outside the bathroom at this moment? She'd already looked. The plunger was the best weapon in here. Even the toilet tank was one piece, so she couldn't use the lid to hit someone.

She was defenseless and cornered, and Pete was screaming so loudly it was splitting her eardrums.

"Oh, God, stop, baby. Stop crying."

Someone banged on the door.

Pete screamed even louder.

Zoey grabbed the plunger and ducked, covering Pete's

body. *Oh, God, oh, God, oh, God.* Would the tub catch the bullets if they were shot at? Did it matter? It was only a matter of time until—

"Zoey!"

Pete was still screaming in her ear, so Zoey raised her head to listen.

"Zoey, it's me. It's okay. It's Dante."

She dropped the plunger and scrambled from the tub, nearly falling on the cold, slick floor tiles. "Dante?"

"Yeah, bella, it's me."

"Dante, oh, God, Dante." She was fumbling with the lock on the door, a flimsy little thing that wouldn't have held off anyone, let alone a bunch of killers, but she couldn't get it open. Her eyes were flooded with tears that she couldn't stop, couldn't control.

"Bella?" His voice was hoarse, weary.

Pete let out another banshee yell from the tub.

"I-I'm sorry, I've almost got it."

Her fingers slipped on the latch, and then it suddenly sprung open. She opened the door and half fell into Dante's arms.

"Oh, God, I thought they'd killed you. I didn't know what to do, and Pete started having a tantrum, and I couldn't quiet her, and all I could find was a plunger. I tried, Dante, I tried."

"Hush," he said in his husky voice. "It's okay, I've got you now."

Her hands slid across his chilly, wet waist, and then he was kissing her, his lips cold, the stubble on his cheeks scraping her chin. And she didn't care. He was alive.

They were all alive.

He shuddered and pulled her against him, and even with

Pete screaming her lungs out in the background, Zoey was aware that they were both nude. She'd grabbed a blanket when she'd run, but it was still in the tub with Pete.

She pulled back a little, bringing up her hand to stroke his cheek. "I don't think—"

She stopped. There was blood on his cheek. She turned her hand to look and the blood was all over her palm.

Oh, God. "Dante . . ."

She looked down. Blood was streaked from his waist to his knees, long rivulets running through the hair on his calves and dripping to the floor. There was a dark, ragged gash just over his waist.

"It's okay," Dante said.

No, this quite obviously *wasn't* okay. For a moment she felt dizzy. Then she blinked and made herself think. "Sit down. No, better lie down."

"Here?" he asked.

She looked at him fiercely. "Do you want to fall and hit your head?"

His exhausted eyes widened. "No, ma'am."

Zoey strode to the tub and snatched up the blanket, laying it on the floor of the bathroom. "Here."

Dante groaned as he lowered himself to the blanket. Next to him in the tub, Pete went into a paroxysm of grief and rage. She had pulled herself up to stand, holding on to the edge of the tub, and now she flung herself against the side of the tub, screaming.

"Uh, shouldn't you pick her up?" Dante asked from the floor.

"Just a minute."

Normally, she didn't let Pete cry, but at the moment, Pete wasn't the priority. Zoey slammed through the linen closet in the bathroom, gathering supplies. She whirled and piled a set of fluffy, natural-colored towels on top of Dante. They looked expensive and would be ruined by the blood, but she just didn't give a damn.

She handed him another towel, folded into a square. "Press this to the wound and wait here," she said breathlessly and scooped a still-screaming Pete out of the bathtub.

She ran to the bathroom door, Pete on her hip, and stopped. Zoey glanced at Dante on the floor. "You're sure no one's down there?"

"Yes." He looked up at her with steady bitter-chocolate eyes. "Trust me."

She nodded, lips pressed together. Outside on the landing above the main room, everything looked normal. The pile of bedding in front of the fire was crumpled and thrown aside where they'd left it in their haste. Early morning sunlight, bluish and weak, was illuminating the room.

Pete bellowed into her ear as Zoey ran down the stairs. It wasn't until Zoey got to the bottom of the stairs that she saw the blood. A puddle of blood lay on the tiles, as if someone had stood there and poured blood from a pitcher. There was a streak to one side, leading toward the front door. It looked like a body had been dragged outside. Zoey was frozen for a moment by the sight. Then Pete arched her back and tangled a fist in her hair.

"Ouch!" Zoey muttered. "Stop that, you little fiend."

She turned her back on the blood and hurried to the pile of bedding. She had to set Pete down for a second as she rummaged through the fabric. The baby flung herself down again, screaming as Zoey pulled her sweatshirt over her head and stepped into the pair of silk long john bottoms she'd had on the night before.

She grabbed Pete and strode into the kitchen. She'd been tending to Pete the night before and had never got the chance to look in the walk-in pantry. A chair was shoved beneath the doorknob. She stared at it a second, but Dante had said everything was safe. She removed the chair and pulled open the stainless-steel and blond wood door. There were shelves running up to the ceiling. A newish-looking step stool stood in the corner to aid in reaching the top shelves. Unfortunately, though, most were bare. There was a row of condiment bottles—ketchup, Worcestershire sauce, soy sauce, three different barbecue sauces—and a bunch of cans. Pete's crying had died a little bit, but her voice still echoed off the ceiling. She had her hand stuck in her mouth as she wailed. Zoey patted her absently as she stood on tiptoe to look over the cans. In the very back there was a box. Could it be?

Zoey reached for the box. "Look what I found."

Pete blinked tear-stained eyes and stopped midwail to reach for the box of cheese crackers.

Zoey took her out to the kitchen and set her on the floor with the open box. There hadn't been any bandages in the upstairs bathroom, and now she made a quick check of the kitchen cupboards. Nothing. If she didn't find any antibiotic she could just wash the wound with soap and water, but she'd feel better with some bandages. She hurried into the downstairs bath just off the kitchen. The mirrored vanity was empty except for a single toothbrush. She stooped to look under the sink. Ha! There sat a first-aid kit still in plastic shrink-wrap.

She scooped it up and ran out to the kitchen, where Pete

had her entire arm stuck into the box of cheese crackers. The baby squawked when Zoey picked her up, but she quieted quickly enough when Zoey snagged the box of crackers, too. Hauling baby, crackers, and first-aid box, she ran up the stairs.

To her relief, Dante was still conscious when she rushed into the bathroom.

"Hey," he said from the floor. "You're dressed."

"I thought it best," she muttered as she plopped Pete back in the bathtub. It made a nice makeshift playpen so she could concentrate on Dante.

"I think the bleeding's stopped," he said. His voice was matter-of-fact, but his face was pale under his naturally swarthy skin.

"Thank God," Zoey muttered.

She knelt beside him and for a moment felt overwhelmed. They were out in the middle of nowhere and had just been attacked. Someone had *shot* Dante. And even if they could call an ambulance or the police, there wasn't any guarantee that an ambulance could get through the snow. She'd never felt so isolated in her life.

"It's okay," Dante said softly. Some of her panic must've shown on her face. "It looks kind of bad, but it's just a graze. I'm not in shock and I'm not going to die. All you have to do is bandage me up. You can do it. I have faith in you, Zoey."

Her gaze met his. His eyes were dark brown and pain-filled. He seemed to be saying something else, something with a deeper meaning than his words. It was significant, she knew, what he was trying to communicate. His trust was a symbol of something more important.

She inhaled. She wasn't sure she was ready for what

he was telling her with just his eyes, wasn't sure she was even worthy of his trust. Maybe her own uncertainty didn't matter. He stared back at her, his eyes unblinking, his faith unwavering.

It was kind of shattering, actually, to have this much certainty laid at her feet.

Zoey swallowed. "Okay."

Which was a silly, childish thing to say in the face of his declaration. But it seemed to satisfy him. He nodded and finally veiled his disconcerting gaze. He turned his head, closing his eyes.

And as Zoey tore the plastic wrap from the first-aid kit, she wondered what exactly she'd agreed to.

Chapter Fifty-eight

Sunday, 7:58 a.m.

This man is insane, I think," Pratima Gupta whispered to her sister-in-law.

"Insane?" Savita-di hissed back. "It is obvious that he is completely potty."

"Quiet," the potty man said in a voice that was disconcertingly soft. "Or I will cut your nose off."

Savita-di inhaled sharply, her lips pressed together in disapproval. Pratima thought it wise to nudge her sister-in-law in the ribs. Savita-di could be quite imprudent at times, and she would not look at all good with her nose missing.

In the corner, Mr. Neil Senior grunted. He could not do much more than grunt, because he had been trussed like a goat ready to slaughter and a thick cloth gag had been inserted in his mouth. Over the gag, Mr. Neil's eyes rolled rather wildly.

The potty man, meanwhile, had gone back to what he'd been doing before. What he'd been doing all night long, in fact. Sitting in the lone armchair, stroking a very big gun and now and again smiling. It was rather disconcerting how he seemed quite content to do nothing else but fondle his nasty gun and smile.

He was not a tall man for an American—maybe Pratima's own height. His hair was a very light blond, cut quite close to his head. Usually such a color was caused by bleaching the hair, but Pratima thought that the color might be natural in this man. He had the ruddy complexion of a northern European, his face full of sharp angles and hard edges that really did not complement each other well. And to top it all off, he had clear gray eyes that were as cold as granite.

Pratima sat next to Savita-di on one of their motel-room beds. They'd been sitting thus since the evening before, and very soon Pratima would have to make use of the W.C. The potty man had broken into the motel room just after eight p.m. He had demanded the whereabouts of the girl baby, and sadly, the ladies had told him. He was a very frightening man indeed.

Then the potty man had brought the baby boy and his father to the room and imprisoned them here. Apparently, too, he had threatened to kill them all if Rahul tried to obtain help. Pratima was quite frightened for her nephew and his family. Rahul was a good man. She did not want him harmed because of her and Savita-di. But would the potty man leave behind any kind of witness?

She very much feared he would not.

Neil Junior, who had been crawling about the room, now grasped Savita-di's green and brown sari and pulled his sturdy body to a standing position. He swayed and grinned up at her.

"Look! The boy is standing," Savita-di exclaimed as if they were all blind. "What a clever child he is. Do you not think he is young to have learned to stand already, Pratima?"

The baby turned his wide grin on her, and Pratima had to admit that he was a most attractive baby. "He is very intelligent indeed."

"Mr. Neil Senior, look at what your boy does," Savita-di called to the bound man in the corner. "Is this the first time he has stood by himself?"

Mr. Neil Senior made a grunting kind of noise that could be taken either as an affirmative or a negative.

It did not seem to matter to Savita-di in her eagerness to laud the baby. "I think this child is most—"

But she was interrupted by the potty man's soft, emotionless voice. "The FBI agent has the other baby."

They all turned to stare at him with various expressions of dread. It didn't seem to be a question, and besides, they had already told him this information earlier in the evening.

Finally, Pratima Gupta gulped and said, "Yes?"

The potty man cracked the window curtain and glanced out before looking at her. His light gray eyes held the same interest as if she'd been an insect under his shoe. "The blizzard has stopped. How do I talk with him?"

The remaining three adults in the room exchanged glances. Even Mr. Neil Senior looked worried behind his gag.

"I'm not sure—" Pratima began.

"I'll start shooting you, one by one, until you tell

me how to contact him," the potty man said without inflection.

"Ah! This is insanity," Savita-di exclaimed. "Why do you think we can help you find these people?"

"Because the woman with the FBI agent came here before," Mr. Potty said. "Would you like me to begin with your sister?" And he pointed his gun at Pratima's chest.

"Sister-in-law!" Savita-di said before Pratima could open her mouth. "And do not shoot her! She is a good woman, even if she did flirt with my husband once!"

"I did not!" Pratima cried, driven beyond endurance. If she were to die in the next minute, she could at least set the record straight. "Your husband flirted with everything in a skirt, Savita-di. I am sorry to say this, but it is true, and what is more, you know it. And as the elder brother he had control of the family finances, so naturally my husband bade me be polite to him. If I smiled at your husband, it was because I had no wish to offend him when he made terribly improper advances to me. Advances, I should point out, that I turned down. It was a smile, Savita-di, merely that. Please to get over it!"

There was a silence in the room as everyone stared at Savita-di. Mr. Neil Senior's eyes had widened over his duct-tape gag, and little Neil Junior was watching the Gupta ladies with interest. Pratima held her breath. Perhaps her dear sister-in-law would strike her now. Perhaps she would publicly scorn her.

Instead, Savita-di's eyes filled with tears. "Oh, Pratima, I am a foolish old woman. You are right, my husband was not as good a husband as he should have been. Please forgive me."

"Of course I forgive you, Savita-di," Pratima exclaimed. "If only—"

But here she was interrupted by the potty man clearing his throat. A soft sound, but an ominous one, as well.

"This is almost as good as the movies, but I have work to do," he said in his awful, low voice. "I've decided I should start with you." He swung the barrel of his nasty gun toward Savita-di.

"What, me?" Savita-di exclaimed. "Why should you choose me as your victim? Why not—?"

"My sister-in-law's phone," Pratima said hastily before Savita-di became riddled with gunshot holes. "He has my sister-in-law's mobile phone. You can call him there."

"Pratima Gupta!" Savita-di said in a scolding voice. "What are you thinking?"

But for once Pratima wasn't paying attention to her sister-in-law's unnecessary bickering. The potty man had turned his cold gray gaze on her and smiled. Quite the most terrifying smile Pratima had ever seen in her life.

"Thank you." He took a mobile phone out of his pocket and dialed.

Chapter Fifty-nine

Sunday, 8:12 a.m.

The cell phone rang just as Zoey finished bandaging his side. Dante'd convinced her that he was strong enough to get up off the bathroom floor and limp down the stairs to the pallet of blankets in front of the fireplace. He tried to cover the limp, though. The last thing he wanted to do was let her know that his earlier injury was bugging him. It hurt even more than the furrow in his side. The first thing he'd done was put his sweatpants back on.

Zoey jerked at the tinkling notes from the cell phone, betraying her frayed nerves.

"It's Savita Gupta's cell," Dante said. He reached for one of Tom's sweatshirts that he'd found the night before. "Probably the Gupta ladies want to know when they're getting their purple minivan back."

He pulled the sweatshirt on, careful of the big bandage on his side.

"Oh," Zoey gasped. It was a measure of how wigged out she still was that she didn't even comment about the Guptas' disabled van. She rummaged in his coat pocket and fished out the phone, frowning at the caller ID.

"Hello?" She'd turned to look in Pete's direction—the baby was cruising the couch again—but suddenly froze. Her eyes were focused inward, on the speaker at the other end of the phone.

Dante stilled.

She met his gaze. Her expression was stricken.

"Who is it?" he demanded, not even trying to conceal his voice.

She shook her head, then held out the phone to him, mute.

He snatched the phone out of her hand. "Who is this?"

"My name doesn't matter," the male voice on the other end replied in ridiculous cliché. "I have the old Pakistani women—"

The caller was interrupted by an indignant squawk on the other end of the phone.

The caller sighed. "I am corrected. The *Indian* old women. Also Mr. Janiowski and his baby son. I will kill them if you do not give me what I want."

What a pompous prick. Dante felt his jaw tighten, but he kept his voice carefully even. "What do you want?"

"Ricky Spinoza's child."

The answer was what he'd been expecting, but it was a blow nonetheless. Dante looked to where Pete was squatting on short toddler legs to pick up something miniscule from the rug. "How?"

"Come here, to the motel where the Indian women are—"

Dante was already shaking his head. "I can't get through on these roads. The snow—"

"Your problem," the voice said indifferently. "Park outside the motel and call me. I'll give you instructions."

He disconnected.

"Asshole," Dante muttered. He rummaged through the pile of clothes next to him, looking for some socks.

Zoey was staring at him. "What? Who was that?"

Dante sighed. His leg really did hurt like a bitch, but obviously he wasn't going to be able to sit around. "Muscle. Probably Tony the Roses's, but he might be connected to the FBI traitor. That seems unlikely, though. This guy didn't sound like he was trained by a bureaucrat."

He found a pair of socks and pulled them on, conscious that Zoey hadn't moved. She was watching him intently. If she lost trust in him now . . .

"But what did he want?"

He looked up and met her beautiful blue eyes. "Pete. He's holding the Gupta ladies, Neil, and Neil's son. He wants to make an exchange of some sort."

He waited, hoping against hope that she would trust him. His track record to date wasn't particularly sterling. He wouldn't be entirely surprised if she grabbed the baby and ran. Disappointed, sure, but not surprised.

But she simply sat on the couch and laid a light hand on Pete's oblivious head. "What are we going to do?"

That *we* burrowed into Dante's heart and made a home for itself. Now he just had to make sure he didn't fail her trust.

"Keep Pete safe no matter what." He held her gaze. "I

don't know what I'll do exactly. Figure out a way to get the others away from him without handing over Pete."

"Okay."

He stood, aware that he wasn't in top shape at the moment. His side burned, and his leg was starting to stiffen up. "First we need to find some transportation. Those assassins found us somehow. My BMW may have a tracker on it. I can't think of any other way they could've found out where we are. We're going to have to leave my car behind. I guess we can take the hit men's truck."

She glanced at the window, out in the direction of the car. Dante felt a pang of regret. He loved that goddamned car, bullet holes or not.

"You'd better get dressed," he said. "Check the kitchen, bring whatever food and supplies you might need for Pete."

"Okay." She turned toward the kitchen and almost tripped over his gun holster. Zoey bent to pick it up. "Ouch."

"What is it?" Dante took the holster from her. Something small and black was poking out between where the straps were stitched together. Dante reached for his trench coat. He had a folding knife in an inside pocket.

Behind him, Zoey said, "I think something broke on it. I'm sorry, I . . ."

Her voice died away as he pulled apart the edges of the leather and picked out a tracing chip with his fingernails.

Zoey's eyes widened. "Is that—?"

"Yeah, it is." Dante felt grimly triumphant as he examined the chip. "Guess it wasn't the BMW, after all. It makes sense. Even if I ditched the car I'd always have my gun on me."

"What are you going to do with it?"

He shrugged and placed both the chip and the gun holster on the fireplace mantel. "Leave them here. I'm not taking the chance that there's another tracer on the holster."

"But how will you carry your gun?"

"In my coat pocket. Listen, let me worry about my gun. You get yourself and Pete ready to go. I'm going to double-check the BMW."

"Okay." But still she hesitated, looking worried.

"Look." He touched her shoulder gently, hating to see the shadows in her eyes. "I need to take a look at where DiRosa's man is holding everyone in the motel, examine the layout a bit more, see what I can do. But I'll come up with a plan. Believe me, I'm not giving up Pete."

"I know," she said simply.

She took two steps until she stood directly in front of him. Until her blue eyes were only inches from his. "I trust you, Dante."

Then she kissed him, her lips soft and feminine and strong on his, and in her kiss was everything he'd ever longed for in life: trust, need, and want.

Maybe even love.

Chapter Sixty

Sunday, 9:34 a.m.

$\mathcal{T}$wo fucking months of twice-a-week anger management classes and this was what it got him: tied up in the
corner like a chump while a hired pretty boy gunslinger
waved a Glock in his face.

Neil twisted his hands behind his back, but the asshole
had used duct tape, and the tape only tangled further. Fuck.
If he got out of this alive he was quitting the fucking anger
management classes. The coffee had sucked anyway, and
they'd always had Fig Newtons to eat. He fucking hated
Fig Newtons. Ash would just have to learn to live with his
natural aggression.

And thinking of Ash made him realize how worried
she must be right now. About the only thing halfway bad
you could say about Ash was that she was a worrier. After
he'd found Neil Junior, Neil had called Ash last night,

just so she wouldn't worry. He'd told her exactly where he was, mostly because she'd demanded the information. What was more, he'd promised her that he and Neil Junior would be home by two in the morning at the latest. Only of course they weren't. There'd been that blizzard and the strange rice pudding, and then Neil had decided to take a little nap before driving home. He'd woken to find Pretty Boy standing over him, the Glock nearly up Neil's nose.

So now he and Neil Junior weren't home, and Ash was bound to be worrying, and that just wasn't good. Last time he'd screwed up with Ash, she hadn't talked to him for a month, just sent him fucking cold looks that still made him shiver. And he'd never even figured out exactly what he'd done wrong that time. This time he knew, which made it ten times worse.

The old ladies were sitting on the bed next to each other, aiming identical death stares at Pretty Boy. They hadn't been real pleased when he'd called them Pakistani. Pretty Boy was still lounging in the only comfortable chair in the room, stroking the Glock like he was going to whip out his dick any moment and come all over it.

Fucking asshole. Probably didn't have a clue how to do it with a woman. Or a guy, nothing wrong with that. Neil's cousin Bernie swung that way, so he'd had to learn not to say "queer." "Fag" was still okay. At least he thought so—he'd have to ask Bernie. Anyway, Neil was betting this motherfucker didn't know how to get it on with anything warm, woman, man, or farm animal.

Pretty Boy's eyes flickered over as Neil Junior dropped to his hands and knees and scooted toward Neil. His son grabbed the front of his shirt and crawled into his lap—what there was of it, considering that Neil had his knees crunched nearly to his chest by the duct tape. Neil Junior grinned up into his face and patted his cheek with a grubby paw. The kid was fucking cute, anyone but a stone-cold killer would admit that.

Problem was, Pretty Boy obviously *was* a stone-cold killer.

The guy glanced over now with his fucking creepy light-gray eyes and said, "I am told that one can push a thumb through the top of a baby's skull if the bones are not yet fused. Do you think your son's skull is fused?"

The ladies gasped, the round one making a little scream. Neil growled and lunged at the asshole. If he could get his hands on Pretty Boy, he'd fucking kill him with his bare hands. But bound as he was, Neil could move only a few inches, jiggling Neil Junior on his lap. The baby laughed and bounced. Probably wanted to play horsy.

Pretty Boy smiled like Freddy Krueger on crack. "Maybe I will let you watch. Maybe—"

But the rest of his sentence was cut off by a loud knock on the door. Everyone swung in that direction, staring.

Pretty Boy motioned with the Glock. "See who it is," he told the taller lady.

Her eyes widened, but she moved toward the door. Neil bit back a groan. If this was that FBI agent's idea of a fucking plan, they were all in trouble. Sure enough, Torelli stepped in the room.

"Where is the baby?" Pretty Boy asked.

"Safe," Torelli said. He walked to the bed and sat down on the end. Neil noticed that he was limping a little.

Pretty Boy's eyes narrowed. "I told you to bring her here."

Torelli shrugged. "I don't trust you."

"You doubt my honor?"

"Yeah."

Neil tensed, because it looked like Pretty Boy just might start shooting right then and there. But then the fucker smiled a nasty little smile. "You are smart."

Torelli nodded. "You don't need all these hostages. Let me take the baby outside."

"No."

Torelli sighed. "Look—"

Another knock sounded at the door. Everyone looked around.

Pretty Boy motioned with his gun to the tall Indian lady. She went to the door.

There was a murmur, and then the Indian lady stepped back from the door to reveal a hugely pregnant dishwater blonde in a flowered smock and stretch pants. She wore glasses, and her hair was cut short like a man's, and she looked kind of like an accountant.

Neil groaned.

She swayed into the room, her belly leading the way.

Torelli stood. "Ma'am—"

The dishwater blonde frowned. "Which one of you is the guy who's holding the baby hostage?"

Pretty Boy said, "Who are you?"

The blonde turned to him and pushed her glasses up her nose with her left hand. A big pink diamond sparkled on her finger. "You the tough guy?"

"Yes, I am." Pretty Boy smirked. "What do you care?"

Neil Junior grinned. "Mama!"

And Ashley brought the Uzi in her right hand up from where she'd been concealing it behind her back and emptied the clip into Pretty Boy. The room kind of shook with the percussion. Pretty Boy slumped over and dropped his gun. He was very dead.

Torelli lowered the Glock he'd drawn. "Huh. So much for my cunning plan."

Ashley put the Uzi on the bureau, scooped Neil Junior out of Neil's lap, and planted a big kiss on the baby's cheek. "That's right, baby, it's Mama."

The taller Indian lady sat down hard next to her sister-in-law. Both ladies were gaping.

"Neil, honey," his wife said to him. "I don't want you working for Uncle Tony anymore. I don't think it's good for our family."

Neil would've told her that there was no way he was going back to her crazy uncle, but the fucking gag was still in his mouth.

The shorter Indian lady gave herself a little shake and turned to her sister-in-law. "I think you should be the one to tell Rahul about the mess in his motel room."

Chapter Sixty-one

Sunday, 10:37 a.m.

*A*shley Janiowski was the scariest pregnant lady Zoey had ever seen. Of course Zoey's perception might've been colored by the knowledge that Ashley carried an Uzi in her purse and had just blown away a man without even blinking.

"I can't believe Uncle Tony sent Rutgar after his own grand-nephew," Ashley was saying as she rubbed her swollen stomach under a pink and white flowered maternity smock. A cartoon mouse on the front held a sign that said BABY ON BOARD! "That's cold, even for Uncle Tony. That's really cold."

They were all sitting in the Agrawals' living room, making it pretty cramped. Mr. Agrawal had taken the news that he had a corpse in his motel pretty well, considering. He'd turned a little gray, sat down hard on a chair in his living room, and stared into space for a bit. Dante had asked him to wait on calling the police to report the hit man's death, and Mr. Agrawal had merely waved a hand kind of vaguely.

The three Agrawal children were alternately playing with Pete and Neil Junior and watching a cartoon that involved a boy scientist with a weird German accent. The Gupta ladies were helping their niece set the table for brunch. Neil was sitting next to Ashley, alternately basking in her wifely concern and being blasted by her displeasure. She seemed to vacillate rapidly between the two.

And Dante lounged in an armchair, his body relaxed but his eyes intent. Zoey frowned. He'd been limping, but he refused to let her look at his leg or side. She only hoped that he wasn't slowly hemorrhaging to death in his masculine stoicism.

"And you!" Ashley suddenly rounded on her husband, the pendulum obviously swinging back to displeasure. "What were you thinking, doing a job with Neil Junior in the back of your truck?"

Neil looked a little like a deer in the headlights. If he hadn't been the one to snatch Pete in the first place, Zoey might feel a bit of sympathy for him.

"It was a little job, Ash, just a fucking little job. How was I to know that—"

Ashley let out a snort like a displeased pregnant buffalo. "That the FBI would double-cross Tony, and you'd arrive during a shootout between the FBI agents, and have to snatch a baby, putting Neil Junior in danger? I don't know, Neil, maybe you should've thought ahead, you know?"

Ashley pushed up her glasses and shot a glare at Dante.

Dante raised his eyebrows. "I wasn't the one shooting,

Mrs. Janiowski." He looked at Neil. "So you arrived in the middle of a shootout?"

Neil nodded, keeping a wary eye on his wife. "More like a fucking bloodbath. There were two Feebs down, and the third bought it as I walked in."

Dante's eyes narrowed, and Zoey remembered that the "Feebs" had been his coworkers. But his voice was mild when he asked, "How do you know the shooters were FBI, too?"

Neil snorted almost as explosively as his wife. "Suits, fucking military-cut hair, and the dead Feebs had let them in the room, there wasn't no fucking forced entry. Didn't take an Einstein to figure who they were."

Dante nodded.

"Listen." Neil sat forward on the couch. "I didn't go there to take the kid, swear on my mother's grave—"

Ashley shook her head angrily and muttered something about Neil's mother, but he raised his voice over hers.

"Tony sent me there to make sure this FBI guy had done the job he promised and had had Spinoza offed."

Dante looked up sharply. "The FBI agent was going to kill Spinoza for Tony the Rose?"

"That's what he'd promised." Neil shrugged. "I don't know if Tony had paid him or had something on the guy. Don't make any difference, because he must've backed out of the deal."

"But why would the FBI agent have his own agents killed?" Zoey asked.

"SOP," Neil said. "Standard operating procedure. You kill the guards, and then it looks like the place has been stormed and hit men killed the snitch. Only, as it turned out, the snitch wasn't there to be popped, get it?"

"Oh." Zoey nodded and then shivered. If Nikki and Ricky hadn't fought and then sneaked out of the apartment, they would've been dead, too.

"Anyway," Neil continued, "I get there, the snitch isn't there, the Feebs are having a massive layoff of staff—you should pardon the expression—and the only other person in the apartment is the fucking kid. What do I do? You want I should go back to Tony the Rose empty-handed?" Neil shook his head. "I don't think so."

"You aren't going back to Uncle Tony at all, Mr. Boo," Ashley said fiercely. The pendulum had swung again. "I don't want you anywhere near that old fart."

Neil looked at his plain little wife, his big, beefy face creased sheepishly. "I gotta report to Tony sometime, hon. Tony don't like people walkin' out on him without his say-so."

Ashley frowned, looking uncertain.

Zoey cleared her throat. "If Tony were in prison, that wouldn't be such a problem, would it?"

Everyone looked at her.

She shrugged. "I mean, he'd have other things to worry about instead of Neil."

Dante shifted in his chair. "She's got a point."

Ashley narrowed her eyes. "How do you figure Uncle Tony's getting in the pen? There's no trial without Ricky the snitch, and Ricky's kid is right here." She nodded with her chin to Pete, playing on the floor with the rest of the children. "Will he take your word that she's safe?"

"No." Dante's eyes were locked with Ashley's. "But if I can get Pete back before nine o'clock Monday morning, Ricky will testify."

"Nikki will make him do it," Zoey murmured. "Believe me."

"How're you going to get that baby through both Uncle Tony's men and those crooked FBI agents?" Ashley scoffed. "'Cause don't think that Uncle Tony won't be waiting for you all to show up."

"I know," Dante said. "But there might be a way to do it. If you're willing to help."

"Bring down my uncle Tony?" Ashley's eyebrows rose behind her glasses.

"Yes."

Neil looked concerned. "Now, wait just a minute. Tony the Rose is the biggest, meanest fucking outfit boss in Chicago. Don't nobody cross him."

Ashley poked her glasses. "Yeah, well, Uncle Tony sent a hitman after my Mr. Boo and my baby Neil. He's goin' down."

Zoey grinned. "You go, girl."

"All is ready!" Mrs. Savita Gupta called from the dinner table. "Come! Come, sit down before the food grows cold."

They all rose to go eat brunch. Dante was moving slowly, and Zoey hurried to his side to help him rise.

He arched an eyebrow at her. "You okay?"

"Better than you," she retorted. "I'm not the one limping."

He shook his head. "I'm okay."

She frowned, but there was an even bigger worry on her mind than Dante's wounds. "How can you go back to Chicago with the corrupt FBI agent still after you? He tried to have you killed this morning, Dante."

"I know," he said as they moved into the dining room. "I can handle him."

"But he's got the rest of the FBI believing you killed your colleagues. He planted evidence against you, and you aren't even sure who he is."

"Hush. I have a good idea who it is." He lowered his head to brush a kiss over her lips, silencing her. "Besides, I have a friend I can call for backup. And I have a plan."

"A cunning plan?"

He raised his head. Everyone was staring at them, and Zoey thought Neil might be blushing.

"Yeah. A cunning plan." Dante looked at Mr. Agrawal. "Do you have a computer I can use?"

Chapter Sixty-two

Monday, 8:53 a.m.

*T*his is the stupidest cunning plan in the world," Zoey said to Dante as they walked up Jackson Boulevard.

He'd had problems finding a parking spot in downtown Chicago, so they were later than he'd wanted to be. They were walking at a rapid though not hurried pace, and his injured thigh was killing him. "Gee, thanks."

"I mean, you're an FBI agent. Couldn't you have come up with a plan that involved secret codes or explosives?"

Dante felt his mouth curve. Zoey had been babbling since they'd hit the outskirts of Chicago. She was obviously nervous and probably scared, but she hadn't said anything about turning back, and for that he was immensely grateful.

"I'm fresh out of explosives."

"Or bazookas," Zoey muttered. They turned the corner

onto North Dearborn, and the federal courthouse came into view. "A plan with bazookas would've been good."

Dante stopped and pulled her into the shelter of a building entryway. "Bazookas are kind of hard to get past a federal courthouse's security."

Her big blue eyes searched his. "Oh, God, Dante, what if—"

He kissed her, feeling the softness of her lips beneath his, wishing desperately that he could just take her away from here, take her to bed and forget this whole thing.

But he couldn't.

Dante raised his head, staring into her face, painfully conscious that if things didn't go as planned this might be the last time he looked into her beautiful eyes. There were a million things he wanted to tell her, but if he did it would only worry her further.

He smiled. "Nothing will go wrong. Trust me."

She frowned fiercely. "It had better not. You promised me a date at the Field Museum."

"And I'll keep that promise." He brushed a kiss across her cold forehead. "Follow the plan. If something happens, don't forget—"

She gave a muted scream and hit him on the chest. "You just said nothing would go wrong!"

He caught her fist. "And it won't. But if it does, promise me you'll get to a safe place."

"I promise," she muttered grudgingly.

She was still scowling, and the frigid wind had turned her nose red, and she was the most beautiful woman he'd ever seen.

"Good."

He kissed her hard and turned to stride toward the

federal courthouse. He stored thoughts of Zoey away in a
corner of his brain and concentrated on the first part of his
plan: getting in the building.

The ground floor of the courthouse was almost all glass
walls, and the security guards could be clearly seen from
the outside of the building. Dante walked in the double
glass doors and headed toward the security setup. His step
was unhurried, neither fast nor slow. The elevator banks
were behind the security guards; in order to go anywhere
within the building, you had to go past them.

To the side was a separate setup for U.S. Marshals, FBI,
and other law enforcement personnel who carried weap-
ons. A Latino flashed a badge and showed the security
guard his piece. Behind him was a tall man in cowboy
boots patiently waiting his turn. Dante looked away. He'd
deliberately decided not to try and bring in a weapon.

There were a couple of people ahead of him in line.
Dante watched as a chunky African American woman laid
her briefcase on the scanner belt. She walked through the
arch and picked up her briefcase on the other side, and
then it was Dante's turn.

He kept his face neutral. If the traitor FBI agent had
alerted the security desk, if they had a BOLO out on him,
this plan might be over very, very quickly. But the security guards barely glanced at him before waving Dante
through.

He strolled to the elevator banks, where the African American woman waited with several other lawyer
types. Two women chatted at the back of the elevator as
it ascended, and the smell of someone's coffee pervaded
the space. Dante had a fleeting wistful thought that he

should've gotten coffee this morning. He rubbed his thigh, trying to ease the aching muscle.

Then the doors opened on the court floor. The hall was crowded with reporters and their crews, cameramen fiddling with their equipment, their faces bored. Dante wove through the crowd, his heart beating harder as he made the doors to the courtroom. He took a deep breath, pushed open the first set of doors, nodded to the guard inside, and pushed open the inner doors to the courtroom.

". . . in contempt of court if you continue to refuse to testify, Mr. Spinoza," the judge was saying. She was a middle-aged woman with blazing red hair and a high but commanding voice.

The courtroom was a dark wood paneled room with seating for about a hundred spectators. Every seat was taken, many with sketch artists, busy over their tablets. Tony the Rose sat at a front table, identifiable by his red bull neck. He was flanked on either side by gray-haired men in dark business suits, obviously his lawyers.

Ricky the snitch was on the stand, looking weasely and mutinous at the same time. "I can't testify, Judge, you know that. They took my baby, an—"

"You've agreed to testify, Mr. Spinoza. Failure to do so will put you in contempt of court. I trust the district attorney made this clear to you when he asked you to testify."

"But Judge," Ricky whined. "I can't testify when Tony's got my kid!"

Tony the Rose stirred. "I ain't got his kid."

The judge frowned. "Mr. Franklin, if you can't keep your client from speaking out of turn, I shall have to cite you in contempt of court, as well."

By now Dante had neared the center of the courtroom.

"Actually, Your Honor, Tony doesn't have Petronella Hernandez."

Every head in the courtroom turned in his direction as Dante continued, "In fact, she's—"

But that was as far as he got before Jack Headington shot him twice in the chest.

Chapter Sixty-three

Monday, 9:15 a.m.

$\mathcal{Z}$oey was getting off the elevator when she heard the shots. Her heart started beating in triple time as she shoved through the masses of people milling in the hallway outside the courtroom. If Dante were shot, if he were killed, she didn't know how she'd live.

He couldn't be shot.

She pushed through both sets of doors into the courtroom. Inside all was chaos. A guard was just inside the doors, his gun drawn. He swung around at her entrance, but she darted past him. There was a knot of people in the aisle, and she hit at shoulders to make them move.

"Dante!"

She shoved aside a tall man in cowboy boots who turned a surprised face toward her. She barely noticed.

Dante was in the middle of the knot, lying on the floor, his eyes closed.

"Dante!" Zoey sobbed and flung herself to her knees beside him. "Dante!" She shook his shoulder.

His eyes popped open. "Ow."

"Dammit, Dante," Zoey sobbed. "I thought you were shot. I thought you were dead."

"I was shot," he wheezed. "Thank God for Kevlar." He pulled aside his shirt to show two bullets flattened against the vest underneath. "Shit. I think I may've broken a rib."

"Arrest him," a man hissed.

The knot of people around Dante cleared, and Zoey could see a tall, balding man near the front of the courtroom. Both of his arms were held by men in uniform.

One of the guards standing over Dante looked up. "I've patted him down. This guy's not armed, Mr. Headington."

"He's a known felon, an FBI agent gone bad," Headington said very quietly. His voice seemed hypercalm. "Arrest—"

The judge brought her gavel down with a loud *BANG!* Everyone jerked to look at her. "How dare you shoot an unarmed man in my courtroom, Special Agent Headington?"

Headington opened his mouth, but the judge had turned her critical gaze on Dante. "And you, sir. Who are you, and what do you know about Mr. Spinoza's baby daughter?"

Dante groaned and slowly got to his feet. Zoey wrapped her arms around him in case he went back down again. She wished she could just tell him to stay on the floor, but that might be detrimental to his masculine ego, what with all the law enforcement types in the room.

"I'm Special Agent Dante Torelli," he said. He didn't

shout, but his voice carried clearly throughout the courtroom. "And Petronella Hernandez is in this courtroom."

Several people gasped. The Mrs. Guptas stood up from where they'd been sitting at the back of the courtroom. Mrs. Pratima Gupta held Pete up high, and the baby beamed. On the stand, Ricky burst into tears, and for the first time since she'd met him, Zoey felt a grudging sympathy for the guy. At least he'd been truly worried about Pete.

Tony the Rose stirred. "You don't wanna go testifying against me, Ricky. Might not be good for the baby's continued health, y'know what I mean?"

The judge slammed her gavel down. "Mr. Franklin, please inform your client what the punishment is for threatening a witness in a federal case!"

"Yeah, you do that, Mr. Franklin," came a voice from the back of the courtroom. Ashley Janiowski waddled up the aisle, looking very fierce for an incredibly pregnant woman. "But Uncle Tony's not going to be hurting any babies anymore, are you, Tony?"

"Ashley, whatcha doin'?" Tony demanded.

"I'm making sure you don't come after me and mine, Uncle Tony," Ashley said. "For shame, sending a crazy hit man after baby Neil Junior."

Mr. Franklin, the defense lawyer, who didn't look like a man particularly bothered by small things like murder, actually leaned away from Tony the Rose. "Tony, you sent a hitman after a *baby*?"

"'Course I didn't," Tony squeaked.

"Don't you lie to me!" Ashley shrieked. The judge started pounding her gavel, but Ashley yelled right over her. "You even think about hurting another baby and I'll give evidence myself."

The judge froze, her gavel still in the air. Apparently she was as stunned as the rest of the room by Ashley's pronouncement.

Tony the Rose turned a deep shade of maroon. "Ashley Madonna Janiowski, family don't tell."

Ashley narrowed her eyes and hissed like a very pregnant cougar. "Family don't send hit men after family, Tony DiRosa. Don't think I'm not telling Mama about what you did."

Tony opened his mouth, but nothing came out, except maybe air, because as everyone watched he seemed to deflate in his chair.

For a moment the courtroom crowd was mesmerized by Tony's downfall.

Then Jack Headington sputtered to life. "Torelli may have brought the baby in, but he's still wanted for murdering fellow agents, for taking mob-related bribes, and for—"

This time it was Dante who cut him off. "I was sent to the Chicago office specifically to uncover ties to the mob, and I did, Your Honor. Jack Headington was the mob connection within the Chicago office. He was the one who passed information to Tony the Rose and others. He was the one who told Tony where Ricky Spinoza's family was being held in protective custody. He was the one who planted evidence that I accepted bribes—bribes he himself accepted. And he was the one who set up FBI special agents in his own office to be murdered by crooked FBI personnel he had on his private payroll."

Dante paused for breath, and everyone turned to Headington, as if they were at a particularly deadly tennis match. Zoey expected Headington to deny everything, to maybe panic and try to run.

Instead he laughed softly. "Dante, Dante, Dante. I have twenty-five years of experience in the Bureau, an exemplary service, and a wall of commendations to prove it. Accusing someone else of your own crimes is the oldest trick in the book."

"Yeah, it is," Dante said. "And you'd certainly know, wouldn't you, Jack? But I have more than accusations. I have proof."

He reached into his coat pocket and pulled out a computer disc. "You might've killed Kevin Heinz, but not before Kevin found your money trail and e-mailed it to me."

Headington's face turned gray.

And then the disc Dante was holding broke apart and a piece fell at his feet.

Dante looked down. "Oops."

Everyone stared at the broken disc.

"There's no way we'll take evidence solely on your say-so," Headington whispered silkily.

Someone sighed. Zoey turned.

The tall man in cowboy boots stood behind her, his arms crossed. "Always trying to impress."

Dante frowned. "Hey, what were the odds the disc would get shot?"

"Show-off." The tall man shook his head. "Your Honor, I'm Special Agent John MacKinnon, and I have all of Torelli's evidence on my office computer. I'm here to arrest Jack Headington." He waved to four men behind him. "Take him in, guys."

This time when the court erupted into shouts, the judge didn't even bother using her gavel.

Chapter Sixty-four

One month later . . .

"This is our third date to the Field Museum," Zoey panted as she and Dante crashed through his apartment door. "And we never get past Sue the T. rex."

"Bitch, bitch, bitch," Dante murmured against her neck. She'd noticed in the last month that he seemed to have a thing about her neck.

Not that she was complaining. She heard a slam as he kicked the door closed with his heel. Dante had a lovely newly renovated apartment in Wicker Park, which had surprised her the first time she'd seen it. For some reason she'd assumed that he'd lived at the red brick apartment where he'd been guarding Pete, Nikki, and Ricky. Actually, she was a little envious of his apartment. The floors and woodwork were all honey oak, and the living room had an enormous bay window that overlooked a garden courtyard.

"No, but really," she said as she tilted her head back to give him better access. Dante was very, very good at neck kissing. "We should at least"—she gasped. *How* did he always find that exact spot?—"at least get to the Egyptian tomb next time."

He pulled back to look in her face. "Did you pack a lunch today?"

"Well, no." She played with his tie. There was something about undressing a man in a suit and tie that was kind of kinky.

She loosened the tie.

He was grinning at her in a perfectly obnoxious way that if she wasn't so interested in jumping his bones she might've taken issue with. "Then you didn't expect to see the whole museum."

She pulled the tie from his collar. "Yes, but it's the principle of the thing. You ask me on a date to the museum—"

He rolled his eyes. "You demanded we go again."

"*Whatever.*" She started unbuttoning his shirt. Really, it was like opening a Christmas package. "We go in and pay the ridiculous entrance fee and we don't get twenty steps inside before you say something dirty in my ear and we have to turn around and rush out again. The ticket people probably think we're nuts."

"So we have a museum fetish." Dante shrugged out of his jacket and shirt. "Perfectly normal."

For a moment she was distracted by the sight of his naked torso. It was smooth and muscled, and it gave her a thrill each and every time she saw it. Zoey ran her fingertips over his side, just above the waistband of his trousers.

She was checking as she always did for the slight bump of his scar there. Eventually there would come a time when she didn't have to see for herself that the scar was healing—had healed—but for now his wound was still too new to her.

"How do we know it's a museum fetish?" Zoey asked. Dante reached for her and raised her arms so he could pull off her sweater. "I mean, we never get past Sue. Maybe it's a dinosaur fetish."

"Dinosaur fetish," Dante repeated, eyes fixed on her breasts. Her sweater had been really bulky, and Zoey had decided not to wear a bra today. He blinked and met her eyes. "Then that puts you in a difficult position."

Zoey arched her eyebrows at him as she shimmied out of her jeans. "What do you mean?"

"I mean," he said as he put his hands around her waist and lifted her up to sit on his entryway table, "that there must not be many guy dinosaur fetishists in the country. I might be the only one."

"And?" She wiggled a little on the table. It seemed quite sturdy, and she wondered why they'd never tried it before.

But Dante was no longer smiling. In fact, he looked a little nervous. "And maybe you should stick with me."

"Stick with you?" Oh, God, was he saying what she thought he was saying?

He nodded. "Permanently."

"Permanently . . ." Her mind went *pink!* just like a lightbulb burning out.

"Christ." He raked a hand through his hair, looking adorably sexy, bare-chested and with his hair sticking up. "Will you marry me?"

"*Marry* you?"

"Oh, God, stop repeating everything I say." He hooked his fingers under the waistband of her panties and drew them off. Zoey lifted her hips to help out, because she wasn't that far gone. "I know we haven't known each other all that long, but I love you, and I'm almost sure you love me."

He looked at her.

She shrugged and nodded.

He tossed the panties to the floor, widened her legs, and stepped between them. "Good. You love me, too. I've got a steady, pretty good-paying job. The FBI might not be your favorite federal organization, but you have to admit you can't beat the benefits."

He looked at her again.

She raised her eyebrows and began fiddling with his zipper. This was certainly getting interesting.

He frowned and hurried on. "I've been cleared of all the charges against me and even been commentated for my undercover work. Headington's been charged with all sorts of crimes, Pete's safe and happy with Nikki and her jerk of a boyfriend, Charlie Hessler's going to recover enough to take early retirement and go fishing; and Tony the Rose has been convicted. Heck, you even got your Prius back from impound. Life looks pretty good right now—"

He sucked in his breath because she'd lowered his trousers zipper and inserted her hand into his briefs to stroke him. He felt hot and hard and just the way she liked him.

She bit her lip.

He kept his eyes on her face and finished almost desperately. "And I really, really think we should get married,

preferably before you meet my huge family and they scare
you off."

"Hmm." Zoey took a condom from his trousers pocket
and thoughtfully rolled it onto his cock.

He groaned.

She smiled and kissed him softly on the lips.

His eyes fluttered close—really his eyelashes were the
prettiest things—and whispered against her lips, "Please,
Zoey?"

He crowded closer and nudged her just *there*. She
sighed. What would it be like to be married to a neat-
nik who listened to Frank Sinatra and drove an eighty-
thousand-dollar BMW with bullet holes in the doors?

"Please, Zoey?" he murmured as he entered her, slow
and strong, and so very, very good. "Marry me?"

She wrapped her legs over his hips, her arms around
his shoulders, and leaned in to bite him gently on the ear-
lobe. For a second she savored the moment. Dante's breath
coming roughly in her ear as he began to slide in and out
of her, his strong, warm body holding her, all his will and
heart and mind bent on one task: to make love to her.

He was right. Life was pretty good right now. Actually,
it was downright wonderful.

She kissed his ear where she'd bitten it and whispered
softly, but clearly, "Yes."

Chapter Sixty-five

Meanwhile, somewhere across town . . .

Pratima Gupta sighed and lowered her spoon to the dish of rice and milk in front of her. "We have done it, Savita-di, we have done it!"

"Yes," Savita-di replied, but her face was not wreathed in the joy that Pratima expected.

"What is the matter?" Pratima asked. "Is not our restaurant a glorious success?"

"Ye-es," Savita-di said.

"Are not the tables filled every night with patrons who groan, their bellies are so full?"

Savita-di frowned. "Ye-es."

Pratima leaned forward across the desk in their shared office. Beyond the door, the voices of their cooks, waiters, dishwashers, and busboys rose and fell, a reminder of the success she claimed.

"Do we not have protection from the so-strong Mr. Neil Senior, so that we do not have to fear thugs invading our kitchen anymore?"

"Ye-es."

"And is not our kesar kheer the finest—the very finest— in all of Chicago, perhaps in the entire US of A?"

"Ye-es."

Pratima threw her hands up in the air. "Then tell me, Savita-di, what could possibly be the matter?"

Savita-di slammed her hands flat on the desk, making the bowl of kesar kheer shiver. "The kesar kheer, Pratima, the kesar kheer! It is not entirely perfect."

Pratima's mouth fell open. She looked at the blue bowl of delicious pudding that sat on the desk between them and then she began to slowly nod. "It is not quite tasty enough."

"It is not quite spicy enough."

Both ladies examined the bowl of kesar kheer. Savita-di took a spoonful and tasted it, her eyes closed, her eyebrows knit.

Pratima held her breath.

Then Savita-di's eyes popped open. "It needs carda-mom. A *better* cardamom than we use."

Pratima stared at Savita-di. "The very best cardamom is Grade Number 1 Short Mysore Cardamom from Mumbai. It is very expensive."

Savita-di stared back, a dawning excitement in her eyes. "Yes, but not as expensive as Grade 1A Very, Very Fine Mongra Kesar."

"True, Savita-di, very true."

"And do you not have a nephew's nephew who lives in the city of Mumbai, Pratima?"

"Yes, I do."

"And could not this nephew's nephew be made to understand how very important it is to fulfill the wishes of his uncle's aunt?"

"I believe so, Savita-di."

The two ladies stared at each other a moment longer, then Savita-di leaned toward her sister-in-law. "Then, Pratima, what we need to make our kesar kheer the very best kesar kheer in all of Chicago—possibly in all the US of A—is Grade Number 1 Short Mysore Cardamom from Mumbai!"

Mrs. Savita Gupta and Mrs. Pratima Gupta's Top Secret, Very Special Kesar Kheer Recipe

¼ cup shelled pistachios, the best you can buy,
  with nine reserved
½ cup basmati rice, picked through and rinsed
4 cups whole milk
6 whole cardamom seeds, preferably from Mumbai
½ teaspoon Grade 1A Very, Very Fine Mongra
  Saffron (or, if you must, regular saffron)
½ cup white cane sugar

First, examine your pistachios. Are they indeed the very best you can buy? If so, soak these pistachios in enough water to cover for about four hours, or perhaps overnight if it is late and you are sleepy. Now take the rice and place it in a saucepan. Add half of the milk and heat, stirring slowly while thinking about how good this pudding will be to eat and how very envious your sister-in-law will be when she tastes it. Cover and cook the rice and milk for twenty minutes until the rice is soft. Then add the saffron, cardamom seeds, the sugar, the pistachios, and the remaining milk. Simmer gently for about sixty minutes or more, stirring now and again, until the rice is the thickness that you desire. Pour the pudding into a lovely dish and decorate using the remaining nine pistachios and your best artistic sensibilities.

This delicious dish makes eight servings—unless your greedy nephew comes to dinner, in which case it is probably closer to six—and may be served hot or cold.

THE DISH

Where authors give you the inside scoop!

From the desk of Julia Harper

Dear Reader,

So many books to read, so little time! Do you find that you have trouble deciding which book to pick up next? Should you read that cat mystery your mother keeps shoving at you or the new zombie book your sister loved so much? And then there are those ubiquitous lists of "classic" books that you must read before you die. What is a reader to do? Well, never fear, I've just made your reading decisions a little easier with the following comparison of my new book, FOR THE LOVE OF PETE (on sale now), and one of those books you really should've read in freshman lit:

A Handy Dandy Guide, comparing my new book, FOR THE LOVE OF PETE, with William Faulkner's AS I LAY DYING

	AS I LAY DYING	VS.	FOR THE LOVE OF PETE
First line of book:	*Jewel and I come up from the field, following the path in single file.*		*Things finally came to a head between Zoey Addler and Lips of Sin the afternoon he tried to steal her parking space.*

Heroine:	**Addie Bundren**, who is dying	**Zoey Addler,** who is *alive* and on a mission to rescue her kidnapped baby niece.
Hero:	Several choices here, but I'm going with **Anse Bundren** who needs false teeth.	**Dante Torelli,** hot, if uptight FBI agent. His teeth are all intact.
The Plot:	Well, Addie dies and her family has to bury her. They're not very good at it.	Dante Torelli is an undercover FBI agent assigned to protect a mob informant and his family. But the informant's hiding place is blown and a baby girl is snatched by a ruthless hit man. Now, Dante must save the toddler, uncover the traitor in his department, evade various bad guys, and deal with Zoey, the toddler's sexy aunt, all before the biggest mob trial in Chicago's history, set to begin in just three days.
Love Scene:	I'm not sure there is one, but Addie did once have an affair with the preacher who's going to bury her.	Woohoo!

| Ends: | SPOILER ALERT! One of Addie's sons gets sent to an insane asylum, but at least her rotting body is saved from a flooding river by another son. Yay! | Happily (and with more hot sex)! |

There! Didn't that make your decision a little easier?

xxoo,

♡ Julia Harper

www.juliaharper.com

♥ ♥ ♥ ♥ ♥ ♥ ♥ ♥ ♥ ♥ ♥ ♥ ♥ ♥ ♥

From the desk of Lisa Dale

Dear Fellow Bookworms,

Do you ever get the feeling that life is too complicated? That you just want to get back to the things that matter most?

I do. That's why I wrote my first novel, SIMPLE WISHES (on sale now), about a woman who makes an impulsive mistake that forces her to leave her New York City apartment and escape to her deceased mother's cottage in the country.

It probably won't surprise you that I wrote much of the novel in my grandparent's cabin on a drab dirt road in Pennsylvania. Every morning, I would get up, make tea, do a bit of reading, and write. You can see pictures of the cabin on my blog, www.Book Anatomy101.com.

Some of the stories in SIMPLE WISHES come from real life. For example, once, my grandfather's collie ran away and I was the lucky one to apprehend the fugitive. When I found him, he was barking and running in circles around a tree. I bent down to grab his collar and when I looked up, there was a *huuuge* black bear staring down at me from a branch above my head! Gives new meaning to the phrase: *barking up the wrong tree*.

Unlike me, the hero of SIMPLE WISHES, Jay Westvelt, is totally accustomed to living in the middle of nowhere. He's a rough-around-the-edges recluse and a brilliant artist, and he's intrigued when a prickly yet captivating city slicker moves in next door. Adele has to admit her attraction to Jay, but because she plans to return to the city, she can't let herself fall in love. She vows their relationship is nothing more than a fling—but little does she know that Jay has vows of his own.

SIMPLE WISHES is about what's most important to us as women—getting over the past, and sorting the things that matter from the things that don't. I'd love to hear about your simple wishes. Visit my Web site at www.lisadalebooks.com and leave a note on my "Wishing Well" to share a kind wish for yourself, your friends, your family, or the whole world.

Happy reading!

Lisa Dale

♥ ♥ ♥ ♥ ♥ ♥ ♥ ♥ ♥ ♥ ♥ ♥ ♥ ♥

From the desk of Amanda Scott

Dear Reader,

Lady Sibylla Cavers of BORDER MOONLIGHT (on sale now) has to deal with Simon Murray, Laird of Elishaw, a man who never forgets a wrong . . . or forgives one.

However, Sibylla, like most of my heroines, is a capable, intelligent woman who knows her own mind. By the time she's finished with Simon, he's not sure which end is up. That is not to say she wins every battle, but she does hold her own.

I think the reason I enjoy creating strong, independent heroines is that I come from a long line of strong, independent women. Since most of my many Scottish ancestors hailed from the Borders, I often tell people I have horse thieves hanging from nearly every branch of the family tree. I have certainly used many examples from that tree to create my heroines—and a number of my heroes, for that matter.

Thanks to a little nepotism, my triple-great grandfather, Andrew Scott, whose father came to America from the Borders, became, the first—and from 1819 to 1821 the only—superior, or supreme, court judge for the Arkansas Territory. His older brother, John Scott, was one of the first U.S. senators from Missouri and named the state of Arkansas. Their wives were sisters, daughters of lawyer John Rice-Jones, a Welshman who served as commissary general to George Rogers Clark's northwest expedition, among many other accomplishments.

All were strong men, definitely, but their wives and daughters were strong, too. They had to be to cope with those men. One of my favorite stories about Judge Andrew Scott concerns a duel he had in 1824 with another judge shortly after Arkansas outlawed dueling. After an argument over a game of whist, they fought their duel on "Mississippi soil" in order not to break the law. Judge Andrew left a letter for his wife, Eliza—the usual "to be opened in the event of my death" letter.

I have a copy of it. After expressions of much

praise to Eliza as the perfect wife and mother, he added a P.S. telling her to give their youngest son, George, (the only son still at home) to the judge's brother to raise.

My grandfather first showed me the letter when I was about ten or twelve. Even then, I did not doubt what Eliza's reaction to that last sentence must have been. It is my firm belief to this day that the letter still exists because of Eliza, not Andrew. He'd certainly have had less reason to keep it, let alone to pass it on to one of his sons to treasure.

Andrew had a legendary temper. During the argument, he is said to have thrown a candlestick at the other judge. But Eliza definitely held her own with him. After she read that letter—and I have no doubt that she did—I'd wager he endured an uncomfortable few minutes at best. My grandfather said she probably "snatched the man baldheaded."

I grew up with many such tales from my grandfather, so perhaps you can understand why, when I need examples of strong women for my heroines, I often look no further than the Scott family history.

Enjoy!

Amanda Scott

http://home.att.net/~amandascott/